LEE SWANSON

THE CALLING OF ALEX TATE

Merchant's Largesse Books

The Calling of Alex Tate

Merchant's Largesse Books

Copyright 2021 by Lee Swanson

Cover art and design by Lee Swanson

First Edition

ISBN-13: 978-1-7362436-1-9

Books>Fiction>Mystery>Crime

Prologue

She sat absolutely still, transfixed by the horror unfolding before her. Tears welled in the corners of her honey-hued hazel eyes and slowly streaked down her unblemished cheeks. Her breathing grew ragged as a sense of constriction enveloped her chest. Around her, the house was settled in utter silence; her parents sleeping peacefully in their upstairs bedroom, unaware of their daughter's increasing emotional agitation.

She wanted to turn the television off, to retreat to her own cozy, safe bed. Instead, she stayed. The tableau playing across the screen of the sixty-inch screen seemed so real she felt she could almost reach out and touch the cold, tortured flesh of the dead girl being hauled from the ravine on a stretcher.

She listened through her headphones while the onsite reporter provided the nauseating details of the grisly discovery in an impassive, factual voice, interrupted at times by the newsroom anchor's supplement of background details into the young woman's disappearance. Their professional detachment juxtaposed with her own extreme emotionality. Her heart was breaking.

It wasn't as if she knew the girl.

Vicki Redmond, she admonished herself, *she is a real person, you know.*

Yes, she could have known Vicki Redmond. They were almost the same age. They could have been in the same English class. They could have played on the same soccer team. They could have been friends, even best friends. But she'll never go to class, or play sports, or be anyone's friend again. She'll be with God and the angels, but that's small consolation to someone whose life was ended so abruptly before its time.

What kind of a person could do such a thing? What kind of sick, demented animal could take a precious life and extinguish it so horribly? No, not an animal, she thought, *even an animal doesn't kill so wantonly.*

She shuddered involuntarily, fighting the revulsion that festered in the pit of her stomach like a poisonous viper, seeking to find its way out.

As the 11:00 p.m. news proceeded on to the next segment, a scandalous bit about another Seattle city councilman caught taking a bribe, she was finally able to turn the television off. She sat in the darkness for long minutes, pondering. Despite being only seventeen years old, she was not a person to ignore wrongdoing. But this was not an instance of confronting a pathetic senior bullying a freshman at school. Rape and murder were beyond her ken, something her upper middleclass upbringing had not prepared her to confront.

What am I going to do, make a poster saying, 'Murder of Women is Wrong!'? Organize a club at school? Write a letter to the mayor? How can I be so pathetic, so hopeless?

She pressed the 'off' button on the remote and the screen became dark; dark as the room; dark as her thoughts. Time passed interminably. Her sense of despair and powerlessness grew. Suddenly, a thought flashed into her mind as if a product of divine intervention. Relentlessly, the thought became an idea that began to coalesce in her mind into a plan of action. If anyone would have been watching the tall teenaged girl, they would have seen a grim smile settle on her full, pink lips. She mounted the stairs to her bedroom with a new purpose in her life.

Alex Tate had recognized her calling.

Chapter 1

"I'll be leaving now, Mr. Harrison, unless there's anything more you need?"

Startled, Walter looked up from page seven of the Kelly's homeowner's policy he had been carefully proofreading. He glanced out of his second story window into the leafy canopy of the row of box alders that separated the Morrison-Worth building from the street. He saw it was still light but, checking the antique Hermle Mantel clock on his office credenza, he was surprised to see it was already past six p.m.

"No problem, Marianne. I'll be right behind you. See you tomorrow, OK?"

Walter watched the shapely young blond walk briskly toward the door and, not for the first time, imagined her strutting down a Victoria's Secret runway in a similar manner. Sighing to himself for his lecherous digression, he sharpened his already stiletto pencil and turned his attention back to his work. Although a few of the consultants in the office gave him a hard time about preferring to review documents in hard copy, Walter still preferred the reassuring feel of a #2 medium lead on crisp white bond paper to the impersonal touch of a keyboard.

If there is one thing I learned from dad, it's that you the job always gets done better if you stick with what you know.

The vivacious secretary turned and flashed a winning smile back at her boss as she opened the door to leave, her perfect teeth silent testimony to her orthodontist's skill and her father's willingness to spend lavish amounts of money to make his little princess the envy of her circle of similarly indulged adolescents growing up on the Lake Washington shoreline of Mercer Island. While most of her friends had used college as a springboard into successful (and unsuccessful) marriages to aeronautical engineers, software designers and, in one case, a rather delicious family psychiatrist, Marianne Peters had decided to enjoy Seattle's flourishing single's scene for a few more years before settling down to the battle against stretch marks, borderline alcoholism, and vague suspicions of their partner's infidelity that seemed the favored pastimes of her female social set.

Besides, being the Girl Friday for Walter Harrison wasn't too bad of a short-term gig. He was a great boss: understanding; polite, but not stuffy; and seemingly interested in her opinions on things.

Plus, she thought with a wicked smile, *he is a definite yummy muffin. Nice butt too.*

Although he had to be in his mid-thirties, he had the kind of body that was meant for a three-piece suit like the dark blue pinstripe he was wearing today. Seated, his toned stomach was evident as there was not the tiniest hint of tummy fat. His six-foot plus frame was muscular, but not overly so. His face was angular, with a slightly aquiline nose swelling to prominence below rather shockingly green eyes. At her job interview, she had wondered whether he wore colored contacts, necessitating her having to ask him to repeat his question because of her lack of focus. Now, she knew they were real, just as she knew his deep tan was authentically achieved through time in the sun rather than the tanning booth. Full lips, white teeth, and a ready smile completed what any young woman would consider a quite tasty package.

She also knew he was heterosexual, his involuntary glances at the fullness of her white silk blouse while shaking hands at the interview had confirmed that quite clearly. So had her awareness that he often appraised her body when he thought she wasn't looking. When she first went to work at International Underwriters a year and a half earlier, she had waited expectantly for an offer of a drink after work or possibly a dinner date. When nothing was forthcoming, Marianne had felt somewhat crestfallen, but brightened up when she realized he might be hesitant to mix business with pleasure or risk a future grilling by Human Resources about a sexual harassment allegation if things went sour between them. Then, she had toyed with the notion of laying down a few broad hints that she was both available and very interested.

- 4 -

When she conveyed this plan to Cath Cartwright at a raucous hen party at the glitzy *Noc Noc Club*, her thoroughly drunk friend had solemnly waved her index finger from side to side and exclaimed in a too-loud voice, "Girlfriend, don't play with fire! Walter Harrison is one frat boy who just refuses to grow up. Believe me, I've got the scoop first hand."

She stared solemnly into Marianne's eyes for a full five seconds before she circled her fingers and slowly moved her hand in a pumping motion, then burst into hysterical laughter that showered Marianne with residue of gin and tonic. A few days later, Cath soberly re-confirmed her earlier warning. Over the course of the next few weeks, some of her other friends gave her a similar vibe about the shaky reputation of her attractive boss.

Marianne got the message: Walter Harrison was a bad boy. The kind you should fantasize about with a nice glass of red wine and a vibrator, rather than risk getting really hurt by in person. Still, if he ever did ask her out, she would probably say yes.

I'd just be very, very careful, she promised herself solemnly.

Almost an hour later, Walter placed the meticulously corrected policy into his secretary's inbox, turned off the lights, set the security alarm, and pulled the door shut behind him. Despite the encroaching darkness as the sun settled slowly into the cool waters of Puget Sound, it was surprisingly balmy, especially for mid-May. For someone unfamiliar with the idiosyncrasies of the climate of Seattle, a late spring evening in the mid-seventies might be considered mundane, not worthy of note. For a lifelong resident of the city like Walter, however, weather like this was exceptional, guaranteed to put a smile on all but the crustiest of grouches among the city's half million plus population. And Walter was definitely not the curmudgeon type; habitually, he was definitely a "glass half full" sort of guy. As a boyish grin of unfettered delight spread across his face, he turned up 8th Avenue, whistling a half-forgotten 80s classic as he strode purposefully toward the parking garage.

Suddenly, he remembered he was entertaining tonight.

Retracing his steps to the corner of South Stacy, he pushed open the heavy door of Wolf's Deli, smiling faintly at the oddly feminine tinkle of the little bell that announced his entry. Pete Wolf, the son of the deli's owner stood massively behind the counter. Noticing the store was empty of other customers; Pete grinned at Walter and yelled, "Hey, Walt, how's it hangin'?"

"A little to the left, if you have to know," Walter laughed, replying in the same flippant manner.

"Pulling to the left, eh? I know a redhead who can help you correct your alignment."

Walter knew Pete could keep up this testosterone-soaked banter forever, eventually devolving to include sisters, mothers and, once, even Walter's grandmother. In the seven years he had worked at the International Underwriters Insurance office up the block, there were very few weeks that went by without at least two to three stops at the deli before heading home. The building in which the business was housed was both trendy and chic, but in a distinctly masculine manner. In the last century it had been a part of a warehouse complex storing mining goods and supplies waiting to be transshipped to Alaska; there, they would be multiplied in price ten or twenty-fold and sold to optimistic prospectors seeking their fortunes in the Klondike goldfields. Today, the structure retained much of its rustic charm with a huge block and tackle hanging massively from an open-beamed ceiling, dangling hawsers, and faded signage claiming the virtues of goods that had been out of production since the First World War. On the floor's massive oak planks, goods were displayed on hundred-year-old, wooden packing crates. Contrasted against these features of period décor were a series of modern refrigerator cases, housing what many of Seattle's discerning gastro-snobs considered the finest range of deli products in the city.

Even more incongruous to the deli's fashionable reputation than its décor was the appearance of the owner's son. At six foot, seven inches, pushing three hundred and forty pounds, and with a meat cleaver in his hand, Pete could have easily stepped from any horror film that centered on a cannibalistic, murderous behemoth. Belying his physical appearance was his gregarious, fun-loving nature, which

Walter likened to an overly-friendly Great Dane that continuously wanted to show its affection by dry-humping your leg. Everyone who came into Wolf's Deli preferred to be waited on by Pete to his father, Jimmy, who always looked like he'd just been gargling with lemon juice right before he asked if he could help you. Walter was no exception.

His acquaintance with Pete was compounded by frequent Friday or Saturday nights at Flanagan's Pub or one of the other drinking holes that lined the regenerated waterfront of Seattle. The fact Pete could take it as good as he gave it had bonded the two men in an enjoyable, yet somewhat superficial, friendship.

"Can I get two good salmon filets, a pound of your Bavarian potato salad, and a raspberry cheesecake?" Walter asked.

"Not the salmon again! What's her name this time?" Pete asked, though simultaneously efficiently gathering Walter's order.

"Your mother, wise ass. Although I'm sure she'd do me for a PBJ," Walter retorted.

"All right, shithead, be that way. Keep it a secret. Bet she's ugly as hell though. That'll be twenty-four fifty," Pete growled with overly-affected surliness.

Picking up his bag of groceries, Walter walked toward the door.

Taking the knob in his hand, he turned toward Pete and said, "Yeah, I know she's got a face that would stop a clock, but it's not polite for a fucking son to be talking about his mother that way."

Ducking through the door and exiting at a trot, Walter only faintly heard Pete's good-natured "Bastard!" before heading back down Stacy Avenue to the parking lot. Throwing the grocery bag in the back seat, Walter started the car, adjusted the radio until he heard Steven Tyler of Aerosmith extolling the benefits of "Love in an Elevator," and headed home.

Walter drove out of the center of the city and into the suburbs to the north. Soon, he had passed into an area of mature trees and large rambling houses built to encompass the families with double-digit children that had been commonplace during its Victorian heyday. Many of the homes had seen better days, those with peeling paint and sagging roof joists as prevalent as the ones with pristinely manicured lawns and BMWs in their driveways. To the casual passerby his house, 107 Locust Lane, was certainly closer to the latter category than the former.

"A Real Fixer-Upper," isn't that what the real estate agent had optimistically called it? At almost four thousand square foot of floor space, the house definitely required an owner who either had a hefty annual maintenance budget or who was a devoted handyman. Clearly, the previous resident had been neither. Between missing shingles and damaged guttering, decay had begun to beset the house's upper siding and gingerbread woodwork. In several other places, primarily around doors and windows, the paint had been worn away to expose bare wood to the ravages of the elements. Luckily, rot had not penetrated into the timbers of the house at the time of Walter's first viewing of the house, but he knew it soon would.

Who in his right mind would buy this heap? he had asked himself incredulously.

Yet, the house possessed an attraction that drew Walter to it as a snake charmer's flute fascinates a cobra. He loved the twin turrets that arose from the corners of the house, giving it a distinctly chateauesque appearance. Inside, the sweeping grand staircase, oak floors, and marble and tile fireplaces were enthralling, or at least would be when restored. To architectural purists, the garage attached to the house in the 1960s would be considered an abomination, destroying the ascetic integrity of the house. Walter, however, was more practical, recognizing the value of moving seamlessly from his car to the house free from both Seattle's prodigious precipitation and his neighbor's prying eyes.

Even more than the dormant grandeur of its interior features, what Walter had found the most irresistible about the house was the unusual arrangement of the basement space, which was divided into two completely separate areas by the vagaries of the plot's substrata. One set of stairs led from the central hallway to a wine cellar under the right side of the house. Not a wine aficionado himself by any stretch of the imagination, he nonetheless saw the value of retaining the original intent of the space for a few bottles for special occasions as well as for cases of beer, his much-preferred beverage of choice. Through a door in the kitchen, a second set of stairs descended to another basement area, this one much more spacious. Although it had previously been used for general storage, Walter envisioned a purpose far more ambitious, one far more pleasurable than utilitarian.

Excited by the house's potential to make his dreams into realities, Walter made an offer that very day which was readily accepted. Now, three years after its purchase, the house had been lovingly restored and, as Walter liked to think, reflected much of its past glory. He had done much of the work himself, using carpentry skills he had learned from his father, who had been a master cabinetmaker. He had also made some modifications that facilitated his own unique requirements.

Dad had always said, "Have pride in your work, son, and people will respect you for that," he remembered nostalgically.

As he pulled into his driveway and gazed at his nearly fully-renovated home, he hoped his father would have appreciated his efforts. Approaching his garage, Walter pushed the button on the door-opener and decelerated, slowing to allow the door to raise enough to allow the Kia Sorento to enter safely.

Oh shit, what if she doesn't like fish? he swore to himself, suddenly panicking about his imminent date. *Well, if she doesn't, she's just going to have compromise this once.*

Whistling again, he stepped through the door from the garage, down the short hallway, and into the spacious kitchen. Setting the bag on the grey-veined marble countertop, he rummaged about in the refrigerator, eventually extracting a Budweiser from among the varied import and domestic offerings. Hearing the expectant series of anxious yelps from the backyard, Walter opened the French doors onto the patio and Mike, his four-year-old Labrador retriever, bounded into the kitchen. After a series of excited laps around the large central island in the strange language of canine greetings, the dog jumped up and, placing his forepaws on Walter's chest, proceeded to liberally wash the man's face with its wet sloppy tongue. Laughing as he tried to evade the dog's frantic slurps, he scratched his friend vigorously behind the ears, eventually persuading the dog to get down. Walter opened the pantry, extracted a can of Alpo Prime Cuts, found a fork in the sink, and scooped the food into the dog's bowl. Mike immediately lost interest in play as he wolfed the food voraciously.

Walter left the dog to finish his dinner and, pulling hard on the beer, moved to the living room, picking up the satellite remote control as he passed the coffee table. He turned on Sports Center and flopped down on the overstuffed sofa. After enduring the grim details of the Mariner's fourth loss in a row, he opened the patio doors again, stepped outside, and turned the gas lever to the barbeque into the "on" position. Lighting the fire, he placed the delectable salmon filets on the grill and seasoned them liberally with salt, pepper, and lemon juice, quickly cooking them through to perfection. Mike explored his backyard domain, every once in a while, turning his attention to the barbeque and what, to him, must be the overpowering scent of meat. Soon, Walter's stomach began rumbling as well as the smell of the fish engulfed his own olfactory glands.

Moving the perfectly cooked fish into the kitchen, he closed the doors, leaving Mike outside with a somewhat dejected look on his face. Walter placed the salmon on two plates next to the carefully mounded heaps of the potato salad. He transferred the plates to a serving tray and added a bottle of wine and two glasses. He then opened the basement door, turned on the light and, grabbing the tray, descended the steps into what, for the terrified teenaged girl caged inside, was the deepest, darkest circle of hell – their date.

He smelled her before he heard her. The toilet reeked with the nervous fruit of her watery bowels and the acrid waft of her vomits, the stink was intensified by the nauseating stench of her fear-induced sweat.

My God, he thought, *she has to do better than this.*

Then the whimpers started; low, from the back of her throat. He grinned. At least she'd finally learned not to scream. That had taken some time, but it was surprising how effective the pliers had been as a means of positive reinforcement.

He laid the tray on the small table in the center of the spacious room and ran back up the stairs, returning a few seconds later with a can of room freshener. Holding the button down firmly, the odors in the room were gradually supplanted by the cloying fragrance of the freshener.

"Heavenly Lilac," he read aloud, "God, you're going to think I'm my grandmother."

The girl in the room-sized cage didn't think that at all. In fact, she thought very little about anything anymore. At first, her thoughts had been wholly about escaping, returning home and never, ever, turning her computer on again.

How could I have been so stupid? she thought numbly.

She'd seen the presentations at school, listened to old Mrs. Harney preach on in health about how you should never make contact with anyone you didn't know on the Internet. She remembered how she, Sharon, and Tammy had laughed, saying the Internet would be the only way Harney would ever get any masculine attention. Besides, what was the problem with chatting, it wasn't like some perv could crawl through the screen, could he? And she certainly wasn't going to give anyone her address, she was certainly too smart for that.

Yup, straight A's again, mom, aren't you proud of me?

She hiccupped at the thought of her mother, not realizing tears were streaming silently from her eyes.

But Nick had been so different, she thought; so cute and so shy. She had met him on a Shakespeare discussion site, when she was trying to gain some insight into *Twelfth Night* for her term paper.

From humble beginnings.

Over six weeks' time, their brief chats had increased to hours spent in conversation each night. The pictures he sent showed a dark-haired serious boy, with brown eyes that were like deep pools of dark water in the moonlight. She had sent him her favorite picture of herself, the one of her in the short, yellow sundress, relaxing in the park. Her long, blond hair was streaming luxuriously in the wind, a delighted, toothy smile frozen on her face. Nick had said she was the most gorgeous girl in the world. Who was she to argue, she had thought, wasn't she attracted to the most handsome boy?

Although she had vowed to remain anonymous, she felt she and Nick had a very real connection. She couldn't ignore the premonition that she may have found her soul-mate, her one true love, just as Viola felt when she first met Orsino in Twelfth Night; and Viola had been masquerading as a boy, hadn't she? She sighed to herself as she thought of the scene at the end of the play where Viola and Orsino had dropped their pretenses, admitting to their great love for each other. She had smiled faintly as she thought of the same thing happening between her and Nick.

That night, she had asked Nick if he had a webcam. He replied, yes, but he seldom used it as his computer was ancient and had very limited virtual memory. She had told him it was OK, but she would really like for them to see each other in real life. He said he would give it a try. She waited impatiently, staring at her screen, then suddenly a rather grainy image of Nick appeared on screen. OMG, she had thought, he's gorgeous!

She had smiled into her webcam and said, "Look at you!"

He beamed at her and appeared to be talking, but no sound came from her speakers.

She typed, "Is there something wrong? I can't hear you."

His return text read, "I can't hear you either. Let me try adjusting things."

Suddenly, his image disappeared.

She typed, "Are you still there?" then realized the connection had been lost.

She tried to reconnect repeatedly, but with no luck. Nick was gone.

Over the next three days, her concentration in school became increasingly worse. Mr. Sorenson, who had grown accustomed to her active participation in American Government class, asked her if anything was wrong.

She gave him a pitifully wan smile and replied, "No," she was just under the weather.

She couldn't tell him she was dying of a broken heart, perhaps never to hear again from the boy she possibly loved.

After dinner that night, her mother echoed Mr. Sorenson's concerns. Again, she lied, telling her mother she just had been under a lot of pressure at school, especially with her term paper in English due the following week. She kissed her mother, told her not to worry, and trudged up the steps to her room. Her term paper had been the last thing on her mind, however, as she booted up her computer.

"Oh, my God!" she thought ecstatically. Opening her IM, she had seen Nick was online.

"Hi, stranger!" his message to her beat hers to him by a millisecond.

"Where have you been???!!!," redundant punctuation reflecting the depth of her relieved emotion.

"Well, I told you my laptop is crap. Adjusting the webcam settings crashed it. I asked a computer geek friend of mine to repair it, but I just got it back today. Do you want to chance the webcam again?"

She remembered the three impossibly lonely days that were the result of their last attempt at video and typed, "No way!" She went on, "I've been thinking."

About what?" he queried.

She took a long breathe, and then typed, "We should get together."

"You mean for real?"

"Yes," she typed, "in person."

"But aren't you afraid?" he asked. "I mean, you've seen the videos in school, where everyone on the Internet is a rapist, a mass murderer, or both?"

"Are you afraid of little old me?" she replied, trying to repress her giggles so her mom wouldn't burst in the room to try to discover what was so hilarious about Shakespeare.

"Well, no," he typed. "I was just thinking about you."

Her heart swelled as she basked in his concern. "Well, we could meet up at a mall. Which one is closest for you?"

"How about Westfield Southcenter?" he asked.

"Wow, that's too far for me," she said, "I only live a couple of blocks from Northgate. Could you get there?"

"Sure. Would 6:00 pm on Saturday be alright?"

"That would be great," she emoted. "How about by the pretzel place in the food court?"

"Fantastic," he replied. "Now, what about Tammy's new boyfriend, or has she dropped him since our last chat?"

The rest of the evening's chat had only reinforced her growing feelings for Nick. He was funny, but clearly was not just trying to get laughs from her like some of the boys at school who thought they were God's gift to comedy. He asked frequent questions, but did not push her for answers. Mostly, it just felt like he was a guy who put her at the center of his universe. How can I wait two whole days? she thought miserably.

Friday passed like a blur. Her teachers were relieved to see her return to her old self, and Tammy and Sharon joked that only a guy could cause such extreme mood swings in a teenaged girl. She said nothing and just smiled mysteriously, however. Her last real boyfriend had been Robbie Simpson in her junior year and that had ended after just a few months. Anyway, the difference between Nick and Robbie was, like, a million miles.

She wished she could tell Tammy especially about Nick. Her best friend had always been there for her in the past, but she felt all that was going to happen was that she was going to have to listen to an earful of shit about the dangers of meeting up with a guy she had met online.

"My God girl," she'd say, "Have you been sleeping through those videos in health class that show what happens? You must be out of your fucking mind! There is absolutely no way you're going to meet this guy unless I'm there, and I'm bringing a baseball bat!"

No way, she had thought. *I love you Tam, but I'm not going to let you spoil any chance I have of a relationship with Nick.*

After completing her Saturday chores around the house in a whirlwind of activity, she got down to the serious business of getting ready. She bathed, and then washed and dried her hair. After putting on her favorite cream-colored, lace bra and matching panties, she was met with a dilemma.

"Jeans or skirt?" she wondered aloud.

She chose the blue skirt, deciding it was better to be a little overdressed than too casual. Wriggling into the new coral peplum top she had got on sale from Lulu's, she began to do her makeup and hair. Forty-five minutes later, she looked in the mirror. "Not bad at all," she said aloud.

She was ready.

Since the weather was glorious, at least by Seattle standards, she decided to walk to the mall. Twenty minutes later, she was inside, working her way through the crowd of people at the food court. She glanced at her watch and saw she was ten minutes early. Ordering herself a lemonade, she settled down to wait for Nick.

Two hours later, she was still waiting. She had tried the number he had given her on her cell phone repeatedly, each time only getting connected to a voicemail. The messages she left ran a gamut of emotions; humor, concern, anger, resignation. Finally, she decided there was no sense prolonging her agony, there was nothing left for her to do but to go home.

She walked dejectedly through the thinning parking lot and down 103rd Street. She wished she had brought her light jacket, as the growing twilight had brought on a proportionate drop in temperature.

What was one more stupid mistake?

Wrapping her arms around herself, she continued walking, imagining Nick's arms around her instead. She was miserable, why the fuck hadn't he come?

As she approached her street, she noticed a middle-aged man get out of a black SUV ahead of her. Somewhat wary, she relaxed when he opened the side door and a black Labrador bounded out. Obediently, the dog sat beside the man as he attached a lead to its collar. Her love for dogs, and Labradors in particular, overcame her earlier caution and she gave the man a tentative smile.

Looking into the SUV, the man asked the dog, "Now, where did you put the ball, Mike?" He then looked at her and asked," Do you mind holding his leash while I find his ball?" As she moved forward to take the leash from the man, he whirled behind her. She suddenly felt a sharp pain in the back of her head. Losing consciousness, she felt herself being pushed into the back of the SUV.

She awakened in the cell. She screamed for what seemed like hours, but nobody came to her rescue; not her mom, not Old Lady Harney, not even goddamned Orsino. Then he came, and she wished with all of her heart she was alone again. Nick. No, not Nick, but the man who had passed himself off as Nick. The man who had taken her dreams and perverted them, just as he had her body. She had fought him, but he was too strong, too violent, too everything.

Now, she didn't care, she just wanted it to be over. To separate herself forever from the sick fuck who now controlled her life.

Walter said, "Look at you! I told you to be ready at eight. You're a disgrace, what self-respecting guy would want a girl who looks like that? Now, at least put on some lipstick and try to make yourself look halfway presentable."

He watched as the girl moved listlessly to the mirror and did as she was told. Fishing in his pocket for his keys, he opened the cell door. Retreating to the table, he beckoned the girl forward to be seated at the table. Moving as if in a trance, the girl stumbled towards the table, dragging the heavy chain firmly shackled to her ankle across the floor after her as she did. She sat down.

"I hope you like salmon," Walter opened.

She just stared at him vacantly. Shrugging his shoulders slightly, he reached for his cutlery. Cutting a bite of salmon, he gestured with it towards her, and then popped it in his mouth. Smiling at her encouragingly, he gestured with his fork for her to begin eating as well. She remained motionless, mesmerized by the horror of her obscene predicament. Suddenly, he brought the tines of his fork down hard on the back of her hand, deeply piercing into her flesh.

She screamed, but muffled it behind her good hand as his eyes clouded with the threat of further punishment.

"I hope you like salmon," Walter repeated.

Fighting back her sobs, she replied, "Yes, thank you, very much. I do like salmon."

Walter was proud of her. She had learned very well, the best so far. Maybe she was the one, the special girl he had been looking for all his life. Well, he certainly hoped she appreciated his efforts. Firstly, finding the rambling Victorian at an affordable price. Secondly, building the sturdy cell, he had even plumbed in a toilet and sink. Thirdly, insulating the whole basement so that even KISS at full volume on his stereo couldn't be heard from outside. And then the wooing. He had played her like a rainbow trout on the line, never being too aggressive, waiting for her to suggest their relationship should progress to the next level. He was ready for her suggestion to use the webcam.

Shit, he thought suddenly, *I would have been screwed if she could read lips.*

He made a mental note to change the video and photos he used to a boy who at least spoke English as he kept up a steady stream of small-talk with his terrorized dinner companion. She replied woodenly, knowing that silence would bring painful retribution.

That's my girl, he thought with contentment.

After dinner was always the best time.

She asked, "May I use the bathroom, please?"

He responded positively to her polite request. As he cleared the dishes back upstairs, she walked shakily into the cell, leaned over the toilet, and vomited until nothing was left in her stomach, except for the hopelessness of her situation that had settled into its pit like a rock. She wiped her mouth and walked back to her seat. Walter returned to find the girl sitting stiffly at the table.

"Well?" he asked.

She looked at him dumbly, bottom lip quivering. She knew what he wanted and had little choice but to give it to him. She slowly stood up. Reaching under her skirt, she pulled her panties down, letting them fall to the floor. She stepped out of them and moved to the back of the overstuffed chair, leaning over it so he couldn't see the tears rolling silently down her cheeks. He leaned over, retrieving her by now badly soiled underwear. He threw them down in disgust.

What a disappointment, he thought, *I can certainly do better than this.* "

Just like a bitch," his dad had said repeatedly after a bottle of Crown Royal or two, "Doll themselves up to look like a million dollars to catch you, then let themselves go to hell as soon as they do." He took a long, hard appraising look at the frightened young woman whimpering in front of him. He had liked her so much, but he now sadly realized she wasn't the girl for him.

Moving noiselessly to his work bench, he picked up a seven-inch Phillips screwdriver.

Right tool for the right job, that's what dad always used to say, he recalled.

Moving behind the girl, who blubbered quietly at the expectation of his violent assault, the inevitable end to all their "dates," he said, "Amy?"

Amy Reiss turned slowly, dimly realizing it was the first time he had ever called her by her name since the beginning of her ordeal. Walter reached to caress her hair, a look of regret on his face. "Amy, I want you to know I really like you," he said, then he buried the screwdriver into her right eye socket up to its handle.

Even before her body had ceased its involuntarily convulsions, he had begun the clean-up.

First things first, dad had said repeatedly, and he was always right. A little clean-up here and, then, time to go shopping again.

Chapter 2

John Caldwell awoke to the persistent wail of the chorus of "Baby, Come Back to Me," coming from his phone lying on the night table next to his bed. Moving with surprising swiftness for both his weight and the time of night, he swung his legs out of the bed and grabbed his cell, hitting the answer key in one semi-coordinated movement.

"Caldwell," he growled, minimizing his words to reflect both his irritation at being called in the middle of the night as well as being woken up.

His wife Claire raised her sleepy head slightly off the pillow in annoyance for approximately the same reasons.

A couple of seconds later, he put his hand over the receiver, turned his head to the left, and whispered, "Sorry, honey. Business."

The frown creasing her attractive forehead deepened. Being married to a senior detective in the city's Sexual Assault and Child Abuse Division, her beauty sleep was all too frequently interrupted by phone calls in the middle of the night, but she didn't have to like it. She conveyed her displeasure by staring at her husband and squinting her eyes down hard, the Claire Caldwell version of the evil eye.

John, however, took no notice. He mumbled a few words into the phone, the scarcity of which an indication he was listening to someone at the other end who had his or her shit together.

He conveyed a brisk, "All right then, see you in a half hour," into the phone and ended the call.

He switched on the corner lamp, moved to the closet, found a white, cotton long-sleeved shirt, and began dressing.

Claire asked, "Who was it?"

John turned to her and said, "Frank Chapman."

His look said it all.

"Oh John," her heartfelt concern overwhelming her earlier predilection toward bitchiness, "Not another one?"

"Yeah," he said, "They think it's the girl from Northgate, Amy Reiss, or at least it matches her general description. A couple of hikers found the body in Lord Hills Park, up by Monroe, last night. Snohomish County Sheriff's Office called Homicide and they called Frank. He and I are headed up there."

While he was concisely relaying what information he could tell his attentive wife, he looked at her as she absent-mindedly chewed her lip. He never knew what to say; if she wanted to hear more, less, or nothing at all.

She said, "All right. Please be careful climbing around out in the woods. Wear your boots and remember to dress warmly. It could even be raining up there, you know."

John smiled at her motherly caution, walked to her side of the bed, bent down, and kissed her on her forehead. "Thanks – see you later. I'll call if I'm held up for dinner."

"Thanks for that. Please do, you know I worry about you, "she said.

It took a long while for Claire to drift back into sleep. She worried increasingly more about John these days. He was carrying two hundred and forty pounds on his five-foot ten frame and it wasn't all muscle by any stretch of the imagination. Earlier in their marriage, he had bounded up the stairs two at a time, impatiently waiting for her to follow. Now, he often paused halfway up, taking a deep breath or two before trudging to the top landing. Although he told her the physician had given him a clean bill of health at his last physical, she suspected he was not relaying the whole story. At the very least, he should have gotten a stern lecture about the additional weight he had put on around his middle. The wrinkles around his eyes had also become more pronounced, although she wasn't sure if they were real or if it was her imagination. She had no doubt about his receding hairline, however, or the growing bald spot on the crown of his head. He was clearly aware of that as well, as he had taken to wearing his Mariner's cap just about any time they went out. At forty-seven, he was well on the way to an early heart attack, stroke, or both. She knew a serious talk was in the offing, as did he, one that neither of the Caldwells were looking forward to.

Claire wished her healthy lifestyle would somehow inspire him to make a bit of progress on his own. Claire was five years younger than her husband, but a casual observer might have guessed her age as twenty-five. A sixteen percent body fat content was the result of at least an hour of strenuous cardio each day. Pilates, yoga, and strict caloric intake kept her perfectly toned. Strength training and modern dance rounded out her weekly exercise routine. Her perfect skin was cared for with similar dedication. Claire was one of the few women her age who could chance stepping out to the supermarket without an hour spent concealing the ravages of time in front of the makeup mirror. A quick brush through of her shoulder-length brunette hair and a little lip gloss and Claire looked ready for a fashion magazine photo shoot. She was just as beautiful on the inside as on the surface. Compassionate, vivacious, comfortable in any social situation, Claire Caldwell was considered their best friend by most of the women she knew. She had talked through many of their problems, some of which were incredibly intimate and/or embarrassing. Was it her turn now?

Maybe I should talk to somebody about John? she asked herself.

Her concern for her husband was fast overcoming her natural reticence to burden others with her own troubles.

She also suspected he had secretly started smoking again. It was hard to tell, as so many of his fellow officers smoked that she couldn't wait to shower the reeking residue off after returning home from one of his department functions. If he was, she couldn't condemn him too much considering the terrible cases he worked. John was always talking about retiring and moving away from the city. Claire just hoped he'd live long enough to do it someday.

Unaware of his wife's thoughts of concern transpiring in the warm bed he had just departed, John turned the light off and exited their bedroom, softly pulling the door shut behind him. He passed swiftly down the dark hallway of the house, so familiar with the location of each piece of furniture that he navigated around it unconsciously. Entering his office, he turned on the light, went to the gun safe and retrieved his department-issue .38. Ensuring it was loaded; he exited the house, locked the door, and got in his car.

He met Frank Chapman in the parking lot of the North Precinct building on North College Way twenty-six minutes after being awakened. He grinned as he saw Frank had used the time it had taken him to get there wisely, as he was carrying a Dunkin' Doughnut's bag and a coffee carrier. Getting into the unmarked department vehicle, John turned to Frank and asked, "Bavarian Cream?" Frank merely grunted and offered him the top of the opened bag before turning the ignition key. John reached in and withdrew his favorite, thinking at least everything didn't suck this morning.

The two men travelled in comfortable silence, sipping hot coffee, and munching the doughy belly busters. Both were in their mid-forties; both had been policemen for all of their adult lives. They knew there would be no silence in the vehicle on the return trip, especially if it was the Reiss girl.

As the sky became increasingly lighter, they turned off from 522 and headed north, toward the Temple Pond viewpoint. As they turned off Pipeline Trail, they saw the bevy of police vehicles that inevitably populated any major crime scene. Getting out of the vehicle, John stretched his legs and breathed in the cool, crisp mountain air deeply. He gazed at the gorgeous evergreen backdrop and the broad trails that radiated in every direction, beckoning hikers and nature enthusiasts to explore their hidden destinations.

God, he thought, has it really been almost seven years since Claire and I took the kids up here to the equestrian center?

It had been a great day and he wondered if he should suggest coming back again.

Probably not, he reconsidered, as what he was about to see would surely dampen any enthusiasm he could muster for a return visit to the site anytime in the near future.

The two King County officers approached the small crowd down near the pond's shore. After brief introductions and a quick exchange of information, Frank and John walked attentively toward the area outlined in yellow and black police tape. They crossed over the barrier and there, beneath a small Douglas fir sapling, they found the body.

She had been wrapped in black plastic garbage sacks, secured by "hundred-mile-an-hour" tape. Someone had cut the bag open. John hoped it had been the CSI unit, but presumed there was not a chance in hell of that; instead, it had probably been the hikers trying to ascertain what they had discovered. In that case, the evidence at the crime scene was already degraded.

Oh well, he thought sourly, *no use crying over spilt milk.*

John looked at the remainder of the girl's ruined face and said to Frank, "Yeah, I would guess it is Amy Reiss. Blond hair, nose piercing with a little silver stud, about the right height and weight too. Blue eyes. Sorry, eye."

Bavarian cream mixed with sour stomach acid danced excitedly just below his esophagus as he stared at the girl's ruined right eye.

Frank asked Dan Smith, the Snohomish County assistant coroner, "Any other signs of trauma, other than the eye?"

Smith replied, "Quite a few; only none serious enough to kill her. Most noticeably, several swollen welts on her thighs, stomach, and buttocks. I would venture a guess they were caused by a pair of pliers, see the marks from the gripping surfaces?"

The coroner's gloved hand gingerly lifted the girl's blouse to expose her stomach.

Frank and John nodded in unison as they peered closer at the series of dark corrugations that formed on each side of the welts. John turned his head and stared at Frank, who only sighed and nodded his head in unspoken agreement.

Smith, noticing the silent exchange, observed, "You've seen this before, I take it?"

John eyed him speculatively and said, "Yeah, too many times. Two girls, three counting this one."

Dan ventured, "Enough to substantiate calling him a serial killer, no doubt. Well, that will certainly screw the pooch. Some demented asshole craving publicity and a multitude of idiot reporters willing to give it to him. Just like Green River."

Yes, John thought, *I do remember that shit show.*

Gary Ridgway, whom the press had dubbed "The Green River Killer," had sexually assaulted and murdered at least forty-nine women in the Seattle area during the 1980s and 90s. Later, he confessed to almost twice that number. When John had joined the force in March of 1990, the news that another woman, Marta Reeves, had been reported missing elicited a hush in the squad room, a shaded look passing from veteran to veteran. All joking and idle conversation stopped and everyone unconsciously pricked up his or her ears, hoping she wouldn't eventually wind up as the latest name on the long list of victims. But she was, and she wasn't the last one either. In August 1998, Patricia Yellowrobe was reported missing but, by then, John Caldwell was one of the veterans who exchanged looks with others on the force who sensed she wouldn't be found alive. When Ridgway was apprehended leaving his job at the Kenilworth Truck factory in November of 2001 and soon after confessed to the murders, the city breathed a collective sigh of immense relief.

Now, it could all be starting again, he thought with a sick feeling in his stomach that had nothing to do with the doughnuts he had eaten earlier. *What if it was a copycat?*

Tracy Ann Winston, one of Ridgway's early victims, was abducted from Northgate Mall, just as Amy Reiss had been. He prayed to God it was a coincidence, rather than some part of a sick pattern of hero worship and homicidal emulation.

After confirming with Dan that he would send them a copy of the autopsy report, John and Frank returned to their car. Opening the passenger door, John took one last look panoramic view around the park.

"Got any cigs?" he asked Frank.

"Shit, if Claire finds out I'm your connection, she'll kick my ass up around my shoulder blades," Frank retorted, but still tossed him a Marlboro.

"Light?" John asked hopefully. Frank groaned and lifted his eyes toward the sky, seemingly asking for patience from heaven. Then he dug in his pocket, producing an ancient Zippo. Accepting the light with a slight nod of his head, John took a deep drag. Gazing back toward what had once in his memory been a peaceful, picturesque setting, he saw the black body bag holding the tortured remains of what had been a beautiful young woman being moved into the ambulance.

No, I won't be bringing Claire back here ever again.

On the ride back to Seattle, the two men efficiently summarized what they knew about the murder of Amy Reiss up to this point. She had disappeared sometime after telling her mother she was going to Northgate Mall on May 16th, at approximately 5:15 P.M. Her body had been discovered yesterday, May 28th at 3:10 A.M.

You poor girl, John thought sadly, remembering the sight of the girl's corpse, *what did you go through over the past twelve days?*

Dan Smith had estimated time of death approximately five to six hours prior to the discovery of the body, as rigor mortis had set, but her body temperature was still in the high-eighties, despite the frosty morning. She was clothed, except her underwear and shoes were missing. Although confirmation would have to wait from the crime lab, sexual assault was highly likely. There were approximately thirty of the welts, probably caused by pliers or a similar device. Additionally, her left ankle had an area approximately two inches wide that was rubbed raw. The ruptured right eye and mass of blood on the right side of her face alluded to cause of death. Although the CSI team had not concluded their sweep of the area, they had turned up nothing significant so far. Temple Pond 1 was a popular picnic site and John remembered it had been crowded the day he and his family had visited the park. Consequently, the chance of identifying footprints or tire tracks as positively belonging to the murderer would be slim at best.

So, John concluded, *unless a witness to the dumping of the body materializes, or the guy accidentally dropped a business card, we only have one thing to go on. The fact he will probably do it again.*

Frank broke into his bleak reverie, asking, "What about trying to connect her to the other two girls?"

Startled from his thoughts, it took John a few seconds to register Frank's question.

He then said, "Yeah, well not much there either. Angela Simmons disappeared last November, but her body wasn't found until January up by Lake Roesiger. Vicki Redmond was reported missing on February 15th; body discovered February 25th at Squak Mountain."

"Well," Frank began deliberately," We have three girls, ages seventeen to eighteen, who have been abducted from Seattle over the past ten months. Item one: He likes 'em young and pretty. Item two: He kept at least two of the three girls alive for between one and two weeks. That implies he must have some place where he can keep them, doing what he does to them unheard and undisturbed, because you can bet that they were raising holy hell. Item three: he has some way to gain their trust; these girls were snatched from good suburban neighborhoods in the early evening. They wouldn't just get in a car with some guy unless they either knew him or trusted him."

"That is, of course, if we are attributing all three murders to only one demented asshole," John interjected.

"Would you rather we had three? Because committing even one of these murders would definitely qualify you as a member in good standing of the Demented Asshole club. Why would you even question that at this point?" Frank asked sarcastically.

"Well, the murder weapon for one," John replied." "Vicki Redmond had been bludgeoned to death, probably by a carpenter's hammer. As best the crime lab could determine, Angela Simmons was killed by multiple stabs to the chest from a small, round extremely sharp object. One of these must have perforated her heart, judging from the damage to her ribs. The weapons seem unconnected, contradicting the idea they are victims of the same man. In almost all cases, serial killers like to stick to the same MO; they get comfortable with one weapon and stick with it. That's why we really didn't connect the first two girls. This one just doesn't seem to fit either."

Thinking deeply before asking, Frank said, "What did you make of her eye?"

John replied, "Well, it looked like he had used a lot of force to stab her. The eyeball was pretty much missing, as if the handle of the weapon had been pushed all the way into the socket. The entry hole into the brain appeared about a quarter inch in diameter. At least she would have died instantly."

Frank said, "All right, listen to this. We figured the second girl was killed with a hammer. What if Angela Simmons was murdered with a carpenter's awl? Following that line of reasoning, it would make sense the Amy Reiss' murder weapon is a screwdriver, probably a Phillips."

"Oh shit, I can see it now, the 'DIY Killer,'" John interjected.

"Fuck off," said Frank, pulling the Ford into the department parking lot, Frank turned toward him and stated emphatically, "You know this works, John."

John sighed. "Yeah, it does, Frank, but what are we going to do now, stake out every Home Depot and hardware store in the State? Besides, he doesn't have to buy a new tool for each murder, he can reuse them. Hell, he may have a garage full of tools already," he said morosely.

The two men entered the building and, after a necessary stop in the men's room, went to Frank's office. Immediately, they became absorbed in formalizing their previous suppositions. Time seemed to melt away as they pondered and discussed the cases, searching for anything else that might link the girls and allow them to narrow down their search parameters.

Suddenly, John's phone rang. Frank looked up and grinned at John's annoying ringtone. Mouthing, "Go to hell" at him, John looked down at his watch, which read 7:35 PM.

Groaning to himself, he spoke into the receiver, "Hi honey, sorry about forgetting to call."

Frank, sensing John was getting an earful, turned and concentrated keenly on the map of Washington State hanging behind his desk.

Hanging up the phone, John said, "That was Claire. I had promised to call if I was going to be late. She was just informing me that what remained of dinner was in the refrigerator; 'Cold Shoulder,' as she termed it. She said she would be out until about eleven and, if I wasn't waiting at the door with a whiskey in hand for her when she got home, there was going to be hell to pay."

Frank looked at him sympathetically. The day had started early for both of them.

"Well get your ass home then," he said grinning, "If Claire kills you, there's not a court in the state that wouldn't call it justifiable homicide."

John picked up his coat and, briefly turning to flip Frank the bird, started for home.

Chapter 3

Alex tapped the tip of her pen against her perfectly-spaced white teeth; for one of the few times that she could remember in her school career, she was flustered.

Not panicking, she assured herself, *but definitely flustered.*

Her AP English examination lay before her. The grammar portion had been a snap, as had the short answer questions on The Great Gatsby and Frankenstein. But Romeo and Juliet?

Why did teachers always choose Romeo and Juliet, she thought to herself, wrinkling her nose in disgust?

It was as if Shakespeare had only written one play or, more likely, it was the only one every teacher had studied in school. The idea of two young "star-cross'd" lovers making a series of irrational decisions, guided by a bumbling priest and a silly goose of a wet nurse, bothered her. If she knew anything about herself, it was that she was a realist. As such, how was she expected to answer, "In a short essay of approximately three hundred words, discuss what you most admire about one of the characters in Shakespeare's Romeo and Juliet. Ensure you support your views with evidence from the text." Why couldn't they have chosen one of her favorites, Titus Andronicus, Macbeth, or especially King Lear? Why this obsession with two kids who are barely teenagers throwing their lives away, thinking they are in love?

I should protest, she thought, smiling to herself, *I could tell Principal Matthews I was thinking about committing suicide, having been inspired by the Shakespeare selection on Ms. King's reading list.*

Shit, she thought, suddenly snapping out of her dramatic reverie in which the School District had to pay millions of dollars in a class action lawsuit brought by the parents of a multitude of suicidal children. *I've only got forty-five minutes to get it in gear, or I'm going to fuck up my chances of ever getting into Stanford next year. Get a move on, girlfriend!*

Putting pen to paper and beginning to almost noiselessly hum to herself, she began:

"It fits when such a villain is a guest. I'll not endure him."
(Tybalt, I, 5: 82-83)

With these words, Tybalt declares he will defend the honor of the House of Capulet against an abhorred trespasser, Romeo. In seeking to defend his uncle's hearth from the conniving Montague, a boy who will eventually defile Capulet's daughter and rob him of his heir, the much-maligned Tybalt deserves not to be disparaged, but instead to be held in heroic admiration. . .

Exactly forty-four minutes later, Alex put down her pen, sorted her papers, and waited to be excused from the examination room. After she was released, she walked purposefully into the hallway and screamed loudly.

Her best friend in the class, Britt Stevens rushed to her and yelled, "OMG, Alex! Control your crazy, woman!"

Alex just looked at her for a moment, then hugged her tightly and began laughing hysterically. Caught up in the same sense of relief, Britt started crying. Soon, both girls were crying and laughing simultaneously, jumping up and down in a rhythmic celebration of relieved stress.

Eventually, Britt asked in a sobbing voice, "How'd you do, but do I even need to ask?"

Alex said, "Yeah, pretty good, I guess. But, like, what about the Shakespeare question?"

Britt replied, "Romeo and Juliet, yeah? I thought it was great. It was about as easy as it gets. Who did you write about?"

With a triumphant smile, Alex replied, "Tybalt."

"Holy fuck!" Britt's eyes went wide in shock. "How could you say you admire him? He only killed Mercutio, which started the whole predestination thing going. He's the villain, Alex, not someone who should be admired! Are you crazy?"

"He's got balls," Alex said calmly. "He's the only one in the play who isn't two-faced, a wimp, or both. Besides, he had dreamy eyes in the movie."

Britt looked toward heaven and crossed herself, seemingly praying for Alex's misguided soul. Alex hit her on her shoulder and Britt looked at her in alarm. Then, both girls started giggling again and began walking down the hallway.

Alex opened her locker and began gathering the books she needed to take home to study for her next examination. Out of the corner of her eye she saw a large hand tentatively reach around her locker door.

"Hey, Alex," a guy's voice said haltingly from the other side of the door.

Taking a step back, Alex saw the too-adorable face of Bobby Parker. Somewhat embarrassed by her frank stare, he asked, "Um, how'd you do on the exam?"

She laughed, shook her hair and, in her best Scarlett O'Hara impression, said, "Why Bobby Parker, are you talking to little ole me? Why, that exam quite addled my po' tiny feminine brain!" She looked in mock adoration up into his eyes, fluttering her eyelashes outrageously for effect.

"Right," he said, trying to sound confident, but clearly daunted despite her attempt at humor.

Every guy in school recognized Alex Tate was the perfect combination of brains and beauty; well, the beauty part was perfect,

I don't know about the brains. A girl as smart as Alex always makes you feel like anything you say makes you look like an idiot, he thought glumly.

This did not stop him from visualizing Alex on the soccer field, long legs gliding effortlessly down the pitch, beautiful face set in a look of grim determination as she set up for one of her league-leading nineteen goals.

It's not as if she's smokin' hot like one of the babes in one of the Playboy magazines under my mattress, he thought guiltily, *it's just that she's so damn cute! She's definitely the girl any guy would love having next door. Saying 'hi' to her each morning, checking out her bedroom window at night, hoping the shades weren't pulled down all the way . . .*

Abruptly breaking from his appreciative reverie, Bobby saw to his embarrassed horror Alex was still looking at him expectantly.

"Um, Alex, if you're not doing anything tomorrow, some of us are going out to the beach and . . ." his voice trailed off hopefully.

"Oh, sorry Bobby, I've already got plans," she replied, "But if I was going, there is no one I would rather be with than Bobby Parker!"

She put her head on his shoulder to emphasize her statement.

Bobby knew she was only kidding, but feeling the light contact of her body on his made him feel great anyway.

Alex has a knack at doing that, he thought, a smile unconsciously creasing his lips as he looked away, embarrassed once again. The guy who lands Alex Tate will really hit the jackpot. Looking up, he saw Alex had returned to rummaging around in her locker.

"Well, if you change your mind, just text me, OK?" he asked.

"Sure. See ya, Bobby."

She smiled at him encouragingly. Closing her locker, Alex turned and started walking down the hallway. Waving to some people, stopping to chat with others, it was a full fifteen minutes before she exited the building, her purposeful, athletic strides making up time as they carried her swiftly home.

Slamming the door after her, Alex yelled out, "Hi, Mom," as she dropped her books onto the foyer table.

She heard the faint, "In here, honey," of her mother's reply wafting out of the kitchen.

Alex adored her mother, who seemed more like an older sister than a parent. Unlike many of her friends, Alex loved going shopping with her mother, whose sense of style was a slightly more refined version of Alex's own. Both women used make-up sparingly, accentuating their intrinsic, natural beauty. Although her mother had given up a budding career as an actress to become a homemaker and mother, she was still actively involved in the local community theater, the Gaslight Playhouse. Added to her various volunteer projects, she led a varied and full social life. Alex loved her dearly.

After giving her a hug, Alex began to rummage in the vegetable drawer of the refrigerator.

Just as she grabbed a stalk of celery, a pear, and two carrots, her mother asked, "How was the English exam?"

Straightening up, Alex looked mischievously at her mother and replied, "What English exam is that?"

Her mother's feigned look of angry exasperation was good but, to the daughter who was well aware of her parent's acting ability, ineffective. Alex ran to her mother and threw another, less automatic, hug about her waist and cried, "I smashed it, Mom, even the stupid Romeo and Juliet question!"

Her mother joined momentarily in Alex's jubilant exuberance, and then asked, "So, are you going out tonight to celebrate?"

"What, with Calculus and Physics coming up on Monday and Wednesday? You've got to be kidding?"

She left her mother in the kitchen, who voiced a silent prayer of thanks for being blessed with such a conscientious daughter. Alex sprinted up the stairs to her room, her healthy snack in one hand and an energy drink in the other. Placing her snack precisely on her desk, she efficiently stripped off her school clothes and slipped into her favorite sweat pants and a well-worn, oversized Seahawk's jersey. Going into her ensuite, she used the toilet, conscientiously sprayed the room deodorizer, and scrubbed her face and hands until her skin assumed a rosy red glow. Then, scratching herself in a very unladylike manner, she returned to her desk.

As with most brilliant students, Alex was capable of wholly immersing herself in her studies. Complex formulas danced across the neurons of her brain, as she unconsciously consumed her snack. Suddenly, she felt a hand on her shoulder. Startled, she jumped in her seat and let out a little gasp of surprise.

Over her shoulder she heard her mother say, "Oh my gosh, I'm sorry Alex! I didn't mean to startle you, but I've been calling you for ages to come down for dinner."

Alex turned quickly to her clock to confirm whether she had indeed been studying for over two hours. She had.

She then turned in her chair, smiled, patted her mother's hand, and said, "It's OK, Mom. I've just been channeling Albert Einstein. Sorry, for not answering."

The two women went downstairs to the dining room table. Alex yelled, "Yippee, mushroom risotto, my fav! Where's Dad?"

Her father, a carnivore by nature, endured an occasional vegetarian dinner to keep peace with his herbivore offspring. It certainly wasn't by choice, however. Consequently, such a meal usually meant he was unavoidably detained at his office. Her mother confirmed Alex's inference, and then raised a sparkling grape juice toast to Alex's achievement on the exam as her cut-crystal glass sent diamond-shaped reflections dancing across the ceiling.

Somewhat embarrassed, Alex said, "I think I've done well, Mom, but it's not really for sure until I see the results in black and white. Oh my gosh, I hope I haven't jinxed it!" She assumed an exaggerated look of melodramatic concern of impending doom for her mother's benefit, back of her right hand to her forehead, forlorn facial expression, and dramatically arched back.

Her mother laughed delightedly and applauded Alex's theatrical range. The meal then settled down to the comfortable silence and intermittent conversation of two kindred souls, intimately entwined by their love for one another. After washing up the dishes, Alex said, "Mom, I'm going back up to hit Calculus for a couple of hours. After that, I'll probably just put on my IPOD and go to sleep. It really has been an exhausting day."

Her mother kissed her cheek and reminded her that she had rehearsal that evening. After kissing her in return, Alex went up the stairs, forcing herself to go slowly despite the intense ball of growing excitement that was burning in her toned belly. She had something to do, but it had nothing to do with mathematics.

She had a date.

Chapter 4

Alex shut her door and turned on her computer. Waiting for the boot sequence to finish, she thought about him, about Will. Images of exhilarating possibilities played across her mind, eliciting a sweet warmth from her body, a feeling she had never experienced before in her life.

He is so perfect, she cooed to herself.

Although Alex was one of, if not the most popular girl in school, she had never really had a steady boyfriend - that is if she discounted Marshall Jones in the third grade.

It had all started when she and Britt had been accepted into the Running Start program at NSCC, North Seattle Community College, the past year. As an advanced placement junior, she could take up to two courses at the college each quarter prior to high school graduation. Alex had chosen Sociology and Psychology, two offerings not available on her high school curriculum. In particular, Sociology intrigued her and she quickly established an easy rapport with both Mrs. Timmins, the instructor, and the rest of the students, all of whom were somewhat older than her. For her class project, she decided to study the group conventions of online chat rooms.

She knew exactly what type of people she wanted as her test subjects. Guys, but only those fitting her own particular, narrowly-defined demographic. She threw herself into her research with her typically fierce determination and single-mindedness. It wasn't too long before she had found several likely subjects. She chatted with them all. Some she quickly discarded as crass and/or uninteresting; while with others she developed a casual online friendship. Her attention became much more focused, however, when she met Will.

His profile said he was twenty-one, a junior at the University of Washington, studying pre-law. His picture was of a smiling, friendly-faced Nordic, one very fit and handsome. Alex, however, was well-aware of the high percentage of men who completely misrepresented themselves online. Consequently, her initial contact was guarded, characterized by seemingly innocent, but actually highly discerning questions, intending to unveil the true character of Will Hendrickson. Gradually, she relaxed as she grew increasingly more aware he was perfect.

They had so many things in common, it seemed. When she had said she loved 80s rock, particularly hair bands like Poison and Whitesnake, he had been ecstatic. Similarly, her love of hiking and camping had struck a familiar chord. After a month, Will had declared to her that she was his virtual a soul mate.

Alex had been careful, however, despite her obvious attraction to Will. There were so many awful stories to mention about what had happened to innocent teenagers who were groomed by bad people on the internet.

But not every guy on the internet is a depraved pervert, is he? she had argued with herself.

It had actually been Will who had brought the subject up first. She had told him she agreed wholeheartedly, that a person can't be too careful nowadays. This was not what she had actually wanted to say, however.

She had wanted to tell him, "To hell with caution; let's hook-up!" Instead, she had repeated, 'patience is a virtue' over and over again to herself, until her emotionality level dropped sufficiently enough for her to continue a rational conversation.

Alex glanced at her on-screen clock and saw it was nearly their pre-arranged chat time.

Too bad about his webcam being broken, she laughed to herself; *I'd love to see what he looks like in real life. Oh well, she thought, that day is going to be coming real soon.*

Suddenly, she was alerted she had an IM, "would she accept?" She punched the "Yes" button and, a couple of seconds later, read, "Hello gorgeous! Miss me?"

She typed, "Not really, I've just been entertaining a much older man here in my boudoir, giving him two hours of very loving, undivided attention."

His "???" caused her to break out into a fit of giggles, which she stifled into her pillow.

She answered, "Einstein, silly! I've been studying for my physics exam."

He replied, "Well, I'm certainly relieved. I couldn't bear the idea you had traded me in for an older model (lol)."

She laughed again and typed, "Hardly likely, as that would mean you would be getting around with a walker and I'd have to chew your food for you!"

He made no immediate reply and Alex slugged her pillow and whispered to herself, *You fucking dipshit! Think before you type, why don't you? Now, you've pissed him off!*

Eventually though, he replied, "Har har, very funny! But that would be better than having a girlfriend who still wears training pants!"

She typed, "Point well taken. Uh, Will?"

"Yeah, Katie?" came the immediate reply.

She continued, "Do you actually think of me as your girlfriend?" As she typed this, she felt the familiar feeling of warmth start to spread across her body, unexpectedly accompanied by a slight, unexpected moistness "you know where."

He replied, "Yes, Katie, I really do. Over the past month, I have talked more with you than anyone I have ever done before. I feel we've truly made a connection. I've also come to realize I've never been happy with anyone until I met you."

Excitement raged up and down her body like a tangible thing as she typed, "I feel exactly the same, Will. Um, would you like to meet up?" She held her breath in anxious anticipation.

His reply caused a flash of anger to meld with her other emotions as she read, "Sure, I mean, not so sure. I kind of don't know if it will ruin things. What if you don't like me in the flesh?"

Calming herself, she replied, "Don't be silly. I'm a good judge of character and already know who you are, what you are, and what my feelings are towards you. You are the guy I have been looking for, Will, please be confident of that. Are you hesitating because you think I'll be different than what you think?"

"No," he replied, but the minute hesitation was noticeable.

"Well then, it's settled."

"OK, you're right. Would you like to meet at Northgate Mall?" he ventured.

"God, how blasé," she chided, "Do you expect me to say, 'Like, fur shure,' then pop my bubble gum and twist my hair like some Val, or what?"

"OK, I deserve that (lol)," he replied, "Where do you want to meet then?"

"Uh, how about Green Lake Park?" she probed. "It seems kind of appropriate, really. We both love the outdoors and hiking. It will be, uh, romantic, Will. There's a bench in the woods back behind the tennis courts. I can stand on it and you can imagine I'm Juliet on her balcony. When you approach, I can call, 'Romeo, O Romeo, where for art thou, Romeo?'"

"Sounds great, Alex," he replied, "Especially the part about reenacting your favorite Shakespeare play. How about tomorrow at four?"

"Uh, sorry, but I can't. I promised my Mom I'd help her do some gardening in the back yard tomorrow afternoon."

"Next weekend?" he countered.

"No way, mister! I've waited weeks to meet you already and I'm certainly not going to wait one more! Could you meet me there at nine?"

"Kind of late, isn't it," he queried.

"You're right," she countered sarcastically, "I know how university guys are, needing to be in their rooms by nine; putting on their jammies, brushing their teeth, saying their prayers, then falling fast asleep."

"Alright, already, I surrender," he replied. "Make sure you scrub the venom off your keyboard before it starts to melt. See you there at nine. Bye, Katie."

"Bye, Will," she typed, her unfamiliar feelings of desire permeating every fiber of her being.

She logged off and initiated the computer's shutdown sequence. She glanced at her phone and saw she had received several texts. Unexpectedly overcome with weariness, she ignored them. Instead, she put on her pajamas, brushed her teeth, said her prayers, and fell fast asleep, her slumber enhanced by pleasant dreams of what she hoped the morrow would bring.

Alex awoke to bright golden sunlight streaming through her window. Closing her eyes to mere slits, she turned to her window and saw a cloudless sky, although she suspected it would be quite cool, if not downright cold outside. She sensed it was early, confirmed by a quick glance at her clock, which read 7:15 a.m.

Unlike most of her friends who often hibernated on weekends into the afternoon, Alex was invariably an early riser, another trait she shared with her mother.

"Besides," she thought delightfully," I've got another reason why I can't sleep today."

Yawning and stretching luxuriously, she got out of bed and went into her bathroom, emerging a few minutes later freshly washed and considerably more alert. Pulling on her robe and wriggling her size five feet into her fuzzy pink slippers red painted toenails first, she walked downstairs, following the unmistakable scent of freshly brewed coffee.

"Good morning, honey," her mother remarked, temporarily smiling up from the Saturday morning edition of the Seattle News Tribune.

"Hi, Mom," Alex replied, already adding a generous splat of White Chocolate Macadamia Nut non-dairy creamer to her steaming hot mug of coffee.

"There are fresh muffins on the counter. Your father was up early and made a run to the bakery."

"Thanks," Alex said, happily retrieving a banana nut muffin and sitting down across from her mother. After swallowing her first bite of her delicious, hi-carb treat, she continued, "Where's Dad?"

"Mr. Workaholic? Three guesses, and the first two don't count." Although her mother had replied jokingly, Alex perceptively noticed the faint aura of underlying tension that accompanied the remark.

Oh oh, she thought, *Dad must have really caught hell this morning.*

Although their household normally maintained a stable sense of equilibrium, her father's work schedule was always good to set off a few fireworks from time to time.

Sensing further discussion of her father's whereabouts was better left unexplored, Alex asked, "You wanted me at the theater this morning about eleven, right?"

Her mother replied, "Yup, you should be done by about two. Any plans after that?"

"Well, I thought I'd go to the mall to pick up a few things," Alex said, allowing herself a faint smile as she thought about the reason for her shopping. "Then, some of us are getting together out at the beach. I won't be back late, I promise."

"No problem," her mother replied, head already re-buried in the local news section of her morning newspaper.

The thought of querying her daughter more closely never entered her mind, even as she began to read the article about the poor girl whose body had been found at Lord Hills Park. Alex was a sensible and completely trustworthy girl, a fact echoed by many of her friends who envied the fact she had never waited up until 3:00 a.m., sick to the soul her daughter was dead or in the hospital, only to see her sneaking in, drunk and disheveled. Nor had she ever picked up her daughter's dirty laundry, only to find a half-used packet of birth control pills or a bag of weed. Despite the compassion she felt for Amy Reiss and her parents, she couldn't help to also feel a bit of happiness at the fact she had been blessed with her adored Alex.

The morning rushed by for Alex. After her morning ablutions, including a decadently prolonged bath, she dressed casually but fashionably, aware she did not want to cause her mother embarrassment later at the theater. She then got down to the serious business of answering the text messages that had accumulated on her phone since yesterday. Deftly deflecting separate offers to get together with Britt, Gina, and Summer, she grabbed her purse and went downstairs to the kitchen. Guiltily, she wolfed down another of the scrummy muffins. Then, after writing, "I love you both!" on the notice board, she went out the door, walking down the sidewalk toward Yoda, the Jedi Master.

At least that's how she always referred to her beloved Toyota Corolla. Yoda had been her sixteenth birthday present from her parents, the absolute best gift anyone had ever bought her. She started the car and drove the six miles to the theater. Her time there passed pleasurably enough. She liked the hubbub and shared sense of purpose in amateur dramatics, but was sometimes dismayed by the company's disorganization and democratic approach to even the smallest decision.

Oh well, it's Mom's thing, not mine.

She dutifully completed the tasks allotted to her; painting of some scenery flats and helping to mount some spotlights. Finishing, she kissed her mother goodbye and left the theater. Stepping outside, she noticed a family of roiling, dark clouds gathered in the west.

Could be rain tonight, her brain unconsciously processing the possible need for her waterproof jacket.

Her obligations finished; Alex's methodical mind was finally free to turn to her impending date with Will. Despite paying close attention to her driving, she allowed herself to revel in a series of short vignettes, each imagining one small scene in her initial meeting with the person she had spent so much time with in the past few weeks.

She pulled her Toyota into the parking lot and walked purposefully into the mall. She strode through the entrance toward Express, unerringly guided by countless visits to the store in the past. She selected a simple white cami and a pair of jeans, paying for them with cash. On her way out, she went through the fragrance and beauty section, liberally dashing herself with Love Express, a fragrance Britt had been raving about. Crinkling her nose as the heavy, unfamiliar scent wafted about her, she giggled as she thought, "A portent of things to come?" Pausing only to rub the brand's corresponding body lotion on her hands, she left the shop and treated herself to a light lunch at Sushi Maru. "Only one more thing to do," she thought to herself. She exited the mall and crossed the street to the Thornton Place movie theater. After waiting in line for a few seconds, she purchased an advance showing ticket for the new Julianne Hough movie. Placing the ticket in her purse, she returned to her Toyota and left for home.

Her excitement mounted as she began to get ready for her date. Stripping to her underwear, she pulled her new jeans over her slender thighs. She took a quick look at her butt in the mirror and gave herself a joking wink and thumbs up. Her mood turned more thoughtful though as she took off her bra and looked at the reflection of her small, firm breasts. She slid the white cami over her head and pulled it down toward her hips. Looking closely, she could just make out her small areoles through the light material, which was stretched perceptively more by the semi-erectness of her nipples.

God, what a hootchie-mama, she chided herself critically, *but I can't let him off the line, can I?*

Alex spent appreciably more time applying her make-up than usual, going for a heavier, somewhat less natural look. She teased her hair, increasing its normal fullness to approximate a "rock chick" look. Putting a set of large hoop earrings in her ears, she looked in the mirror to view the total package.

Well, he's certainly not going to run away in fright, she smiled.

Completing her ensemble, she wedged each petite foot into a Gel-Noosa Tri, packed her purse, and looked at the clock; it was 7:45 p.m. It was time to go.

Opening the front door, she saw the evening sky was now dominated by the angry clouds that had seemed so innocent earlier. She returned inside and grabbed her jacket. She closed the house door behind her, turning her key carefully to ensure it was locked. As she drove to the park, however, a niggling hint of self-doubt chipped at the upper-right hand corner of her customary self-confidence.

Should she really go through with this? Could she really go through with this? She pulled Yoda to the side of the road and looked at herself in the make-up mirror. *Listen you bitch,* she said fiercely but silently to herself, *this is no time to wimp out now. You've devoted untold hours to this guy, you know he's perfect. Now, get your ass to the park and meet him, for crying out loud!*

Buoyed up by her internal pep talk, she slid the Toyota back onto the street and continued on her way.

She unobtrusively parked her car down a side street off 59th. She knew the short walk to the agreed-upon meeting place would clear her head, give her focus.

She checked the time on her phone, 8:05 p.m., *plenty of time to get there, to be waiting alluringly for him when he stepped into the clearing.*

The visualization of her first sight of him excited her; yet, also relaxed and calmed her. She set off down 59th, quickly crossing into the wooded expanse of Green Lake Park. The wind was whipping up noticeably, corresponding to an appreciable drop in temperature. She registered the shifting weather conditions unconsciously; secure in the fact her waterproof jacket would counter any adverse possibilities. Before she knew it, she had arrived at the bench. She looked around, confirming the late hour, coupled with the likelihood of rain, had emptied this area of the park completely. She leaned back on the bench, idly took out her phone, and settled down to comfortably pass the time.

At a quarter to nine, she put her phone down, too wound up to do anything other than gaze at the pathway leading into the little clearing. Her stomach was churning when 9:00 p.m. came and passed. She put her phone away, vowing not to check it every minute that passed in which Will had still failed to materialize. It began to rain very lightly, a liquid reconnaissance for the full precipitation attack that was certain to follow sometime later in the night.

She heard his footsteps before she saw him, the distinctive tap of the soles of leather shoes. The man coming down the pathway bore no resemblance to the picture of Will that was firmly etched in her mind. He was probably in his late forties, well dressed and well kept.

He approached the bench and said, "Pardon me, are you alright?"

Bravely putting a smile on her face, Alex replied, "Yeah, I'm just waiting for someone. He should be here any minute though."

The man smiled and said, "OK. By the way, my name's Tom, Tom Beach. Do you mind if I sit down? This is one of my favorite places in the park. I often come here at night and imagine it's up in the Cascades somewhere, a hundred miles from civilization. Sorry. Silly, isn't it?"

Alex responded, "No, I don't think so at all. Everyone has places they love and it's a shame they can't be there whenever they want to be." He concurred and they talked, instantly establishing an easy rapport that seemed impossible to achieve in such a few short minutes. Then, phrasing her sentence very carefully, Alex said, "So are you happy I chose this place, Will?"

The man said nothing aloud; yet, the look in his eyes confessed everything. He stood up abruptly and began backing away, apologizing. Alex, however, only smiled and patted the seat next to her gently, an unspoken invitation to him to sit beside her. He looked at her, not believing she was serious. As if she could read his mind, she smiled more fully and again patted the seat.

Hesitatingly, he walked over and sat down. He gazed into her the eyes then, looking like he was about to cry, turned away. Then the words came tumbling from his mouth.

"I'm so sorry for lying to you, Katie. I know I shouldn't have deceived you, shouldn't have even continued our first conversation when you told me how old you are. But you're just the most fascinating person I've ever met; intelligent, witty, and incredibly sweet. I tried to stop, to never even go on that chat site again. I just couldn't help myself. Before I knew what was happening, I could hardly think about anything else except for the next time I would be able to talk to you. Then, when you said you wanted to meet, I knew it was all over. I was devastated, but thrilled as well. I wanted to see what you really looked like in person. I knew I couldn't actually meet you but, if I knew where you were going to be, I could at least see you. I swore to myself that would be enough. Tonight, however, I knew I had to chance talking to you as well. Besides, you wouldn't know who I was anyway, right? Just a quick conversation, I could leave, and you'd be none the wiser. Only, I'd forgotten how perceptive you are. I'm so incredibly sorry, Katie, I'll be leaving now and . . ."

"Shush," she interrupted in a throaty whisper. "You say you recognize how perceptive I am, so did you think your little deception was going to go unnoticed forever? I had you figured out the first time we chatted. Think about it, what did we talk about? Art, politics, travel, and twenty-year-old music, that's what; not the kind of things a normal college junior would find interesting, pre-med or not. I even worked in a few local references only someone who had lived in Seattle during the 1970s would recognize and you know what? You passed with flying colors!"

"OK," he admitted, "But what if I had grown up someplace other than Seattle? That would have thrown your little test out of kilter."

She looked at him with the look one uses on a puppy that trips over its own feet and lands sprawling.

"Do you think a girl needs to reveal her entire repertoire, especially if she doesn't need to?"

He looked at her in silent amazement. He had felt guilty after every one of their chats, thinking it was as if he was grooming her like some pervert, the ones you read about in detective stories. The funny thing was, it was actually her that was grooming him. He didn't know exactly how he felt about that.

Alex stood up and walked to the edge of the tree line. He watched as she took off her jacket and stretched, arching her back and raising her arms enough to show the smooth skin of her tanned back. Returning to him, he was transfixed by the outline of her breasts becoming increasingly more visible as the rain dampened her translucent top. She sat down, straddling his legs and holding her body close to his. She moved her head forward, finding his disbelieving lips and probing her tongue inside them.

She slowly disengaged and rotated her body suddenly off his lap, dropping her jacket on the bench beside him. She trailed her arm lingeringly across his right shoulder as she moved behind him. She moved unhurriedly, as if in a dream. Alex ran her fingers through his still thick shock of hair, pulling at it, seemingly playfully. He closed his eyes in erotic bliss, unaware of what was to come next, but anticipating its pleasure with every iota of his being.

Alex reached carefully into her jeans and pulled the slim box cutter silently from her pocket. Duplicating the sequence that she had rehearsed so often, she slid the blade forward and tugged ever so lightly on his hair, causing him to arch his neck slightly, pulling the skin tightly across his carotid arteries. With surprising and sudden force, she swiftly drew the sharp blade through his soft flesh, severing the left carotid, trachea, and right carotid in quick succession. She pulled the weapon free with a flourish, resisting the urge to shout "Ole!" like a bullfighter as she did so. At first, Tom Beach was unaware his life was soon to be over. He felt no pain, only the pressure that passed across his neck. Before his eyes, however, he saw what appeared to be a bright red aerosol but, what was in fact, his arterial blood. He attempted to turn around, but slid instead to the ground. He saw Katie had moved back to the edge of the clearing. He tried to call out to her, to ask her what had happened, but his breath emerged instead from his severed trachea in the form of bloody froth. He attempted to stand, but his coordination was fatally impaired by approaching unconsciousness resulting from his already considerable blood loss. He fell back to the ground, struggled weakly, and then laid still.

Alex swiftly surveyed the scene. Tom Beach's body was sprawled in front of the bench, lying predominantly on his left side, his right leg at a 225-degree angle to the rest of his body. His right arm was also extended, with his bicep covering the angry gash that split his throat horizontally. The spray of blood that saturated the grass in front of the bench was already dissipating, diluted by the increasingly heavy rainfall.

Oh my God, she thought, stifling her gag reflex as a rancid scent infused the air, reminiscent of the porta- potties at the outdoor concert she had attended last summer. *It really is true what they say about a person's bowels and bladder when they die.*

The horrible smell prompted her to turn away from the body and back to her immediate task.

Quickly pulling a plastic bag from her purse, Alex pulled out a pair of disposable gloves that had been part of a furniture refinishing kit with her left hand as she dropped the box cutter inside with her right. She deftly sealed the bag and dropped it into her purse. She then pulled on the gloves, put on her coat, grabbed her purse and began walking toward the pathway, shoving her hands deeply into her jacket pockets. She rounded the corner and strode onto the pathway at 9:42 p.m., exactly two minutes after the park had become an unexpected crime scene.

Chapter 5

"God damn it, God damn it, God damn it!" Alex kept up her repetitive litany of expletives for miles; yet, unconsciously clocking she would have to humbly seek the Lord's forgiveness in her prayers for taking his name in vain.

She drove aimlessly through the dark suburbs of Seattle.

How could I be so stupid? she asked herself, tears flowing freely down her cheeks.

Her sense of self-loathing transfixed her, leaving her largely unaware of even where she was driving.

She had spent hours planning her meeting with Will, down to the minutest detail. She had explored every possible contingency, formulating a corresponding response that would guarantee her success.

Then, what happened? I get caught up in the moment and leave my DNA all over his mouth, that's what! she answered miserably.

For the past six years, she had hardly missed an episode of CSI, be it Las Vegas, Miami, or New York. Gradually, her avid interest had subtly changed, from viewing the programs as light entertainment to considering them a crash course in forensic science. She had augmented her knowledge by frequenting criminology sites on the Internet. By the time she had decided to put her plan into action, she had a very good working knowledge of how forensic evidence could, and usually did, trip up those who decide to take the life of another human being.

"I had him, I knew I had him," she whispered to herself, unconsciously waiting for a red light to change.

She was certain that when she had turned around and walked towards him, she could have done almost anything and he wouldn't have moved from his spot on the bench.

Why didn't I just move behind him then, cut him, and that would have been that? she asked herself for the umpteenth time. *No trace evidence would have been left to associate me with him. I had been so careful to avoid the blood splatter; so careful not to let him touch me, both before and after.*

"God damn it, God damn it. . ." she began aloud again.

Gradually, her anger with herself abated. She had wanted to make sure he would stay on the bench; not get up to face her as she moved behind him. Sitting on his lap should have planted the subliminal message she wanted him to stay seated, affirming that decision with recollections of conditioning theories they had discussed in her Psychology course. The kiss had been an inspiration in the heat of the moment, to "seal the deal," so to speak. That it had worked to subdue the man was not in question, he had barely moved as she drew the box cutter across his throat. Instead, the questionability of the action centered on the advisability of leaving DNA evidence that linked her to the man she had killed.

Alright, what's the worst thing that can happen? They find the DNA of some girl on the vic's lips and in his mouth. How could it have got there? Quite a few ways, actually. Maybe he has a young girlfriend, a wife, or even a daughter he likes to very affectionately kiss goodbye, her nose crinkled in disgust at the thought of that possibility.

Alternatively, he could have been with a prostitute or even at a strip club before coming to the park. As a result, the CSI team may not make too big of a deal out of it. I mean, wouldn't they be more likely to associate a girl's DNA with a possible victim, rather than that of his killer? she asked herself optimistically.

Well, so what's the damage then? One, I can't take it for granted that my DNA hasn't been entered into CODIS; consequently,

I can never, and I mean never, allow the police to take a blood or saliva sample from me for any reason. Two, I have to be very careful to never, and I mean never, leave stray DNA floating around a crime scene again. Three, to never, and I mean never, be such a stupid dumb shit again.

She permitted herself a little smile after that one.

Somewhat buoyed back to her usual perkiness by her reassuring rationalization of her ill-conceived, spur of the moment actions in the park, Alex began to pull herself back together. She realized she had several necessary tasks to complete before returning home. She turned her attention to the view out of her windshield and soon determined her locale and got back on course. She pulled into the service station where she had planned to use the single, very lockable restroom. Taking her purse, she flashed the young attendant a disarming smile that clearly made his day. Entering the restroom, she locked the door and got down to work. She peeled the plastic gloves off her hands and laid them on the side of the sink. Next, she examined her now bare hands and arms. Encouragingly, she could not perceive any blood on them, nor on any of her clothes, face, or hair.

Good job with that at least, allowing herself a terse self-compliment.

She thoroughly washed her hands with the dermatological soap she had brought in her purse, quickly brushed her still damp hair, and fixed her makeup. Feeling immeasurably better, she turned her attention to the box cutter, still sealed in its plastic bag.

What to do about the knife had always troubled her.

Should I just throw it away? she had pondered, *or clean and return it to the garage?*

She had decided on the second course of action. She took the knife from the plastic bag and removed the blade. She then washed the box-cutter, knowing she would repeat the process much more thoroughly later on. She dried it under the air dryer and placed it into a second plastic bag, returning it to her purse. She dreaded what was to come next, however.

She opened the contaminated materials receptacle. She silently retched as she examined the bin's contents; a few used sanitary pads and various other articles too unsavory to mention. She gingerly picked up a couple of the worst examples of hi-octane menstrual flow and placed them in her own bloody plastic bag. She then carefully placed the gloves and the used box cutter blade into the center of the mess and buried it into the middle of the receptacle's contents. Even if an investigator had the ability to have somehow followed the extremely tenuous evidence trail to this container, he or she would have to be psychic to ignore the most obvious source of the blood in the bag, swabbing it to connect to the crime scene DNA, she thought with satisfaction. She placed the lid back in its place and turned to wash her hands again; if anything, even more thoroughly than she had the first time. Going through her mental checklist, she ensured she had left none of the tasks uncompleted and left the restroom. Before leaving the service station, she stopped to purchase a package of sugar free gum and, popping a stick into her mouth, returned purposefully to her Toyota for the short drive to her house.

"Hi, everybody. I'm home!" Alex sang as she came through the door, knowing her greeting was probably in vain as she was welcomed by the silence of a deserted house.

She imagined her mother would probably be out with her theater friends, reliving in detail every second of the evening's dress rehearsal at Black and White, the neighborhood's trendy wine bar. Her father may have decided to join her mother there or, more likely, met his friends from work at the local sports bar. Alternatively, he may have just decided to call it an early evening since he was by himself. She took a quick look in the garage and was relieved to see both of their cars were missing. She carefully placed the box cutter on the workbench, reminding herself to finish cleaning it the following day. After throwing the plastic bag into the garbage can, she left the garage and went to her room.

She went into her bathroom and carefully removed her outer clothes, placing them in a bag, tying the top closed, and sliding it under her bed.

Tomorrow, those go to the Goodwill collection point, she declared, a bit ruefully as she had really liked the fit of the jeans especially. *There is no way I'm going to risk the chance of a bit of his DNA hanging around here. One forensic faux pas' tonight is already one too many, thank you very much!*

She then started to run a bath. While the tub was filling, she brushed and flossed her teeth, removing all residues, either real or imagined, of Will Hendrickson/Tom Beach. She then wriggling out of her panties, deposited them in her dirty clothes bin, and stepped into the luscious, hot water of her bath, which she had liberally doused with cinnabar scented bath oil beads. Sliding down to where the water fell just below her chin, she smiled blissfully, reveling in her sensual reward for a job pretty well done.

Before she was finished, she heard the door open downstairs.

She answered her father's shout of, "Hi, Alex. Are you up there?" with, "Yes, I'm in the bath." Reluctantly, she left the tub and dried herself, wrapping a towel around her still wet hair. Putting on her robe and bedroom slippers, she went downstairs.

"Hi, Dad," she said, flashing him a tentative smile, "Where you been?" already anticipating the answer from the pungent odor of beer and nachos on his breath.

"Aw, just down with the guys at The Home Plate, watching the Mariners get crucified. How about you?" he responded.

"Well, I went shopping and then I was going to go out to the beach with some friends from school. But the weather was really starting to look iffy, so I went to a movie instead, followed by some sushi. Then home, a bath, and you."

Alex then spent the next five minutes detailing the plot of the movie, which she had actually viewed the previous weekend. Her father's interest in a minute accounting of ninety minutes of cinematic teenaged angst quickly flagged and his relief was visible when Alex excused herself, pecked him on the cheek, and trundled off to bed. Slipping into her pajamas, she said her prayers, including a heartfelt and contrite admission of her earlier repetitious blasphemy and penitent request for forgiveness. She then crawled into bed and snuggled her favorite teddy bear closely. Just before falling asleep, she mentally noted it was church tomorrow and to remember to finish cleaning the box cutter and to drop her bag of clothes off at the Goodwill.

Alex awoke to the sound of incessant rain drumming on her window and her mother calling, "Alex!" She looked at her clock and saw it was nearly nine a.m. She leapt out of bed, put on her robe, and hurried downstairs, simultaneously answering, "Coming right now, Mom!"

As she expected, her mother was already dressed and seated at the breakfast bar, sipping what must be her third cup of coffee by now.

Her mother asked, "Up late last night, sleepyhead?" in a joking; yet, mildly inquisitive manner.

Alex bussed her on the cheek in passing and placed two slices of whole wheat bread in the toaster.

She replied, "Not really, guess I just needed to recharge a bit, what with all the exam stress lately."

"Did you get to the beach yesterday?"

"No," Alex replied truthfully before spinning her response into a little white lie. "After shopping, I saw the clouds welling up, so I went across to Thornton Place and bought a ticket to the new Julianne Hough romcom."

"That genre's not exactly your usual cup of tea, Alex. Any good?"

"Yeah," she said, again stretching the truth a bit. "Not bad actually." She was saved from recounting the plot of the film yet again by her toast suddenly popping up.

After quickly covering the slices with a thin layer of Smuckers strawberry jam, she began to consume them voraciously.

"Hey, slow down, "her mother laughed, placing a hot mug of coffee in front of her daughter. "We've got plenty of time to get to church."

"Dad coming?" Alex managed to ask, a mouthful of toast rendering her normally excellent enunciation only semi-coherent.

"Well, he had a pretty exciting night last night. Combined with the hours he's been putting in at work, he's in pretty rough shape this morning," her mother alluded, in what Alex correctly inferred was a somewhat unforgiving tone.

It was readily apparent she was not happy about her husband begging off from church, a commitment she took very seriously.

"So, it looks like you, me, and God today, Mommy," Alex said, hugging her mother tightly.

Although Alex had called her "Mommy" well into high school, she could not remember exactly the last time she had done so. Tears began welling up in the corners of her eyes at the thought of her daughter's empathetic compassion and unconditional affection.

"I love you so much, Alex," she said, simultaneously offering a prayer of thanks to God for the special gift of her daughter.

"Not as much as I love you!"

Breaking their mutual embrace, her mother dried her eyes and said in a much more business-like tone, "Now, young lady, get upstairs and get ready or we're going to be late." She swatted Alex's bottom lightly for emphasis as she turned to comply. "Honey, please wear that nice white linen suit I bought you. You look absolutely gorgeous in it."

Alex turned back to her mother and wagged her finger in mock censure, saying, "Remember, Mom, 'Women should adorn themselves in respectable apparel, with modesty and self-control' - Timothy 2:9"

Her mother executed a deep courtesy, acknowledging equally her daughter's quick wit as well as her knowledge of the Bible.

Rising, she said, "All right, smarty pants, now shoo!"

In less than a half hour, Alex descended the stairs and the two women exited the house.

Alex asked, "Do you want me to drive, Mom?"

"Oh, that would be great," her mother replied, knowing how much Alex loved driving Yoda, the Toyota.

At the thought of the pet name Alex had given the little car, she suppressed a slight giggle.

Alex looked at her mother quizzically as they got in the car, but she just shrugged her shoulders comically, performing a passable impression of a mime. They drove to the Methodist church in comfortable silence. Getting out of the car, they crossed the parking lot and walked up the steps toward the entrance doors, greeting several people they knew and nodding in a sociable manner to those they did not. Actually, there were very few in the second category as she and her mother had been worshiping there for as long as she could remember.

They exchanged a few affable words with Reverend Roberts, the church's minister for as long as Alex could remember, at the door. They then walked inside the church, moving purposefully to their customary pew. Alex loved the architecture of the building; modern and light; beautiful, yet functional. Since she was a little girl, she had always felt good about coming to church in the building, comfortable that she was in the loving hands of God.

Reverend Roberts gave his welcoming address and directed his congregation to open their hymnals to #2130, "The Summons." Alex loved the hymn, feeling its special significance to her. As she joined the other parishioners in the first few lines, tears of her heartfelt joy flowed unbridled down her cheeks.

Will you come and follow me if I but call your name?
Will you go where you don't know and never be the same?
Will you let my love be shown? Will you let my name be known,
will you let my life be grown in you and you in me?

After a few minutes of the minister's sermon, Alex's thoughts strayed to the night before and her killing of Tom Beach. She still reproached herself for leaving evidence at the site unnecessarily, but rationalized the chance of the police using it to connect her to the dead man were actually quite slim. For the first time since she killed him, she went over the sequence of events in her mind, evaluating the strengths and weaknesses of her implementation of her plan. Aside from her obvious gaffe, she decided, she had not done badly for her first time. She had certainly correctly targeted a man who was misrepresenting himself as a teenager, for what perverted purpose she could only horrifically speculate. She almost became physically ill as she contemplated what might have happened to her if she had not pre-empted his actions.

Thank you, Jesus, for keeping me safe, she offered a fervent silent prayer.

After the services were concluded, Alex and her mother gravitated to Mr. and Mrs. Stevens, and their lovely, vivacious daughter Britt. Alex and Britt were quickly immersed in undemanding, friendly conversation, in contrast to that of the adults that centered on the news of the most recent murder in the city. After a while, mutual consensus was reached to have lunch at TGIF.

After ordering, Grace Stevens remarked, "It's terrible, isn't it, that a person isn't even safe in a local park?"

Alex's mother nodded her head in agreement.

"The fact that a group of young children discovered the body even makes it worse. Imagine how badly they must have been traumatized, poor things."

The adults all looked quizzically at Alex, who appeared quite visibly shaken by the news.

She quickly recovered, however, exclaiming, "My Gosh, how dreadful!" to cover the sick feeling in her stomach that she was responsible for the children's shocking experience.

Just like Mom though, Alex thought proudly, *feeling compassion for all those who involved, not just the most obvious person.*

"Poor things?" George Stevens chipped in, "It could have been their older brothers who did it. Damn kids are too violent nowadays; get it from those videogames. If anyone deserves to be called 'poor,' it's the guy who's lying dead in the morgue this morning. Did the paper say if he had a family?"

Grace Steven's response was lost on Alex, who was weighing whether Tom Beach's transgressions were worse if he left a loving wife and adoring children at home to go out to commit his depravations. She decided they were.

She then realized everyone was staring at her again.

She looked at her mother helplessly who, understanding Alex had been woolgathering, repeated, "Mrs. Stevens asked if you were still thinking about getting a temporary job with the city park service this summer."

Recovering quickly, Alex responded, "Yes, ma'am."

Britt's mother said, "Do you think that's wise, dear, with all of these terrible murders occurring in and around parks? You can't be too safe, you know."

"Oh, Mom!" said Britt, leaping to the defense of her friend, "They'll probably catch the guy responsible by then. Furthermore, none of the people killed were working in the park, were they? Besides, Alex has a mother to look out for her. Your job is to make my life miserable, not hers." She punctuated her statement by blowing her mother a kiss and then flashing her a cheesy grin.

Mrs. Stevens turned to Alex's mother, passing her a look that lightheartedly conveyed, "What's becoming of the younger generation?" Just then, their appetizers arrived and the conversation split into one between the two girls and another involving the two adult women, occasionally punctuated by a comment by Britt's father.

Tuning out the adult's discussion going on around her, Alex smiled at Britt and, assuming a dreamy swoon, remarked, "My hero!"

"You're welcome," Britt replied, flicking a crouton that bounced off Alex's nose. "Doing anything later?"

"Well, I've got a couple of chores to do this afternoon, but how about around four?"

"No probs, my house?" queried Britt.

Alex agreed and their conversation grew into a tête-à-tête about school, music, and boys. Finishing their meals, Alex and her mother bid the Stevens' goodbye and returned home. Stepping through the door, their chorus of "Hellos" was met by silence; it was obvious the house was empty.

"Too tired for church, is he? Probably snuck off to work the minute we left the house," Alex's mother said in a tone that was more reconciled to the inevitable than angry. "Do you mind if I work on my lines for the play, honey? We open next week and I'm still a bit shaky once we get into act three."

"That's OK, Mom; I've got a few things to do myself. I'm also going over to Britt's at four, if that's OK? If you'd rather though, I could stay and run through them with you."

"No, you run along. Your father will probably be along later and I'll make him help me as penance for missing church."

Alex went to her room and put the finishing touches on a collage of Civil War images she was doing for her final history project. She then vacuumed her room, knowing the noise would probably prompt her mother to put on her earphones. She went downstairs and saw, just as expected, her mother lying on the sofa with her earphones in place.

Going into the garage, she retrieved the box cutter and began to clean it more thoroughly. Using a bristle brush and OxiClean, she scrubbed the knife until it was spotless. She had discovered in her research the standard forensic tests for blood residue rely on the detection of hemoglobin, which is the part of the blood that carries oxygen from the lungs to the rest of the body. Oxy cleaners, however, flood the blood deposit with oxygen as part of its cleaning process and, once the protein is saturated with oxygen, it can't absorb any more from the investigator's blood detection tests. Consequently, results are consistently negative. Finishing with her cleaning of the knife, she rubbed it with a light lubricant to prevent rust from forming, placed it back on the workbench, and returned to her room.

Reaching under her bed, she pulled out the bag containing the jeans and top she had worn the previous evening.

She took one last rueful look at the jeans, musing, *this is going to get expensive.*

Placing a few other odds and ends of unwanted clothing into the bag as well, she carried it down to the living room.

Moving to the end of the sofa, she wiggled her mother's foot and said," Mom, I'm going to drop some old clothes off at the Goodwill before I go over to Britt's. Do you want me to pick you up anything while I'm out?"

Her mother responded negatively and Alex left the house.

After dinner that night, Alex returned to her room. After a couple of hours of studying, she fell back onto her bed with a growing sense of self-satisfaction. She felt ready for tomorrow's Physics exam, as well as Calculus on Wednesday. In retrospect, she was also fairly pleased with the killing of Tom Beach.

I deserve a B-, she mused in critical appraisal of her actions. *A few mistakes, but none of them fatal, hopefully. Not bad for a first timer.*

Throughout her life, however, Alex had always been an A+ student; consequently, she knew she would have to up her game in the future. Moving over to sit at her computer she promised herself, the next one has to be perfect.

Chapter 6

John Caldwell was not a happy bunny. His Sunday afternoon routine in late spring involved planting his ass in his recliner with a bucket of beers and catching at least a few innings of baseball before he began the discordant serenade of snores that drove his family running from the immediate area. Instead, here he was, pulling into another crime scene.

Christ, am I the only bastard stupid enough to answer his phone on Sunday? he thought in exasperation.

Even though it was Frank who called, he probably would have told him to go to hell if the murder hadn't occurred almost on John's doorstep. He pulled his Ford into the parking lot next to the tennis courts and cut through the woods to where Frank had said the body had been found. After a couple of minutes, he saw the homicide detective, standing in a ring of barrier tape that cordoned off a rough circle approximately fifty feet in diameter.

Approaching the tape, John said, "Shit, Frank, people are going to think we're an item if you keep calling me out every time you find a stiff. What the hell's up?"

Frank's serious look instantly defused John's bantering sense of irritation.

He began, "I'm really sorry to ask you to come in on your day off, John, but this is a really strange one. A young kid called 911 at 9:25 this morning, hysterical as hell. After the dispatcher calmed her down, she said she and some of her friends had walked to the park to play some soccer. They decided to cut through the trees and saw a guy lying beside a bench. Well, they argued for a while about what to do; they didn't know if it was someone who was hurt or just some wino sleeping it off. Finally, one of the girls got up enough nerve to go over to the guy and tap him on the shoulder. This caused his position to shift slightly and she saw he'd never be able to sleep off what had happened to him; his throat had been cut from side to side. Well, she screamed and they all got out of there fast, running like hell down to the tennis courts. That's when the girl had got herself sufficiently under control to call 911."

"Victim?"

Frank replied, "Forty-six years old, white Caucasian male. Brown hair and brown eyes. Smartly dressed, jacket and tie. Still had a gold wedding ring on his finger and a wallet in his pocket with over a hundred bucks; consequently, robbery seems to be a highly unlikely motive."

John, whose brain had gone into processing mode, interjected, "Splatter pattern?" knowing the spray area from a severed carotid can be impressive. If the pattern was interrupted, say by a person standing in the way, a ballpark estimate might be made of the perp's height and body type.

"Crime scene team has already processed the site; photographs, measurements, etc. Now just waiting on the lab for the results," Frank replied. "Last night's downpour certainly didn't help the quality of the evidence, but the CSI tech took soil samples for analysis, so hopefully we'll have something there."

"Any other evidence?" John asked, knowing already there probably wasn't anything noteworthy since Frank had mentioned nothing to the contrary.

"Nothing of real interest," Frank replied. "The site was pretty well contaminated; first by the rain, and then the kids. By the time we got here, a couple of joggers had also called it in. So, there are at least seven people that we know of who have been stomping around here since the time of death. That makes footprint morphology highly unlikely to turn up anything. The preliminary grid search failed to turn up any artifacts either. No first-hand witnesses have come forward, but the Department will send some uniforms out tomorrow to canvas the area. Hopefully, they'll find something on the body, or from the latent prints they lifted from the bench, but I'm not holding my breath."

"Well?" John asked, with a slightly brittle edge in his voice.

"Well, what?" Frank stared innocently into his eyes.

John took a deep breath and said, "Well, what the hell am I doing standing here listening to you yap when I should be on my third beer by now? Unless I missed the memo, you work for Homicide while I, being of a gentler persuasion, work for Sexual Assault and Child Abuse. From what you said, the guy wasn't a minor and he certainly wasn't fucked to death, unless the perp had a razor for a dick. So, I'm really confused, Frank. Why did you call me?"

A faint smile formed on Frank's lips as he said, "Well, it's certainly not for the quality of your company, that's for damn sure." John's silent glare caused him to continue more seriously. "The vic's driver's license was issued to a Thomas Beach; address 456 Capital Way, here in Seattle. When they ran the license on the system, they got a hit on the sex offender's list. He liked under-aged teenaged girls and boys just a little too much. Swung both ways, it seems, just as long as they were young. He was sentenced to seven years for felony sexual assault of a minor in 2004."

John looked at Frank, still without a clue, and began, "Yeah, so the vic's played around in my neck of the woods. I get it, but what's that got to do with the here and now?"

"Well," Frank replied," He also had a note in his overcoat pocket. It had the names "Will and Katie" at the top, followed by the drawing of a cute little heart and detailed directions on how to get to the park. Any guesses as to where X marked the spot?"

"Here," John stated the obvious.

"Yep, here. So, we can at least infer a few possible motives," Frank continued. "Number one, it could just be a random act of violence; in which case the murderer could be anyone. More interestingly, our boy Tom could have actually had a date with a woman his own age who, when she found out what a slime ball he actually was, decided to off him for the betterment of society. On the other hand, he could have just picked the wrong little kid to play with. Another option is that someone set him up. Maybe the father of one of the adolescents he traumatized discovered who he was and decided to get some sweet revenge. There is a fifth possibility as well, you know."

John said, "Go on, but let's try to get to the damn point sometime this afternoon."

"What if Beach was the one posing as 'Katie?' Now, just suppose there is some degenerate Romeo out there who thinks he has just set up a date with darling little Katie, the girl of his dreams. Arriving at the park, he discovers little sweet cheeks is not a nubile young cheerleader but, instead, is just another old perv. Consequently, rather than whisking her off in his chariot for some S&M fun and games back at the ranch, he slits his throat on the spot. You would think he'd be pretty pissed off, wouldn't you?"

John looked intensely at Frank, face frozen into a frown. Suddenly, he knew he couldn't hold it back any longer. He erupted into loud guffaws so intense his eyes began to water uncontrollably. Immediately, Frank joined him in his hysterical laughter.

The two beat cops assigned to guard the area until CSI was sure there was no more evidence to salvage looked on with irritation.

Well, I'm glad those sons-of bitches think this is funny, the taller one thought, I could be getting off-duty by now.

His partner silently nodded, as if he could read the other's mind.

Finally, gaining his power of speech once more, John said, "Oh, shit, I can see it now. One guy comes here looking for Hansel, the other one for Gretel. Then, it's a Mexican standoff, with both of them realizing they can't get on with what they want to do because the other one is there, cramping his style. Each of them would be shitting himself, afraid his little playmate would show up and he'd have a lot of explaining to do to the upright pillar of the community he imagined the other guy to be. Somehow, it must have come out that they were both child molesters. What Beach didn't realize, however, was that he found the wicked witch instead of a little kid who liked candy."

Frank continued to stare at John as he said slowly, "Take the theory one more logical step, John. We have a man coming to a secluded area of a park late in the evening, expecting to meet up with a young girl. He gets there and finds some guy camping out on his turf. When he somehow finds out the fella had played him for a fool, he is mucho pissed off. So, not wanting to make it a completely wasted trip, he pulls a utility knife out of his pocket and slits the guy's throat. Then he goes home and throws the knife back in his toolbox, hoping for better luck next time."

"The DIY Killer, "John exclaimed, looking in admiration at his fellow detective. "Well, it certainly fits. We've got a perp who preys on young girls, or possibly those who masquerade as one. He arranges to meet 'Katie' at a secluded location, an easy place to overpower her and take her away to fulfill his sick fantasies. Most importantly, he's a violent son-of-a- bitch who uses a weapon owned by just about homeowner in Seattle. Oh yeah, and did I mention he gets away without leaving any apparent clues as to how to nab his fucking self?"

Frank continued, "There's more too. Do you remember the second girl, Vicki Redmond?"

"Yeah," John responded, intently interested to see where Frank's line of reasoning was going to go next.

"Well," he began, "She had all those light slash marks on her thighs and stomach, right? At the time, we thought she was a cutter, using physical pain to obliterate even worse emotional trauma. It could have been something she had started before she was abducted, but it certainly would have made sense after, considering what she had to go through. But what if she didn't do it, what if it was him instead? We found the pliers marks on Amy Reiss, what if the slashes were made for the same reason? If we assume that to be true, they could have been made with the same knife he used to kill Beach."

"So, if the lab finds any residual DNA matching Vicki Redmond in Tom Beach's wound, we can connect the dots, right?"

He looked at Frank, who nodded his head in agreement.

John said, "Look Frank, I really think you've got something here, but there's not much more we can do until we get the lab reports. Let's go over it in detail first thing tomorrow at the office, OK?"

Frank agreed and John returned to his car. Driving home, John couldn't get their conversation out of his mind.

Shit, he chided himself, *let it be for now, will you?*

He parked the Ford in his driveway and went inside. He yelled a tentative "Hello?" but the lack of response indicated his family was evidently out somewhere. Retrieving a beer from the fridge, he settled into his recliner, grabbed the remote, and started to flip through the channels.

After a few minutes, he turned the television off, giving in to the uncontrollable itch to get his mind back on the case. He knew Frank's idea was only a theory but, goddammit, it somehow seemed to fit together. The guy had abducted and murdered at least three girls, what would have prevented him from killing Beach? What do big sharks eat when there's no fish around? Little sharks, that's what.

Suddenly, his phone rang. It was Frank. The lab had found foreign DNA on Beach's body. They estimated it was from a female, approximately fifteen to twenty-five years of age. At Frank's insistent urging, they had compared it to that of Vicki Redmond. Frustratingly, the match was negative.

"That's too bad," John commiserated, "I had actually bought into that theory of yours."

"Yeah," Frank answered. "Then he told me he didn't get the sample from blood residue, but from an oral swab. Seems Tommy boy had been swapping spit with a girl, and not to long before he was killed. Before you ask, they searched for a possible match on the CODIS database. No luck there."

John thanked Frank for keeping him informed and confirmed their meeting for 8:15 a.m. the next day Hanging up the phone, John's feeling of anger rose. He couldn't shake the imagine of Tom Beach kissing one of his daughters, his filthy hands all over her body, forcing her into unspeakable acts to provide him his sick pleasure.

He swore and thought harshly, *If I would have found you with my daughter, you bastard, you would have considered yourself lucky to just get your throat cut.*

Gradually, his rage subsided to a controllable level and he got another Michelob. He returned to the chair, cautioning himself to keep his perspective, to avoid an emotional investment in the case that might cloud his judgment. He turned the television back on and immersed himself into the third inning of the Braves vs. the Giants.

He awakened with a barely suppressed shout, startled. Claire stood over him, clearly upset.

"It's not bad enough you've already put in sixty hours this week, but then you go in on Sunday," she began her tirade softly, then started to hit her stride. "You might as well take a pillow and move into your office! I'm really upset, John, you've got to start cutting back. You're not so young anymore, and it's going to start taking a toll on you. Look at you, it already has. It used to be we'd do something on the weekends, now all you can do is crawl up in that damn chair and start snoring, or go back in to work. It's got to change, John, for your good and ours." She looked at him expectantly, her eyes demanding a reply.

"Sorry," he started, knowing the last thing she wanted right now was an excuse, but unable to think of any response other than meeting her silence with one of his own, a sure way to piss her off even more.

"It's just this Woodsman case is really leading me around by the nose right now." The newspapers had dubbed the killer of the three girls the 'Woodsman,' for his habit of leaving his victims in forested areas.

Well, he thought sourly, *it's better than "The DIY Killer."*

He continued his explanation to his wife, "Now, the guy they found dead this morning in Green Lake Park seems to somehow be involved. The connection is there somewhere, Frank thinks he has found a link, but doesn't have any proof yet. It's just so damned frustrating, honey. Look, I'm really sorry, how can I make it up to you?"

Claire looked at her husband with a mixture of concern, anger, and love. Then, she said, "Well, it's just you and me in the house right now. We could go upstairs and you could try to convince me just how sorry you are, if you catch me drift?"

John rose and, taking Claire's hand, escorted her up the stairs, thinking it would be great if all life's problems could be solved so enjoyably.

Chapter 7

"What the hell did you say?"

"I said, 'Are you hard of hearing, or what?'" replied Pete Wolf, slurring his words slightly in good-natured inebriation.

Walter let Pete's jibe go without retaliation, considering besting his friend's joking insult while Pete was drunk somewhat beneath him. Besides the chance that Pete would actually hear what he said was somewhat doubtful, given the fact the noise level in the bar was approximately that of a 747 taking off from nearby SeaTac. The Mariners were doing better now, only three games out of first place. Still, blowing the Blue Jays out by double figures in both games of a double-header was definitely something to celebrate.

Flanagan's Pub had been their favorite Saturday night meeting place for years. Although it avoided the nouveau trendy look that characterized so many of the places near the waterfront, it was still somewhat upscale, attracting mainly twenty and thirty-something males in search of passable Guinness, terrific nachos, and six big screens constantly tuned to mainstream sports. The waitresses on the weekends were mainly college girls, not quite as photogenic as the Hooter's honeys down the street, but able to hold their own in the semi-sexually suggestive banter inherent in such a predominantly male gathering place. In short, it was a pretty God damn good man-cave.

As the din gradually diminished to an almost bearable level, Walter shouted, "That damn Smoak is killing us though. Two homers tonight! That's what I call hitting! Why in the hell the Mariners ever let him go, I'll never know." He then glanced at his watch and noted the time.

Pete belched loudly and replied, "For once, Walt, you sound like you know what you're talking about. Get the next round, will ya? I've got to take a piss."

"Sorry, man, but I've got to beg off. I got to go in to the office tomorrow and finish up some stuff I've been avoiding all week."

"Alright, you lightweight son-of-a-bitch, go ahead and desert me; but, if I get raped by a truck load of gorgeous blonds on the way home, it will have to rest on your conscience," said Pete, with an air of as much solemnity as he could muster.

Walter sighed, rose, and reached over and ruffled his friend's hair saying, "I'll just have to learn to live with it, I guess. You OK to get home?"

"Yeah, no problem. I took a cab down tonight because I thought I'd have to drown my sorrows after the game. Instead, it's a celebration. What a bitch, eh? Either way I was just gonna get shit-faced. Life's funny, huh?"

Walter laughed and said, "God, now you're turning into a philosopher. Next thing you know you'll be living on a mountaintop in Tibet, contemplating the lint in your navel. Knowing you, though, it's probably more likely it'll be a butt nugget."

Pete's face took on a pained look; however, Walter couldn't readily decide if it was a feigned reaction to what he had said or the sudden realization his bladder was about to explode. Not waiting to find out, he said a quick goodbye and exited the building.

Walter navigated home carefully, trying to avoid drawing the attention of any of the beefed-up police patrols looking for drunken drivers on a Saturday night. He'd meant to only have two, but he should have known better after all the epic drinking bouts he'd shared with Pete. "Yeah, I've got a little buzz, but not bad enough to hurt my driving," he rationalized to himself. Despite his bravado, he was thoroughly relieved when he pulled into his driveway.

He walked across his front lawn to retrieve the newspaper that had missed his front porch by at least ten feet. No major league contract in that kid's future, he thought, grinning. Immediately upon entering the heavy oak door of the house, Walter went to the kitchen and began brewing himself a pot of strong coffee. He then opened the patio doors and let in Mike, succumbing immediately to the dog's insistent desire to be petted and fed. As he waited for the coffee, Walter absentmindedly scratched his Labrador behind the ears while he began to peruse the day's paper.

Unconsciously noting the daily offering of violence in the Middle East and the saber rattling of the North Koreans, his interest was drawn to the local news that a man had been murdered in Green Lake Park. Although the identity of the victim was still being withheld, pending notification of the next of kin, the details of the crime were surprisingly explicit. He read with interest the description of the crime scene, somewhat enhanced by the reporter's liberal use of emotive adjectives; such as, "crimson-splattered," "blood-soaked," and "horrifically distorted." After the usual drivel derived from "concerned citizens" complaining about the deterioration of modern society and the ineptitude of the police, he was engrossed by the reporter's speculation that the killing might be linked to those of the Woodsman. Citing an inside source at the police department, the writer related there was "substantial evidence" certain aspects of the crime, including the employment of the murder weapon, were quite similar. The reporter wrapped up his story by joining the citizen's chorus demanding results from the police, imploring them to "make the streets of Seattle safe once more."

He poured himself a cup of coffee, added a liberal pouring of cream and two sugars, and mused over the story about the murder in Green Lake Park. "Funny, isn't it," he pondered aloud, "That people feel the need to try to wrap up everything into one neat little bundle?"

One thing for certain, he continued to himself, *if they think I'm dropping bodies all over western Washington, their confusion can only make my job easier. And tonight, he did have a job to do.*

I shouldn't have had any work to do tonight though. I should still be at Flanagan's with Pete, having a helluva time. Maybe even arrange a nice date when I got home, except that stupid little bitch ruined everything!

- 76 -

He went downstairs into the basement. He turned on the lights and gazed left to right; taking in the empty cell, his favorite overstuffed armchair, the table with its cold candles burnt down to nubs, the half-eaten meal of Chicken Tetrazzini buzzing with flies, and the workbench with his father's beloved tools.

Oh, yeah, he thought, his anger unabated, *and that whore in front of the table, sprawled all over like she owned the God damned place!*

"Sprawled" was perhaps an understatement, for the girl was horribly contorted in the advanced throes of rigor mortis; her face, or what remained of it, an open wound, punctuated by her mouth, gaping open as if in a rictus of ultimate despair. The pool of sanguine stickiness that surrounded her ruined head measured approximately two feet in diameter; the hand ax that had so violently ended her life lay about a foot beyond, clumped with blood, skull fragments, brain matter, and tufts of her lovely blond hair that was lovely no more.

She had seemed so perfect, he reminisced regretfully as he put on his yellow rubber kitchen gloves and began to wrap the body in plastic garbage bags. Erin Foster had been everything he was looking for; intelligent, opinionated, funny, and very attractive in that "girl next door" kind of way. She had suggested a meeting after only two weeks. He had been reluctant, as it had seemed to him too short of a time to really get to know someone, but she had been adamant. He had taken her without a problem, easily knocking her unconscious with his homemade blackjack while she fondled Mike. He then took her to his house, carried her into the basement, and installed her in the cage, all without her uttering so much as a peep.

Everything according to plan, going off without a hitch, right?

Regrettably, that had soon changed.

Walter had never had a date that was so hysterical. She screamed, she yelled, she moaned; her wailing was non-stop. When he let her out of the cell for dinner, instead of politely sitting down (*he had even pulled her chair out for her, for Christ's sake!*) she had cowered in the furthest corner. Then, without warning, she had ran at top speed for the stairs, whether or not she realized she was still shackled to the chain that was attached to the eyebolt in the cell's floor was debatable. The results of her mad dash, however, were far less uncertain. When she reached the end of her tether, she was jerked off her feet and she fell on her face with a resounding thud. Simultaneously, he heard the resounding pop of what he surmised to be her hip joint dislocating. If he thought her previous screeching was annoying, it was nothing compared to her shrieks now. Blood streaming from her obviously broken nose, she hobbled around the room like a chicken with its head cut off.

Considering it an appropriate analogy, Walter went to his workbench and took his father's hand ax from its place. He hefted it in his right hand, feeling the reassurance of its weight. Then he buried it into the side of Erin Foster's head.

Putting an end to my suffering and torment, he thought sanctimoniously.

He couldn't have cared less about her, only that he had thankfully stopped her relentless racket. He considered whether he should indeed cut off her head, just to make his previous analogy more precise, but he felt she just wasn't worth the effort.

"Fuck!" he spat as he surveyed the disarray. "Dinner? Ruined. Enlightening conversation? Ruined. Sex? Ruined. Ruined, ruined, ruined, and now a job to do to top it all off. Fuck!" he repeated.

He was enraged, but enough in control to realize that now was not a good time to clean up.

Angry people make errors, he admonished himself, thinking of his father.

Clearly, he did not want to make those kinds of mistakes. Consequently, he ascended the stairs, slamming the door behind him. He got on the phone, ordered a large double cheese and pepperoni, broke open a six pack and settled down to watch a movie. By the time the pizza arrived he had calmed down somewhat. Sated by a belly full of carbohydrates, saturated fats, and alcohol, he drifted off into a deep, peaceful dreamless sleep, unencumbered by any remorse for the young girl whose body laid stiffening in the basement below.

Three hours later, he awoke with a start. Looking at his watch, he saw that it was after 11:00 p.m.

Shit, he thought, rising out of his chair and yawning. *If I don't get started, I'll be up all night.*

Walter stretched mightily, hearing his joints pop audibly as he worked the kinks out of his body. He proceeded to the basement where he wrapping the body thoroughly in plastic, then secured it using duct tape. When he had finished, he carried the corpse upstairs and into the garage, tossing it thankfully into the back of his Kia SUV. He wiped the growing perspiration from his forehead and descended into the basement once again. He left disinfectant cleaner soaking on the tiles of the big blood spot where the body had lain, the medium blood spot where she had broken her nose, as well as all the small blood spots that she had dripped about the room. Leaving the actual cleaning for later, he went back to his kitchen and poured the remaining coffee, now cold as a stone, down the drain. He made a fresh pot, then went to the bathroom, changed clothes in the bedroom, and returned to the kitchen just as it finished brewing. He poured the steaming hot java into a thermos.

Best to leave it black, gotta *stay alert for this.*

He returned to his car, raised the garage door and drove out into the moonlit night.

He knew where he was going: east on Interstate 90 toward Issaquah, then a quick right onto Newport Way, and eventually onto the old logging road than snaked through the forest in the direction of Cougar Mountain. A couple of hours max, he promised himself. He drove on; headlights piercing the ebony darkness, whistling what could have been any of a number of tunes, or perhaps a conglomeration of them all. His anger and frustration toward the unfortunate girl who rode lifelessly in the back of the car had long since evaporated, replaced by his habitual good-natured optimism.

Before long, he saw the freeway exit approaching. He left the interstate and continued through a maze of suburban streets until he reached the semi-concealed turn-off to the logging road. It was bumpier than he remembered it, the wheels of his Kia dipping into a series of deep potholes whose mucky bottoms clutched at his tires fiercely. He shifted into four-wheel drive. It would be really embarrassing to get stuck, he thought humorously. Pretty hard to explain what I'm doing out here in the middle of the night if the County Mounties came by. They'd probably think I was poaching, want to look in the back of the car.

"No sorry, officers, I don't actually have a hunting license for that species of animal."

Oh oh, not a good scene.

As he slowly negotiated what had become little more than a trail, his thoughts turned toward his favorite poem, one which he had recalled repeatedly at times like this. Aloud, he began:

"Whose woods these are I think I know.
His house is in the village though;
He will not see me stopping here
To watch his woods fill up with snow."

After about five minutes, he came to a small clearing in which the massive Douglas fir trees had conceded about forty feet of open space. He pulled the car off the road and cut the engine. He checked his watch, which read 1:05 a.m., and smiled. He had made it here in about fifty minutes.

"Good driving, my man," Walter congratulated himself aloud.

He opened the door and exited, again stretching his muscles before getting on with his work. He took a deep breath, feeling the

- 80 -

cool early morning air filling his lungs. He walked to the back of the Sorento and suddenly froze.

"Hey, what's up?" the voice materialized from somewhere to his left, accompanied by the faint sound of footsteps crunching forest detritus.

"Hello?" Walter responded, scanning the tree line, trying to discern the speaker.

Gradually, the outline of two young men became more distinct as they moved his way. This took a bit longer than expected as both men were clearly pissed.

The one on the left laughed heartily as his companion stumbled and fell, uttering a loud, "God damn it!" as he hit the soft ground cover.

His friend helped him up and Walter moved toward them, trying to get as much distance as he could between them and his vehicle that lay shrouded in the dark.

The man who had fallen extended his hand and said, "I'm Jeff and he's Rob."

Walter shook the proffered hand and replied, "Hi, I'm Jack, um, Jack Smoak." Walter groaned inwardly at the thought that the only name he could think of off the top of his head was that of the ex-Mariners' first baseman. "You guys scared the shit out of me; I thought you were Bigfoot, or something! I sure hope you two can help me. I've been driving around for hours trying to find this girl's house on Newport Way. I thought I was following the directions she gave me pretty good, but then I got turned around and, well, you can see where I wound up. You know how I can get back to Newport Way?"

Jeff laughed and replied, "Yeah, but she's probably just playing you, man. We're camped through the trees over there, got plenty of beer and some absolutely righteous smoke. You could join us." Rob nodded vigorously in agreement.

Walter responded, "Thanks for the offer, but I'd really like to find this chick. She was smoking hot and really seemed like she was in the mood to hook-up. So, what do you think is the best way back to civilization?"

Jeff provided Walter with a garbled set of instructions which, if he had followed them to the letter, probably would have resulted in him ending up in Walla Walla. Walter thanked him and got back in the SUV, pulling out his cell phone and feigning a deep and animated conversation. Rapidly losing interest in Walter and drawn back to their encampment by the promise of more liquid refreshment, the two young men melted back into the forest. Seeing they were gone, Walter started the Sorrento and executed a three-point turn, disappearing back up the road in the direction he had come from.

At their camp, Jeff and Rob were hysterical, their laughter interspaced with long pulls on their beers.

Wiping the froth off his lips with the back of his flannel shirtsleeve, Jeff said, "What a pathetic son-of-a-bitch! You'd have to be pretty fucking desperate to get laid to be burning up gas in the middle of the night, trying to follow some girl's directions that were probably bogus in the first place. Shit, that guy probably ain't been alone with a girl for longer than you!"

Rob sparked his joint and laughed at his friend's joke, his smile gradually diminishing as he slowly became aware that he had dissed him as well as Jack Smoak.

As he drove back toward the interstate, Walter's smile had disappeared at a much faster rate than Rob's. He was visibly shaken, realizing how close he had been to revealing his cargo to the two men, to exposing his secret.

Five minutes later, and I would have been pulling her body back into the trees. How could I have explained that? Even worse, what if they would have just stood back there in the woods, watching me, at the same time reciting my license number to the police? Open and shut case, man, open and shut. Damn!

As he got back onto the freeway, his initial pessimism was somewhat replaced by a guarded confidence.

Firstly, he ticked off his points unconsciously on his fingers, *it was too dark in the wood-line for them to make out my plate number, maybe even what kind of car it was. Second, they were both so messed up they probably won't remember shit in the morning. Third, and most importantly, why would they worry about a chance encounter with some guy in the woods? I had just as much right to be there as they did, didn't I? Seems they bought my story too. Could have been worse, though, far worse.*

Despite his returning optimism, Walter knew it had been a close thing. He vowed to himself never to be caught unaware again, at least not unless he was armed. Would he have shot the two men? he considered, and, if so, at what point? Would he have killed them as soon as they came into the clearing or at close range when they were talking? Walter had no answer for his questions, so he drove on, knowing that his plan to be finished with his task in a couple of hours was clearly shot to hell.

At the I-405 junction he turned north, towards Everett. As the countryside surrounding the freeway because less populated, he decided to exit. It was now nearly 2:30 a.m. and the combination of his earlier drinking, lack of sleep, and extended time behind the wheel of the Kia were finally catching up with him. He finished the dregs of the coffee in his thermos, by now nearly as cold as the night. He decided he had to find a place to dump the girl's body soon or he was going to have to find a place to catch a catnap. Suddenly, he saw a turnoff into a small wooded area.

Pretty close to those houses I passed back there, but beggars can't be choosers, can they? he asked himself rhetorically.

Walter pulled off the road and carried Erin Foster's body back about thirty yards into the woods, dumping her corpse unceremoniously into a small ditch.

Bitch! he said once3 more, considering the expletive a suitable eulogy for the girl who had caused him so much trouble tonight.

Returning to his car, he started the engine and began the long drive home, murmuring to himself:

> "The woods are lovely, dark and deep.
> But I have promises to keep,
> And miles to go before I sleep,
> And miles to go before I sleep."

Chapter 8

I should be getting used to it by now, John thought grimly.

The scene was shockingly familiar: the cool, crisp, early morning air, a grove of trees, a young girl's mutilated body wrapped in black plastic bags. He lit another cigarette, his fifth one this morning. The nicotine-rich smoke curling caressingly into his now nearly creosote-free lungs. He'd given up the habit five years ago, a New Year's resolution he had actually kept. The stress associated with his recent series of early morning rendezvous with dead bodies, however, had triggered a craving he had found impossible to deny.

Claire will blow her top if she finds out, he reflected. *Just what I need, something else to worry about.*

He looked over and saw Frank having a powwow with a deputy from the Snohomish County Sheriff's Office. Every now and then, they'd gesture at Dan Smith, the County Coroner, who was completing his preliminary examination of the dead girl's body. It was clear beyond a shadow of a doubt they had found Erin Foster. She was wearing the same red gingham shirt, beige cardigan and floral shorts that had been detailed on her missing person's report. Blond hair, green eyes, about five foot five; everything about her matched the description except the massive trauma that cleaved the right side of her head.

Two other officers barred the growing crowd of interested onlookers, preventing them from inadvertently tromping over the crime scene. There were about thirty of them now, gawking and gesturing, roughly three times as many as when he and Frank had arrived.

"Well, I hope they're getting their money's worth," he said under his breath, disgusted with people's morbid curiosity. "Bastards."

Frank turned away from the deputy and walked over to John. He said, "Woman taking her dog for a walk found her. Luckily, she didn't disturb anything, just went inside and called the Sheriff's Office. I'd wager that, beyond a shadow of a doubt, we've got another one, John."

Temporarily curtailing his pre-examination of the corpse, Dan rose, stretching to relieve the muscles that were tightly knotted from working in the cramped confines of the drainage ditch. He approached the two detectives and said, "Hey, John. Do you think I can bum one of those?"

Frank looked at John quizzically, who guiltily offered his pack of Camels to the coroner.

"Claire's gonna be pissed, man," Frank said with exaggerated solemnity, "but at least you've discovered the self-respect to buy your own."

John's responding glance clearly communicated an unspoken "fuck off."

Dan lit his cigarette and, taking a long draw, said, "Well, I figure she's been dead between one and two days, as full rigor has set in. Cause of death seems pretty obvious. Some minor abrasions and bruising, particularly to the lower extremities. The left leg is oddly distended and rotated, appears to be a dislocated hip. Considering the deep lacerations on her left ankle, her hip injury probably resulted from struggling against some sort of manacle or other metallic constraint. No apparent signs of sexual assault, but we'll see if the lab evidence provides confirmation of that. The patterns in which the garbage bags are secured by the gaffers' tape clearly indicate it's your guy."

Frank observed, "A couple of the other girls looked like they'd been restrained as well. Easy to understand why he does it, though. Can't think they'd be too keen on sticking around."

Guardedly, John asked, "Any evidence of deliberate marks on her? Remember the pliers he used on Amy Reiss?"

Dan shook his head and said, "No, nothing like that this time." He ground out the end of his cigarette under his heel. "Can I get another one, John?"

"Yeah, they're the best kind, aren't they? Somebody else's." Frank looked at him in surprise then, seeing a sheepish grin spread across John's face, smiled at the self-deprecating remark.

Unfazed by either John's sarcasm or the apparent joke between the two detectives, Dan took another cigarette and stuck it behind his ear, said "Thanks," and returned to his work.

Suddenly, the two men noticed one of the patrolmen who had been maintaining crowd control advance toward George Ealing, the deputy sheriff. Frank and John exchanged a quick glance and began to match his approach step for step.

Arriving simultaneously, they heard the patrolman say, "There's a guy back here says he saw a car over here late last night. You want to talk to him now?"

An electric charge seemed to rend the atmosphere around the men as the thought that an actual lead in the case might be in the offing. After Ealing told the officer to bring the man to his car, Frank asked," Mind if we sit in?"

Ealing replied, "I guess not, Frank, but let me handle the questioning, OK?"

The two Seattle detectives got in the rear seat of the police cruiser and watched as the patrolman returned with an older man, approximately fifty years of age. Ealing let him in the front door of the passenger side of the car, getting in the driver's seat himself.

Ealing said, "Thank you, Mr. Anderson, for volunteering to help in our investigation. I'd like to introduce Detectives Chapman and Caldwell who'll be listening in as well."

Anderson nodded, "Chapman, yeah, you're the fella who's working on the Woodsman case, aren't you? So, you think that son-of-a-bitch killed this poor woman too, huh?"

Ealing replied before Frank had a chance to. "Well, it's way too early to say, but they've got to explore the possibility. Now, Mr. Anderson, will you tell us what you saw?"

"Well, I own the farm down the road over yonder there." He pointed at a picturesque, white painted farmstead across the road about five hundred yards from the clearing. "It was almost three in the morning and I'd just been out to my barn to check on a cow that's about to calve. I shut the barn door and lit up a cigarette. I was just walking back toward the house when I saw the lights of a car pulling off into the woods here. I thought it was probably some kids hunting for a place to make out, most likely. Well, I stood there finishing my cigarette - my wife, Bonnie, won't let me smoke in the house, you see. Suddenly, the car reversed back out and took off down the road the way it had come. I thought to myself that was pretty strange, but maybe the girl wasn't on the same wavelength as the guy and had told him to go to hell; that a burger and a movie wasn't gonna get him 'that.' Anyway, I went to bed and didn't think anything more of it until I noticed all the ruckus over here this morning."

OK, now for the million-dollar question, John unconsciously held his breath in anticipation.

Ealing asked it. "So, Mr. Anderson, can you tell us anything about the car?"

Anderson replied, "Well, it's kinda far away, but there was almost a full moon last night. By that time of the morning, the cloud cover had broken up and it was fairly clear. Yeah, I saw him pretty good. A big black SUV. Could have been a Chevy, but I wouldn't swear to that. Definitely a black SUV though."

"License number?" Ealing prompted.

Nobody's that lucky, John thought sourly.

"Nope, sorry," Anderson continued, "Way too far away to see that with these old eyes."

Ealing thanked Anderson, took down his details, and gave him his card in case he thought of anything else.

Suddenly, despite having been asked by Ealing to leave the questioning to him, Frank blurted, "You said 'him,' Mr. Anderson. Was that because you could tell it was a man?"

"Sorry 'bout that," Anderson responded. "I just assumed it was a fellar. Wouldn't seem to make much sense that a gal was murdering people, would it?"

Frank shook his head ruefully, avoiding Ealing's steely gaze of condemnation. All the men then got out of the car and the police officers stood in a loose cluster, watching Anderson walk through the throng back toward his farm.

Frank was the first to speak. "Sorry about that Sheriff, but I hoped he might have noticed something about the driver."

Ealing held up his hand to indicate it was water under the bridge, but his facial expression still alluded he was somewhat pissed off.

Frank ignored the unspoken censure and continued, "Well, it's not much, but it's really the first bit of hard evidence as to the killer's identity since we've started. It would make sense to have the lab guys take tire track impressions, wouldn't it?" he suggested, careful not to step on Ealing's toes again.

"Yeah." the deputy sheriff replied curtly. "Well, I'm going to see if Dan's turned up anything more. You guys coming?"

John looked at Frank, who shook his head "no." "Naw, if he would have found something interesting, he would have come over. I think we'll head on back now, but let us know if anything pops up. Hey, thanks for everything." The men shook hands and Frank and John returned to their unmarked Ford.

"So, what do you think?" John broke the silence within the first mile of their return journey.

"Well, I think you better get some Tic Tacs before you get home, or Claire's gonna know you're smoking again."

"Yeah, thanks. I'd almost forgotten about it; but, how about the case?"

"Well," Frank began, "Something just doesn't seem right about it. We know our guy likes to hold onto them for a while; at least a week. Erin Foster's only been missing a couple of days. Another thing; he likes to mark 'em up, remember that's where we got the idea of calling him "'The DIY Killer'."

"Where you got the idea, rather."

"Yeah, I'll take the credit. It seems like he was in a real hurry with this one all around."

John said, "OK, so something happens that makes him kill Erin Foster before he really wanted to. So, why does he hold onto her so long? We found Vicki Redmond and Amy Reiss before their bodies were even cold. Is it enough to suggest we have a copycat rather than the real deal?"

Frank replied, "No, the way he wraps the body is distinctive, original. The hundred-mile-an-hour tape is wrapped at least three turns around the bags at the throat, the waist, the thighs, and the ankles. No one outside of police channels knows this is part of his signature move, so I would definitely say this is the work of our guy."

"All right, so we have a single killer who's acting somewhat out of character. How about the dump site? Always before, he dropped the bodies in a forested area, not a miserable little bunch of piss pine a hundred feet off a road. Was he in a hurry to get rid of her or could it be that this is not really where he planned to dump her?" What if he couldn't get rid of the body where he really wanted to for some reason?

"And that reason would most likely be that he was disturbed at his work, or his preferred site might have already been occupied by someone who might consider sharing his campsite with a girl's corpse a bit unsettling," Frank continued John's line of reasoning for him. "OK, so we ask the TV stations to appeal for anyone who saw a black SUV behaving strangely last night to contact us, right?"

"Definitely sounds like a plan, Frank."

"Something else bugging you, John?"

"Yeah," John replied, turning a new thought over in his head." What about Tom Beach? If the same guy killed him, it's another break in his pattern. Two bodies in less than twenty-four hours? Either he's decided to put in some overtime, one or both of them weren't planned, or it's not the same guy. Connecting Beach to the Woodsman was pretty tenuous in the first place, wasn't it?"

Frank said, "Yeah, I'll admit it, but it did seem pretty convenient. Oh well, what the hell, back to the drawing board on that one."

In a short while they arrived back at the precinct building. Going to Frank's office, they were surprised to find two people waiting for them, an older man and a younger woman, both of whom were clothed in the unmistakably conservative suits and professional demeanor of federal agents.

The man rose from the chair in which he was seated, extended his hand, and said, "Good morning, Detective Chapman, I'm Special

Agent Martin Burns and this is Special Agent Cecilia Rhodes. We're here from the Bureau to assist you with the Woodsman case."

Frank introduced John to the two FBI agents and hands were shaken all around.

He then asked carefully, "Are you assuming jurisdiction then, Agent Burns?"

Burns met Frank's steady glare and replied slowly, "No, not at this time at least. We're only here to help out, if you'll have us." He spread his hands in supplication, and then turned to his female companion. "Cecilia is one of our best profilers. If you can bring us up to speed with what you know, she'll try to give you some insight into what makes this guy tick. I hear you've got another victim this morning, right?"

Concisely, Frank summarized the case so far, including what they had found out that morning. He provided all the facts, only omitting the unsubstantiated speculations he and John had shared. When he had finished, Special Agent Rhodes spoke for the first time.

"Thank you, Detective. He seems to pretty well fit the generic profile: Male, apparently intelligent and cruelly sadistic. His use of what appears to be common tools to torture the girls reflects his deep-seated rage and perhaps a need to control his victims. It could also be connected to his job or even a hobby. The tools may even be connected with one of his parents, most likely his father, considering them to be rather gender specific for the previous generation. He could be subconsciously relating their use on the girls with the thought of using them to punish his father, whom he hates. If so, it is possible he was psychologically, physically, and/or emotionally abused as a child. If this is true, we should be exploring the possibility he may have been institutionalized or made a ward of the court in his youth."

Frank looked at John and raised his eyebrows, as if to say, *not just another pretty face, eh?*

Rhodes smiled bemusedly, as if she had read Frank's mind. "Miss Multnomah County 2001 and second in my class at Quantico. The total package, don't you think, Detective Chapman?"

Although Frank succeeded in keeping a neutral expression, a wave of crimson slowly ascended his neck. Rhodes didn't press her advantage, however, and continued her analysis of the perpetrator of the crimes as if nothing had happened.

"So where does that leave us, gentlemen? Firstly, we are looking for a male, probably in his twenties or thirties. We can assume he lives in the greater Seattle area, although he is comfortable in traveling to nearby areas to get rid of his victims' bodies. He is probably unmarried and has a track record of a series of unsuccessful and unfulfilling relationships."

She glanced rather pointedly at Frank Chapman as she said this, unable to resist the opportunity to needle the man whom she felt was a dyed-in-the-wool chauvinist.

"He is employed in a relatively well-paying job, evidenced by the SUV he drives. Finally, he takes the girls to somewhere that he feels very safe from discovery, primarily because it appears he doesn't gag his victims; God knows a girl abducted by a psychopath is going to make a helluva racket. That is about everything I have for now, gentlemen. Any questions?"

Frank responded first, "No, thanks Ms. Rhodes," he stressed the "Ms." "So it looks like we need to start by screening the DMV database to compile a list of black SUVs registered to young male yuppies in Seattle. We should be able to compile a pretty concise suspect list from that; say, about a hundred thousand maybe. Then we just have to put feet on the street, checking each and every one of them. Sorry, I really do appreciate the help but, unless we get something more definitive to go on, we've got exactly a one in a million chance of finding this guy."

John said, "We do have something else. A couple of nights ago a guy had his throat cut in a city park. Seems he was a convicted pedophile who liked both genders. We found a note on him with directions to the park and two names, a guy and a girl, and a heart drawn around them. Neither of the names was that of the vic. So, we thought that maybe he had set up a meeting with what he thought was a teenager but, in reality, proved to be the Woodsman, who was then pretty pissed off at being duped. The wound would seem to indicate it was made with a box cutter, which is pretty much a standard toolbox item. Do you think there's any chance this scenario isn't as farfetched as it seems?"

Rhodes thought a moment and said slowly, "Well, credit to you for thinking out of the box, detective, but no, I don't think it's the Woodsman's work. For one thing, I can't believe he wouldn't observe the meeting place very carefully in advance. If he didn't see his intended victim present, he probably wouldn't have made his presence known, let alone reveal he was the other man's "intended." The man just seems too careful than to make that kind of rash miscalculation. Also, in most of these cases, the murders are somewhat ritualistic; this sounds more like a spur of the moment idea to me, as you described it. Finally, you reported Vicki Redmond had a series of wounds of slashes on her body that looked like they were made with a box cutter or some other extremely sharp object, right?"

Frank nodded his head affirmatively and she continued.

"Well, the evidence so far seems to indicate he is working his way through the tool chest, using each once and then going on to another instead of using that same one again. I would infer this is part of his MO, a part of his rulebook, so to speak. Consequently, I can't imagine him using the box cutter again. Sorry, but in my opinion it's not the same perpetrator."

Somewhat chagrined at Rhodes' quick dismissal of a link existing between the crimes, John nevertheless put on an appreciative smile and thanked the two FBI agents. Frank echoed his gratitude and, there being little else to say, the meeting broke up, with Frank promised to keep the Bureau agents informed of any new developments in the case. The agents left Frank's office, as did John who migrated to his own after stops in the restroom and at the coffeepot.

For the rest of the morning John waded through the mass of paperwork that was threatening to overflow his inbox. Having almost reached the sediment at the bottom of the tray, Frank's thoughts were beginning to stray to plans for a meatball sub lunch when Frank's head peeked around the corner.

"Hey, grab your jacket and move your ass, "Frank said unceremoniously.

"Huh?" was John's astute response, thoughts of succulent meatballs stubbornly still demanding his attention.

"The Chief's called a press conference to discuss the Woodsman case. I've been briefing him for the past hour while you've been fucking around in here. So come on already!"

John grabbed his jacket and strode briskly with Frank to the parking lot, slipping into his jacket as he walked. They got into Frank's car and drove the short distance to city hall. The two men walked quickly into the building, showed their badges to the security officer, and moved to the briefing room. John seated himself quietly at the rear of the room; however, Frank moved to the front of the room, sitting in one of the chairs facing the audience composed primarily of reporters.

Chief Applebee took the podium and in a brisk but somewhat reassuring voice brought the members of Seattle's diverse media services up to date with a thoroughly edited version of what Frank had told him a few hours before. He concluded with a call for anyone having information pertaining to the case to contact the department on a number John recognized as Frank's direct line. In particular, he asked that anyone who had seen a black SUV engaged in suspicious behavior the previous night to call immediately. Then, he asked for questions.

Though several hands went up simultaneously, Seattle's senior police officer focused only on those belonging to the first-stringers, the city's media elite. He smiled at Melissa Black, senior correspondent for the Seattle Tribune and motioned for her to stand.

She did this quite elegantly; betraying vestiges of a Vassar education that somewhat conflicted with nearly forty years of reporting from locations from Beirut to Belfast.

"Chief Applebee, is it true the FBI will be assuming jurisdiction over the investigation?"

Although it was apparent the reporter had hit a somewhat sore nerve with her question, Applebee responded in a friendly manner, "No, Melissa, Seattle PD still has jurisdiction on the case. The FBI is acting solely in an advisory capacity. Next question?"

The Chief fielded the series of questions efficiently, deftly evading those from reporters he sensed sought information that would compromise the case or those whose inquiries were deliberately provocative. At the end, he thanked them for coming and departed through the exit reserved for city government officials who wished to avoid further questions.

This left the predators to seek out alternative prey. John groaned as he saw Melissa Black approach. He knew she knew who he was; over the years they had spoken officially on several occasions. Familiarity still didn't make fielding her questions easier; he always felt like he was back in high school, squirming under the close scrutiny of Miss Hopkins, the math teacher.

"Hello, John. I might have known you'd be associated with this case."

"Hi, Melissa. How have you been?" His attempt to deflect her attention into inane conversation was futile, however. Whereas other women sixty plus years of age might be willing to discuss their grandchildren or their various aches and pains, Seattle's Grande Dame of News focus was as sharp as a new scalpel.

"Cut the crap, John. You really don't have anything, do you?"

He figured there was no sense in trying to pull the wool over her eyes, so he responded with a frank, "No, nothing beyond the general description of what might be his car."

She fixed him with a penetrating stare and asked slowly, "So you're not holding anything back from me are you, other than the fact that you're smoking again?"

Shit! thought John. *Is it that easy to spot?*

He knew that Melissa's powers of perception were legendary, but he knew from experience that Claire's would give her a run for her money.

He then said, "No. Melissa. That's it," bid her goodbye and joined Frank who was waiting undetected by the door.

"Setting up a date, Romeo?" Frank asked jokingly.

"Screw you," John replied. "That old bird could probably chew both of us up and spit us out, then look for more. No, she was just trying to find out if the Chief was holding anything back. Let's get the hell out of here, OK?"

Getting into the car, John said, "There is one thing though."

Frank looked at him with sudden interest, gesturing for the other officer to continue.

"Can we stop at Mazios'? I've been listening to a meatball sub calling my name since before noon."

Chapter 9

Jeff Stasiak took a long hit on the bong and passed it to his friend even before the deep gurgling sound had subsided. Both he and Rob Tucker were pretty high, but not so far gone to not laugh at the old cop's heartfelt plea for assistance from the community.

"Screw him," Rob laughed, "Who the hell is going help the pigs anyway?"

Jeff replied, "'s good, brah, but ya gotta admit it's pretty messed up what's happenin' to those girls."

"Yep. Pretty fucked up!" Rob agreed solemnly, then burst out laughing uncontrollably at nothing in particular.

Suddenly, a very dim twenty-watt light bulb sputtered to life inside Jeff's drug-addled head. "Hey, was that dude we ran into in the woods the other night drivin' an SUV?"

"You mean Jack Smoak?" his friend replied, laughing at the name "Smoak." "Smoak my dick, more like it," he quipped, giggling some more at his own joke. Then, realizing the word homonym "smoke" had other connotations, he looked frantically about the room before realizing he already held the bong in his lap.

"Yeah, him," Jeff answered slowly, ignoring the sarcastic bit of Rob's response. "Man, what if he was this serial killer? We'd be like famous and shit if we helped the cops catch him. Maybe even get a reward and shit."

He lifted his hand to high five his friend, but was left hanging by Rob who was taking another deep drag of hashish.

"Naw, man, it ain't him," Rob responded with surprising conviction in his voice.

"Why you say that, man?"

"Well, "began Rob, speaking slowly as if to a child, "If Smoaker was a serial killer, he would have been all cool and shit, like Jason or Michael Myers in one of those horror flicks. But he was just some pussy-whipped dud, wouldn't even take us up on freebie smoke and beer. That's why . . ." he pointed his index finger at Jeff, simulating a handgun for dramatic effect, ". . . the asshole ain't no serial killer!" He squeezed off an imaginary round at his friend's head for further emphasis.

The gears ground slowly in Jeff Stasiak's heavily impaired brain as he considered the somewhat faulty logic of Rob Tucker's reasoning.

After a few minutes of silence, he turned to his friend and said, "Yeah," reaching out his hand for the return of the bong.

Chapter 10

"I'm really excited about going there, but I'm scared too, if you know what I mean?" Alex's slim fingers flew across the keyboard. In the back of her mind, she acknowledged her mother's wisdom in ensuring she learned how to touch type at a young age.

"Yeah, I really do, Chloe," responded Justin after what, to Alex, was an agonizingly long pause. "When I first visited the UW campus last year I was, like, totally scared. It was, well, like I was on some alien planet. I didn't know anyone, or anything. It was really overwhelming."

"Well, I guess if you survived, I should be able to as well. So do you live off campus or in the dorm?"

"In the dorm this year, but a couple of friends and I are thinking about renting a house in town next year. Most of the affordable places that are available are real shit holes, but it's got to be better than in student housing."

"Yeah," Alex typed, somewhat disengaged temporarily from their conversation as she simultaneously scrutinized Justin's grammar, syntax, and vocabulary choices. At the beginning of the year, Mrs. King had been overjoyed Alex had shown such an aptitude for the analysis of English language. Alex had augmented what she learned in class with additional research on the Internet. Now, she felt she could pretty well tell who she was really talking to, regardless of who he portrayed himself to be.

I don't know, I'm just not sure, she mused to herself, chewing on the corner of her lip unconsciously.

"???" appeared on her screen.

"Sorry," she wrote, "I just had to put the cat out."

Her lie constituted the first thought that came into her head.

Why the hell did I say that?

"Oh, what kind of a cat do you have?" his fascinated reply was surprisingly immediately.

Crap! Now I'm going to have to create a complete persona for a pet I don't even have. Teach you to lie, Alex!

"Um, his name is Macbeth and he's a four years old Seal-Point Siamese. So which dorm do you live in?" she asked.

Well, this will settle it, she thought, somewhat spitefully. *If he replies in a reasonable amount of time with a plausible answer, he just might be what he says he is. On the other hand, if he has to take the time to research his answer first, it's just another nail in his coffin. Literally.*

Alex stared at the clock widget on her computer screen, watching the seconds tick by. She could imagine his panic as he furiously waited for the UW homepage to appear, then navigated to the housing and residence menu, and then choose a plausible hall, one that wasn't female only at least. Exactly two minutes and thirteen seconds later, the words "Stimson Hall" appeared on her screen.

Too long, baby, she murmured to herself, *too damn long.*

She slowly nodded her head, typing, "Oh, is it nice? What floor do you live on? Do you have much of a view?" simply to keep him occupied while she considered the sum total of her investigation into 'Justin Hale.'

She was now certain he was not the nineteen-year-old PE major he was portraying himself to be. His grammar was too polished, his vocabulary too extensive, to be a normal college freshman trying to chat up a high school girl to get a quick roll in the hay. She had tried to introduce every topic in her conversational repertoire guaranteed to get a teenaged guy talking; sitcoms, computer games, basketball sneakers, even films with Bruce Willis blowing up half a city to "save" his little boy. Justin would answer politely, but then deftly steer the conversation toward learning about her feelings, dreams, relationships, and pet peeves.

God, if he's not a perv, he's probably a keeper.

But he is a perv, she thought resolutely, recalling his insatiable appetite for pictures of her.

They had first exchanged photos on their third meeting online. She had supplied a candid shot Britt had taken of her at the park, swinging. His revealed a good-looking guy leaned up against a Chevy Camaro, definitely chick bait, she had thought at the time. Since then, however, he had cautiously asked she provide additional photos, posed to his specifications. Sure, they had all been innocent enough, nothing overtly sexually suggestive or anything, but she definitely had an idea about what he really wanted.

Just then, Justin's replies appeared on her screen. Getting back into character for her role as the wide-eyed innocent Chloe, Alex cooed, "Oh, it looks really great, Justin! I hope my dorm room is half as nice as yours. Well, it's been so wonderful to talk to you again. It feels like I've known you forever, even though it's only been three weeks. I've never really known anybody like you. Really!" she feigned gagging at the saccharine quality of her gushing comments.

His reply was now immediate. "I feel exactly the same way. It's like I can talk to you about anything, Chloe. Thanks so much for being so special."

"Back at you," she answered. "Well, I have to work tomorrow, so I've got to be going. I don't want to though; I just want to talk to you forever. Can we talk again tomorrow, say at nine?"

"Of course, Chloe, any time you want, I'll be here. Yeah, I know the feeling about not wanting to hang up, I always feel so sad after you go. I don't want to get you in trouble though; it would kill me if I thought I was hurting you. Bye."

She typed, "Bye, Justin XXX," finally logging off and shutting down her computer. She stood up, stretched, and went for a tinkle. Returning, she looked at her clock and swore silently, acknowledging that it was very late. She undressed, put on her pajamas and went back into her bathroom to brush her teeth and wash up. Despite her best efforts though, she felt somewhat dirty still, psychologically soiled by her conversation with a man who she now believed deserved to die, and soon would.

Just a few more chats, then I'll ask him to meet. I've just got to make sure everything is perfect this time. No more mistakes, right? she cautioned herself.

She said her prayers, asking God to keep her safe and to help her accomplish the task before her. She shut off her light and crawled into her bed, fading into sleep mulling over Justin's last comment, that it would kill him if he thought about hurting her.

Did he suspect something? Alex, he said his name was Justin, not Nostradamus.

Giggling at her own joke, she fell into a sound and dreamless slumber.

Alex awoke to a glorious morning; sun shining, birds singing, a slight nip of cold in the air.

One of those mornings that make you thankful to be alive.

After a quick breakfast of coffee, orange juice, and toast with orange marmalade, she went back upstairs and finished getting ready for work.

She yelled, "Bye Mom, see you later," as she rushed from the house, ran up the driveway, got into her Toyota, and drove the short distance to Magnuson Park.

She greeted Dimitri Johnson, the willowy young man with coffee-toned skin who had drawn the early shift that morning.

Better him than me, she thought with somewhat self-centered logic.

Although Alex loved early mornings, being at work at 4:00 a.m. was more like getting up in the middle of the night. As Dimitri walked purposefully toward the park's bus stop, Alex surveyed her now singular domain. Even though she knew it was just a summer job bridging the time until she left for Stanford, Alex couldn't help feeling somewhat proud of herself as she strode purposefully to the public boat docks, which waited expectantly for the arrival of their boat ramp ranger who would bring them to life.

"That's me!" she told a frolicking squirrel as she passed it, gesturing at herself with her thumb for emphasis before erupting into a fit of the giggles.

Later, standing on the ramp and surveying the panoramic vista across Lake Washington, she was nearly moved to tears by the beauty of her workplace.

Amazing, I'm actually getting paid for this!

Her reverie was short-lived, however, as a steady stream of boaters made their way to the ramp. Alex was indeed in her element; capably coordinating ramp traffic, efficiently collecting fees, and generally impressing the park's patrons with her ready smile, helpfulness, and air of competence. Time passed quickly and, before she knew it, her stomach began to grumble mercilessly, signifying it was time for lunch.

She was just retrieving her retro Hello Kitty! lunchbox when she heard a familiar voice say, "Hey, working girl!"

She turned around, already having recognized Britt's lilting soprano voice. Alex waved and Britt ran to her, catching her in a bone-crushing bear-hug.

Finally breaking away, Alex asked, "What are you doing here? I thought you were staying with your aunt in British Columbia for another week."

"Well, I was, but my mom fell down the stairs at Simplicity Boutique and actually broke her leg. Can you say lawsuit? Seriously, I had to come back to help out, at least until she's off her crutches."

"That's great, I mean, that's terrible. Uh, whatever. I'm just so happy to see you!" said Alex, absolutely ecstatic at her friend's unexpected appearance.

"Oh, Alex, we've just so got to get together tonight! You've got to tell me all the goss! Is Jackie still mooning over Brett? Oh my God, what a sad-o!"

Alex always found Britt's laughter contagious and right now was no exception. Her mirth was interrupted, however, as she saw a pickup pulling a fire-engine red Baja 252 approach.

Alex said, "Uh, excuse me, but I have to get back to work. Look, I can't get together tonight, family thing you know, but how about Saturday? We can do movie night, OK? Load up on a bunch of teen slashers and then spend the rest of the night debating which of the big boobed bimbos most deserves to die. What do you think?"

"I think I love you, Alexis Marie Tate! I've missed you so much! Look, do you mind if I lay out over there for a bit? Even if we can't talk, I just want to be near you. I won't bug you, promise!"

Alex's, "Of course, silly!" precipitated another of Britt's python-like embraces.

Quickly disengaging herself, Alex hurried over to the speedboat owner and his wife who had just stopped their vehicle. After collecting his launch fee, answering a question about closing time at the park, and flashing him her famous Alex Tate smile, the middle-aged man and woman were thoroughly won over, the woman commenting, "It's so nice to meet such a polite, helpful young lady!"

Alex blushed profusely, thanked the woman, and returned to find Britt shimmying out of her tee shirt and board shorts, revealing an absolutely to die for Dolce and Gabbana Kelly green and silver bikini.

Alex looked her up and down and said, "Damn girl, you've been working out! Look at those abs!"

It was Britt's turn to blush a bit, and then reply, "Thanks, there wasn't much else to do at Aunt Dana's house, except to go all athletic and shit. OK, I swore I wasn't going to distract you from your work, so shoo!"

"Hey, I was just getting ready to have lunch when you showed up. Want to join me?"

"Oh yeah," Britt's voice was dripping with contrived sarcasm, "First you compliment me on my absolutely smokin' hot bod, then you want to pork me out with a bunch of empty carbs." She hesitated slightly for effect, then asked, "Um, got Oreos?"

Alex's nod of affirmation was met by Britt's frantic grab for the lunchbox and repetitive whine of "Me! Me! Me!" Soon, the two girls were woofing down a massive mature cheddar and humus sandwich, two oranges, and a generous helping of their mutually favorite cookies.

After they finished, Alex conscientiously placed wrappers and napkins in the trash and returned to her job. Meanwhile, Britt spread a blanket near the water, and then stretched out luxuriously to begin serious work on her tan.

Alex thanked her friend for being so understanding then spent the remainder of the afternoon directing traffic on the boat ramp. Guiltily, she did sneak a few moments to converse with Britt every now and then, but compensated for her slight transgressions by making a thorough sweep of the litter that inevitably became impaled in the shrubs that bordered the parking areas.

At about three, Britt came over to Alex and announced she had had all the sun she could take. Sure enough, her body had assumed an attractive golden glow; however, it was apparent it was a look that further exposure to the ultraviolet rays would turn into a much less flattering angry red burn. Reaffirming their plans to get together Saturday evening, they said goodbye and Britt left the park.

Alex was somewhat preoccupied for the remainder of her shift. She was happy her BFF was going to be around for the whole summer, but realized also Britt was going to be one more drain on the amount of time she had available to do the things she needed to do.

I've got work, home, and preparing to get away to college. Shit! she swore to herself. *Not to mention taking care of Justin and the others. How's a girl supposed to have a social life too?*

Her relief showed up and Alex left for the day. She drove home and was delighted to find her mother was home. She rushed up to her and, giving her a hug, told her the news about Mrs. Stevens and Britt.

"Poor Grace, "remarked Alex's mother. "I'll give her a call right away. Perhaps I'll make a nice casserole and drop it off to her tomorrow afternoon too. It must be really painful if she needed Britt to come back home. I'm sure you're glad she's back though."

"Of course, but I wish it wasn't for such an awful reason," observed Alex. "Oh, by the way, do you mind if Britt and I do movie night on Saturday?"

"Not at all, honey. You can have Britt bring her church clothes and we can take her to morning service."

"Thanks, Mom. I'm going to go take a shower before dinner, OK?"

Not waiting for a response to her somewhat rhetorical question, Alex headed upstairs. Closing her door, she quickly stripped off her sweaty clothes and stepped into the shower. She loved the feeling of the slightly cool water caressing her body, washing away her worries as thoroughly as the day's perspiration and grime. Feeling tremendously refreshed, she dressed and went down to dinner.

At the table, talk centered around Grace Stevens' unfortunate accident and Alex's day at work.

Suddenly, Alex's father asked, "Are you going to be able to get away for the 4th of July? I thought we'd spend a few days at that little bed and breakfast in The Straits we stayed at a couple of years ago, what do you think?"

Her mother avoided making eye contact with Alex's furtive glance. Alex knew her father didn't get much time off, especially now that there were such serious problems at his work. She also realized that this was a special summer, her last at home before heading off to Stanford. Nevertheless, she had made a commitment and her parents knew her well enough to know she did not take her responsibilities lightly.

She took a deep breath and began, "Um, sorry, but I'm already scheduled for the day shift every day over the holiday weekend. It's the busiest time of year and, besides, quite a few of the summer hires have already requested days off." She repeated herself, "Sorry."

Although her father said he understood, his eyes conveyed a less open-minded attitude. The remainder of the dinner passed in somewhat uncomfortable silence. While Alex and her mother cleared the dishes, her father retired into his office. Once they were alone, Alex whispered, "Gosh, I'm sorry about hurting his feelings, Mom, but the 4th is only a few days away. If he had thought about planning something, why didn't he mention it before?"

Her mother took Alex by the hand and answered, "I'm sorry about letting him blindside you like that, sweetie, but he wanted to make it a surprise. He only mentioned it to me a day ago anyway. You know he's been so preoccupied with his job recently, he probably forgot about taking your work schedule into account. Don't worry about it, Alex, I'm sure he understands."

After finishing in the kitchen, Alex went to her room, feeling fatigued as well as still somewhat depressed for ruining her father's plans. She picked up her phone and dutifully answered some texts, then turned on her computer so she could do the same for the large number of e-mails she knew were awaiting her. Suddenly, she noticed the instant messenger notice was flashing.

Oh, crap! She thought, hitting the 'accept' button inordinately hard.

"Hi. Did you forget about me, Chloe?"

She swore again.

Justin.

She'd forgotten all about her promise to talk with the son-of-a-bitch tonight.

Oh well, back on the clock, girlfriend.

She typed, "Hi, yourself. Of course, I didn't forget, silly. I just had to help my mom with the dishes."

Watch it, she cautioned herself, *don't start overlapping fantasy with reality.*

"Yeah, I figured it was something like that," he wrote.

You did, did you? You egotistical bastard! Alex thought to herself, absolutely fuming. *I'm beginning to really hate you. How dare you make assumptions about my family life!*

The urge to tell him the same in no uncertain words was strong in Alex and extremely hard to resist; however, she stifled her anger and instead wrote, "Sure, you know how parents are, they feel they have to give you jobs to do while you're growing up, 'builds character and a strong work ethic!'"

"LOL"

Oh, God, I don't know if I'm going to be able to do this tonight. Maybe I should just beg off, say I've got a headache or something?

Biding for time while she decided, she wrote, "So how have you been?"

"Um, fine, not really doing much, except thinking about you, that is. Um, can I ask you something, Chloe?"

What now? Has he finally mustered up enough nerve to ask for some nudie pictures? If he does, what should I do; tell him to go to hell, give him a taste, or go all the way? Think, Alex, what would Chloe do?

She typed, "Sure???"

"Well, I was thinking, how would you like to meet up somewhere?"

What the hell?

The suggestion hit her like a frigid shower, instantly dispelling her pouty mood and fine-tuning all of her senses to a pinnacle of attentiveness.

He's not supposed to suggest getting together; that should be left to the girl, so as not to scare her off. A basic rule of Sexual Offender 101 and he broke it! What kind of idiot am I dealing with here?

Well, the cat is definitely out of the bag; he has asked and I have to say something. Her mind raced, definitely shifting into overdrive. *I can't really tell him no, can I If he thinks I'm a dead end, he might just drop me and move on to some other poor girl who might fall for his shit. No Alex, you started this and you have to finish it.*

"Oh, Justin, that would be wonderful! I've waited so long; afraid you'd never ask!" She promised herself an hour of self-flagellation for that one, like the crazy monk in the Da Vinci Code.

"The only reason I haven't asked already was I was afraid you'd say no," he responded. "I didn't want to move things along too fast, but I just can't wait any longer to see if you're as beautiful in person as you are in your pictures. OK, I know you're really into fitness, so would you like to meet for an early morning jog on Saturday? I know this sounds like a really crazy first date, but I thought it would be a really good way for us to get to know each other. Anyway, we would still have the rest of the day to do more traditional first date stuff, at least if you're not sick of me by then. What do you think, am I just being stupid or are you somewhat intrigued?"

Alex sat back in her chair, dumbstruck.

This is amazing! Not only can I keep him on the hook, but I can also land him! A secluded jogging trail in the early morning will be the perfect place to bring this to a successful conclusion; an end to this freak and maybe a chance to get one more in before going away to university. Perfect! A chance to kill two birds with one stone, literally and figuratively.

"Justin, you sure do know your girl! I've got a slight problem, however. You know that part-time job at the mall I told you I had? Well, I have to work on Saturday. So, an early, early morning jog would be great, but then I'd have to get back home in time to make myself beautiful for work. I know, I'm such a hopeless Barb!"

"Uh, what time is 'early, early'?"

"Say, about five or so?"

"God, girl, you really are a fanatic! OK, so where do you want to go?"

"Um, they say Monaco is lovely this time of year, or perhaps Paris, dahling?" Alex responded jokingly, happy that her mojo seemed to be rekindling. "All kidding aside, have you ever been to Discovery Park? It's a great place to run and it's not too far from my house."

"Sounds great to me; I really like it there too. What do you think about meeting up at the south parking lot?

A bit too public for my real purpose, but how can I tell him I'd like a more remote place so no one will be around when I end his miserable life?

To him, she replied, "Could we meet at the Environmental Learning Center parking lot instead? I'll be coming in on Government Way and that way I won't have to circle all the way around."

"Sure, anywhere you want is fine with me."

Just to show she wasn't completely self-centered, she gushed, "My hero! That will be perfect! Oh Justin, you've made me so happy!"

To Alex, the rest of their conversation was painfully inane.

Why can't you just shut up and let me get on with planning how I'm going to kill you, you asshole?

Finally, unable to continue the charade that she adored the ground that he walked on any longer, Alex said, "I'm really sorry, Justin, but could we call it an evening? I've had a really long day and I'm just about nodding off as we speak. Sorry to be rude, but I've got work tomorrow."

"Oh, I'm the one who should be sorry, Chloe. It's just that I feel such a connection with you, almost as if we were meant to find each other. Do you feel that way too?"

"Yes, Justin, I really do. Maybe it's just karma that we found each other."

"Yeah, an Act of God or something. Well, sweet dreams, Chloe. I know mine will be that way, since its only two days until I actually get to meet you face-to-face."

"I can hardly wait, Justin. Bye for now."

Hitting the 'disconnect' button with a vengeance, she thought about how true her last words were; she really couldn't wait until Saturday. The day she would rid the world of another one of these predatory bastards, men who don't deserve to live.

An Act of God? Yeah, an Old Testament God who would smite the unrighteous from the world. And I'm in a fucking smiting mood myself, she thought to herself with satisfaction.

Alex knelt by her bed.

With eyes closed and hands clasped fervently, she whispered, "Please Father, keep me safe in everything I do. Give me strength to accomplish those tasks that help to restore goodness and beauty to your world. And God please forgive the man who calls himself Justin. He is a sinner and undeserving of your love but, if he accepts you into his heart, he may still be worthy of redemption. In Jesus' name, Amen."

Even though she was weary beyond words, Alex had a hard time getting to sleep. For the first time in as long as she could remember, she worried things were slipping beyond her control.

Chapter 11

The next morning, Alex's mother observed, "Honey, are you alright? Your eyes   look really puffy this morning."

Alex swallowed the large sip of orange juice she had just taken and then replied, "It's OK, Mom. I just didn't sleep so well last night."

"Do you think a fulltime job is too much for you, dear? I don't want you making yourself ill, you know."

Alex gave her mother a hug, and said," Don't be a worry wart, Mom. I'm fine, I really am. By the way, I have to cover the early shift tomorrow."

"What time do you need to be there, honey?"

"Well, the park opens at four, but I need to be there a bit before that."

"Before four! Sweetie, you're already looking like the walking dead! I know you're an independent working woman, fully capable of making her own decisions, but if you're not in bed by nine tonight, I'm going to paddle you. And don't think I won't!"

Alex giggled and replied, "Yes, ma'am."

"All kidding aside, Alex, please take care of yourself. Even though you're seventeen, you'll always be my little girl."

Her mother's worry was clearly evident in her eyes.

My God, she thought, do I really look that bad?

Alex kissed her mother goodbye, promising she would indeed look after herself. She grabbed her lunchbox and left the house.

Driving to work, Alex's thoughts wandered off to her impending assignation with Justin. Her first thoughts centered on the inevitable, what to wear.

Well, I know it's going to be chilly that time of the morning, so I can't go too skimpy or I'll be shivering too much to do anything. My old pink Soffe fleece hoodie will definitely help with that, especially if I throw it on over a sports bra, maybe the one from Under Armour. Warm and wicked, that's me. Now shorts or sweats? Gotta be shorts, girl. Sometimes you have to suffer to be sexy, you know."

She grinned; somewhat relieved that, come what may, she was at least going to be looking good. She regretted she'd, at a minimum, have to trash can the hoodie. But she'd had it for two years now and it was starting to look the worse for wear a bit.

It's at least better than throwing away something brand new. Besides, it would be a good excuse to go shopping for something to take to Stanford with me, she thought happily.

She was very familiar with the layout at Discovery Park, as it was one of the places she and her friends often chose to hang out, especially during the summer. She recalled it had once belonged to the army, when it had been known as Fort Lawton. Now, it was Seattle's largest park, with miles and miles of jogging trails, passing through several secluded wooded areas that would suit her purpose well.

But, which one in particular would be best?

After mulling several possibilities over in her mind, she suddenly knew the perfect place. The old cemetery. Secluded, off the beaten path, romantic in a gothic sort of way; she could surely lure him there, especially if she hinted at the possibility of a little hanky panky. She suddenly realized she was already at the entrance to Magnuson Park.

Gosh, time flies when you're having fun.

The day passed easily, a routine succession of simple tasks that eased her mind like a full brain massage.

I love this place so much! she observed ecstatically, for perhaps the tenth time that day.

The deciduous big-leaf maples and red alders were perfect accent pieces to the Douglas fir and western red cedar that dominated the planting. Further on were the wetland areas, created after the land had been returned to the city by the Navy. The area abounded in birds, and the variety of the trills of their calls never ceased to entertain her.

No matter what, I'll never bring one of them here, she vowed solemnly.

By the time she broke for lunch, the day had turned into an anomaly for Seattle this early in the summer, mid-nineties and oppressively humid. Alex's uniform top clung to her skin unpleasantly, sticky and irritating. She made a mental note that, if the weather continued like this, she would have to bring her alternate top so she could change at midday.

And definitely a can of deodorant, she thought, not having to crane her head too far to begin to catch the somewhat pungent scent of her underarm. *Don't want anyone to complain the boat ramp warden is a stinky girl,* she thought, only half-jokingly.

After eating her tuna and mayo sandwich, a red delicious apple, and the end of the Oreo pack, a sudden weariness spread through her body. She readily recognized the feeling as postprandial depression, the feeling one gets as the body digests food, but it was probably intensified by her lack of sleep the night before.

See, biology class had some relevance after all.

She stretched and stifled a yawn; guiltily hoping the afternoon's business would be light; however, as if in response to her contemptible slothfulness, she almost immediately saw a Ford SUV pulling a fifteen-foot Sylvan Alaskan Deluxe approach.

Ignoring her body's urgent siesta request, Alex jogged over to where the man had stopped his car. She politely greeted the middle-aged man driving the vehicle, who rudely ignored her as he dug in his back pocket for what Alex logically assumed was his wallet. She shifted her glance to the passenger seat where a rather severe looking woman of the man's approximate age leaned back into the headrest, a hand shielding her eyes from the dazzling sunlight that pierced the windshield as if from a blast furnace. Two pouting, pre-teen children in the backseat rounded out the Sylvan's boorish crew roster. Completing her clockwise panorama, Alex was startled to see the man looking down her uniform shirt at the triple bands of her tanned chest, the creamy white tops of her breasts, and the sweat sodden white lace of her bra, his leer as wanton as if he were staring at a delectable parfait sundae he couldn't wait to taste.

Despite her embarrassment, Alex took the twenty-dollar bill from the man's outstretched hand, stood up straight, smoothly made change from the Park Service wallet she wore attached to her uniform belt, and then scribbled a receipt. All the while she could feel the man's eyes violate every inch of her skin, even those that were concealed by her uniform. Whereas she previously had felt somewhat grubby from perspiration and a day's accumulation of workplace grime, she now felt as if she had immersed herself in a fetid cesspit. Her stomach began to churn at the intense sensory imagery of her thoughts. It was all she could do to keep from leaning forward and drenching the man in the semi-digested remains of her lunch; except, (a) it would probably get her sacked from her job and (b) the lecherous bastard would probably enjoy it.

Instead, she turned back to the driver and, rather than leaning forward, reached stiffly through the window with the hand that held the man's change and receipt. Rather than simply taking the money, however, he placed his hand lightly over hers, the tips of his fingers caressing her from the wrist downward. Alex jerked her hand away as if she had contacted a raw electrical wire, as the malignant shock of his touch electrified her entire being. The money fell from her grasp, spilling to the floor of the vehicle.

As the woman in the passenger seat turned her head toward the commotion, the driver yelled, "You clumsy little slut, pay attention to what you're supposed to be doing, will you! You're supposed to be working, not dreaming about spreading your legs for your fucking boyfriend!" The woman glared at Alex poisonously as the two children chortled, both at what Alex assumed to be her mortification and their father's liberal profanity.

Angry tears welled in Alex's eyes as the SUV rolled ponderously toward the boat launch. Although the remainder of her shift passed uneventfully, the near-spiritual reverie she had felt throughout the morning had been destroyed. For the first time since she had been hired, Alex felt glad to leave Discovery Park.

Alex drove home automatically, navigating unconsciously through a mist of angry tears. What disgusted her wasn't that a man had been undressing her with his eyes. She had been conscious of boys ogling her since she had first felt her little girl cami tops start to tighten across her blossoming chest. Nor was she a prude herself, readily engaging in bawdy banter with her friends as they checked out the studs sauntering down the high school halls. What both horrified her and totally pissed her off was the instantaneous certainty that the man was a predator. She recognized the fact in his leering eyes, in his uninvited touch. Presented with the opportunity, she knew he would take what was not readily offered, forcibly if necessary, devastating unsuspecting young innocents without regard or compassion. Habitually misrepresenting himself to his wife and children as a loving husband and father, Alex shuddered with revulsion as she envisioned babysitters and, later, his daughter's friends confronted with the man's appalling advances, such as Alex had experienced that day. Tears again formed in her eyes at the realization that his sickness would not end until tragedy, or a series of tragedies, eventually exposed his crimes to the light of day.

If his wife suspected, would he be able to allay her suspicions with plausible explanations? She suspected as much, given the woman's overt hostility toward Alex in support of her husband's outburst. Would his children open up to their school counselors, accusing their father of unspeakable acts? Given her own experiences with well-meaning but inept school staff, she would probably think not. Social workers? Police? Over-worked, underpaid, calloused and jaded by years of experience with slick attorneys and liberal courts.

Who then? she asked, murmuring softly to herself. *Who can stop this man's transgressions against the innocent, against the vulnerable, against the very laws of God himself?*

She was aware; however, the question was purely rhetorical. She knew the answer.

Alex had begun her journey home feeling disheartened and ineffectual. By the time she arrived, however, she had regained her inner strength and determination. Since she had become aware of her unique calling, Alex had seldom doubted herself until today. Now, however, she felt a renewed strength of purpose, a vindication of the righteousness of her cause. She parked her car on the driveway and literally skipped up the sidewalk and through the front door. Pushing it shut behind her, she heard the hum of the vacuum emanating from the rear of the house.

Following the sound into the family room, she threw her arms around her mother in an affectionate, yelling, "I love you!" quite a few decibels above the din from the vacuum.

Her mother toggled the switch on the machine to off and turned to behold her radiant daughter. She took Alex's face between her outstretched hands and exclaimed, "Why are you so bubbly? When you left this morning, you looked like death warmed over. Now, after a full day of work, you're like the Energizer Bunny!"

"Oh, I'm just happy, Mom! You know how sometimes you let life's injustices just get you down? Then you realize you have it in your power to make some of them right. That even though you can't change everything, you can change some things, right some of life's wrongs."

Alex's mother looked at her appraisingly and said, "Wow, that's quite a strong declaration, honey. Something you want to talk about?"

"Not right now, mom. But if I do, you'll be the first to know."

Her mother sighed and moved one hand to her daughter's golden-brown hair, the other dropping to her side. Even though her daughter was bright, bubbly and gregarious, she knew Alex kept her cards close to her chest, preferring to keep her own counsel rather than asking either her opinion or that of her father. Especially her father. It seems as if a gulf had been growing between the two people whom she loved most in the world recently. It was nothing overt, nor, to the best of her knowledge, predicated on a defining moment. Instead, it seemed as if their relationship was increasingly characterized by one-word responses and a noticeable reduction in the amount of time they spent together in the same room. Alex's mother hoped it was just a phase one or both of them was going through and not a symptom of some deeper, underlying problem. Perhaps it was the pressures of her husband's job, or Alex's work and preparations for university. She offered a prayer that it was not something that would disrupt the loving atmosphere of her previously tightly knit family.

She shook herself from her concerned reverie and exclaimed lightheartedly, "Unless the Greens next door have taken up hog farming, that rancid odor that seems to be spreading throughout the house must be emanating from my beautiful daughter. Young lady, get up those stairs and into the shower right now before we have to have the house fumigated! We'll decide later whether to burn your clothes or bury them!"

Alex grinned and backed away from her mother, frantically fanning her left underarm with her right hand toward her. Playing along with her daughter's slapstick humor, she grabbed her throat and pretended to faint on the sofa. Laughing uncontrollably, Alex curled the fingers of her right hand into the shape of a gun, took aim at her prostrate adversary, and pretended to pull the trigger. She then raised the barrel to her lips as if to blow the imaginary smoke away; instead, she sniffed, mimed retching and, clutching her own throat, began an interminable sequence of dramatic death throws. As Alex made a final full-body convulsion, collapsing on the floor with her pink tongue lolling from the side of her mouth, her mother arose from the sofa, giggling and applauding ecstatically.

Just then, Alex's father entered the room, prompted from his office by the commotion. Looking from his guffawing wife to the prone figure of his daughter, he asked in a quizzical voice, "Did I miss something?"

"Only a performance deserving of a best actress Tony, that's all dear," answered his wife, wiping tears from her eyes.

At that, Alex sprang from the floor and rendered a demure curtsy. Without uttering a word, she ran past her parents into the hall and up the stairs, two at a time.

After hearing the slamming of her door, her father looked at her mother and asked, "What's up with her?"

"Sometimes I truly wish I knew," she responded, with a hint of concern in her voice that made her husband look at her searchingly before returning to the unfinished work in his office.

Alex's shucked off her work uniform and stepped into her shower. As the steaming water pelted down, she scrubbed every inch of her body almost brutally, raising a pink glow on her fair skin. Toweling off, she dressed casually – underwear, t-shirt, and shorts. She then spent the next hour responding to texts and engaging in a short telephone conversation with Britt before being interrupted by her mother's call to dinner.

After eating, she told her parents that, because of her extremely early start time tomorrow, she was going to turn in early to get a good night's sleep. This wasn't far from the truth, as she knew she needed to be at full faculties for the task that lay ahead of her. In her room, her previously light-hearted mood gradually dissipated, replaced not by her earlier sense of despair, but rather by a serious sense of purpose. Tomorrow morning, she knew she would be placing herself in extreme danger again.

This isn't a game and I can't call 'time-out' if things suddenly stop going my way. Are you really sure you can go through this again, Alex?

Then she thought back to the creep at the park that day and how, someday, he would quite possibly fill some poor girl's life with shame, misery, and despair.

No, she vowed, if you can't be part of the answer, then you're part of the problem.

She mentally reviewed her plan in minute detail, tracing her route to and from Discovery Park on a city map. She had been provided with a detailed map of all the city parks on her first day of work and she now memorized every trail and feature of the site. Alex went to her bathroom, opened her cabinet door, and grabbed a few 4x4 sterile gauze sponges from the shelf. She then took a two-day old edition of the Seattle Post-Intelligencer from her desk and went down to the garage, tossing it into the paper recycle box. Ensuring her parents were nowhere in sight, she grabbed the box cutter, inserted a new blade, and buried the tool deeply in the pocket of her shorts, followed by a couple of plastic Ziploc baggies, another pair of thin plastic refinishing gloves, a small nail clipper, and a bag of Peanut M&Ms she had discovered in her pocket. Next, she went to the laundry room and soaked the cotton sponges thoroughly in bleach before placing them inside of one of the Ziplocs, washing her hands thoroughly in the sink afterwards. Returning to her room, she moved her homemade contamination containment kit to the ample pockets of her hoodie. She packed her chosen running clothes in a sports bag, recognizing she would have to leave the house in her uniform, just in case one of her parents happened to be rustling around the house before she left in the morning.

She looked at her computer rather guiltily, but knew the last thing she wanted to do was to chance an encounter with Justin tonight.

No thank you, she thought to herself.

Instead, Alex laid down on her bed and drew her Bible from her bedside cabinet. She opened its well-worn cover and flipped idly through its pages. Suddenly she found herself turning to the Book of Matthew, Chapter 13:47-50, where she read:

Again, the kingdom of heaven is like unto a net, that was cast into the sea, and gathered of every kind: Which, when it was full, they drew to shore, and sat down, and gathered the good into vessels, but cast the bad away. So shall it be at the end of the world: the angels shall come forth, and sever the wicked from among the just, And shall cast them into the furnace of fire: there shall be wailing and gnashing of teeth.

Alex was much too humble to consider herself even remotely angelic; however, the words certainly seemed to be appropriate toward her impending mission. She put her Bible away and dropped to her knees beside her bed. Folding her hands, she implored God's forgiveness and mercy and asked for him to provide her his blessed strength in what she was about to do tomorrow. She did not question as to whether what she was doing was right or wrong, she felt certain her Savior had already blessed both her past deeds in ridding the world of the wicked, as well as those yet to transpire. She rose quietly, got into bed, ensured her alarm was correctly set, and shut off her light.

That night, Alex slept soundly, confident in the sanctity of what she was about to do.

Chapter 12

Alex awoke with a start, the still faint, yet insistent, chime of her alarm clock demanding her immediate attention, threatening to increase its volume to a loud crescendo that would probably awaken her parents if it were ignored for any appreciable length of time.

That certainly won't do, she thought sleepily, punching down on the alarm button and evoking an almost eerie silence in the house.

The last thing she needed was trying to negotiate through one or both of her well-intentioned parents' bumbling about the kitchen in a semi-comatose state while she tried to get her shit together enough to drive to Discovery Park without being pulled over by a cop who suspected she was drunkenly weaving her way home from a late-night club.

That certainly wouldn't do either. The last thing I need is a police record placing me anywhere near the vicinity of Discovery Park this morning.

Getting out of bed, she made a quick trip to her bathroom, going to the toilet, having a quick wash, and brushing her hair. She considered whether to go the "au natural" look, but then decided a little blue eye shadow and a bit of pink lippy couldn't hurt matters. She then dressed in her uniform and, carrying her Timberlines in one hand and her gym bag in the other, tiptoed out of her room and down the hallway. As she passed her parents' room, she was happy to not hear any waking sounds, just the sonorous drone of her father's second job, sawing z's at the lumber mill. She stifled a giggle and walked silently down the stairs.

She poured herself a glass of orange juice and took an individual container of plain yogurt from the refrigerator. She looked at the coffeemaker with desperate longing, but decided (a), she didn't have the time to brew a pot and (b), the aroma might prompt her parents to come get a cup.

Look, if everything goes all right with this, I'll treat you to a Grande White Mocha Latte at Starbucks on the way home as a treat, she promised herself.

Finishing her meager breakfast, Alex put on her boots, exited the door, and stepped outside.

The chilliness of the morning hit her like a shockwave.

Oh my God, am I really going jogging in the Arctic?

Goosebumps erupted on her bare arms as she quickened to a trot to reach her car a few seconds faster. Once inside, she turned the ignition and the 1.8 liters of Japanese engineering came to life. She turned both the heat and the fan up full blast and rubbed her arms vigorously, the sudden friction diminishing the effects of the cold somewhat. Then, turning on the lights, buckling her seatbelt, and taking one final, cautious glass up to her parents' second story window to ensure the light was still off, she put the car in reverse and eased out of the driveway, over the sidewalk, and into the silent street.

As Alex winded her way across town, she gazed at the dark and deserted boulevards appreciatively. She could not remember the last time she had been in a car at this nether region between night and day. She knew she had never driven herself anywhere at 4:00 a.m. before though. Suddenly, she was startled from her reveries by a tabby cat racing across the street in front of her. She jammed hard on her brakes, avoiding the suicidal feline by a few feet.

Holy crap! she thought to herself embarrassingly, aware that her unexpected fright, combined with the shock of the cold morning air, had almost caused her bladder to spasm.

Oh my God, Alex, that intrepid heroine who strikes fear into the degenerated underworld of the city they call Seattle, races toward her mission, a steel set to her firm jaw, a look of determination in her sky-blue eyes, and wearing a pair of white, yellow, and wet, piss panties! Then she admonished herself sternly, *Girlfriend, you'd damn well better stop joking around and get serious right now!*

The rest of the drive passed much more uneventfully. Soon, she pulled into the deserted parking lot of the Magnolia United Methodist Church. She had thought long and hard about where would be the best place to change clothes. Originally, she had selected a nearby Shell station. Obviously, it would be a snap to take her bag into the Ladies', lock the door, and put on her jogging outfit.

Why, I can even freshen up my make-up, if need be, she had thought practically.

The downside, however, was that a permanent record of her in both her uniform and her jogging gear, as well as her car, would exist on the business' security tape. It wouldn't take too sharp of a detective to put together the pieces of the puzzle once he or she was inspired to search for someone whose early morning activity seemed incongruous. Similarly, she had discarded the idea of parking along a street somewhere. It wouldn't take much bad luck for a garbage man or a paper carrier on his way to work to glance into an unfamiliar Toyota and see a half-naked girl scrambling about.

That image wouldn't fade too quickly.

No, the church had seemed a prudent alternative. No one should be anywhere near the parking lot that time of morning and, even if they were, the clear expanse in every direction would give her time to cover up and/or drive away if she saw someone coming.

Besides, it can't hurt to be a bit closer to God right now, can it?

After taking a thorough look about to ensure she was not being watched by a casual observer, she quickly shucked off her boots and uniform, leaving herself in her sports bra, white athletic socks, and underwear. She opened the sports bag lying in the passenger seat and removed her running gear. She efficiently pulled on her jogging shorts and slipped on and laced her Gel-Kayano 21s. She put on her hoodie, completing her ensemble for the morning's work. Placing her hand on the soft pink cotton at the bottom of the garment, she felt reassured by the light weight, but definite outline, of the box cutter. She neatly folded her uniform and placed it and her boots into the bag, zipping it tightly. She looked at herself in the supplemental make-up mirror attached to her sun visor. It didn't appear she had put on anything inside out. She ran her fingers backward through her hair, breathed a long deep breath, and shook her head vigorously, as if to remove any lingering doubts from her mind. Alex pulled from the church parking lot and drove slowly up 34th Avenue, then down West Elmore Street, searching for a place to park her car prior to making her anticipated deadly rendezvous.

She found a couple of spots between a grey Chevrolet and a black Buick and eased on in, quite easily foregoing the urge to attempt to parallel park, a skill she still had not quite mastered. She took one more look at herself in the mirror, staring into the eyes of the pretty young woman who seemed so unprepared for the task at hand.

She mouthed, *please be with me today, Jesus,* and exited the Toyota, grabbing the athletic bag and depositing it in the trunk for safekeeping.

Alex walked purposefully down South Emerson, turning at the Baptist church, then up 34th Avenue to where it intersected with West Government Way. The cold was already creeping into her bare legs, replicating the pattern of goosies that had earlier formed on her arms as she left her house.

Oh well, I can hopefully get this over with rather quickly; after all, it's not like I'm really going jogging, is it?

As she kept up her brisk pace, negotiating the few blocks to the park in scant minutes, she reviewed her anticipated plan of action. She knew she would arrive by at least 4:45 a.m., believing this gave her ample time to be on site before Justin arrived. She was fairly certain there would be a few parked cars already in the lot, left there the previous evening by people who had decided to share a car as they proceeded with the enjoyment of the rest of their evenings. She would pick one out, start to stretch out in close proximity to it, and claim it as her own when he made his appearance.

And if there aren't any cars parked there, Alex? she queried herself. *Um, uh, you see my car wouldn't start this morning and my mom dropped me off.*

Seemed a bit implausible, but she was sure her mom actually would have done it if Alex had asked.

Luv ya, Mom, Alex thought, her mind quickly returning to examine the eventualities of the scenario.

What if he feels the hood of the car and its cold? Well, then I just tell him I've been sitting here for an hour freezing my tits off waiting for his sexy butt! she thought lamely. *Can't have it all worked out, can I?*

She was sure he wouldn't be too suspicious, however. He was coming here for a terrible, disgusting purpose and she was certain that was what would be the focus of his attention. She also felt sure that, when he approached her, he would be taken aback by her calm acceptance of his true identity, just as Tom Beach had been. He might suggest they get into his car, but that was something she knew she wasn't going to do as it would definitely put her at a disadvantage in the situation.

One thing I'm not going to have to worry about is whether he really wants to do a seven-mile run around the park, she thought with confidence.

Instead, her plan was to ask him to come with her up to the old fort cemetery, just north of the parking lot.

Oh Crap! Should she have assumed a Goth personality in my chats with him? What self-respecting girlie-girl wants to drag her beau to a graveyard at 5:00 a.m. on their first date? Too late for regret, I'll just have to use my feminine wiles to surmount the absurdity of the situation.

As she crossed 36th Street and Government Way transitioned into Discovery Park Boulevard, she posed the question, *what then?'* to herself.

Well, all things considered, the tactics I used with Tom Beach were pretty effective. What perv wouldn't like some teenaged girl voluntarily undulating over his body? Just no kissing this time, she cautioned herself, remembering the taste of the older man's mouth distastefully.

Then pirouette, pull, slash, and jump out of the shower of blood, she enumerated her anticipated actions just as if she were reciting dance steps.

After that, she knew she would want to calmly appraise the scene of the crime, ensuring no loose ends or bits of possible evidence existed that linked her to the crime. Then a fast jog out of the park, a drive back halfway across town, and a stop at a gas station to do a bit of clean-up and a change of clothes. A few minutes at Starbucks to collect her promised latte and in to work early, substantiating her image as an exemplary employee.

Well, that's if everything goes perfectly to plan. Since when did that ever happen? she thought as an unexpected chill of foreboding traveling down her spine, one that had nothing to do with the cold of the early morning air.

A minute more and she was turning into the Environmental Learning Center parking lot. Looking at the Bulova sports watch she had received from her grandmother the past Christmas; she saw it was 4:43 a.m.

I've made good time, so far so good.

She also breathed a sigh of relief when she saw three vehicles already sitting in the car park.

OK, she smiled to herself, *time to go shopping.*

She absolutely couldn't picture herself driving the enormous, white Chevy Suburban. The Nissan Altima was definitely something she could see herself actually purchasing; however, the late-model red Mustang was what ultimately rung her bell. She stepped over beside it and admired its sporty interior, happily ascertaining there wasn't an infant seat inside that would further complicate her explanation. She moved a few yards away and, keeping watch on the approach street, began to simulate a stretch regimen. In a minute or two it ceased to be an act and instead became a warm-up in earnest as the athlete in Alex automatically took control.

She was starting to enjoy the feeling of her warming body when she noticed a tall figure in black hoodie and sweatpants walking at a quick pace down the street perpendicular to the parking lot entrance.

Damn! she thought crossly, *all I need this morning is for every health-conscious person in Seattle to have decided to take an early morning jog in Discovery Park.*

Alex's perceptive brain unconsciously processed the fact the person was male, while it was also evident he was tall and at least reasonably fit, although his bulky sweat clothes prevented her from firmly confirming that assumption as fact. Unexpectantly, he turned into the parking lot, quickening his pace as he saw her.

Better get into character, she warned herself, this could be him, although she wondered why, if it was Justin, he would be walking instead of driving.

Then he waved, apparently recognizing her, although the placement of the parking lot lighting effectively still hid his face from her view.

At least he's prompt, she thought primly, moving more prominently into the glare of the lights and tentatively waving back.

As he continued his approach, he simultaneously reached up with his left hand. The face of a University of Washington class ring caught in the meager light, sending a weak flash toward Alex's slowly comprehending eyes. He then pushed the hood back, leaving Alex silently gaping like a rainbow trout pulled from the water, hooked on the end of a fishing line.

It was Justin.

No, not just 'Justin,' she thought slightly incoherently, the intellectual parts of her brain momentarily sputtering, *but Justin!*

The guy from the pictures she had dismissed as blatant fakery stood right in front of her, clear as day. He was definitely twenty-ish, at least six feet, and assuredly fit. His long, dark brown hung fashionably down around his collar-line, framing his clearly complexioned skin. Dreamy brown eyes looked at her languidly from under two distinctly separated eyebrows. His full lips were parted slightly in a rather quizzical smile, revealing very white, almost imperceptivity crooked teeth.

My God, was all Alex could think, and that was rather inarticulately.

"Um, like do you talk?" he offered tentatively.

"Huh? Uh, yeah," she replied, certain she had made a great first impression with her conversational acumen.

"Is everything OK? Did I scare you? You are Chloe, aren't you?" he offered the questions in quick succession.

Alex looked at Justin curiously, wondering *who in the hell is Chloe?* before realizing it was her, or at least it was to Justin.

"Well, 'Yes,' 'Kind of," and 'Yes again,'" she tittered girlishly as she replied to his inquiries, frantically trying to remember everything she could about her alter ego, Chloe Sanderson. "I was just kind of into my warm-up routine and then, when I saw you walking up, didn't really know what to think. A woman can't be too careful nowadays, can she? Where's your car?"

"Uh," he looked embarrassed. "I got really turned around coming into the park and pulled over into the first place I saw. When I checked the map, I saw it was the North lot and just decided to hoof it here instead. Hey," he *continued rather abruptly, clearly hoping to change the subject from his poor navigational skills, "Is that one* yours?" he asked, gesturing toward the nearby Mustang.

"Of course," she replied rather aloofly, her thespian talents awakening once more. "What did you expect, a mini-van?"

"Not at all," he said, "Just, wow, what a great car, Chloe! Love the bumper sticker as well."

For the first time, Alex glanced at the rear of her adopted car, reading, "Looking for Mr. Right is like looking for a needle in a room full of pinheads!"

Oh shit, she thought, I got lucky there, as she compared the phrase's appropriateness to the one on the back bumper of the Altima that read, "I don't get drunk, I get awesome!"

"Yeah," Alex hoped she was encompassing just the right amount of dejection in her voice, "It's not easy finding a good guy."

Justin said nothing, choosing to phrase his reply in the form of a silent, encouraging smile.

Oh my God, she thought for the first of several times this morning, *is this really the guy I hated so much online that I couldn't wait to kill him? You've definitely lost your way, Alex.*

She returned his smile encouragingly.

"Look," he said, "If we're going to do this running thing, we'd better get started. I know you've already stretched, but I don't want you to start cooling down again. Great way to cramp up. Didn't you bring anything warmer than those," he asked, pointing at her brief runner's shorts.

She was not sure whether he admired her heartiness or pitied her stupidity.

"Nope," she replied, putting up a brave front despite once again conscious of how cold her legs actually were. "You running in that Eskimo get-up?" she pointed at him with what she hoped he would recognize as an outrageously fake disparaging look on her face.

"Yeah, you're right. I'm a wimp," he said, waiting a few seconds before adding with dramatic effect, "but at least I'm a warm wimp!"

Alex laughed enthusiastically, recognizing consciously for the first time this morning that she could really like this guy.

Then she asked, "Well, are we going to run or just stand around gabbing?"

In response, Justin began an easy trot to the edge of the parking lot before picking up one of the park's major pathways, the Loop Trail. Alex easily caught up with him in a few steps, matching his strides with her long, slim legs. They fell into a rhythmic pace that anyone not in excellent fitness would have had trouble maintaining for any length of time. As their footsteps ate up the distance, they fell into an easy conversation, belying the fact they had known each other for such a short time.

Justin asked, "How's the job going? I bet its every girl's dream to be working in a young women's clothing boutique."

"Yeah, you're right about that," she answered noncommittally. "But not much time left before I'm going away to university. I've really been focused on getting ready to begin that part of my life now."

Justin continued, "I was so excited last year about this time too. It was going to be the first time I was ever really separated from my parents, barring two weeks away at summer camp when I was eleven. How are your parents handling it?"

"Well, my dad is so busy with work that he hardly comes up for air, so it's really hard to judge how he's feeling about it. My mom is really supportive and positive, but I see her looking at me every so often with doe eyes, like she's going to start tearing up. One thing for certain though, I'm going to miss her as much or more than she is me, "she continued quite truthfully.

"Wow, you guys must be really close," he inferred perceptively. "So, what do your parents do for a living, Chloe?" he asked.

"My mom is without a doubt my best friend. I don't know what I'd do without her. She's a stay-at-home mom, but she is so active in our church and other community activities that you'd think she was working two jobs."

But she always has time for me, Alex thought, as a knot seemed to grow in her throat, making it hard for her to speak.

Swallowing hard, she continued, "Um, my dad is an executive with a big insurance agency downtown. He like writes people's policies and checks out their claims to make sure they're on the up and up. I've also got an older sister, Jennifer, who works as a costume designer on Broadway in New York."

"Wow again," Justin replied, obviously impressed. "Do you ever get out there to see her? What plays has she worked on?"

Damn it, Alex mentally kicked herself.

That last bit was just too far over the top. She was now having difficulty separating lies from reality with Justin. She hated juxtaposing the false persona she had created for his benefit online with her growing desire to share the truth about her life with someone to whom she felt a definite attraction.

You're going to have to figure this out, Alex, otherwise he's going to trip you up on something and then where are you going to be?

- 134 -

In reality, she had always been truthful to a fault. In fact, the only real lies she could ever remember having told where those associated with her search for pedophiles online.

Yeah, and look where that has got me, running down a path with probably the nicest guy I've ever met, but whom I had every intent on executing less than an hour ago. Some avenging angel, huh?

Alex's self-disgust gradually dissipated as her body efficiently shuttled oxygen and glucose to her muscles, exchanging them for lactic acid. The mood-elevating hormone dopamine flooded her body, giving her a growing sense of euphoria. As they neared West Point Lighthouse, the warming air and lightening sky further contributed to her growing feeling of contentment.

They paused momentarily to look past the lighthouse and across the sound.

"My Gosh," he said," That's absolutely awe-inspiring, don't you think, Chloe?"

Impulsively, Alex reached out and lightly intertwined her fingers around those of Justin. He looked surprised, then smiled at her and momentarily tightened his own grip.

He then dropped her hand and said," Come on, there's still something I want to show you this morning."

As they continued down North Beach Trail, Alex blissfully thought this was the best day she had had in quite a while.

She abruptly realized the strenuous exercise was causing her core temperature to rise, so she unzipped her hoodie, revealing her snug black sports bra and toned and tanned flat stomach. Alex had resisted the fad of having her navel pierced and adorning it with a bit of metal and faux precious stones; consequently, her almond-shaped belly button formed an eye-catching punctuation point an inch or two above the waistband of her shorts. Attracted by her activity, Justin turned his head, smiling broadly and appreciatively at Alex's trim form.

She was absolutely lost in the moment. The growing warmth of the sun was counterbalanced by the slightly cool breeze that blew in off the Sound. She could taste the slight salinity of the spray that permeated the air from the ocean water that lapped peacefully to her left. The vegetative tunnels through which they ran seemed to embrace her, separating her from civilization and transporting her to an earlier, more primeval setting. A few gulls plaintively cawed as they twirled on the updrafts above the water, their sharp eyes scanning the water for the slightest flash of a fin that could signal a fresh victim. Then they would dive, hoping to catch the fish unaware of the danger in which its momentary frolic near the surface had placed it.

Chapter 13

It was with a tangible sense of regret that Alex turned the corner of the trail that moved away from the water, starting back toward the parking lot. The shrubbery embracing the trail grew even thicker as he picked up the pace ever so slightly.

Is he going to try to show me up? a grin spreading across her face. *Will he try to impress me by sprinting the last bit in a macho attempt to prove the superiority of the male gender?*

Her smile widened.

Did I mention to him I was the co- captain of the cross-country team?

Then a sobering thought occurred to her.

What if he's just sick of me and wants to end our time together as soon as he can?

Alex was not normally prone to insecurity, but frantic ideas of how to get Justin to ask her out a second time began to flash across her mind.

She and Justin were running in unison now, matching their steps to each other as they jogged side by side. Abruptly, he stopped. The action was so unexpected, that Alex continued on a few yards before her brain sent the command to her legs to halt. She turned to look at Justin, seeing a sly grin starting to spread across his face. She matched his expression, but not really understanding the rationale why.

He said," Come with me, Chloe. This is where I wanted to show you something really special."

He proceeded up a barely perceivable pathway and through a grove of maples. After a few seconds she followed, her curiosity piqued.

In a few hundred yards, they came to a small clearing. An ancient wooden picnic bench, weathered by the pelting of countless raindrops, was the only manmade feature. His right hand beckoned her to his side and she silently walked to him in response. He then pointed through the trees and out to the water. The early morning sunlight reflected brilliantly off the sound, producing a kaleidoscope of colors. She caught her breath at the beauty of the sight. She then sensed him moving behind her and his arms enveloped her gently. She closed her eyes halfway, enjoying the intensely sensual pleasure of his embrace. Neither of them spoke, as words would have only lessened the perfection of the moment.

Then she felt him move his hands upward, over the top of her sports bra and lightly cupping her breasts. She was abruptly taken aback, but refrained from making any overt protest. Although she was still a virgin, she had let a couple of boys round first and head into second base before. Although she was somewhat uncomfortable with his gentle petting, she had to admit she was finding it quite pleasurable. Suddenly, she felt his hands shift under the bra, pushing it upward and exposing her chest, now covered only by his groping fingers.

Alex turned ninety degrees and shot her left hand into his chest sharply, separating their bodies somewhat. She pulled the bra back down immediately, then gasped at the sudden look of hurt and surprise that came into his eyes.

"Oh my God," she cried, "I'm so sorry, Justin! It was just so sudden that I kind of freaked out."

"Yeah," he replied moodily, rubbing his chest. "It just seemed like a natural thing to do; besides, don't tell me you weren't liking it through the bra."

"Well, yeah," she admitted guiltily. "It's just that I've hardly ever let a boy touch me there, especially not on the first date. I'm just not very experienced, you know, in like sexual stuff."

She felt so embarrassed by her totally lame explanation that she felt like she was going to start bawling.

Oh, that will really improve the situation, she thought crossly to herself.

"OK, I understand, I guess," he conceded, though it was plain to her his anger had not yet fully dissipated.

The silence between them was palpable. The growing bond she had felt between the young man in front of her and herself only scant minutes before was now completely severed by, what she now considered, to be her stupid, immature reaction.

I let Jack Campbell go under my bra when I was a freshman, she recollected with a shudder at the icky sensation of him rolling her nipple between his thumb and forefinger as if it were a booger that he was readying to flick off his finger. *This has got to be better than that, for sure.*

He still said nothing, just looking at Alex impassively. To somehow break the exceeding awkwardness of the situation, Alex suggested haltingly, and in a small voice, "Maybe we should go."

After a few seconds, he replied slowly, "Yeah, maybe you're right." hen, a bit of brightness returned to his face and he smiled slightly. "Hey, no hard feelings, right?" He extended his right hand in the near-universal sign of friendship.

Oh my God, she thought, *is there really some hope of savaging this?*

She moved forward eagerly to accept his proffered handshake.

He surprisingly evaded her hand, however, moving swiftly past it with his own, almost touching his shoulder. Then he brought it forward in a rapid backhand, slapping the right side of her head with a resoundingly sharp crack. Alex's head reeled, the sudden pain causing little black dots to migrate slowly across her eyes.

"You prick-teasing little bitch!" he spoke vehemently, spitting the words out of his mouth with undisguised rancor.

"What?" was the only word her stunned mind could think of to say in response.

"What?" he repeated mockingly. "What the fuck do you think I meant? I'm out here freezing my nuts off when I should still be in bed, curled up next to a girl with real tits. Instead, I'm in this fucking park with a stupid little high school slut who's not smart enough to know the only reason a guy would give her the time of day was if she was using her mouth to suck his dick instead of talking about the pretty fucking scenery or her fucking pointless life!"

"What?" she said again, the sudden shock of the slap, his profanity, and his apparent disgust toward her still paralyzing the intellectual part of her brain.

"I'll show you 'what,' he said grimly, stepping forward and throwing two quick punches into the pit of her bare stomach.

The air expelled from her lungs with an audible, "woof," as she bent over, her stomach retching to oust the meager remains of her breakfast.

She held out her left arm weakly as he purposely approached. He grabbed it and spun it painfully behind her back. He then forced her to the picnic table, bending her over it viciously. She turned her head to the side to avoid taking the force of the impact nose-first.

From behind her, she felt the hand not holding her arm roughly push her cotton shorts and underwear down around her knees. She felt his hand squeezing the soft flesh of her butt, her feeling of shame nearly surpassing her growing awareness of imminent danger.

"You thought you liked your titties being squeezed, bitch," he said in a guttural voice, "Well, you're really going to love this." He then shoved his fingers roughly inside her. She gasped from the shock of the center of her womanhood being violated, her knees buckling involuntarily.

He unexpectantly released her arm and she felt the pressure of the front of his thighs disappear from the lower part of her body. Alex turned around shakily, placing the backs of her legs against the edge of the picnic tabletop. As she reached down to pull her clothes up to cover her nakedness, she heard him say," Don't even touch those clothes, honey, you know what's coming next."

Tears drew patterns down her cheeks; however, Justin had no way of knowing there were far more falling in anger than in pain, fear, or embarrassment.

Her head finally clearing, she saw that he was in the process of pulling a condom over his fully erect penis. Appraising her situation didn't take much time at all; yes, she did know what was coming next. She realized she had lost complete control of the situation from the start, lulled into such a sense of complacency by Justin's appearance and gregarious demeanor that she had completely let down her guard. Playing for time, she said the first thing that came into her mind," Don't do this, they'll kick you out of school!"

His laughter was abrupt and oppressive. "Are you kidding me? How are they ever going to find out?"

She said quietly, "I'll tell, Justin. Don't think for a second that I'd just let this pass."

He smiled at her chillingly. "Oh, you will, will you, and who will that be? UW? Bought this ring at a garage sale for ten bucks," he flashed it at her mockingly. "Do you think I'd be stupid enough to tell some fucking whore my real name either? Why do you think I

- 141 -

didn't drive my car into the parking lot this morning? Just so some little girl wouldn't remember the license number, that's why. Although it's hard to believe you'd remember anything, once I'd fucked your brains out! I even left my real girlfriend asleep in bed. I'll finish with you, hightail it back home, and be lying beside her when she wakes up. Perfect alibi, eh? Now, get out of those shorts and lean back on the table, this is going to be really good!"

He began to approach her.

Alex realized she'd probably only have one chance to gain an advantage over the taller, stronger, man. She nodded her head meekly in an acknowledgement of her apparent submission, lifting her left leg unsteadily and letting her shorts and panties fall over her running shoe. Then, without warning, she kicked out her right leg, sending the two garments into the air, flying toward her attacker's head. He involuntarily raised his arms to bat away the objects flying toward his face. Simultaneously, Alex stepped forward, planting her left foot approximately three feet in front of the man. She then rotated her hips, just as she had done so many times on countless soccer fields, bringing her fully extended right foot through an imaginary ball. Today, however, it was her follow-through that mattered most and the hours of camps, practice, and matches ensured the perfect form of the most important shot of her life. Her foot caught Justin squarely in his exposed crotch, its force knocking him backwards and to the ground. He rolled over onto his stomach, clutching his severely ruptured scrotum, moaning loudly, and writhing in intense pain.

"You fucking cunt!" he spoke gutturally, the hatred in his voice raw and undisguised. "I'll fucking kill you!"

Alex's feelings of being violated were overpowering, the first thing she wanted to do was to regain ownership of her body by putting her clothes back on. She had seen enough horror movies, however, to realize that you never, ever, give up the advantage over your assailant once you've gained it. She moved quickly to the prostrate man, pulling the box cutter from her pocket, and extending its blade. She thrust her knee into the center of his back, forcing him to the ground. She gained grim satisfaction from his muffled cry of pain.

She paused for an instant, wishing she could talk to him, letting him know how badly he had hurt her, scared her, betrayed her, before she sent him to hell where he belonged.

It would serve no purpose, she thought sadly, *he wouldn't even care.*

With that thought etched in her mind, she grabbed the back of his hair firmly, jerking his head back toward her. She then reached under his neck and brought the box cutter pitilessly across his throat, burying the blade in his flesh up to its handle.

She rose off the man and got to her feet, moving away a few feet and picking up her shorts and panties. She extended the distance between them another ten feet as he flipped over on his back, struggling to comprehend what was happening to him. He somewhat assuaged the rapid flow of blood from his severed carotids with his left hand, reaching out toward Alex imploringly with his right while he mouthed the words 'help me' with his voiceless lips.

Really? Are you fucking kidding me? She thought with disbelief, balancing on one leg as she pulled her panties, followed by her shorts, over her shoe. She then changed legs and pulled her clothes up around her waist.

His movements grew weaker as the blood flow to his brain rapidly diminished. Soon, he was motionless. Finally, Alex experienced a tremendous release of pent-up rage toward the young man whom she realized she didn't even know his real name.

She went over and kicked him fiercely in the side twice; simultaneously muttering, "You bastard, you bastard, you bastard," aloud repeatedly.

Alex suddenly got the uncontrollable urge to use the box cutter to cut off his penis, now pathetically shriveled since its blood supply had been so dramatically curtailed, and shove it into his mouth, just as they'd done it in a Mafia movie she and Britt had watched. Even though the thought of doing this inexplicably made her feel somewhat better, Alex realized she had much more important tasks to attend to if she were somehow going to erase any and all connections between herself and what was now her second victim.

Alex looked quickly from side to side, evaluating the area from the perspective of whether she felt safe enough to try to hide her forensic tracks or if she needed to get away immediately to avoid discovery. She decided she was quite fortunate, from the standpoint of her impending task at least. She was at least a hundred feet from the trail, which was totally obscured by the thick tree cover and underbrush.

The only thing that could realistically trip me up would be a dog following the scent of blood.

She mentally made the decision to chance a clean-up after she remembered Discovery Park had a strict leash law and that no dogs were permitted on the beach.

She momentarily completed a deep-breathing exercise she had learned in yoga class.

All right now, she thought, somewhat calmer than she had been a minute previously, *I have to take stock of the situation.*

She quickly performed a self-assessment: the side of her face hurt like hell, her stomach felt like she was having the worst set of menstrual cramps ever, and she knew she was probably in borderline, if not full-blown, shock.

No time for that now, she admonished herself. *Overall, in pretty poor shape, but functioning.*

Considering her situation a few minutes prior, however, her condition was definitely more than she could have realistically hoped for.

She reached into the pockets of her hoodie, extracting her improvised crime scene containment kit, wondering what in the hell she had had in mind when she had included the M&Ms.

Returning them to her pocket, she surveyed the area, thinking, *OK, what exactly links me with his death?* She felt her actions previous to the arriving at the clearing were pretty well covered. They had encountered no one on the jog and, as far as she knew, they had done nothing that would have attracted the attention of an unseen, yet hopefully disinterested observer.

So that just means sprucing things up here and getting the hell back to Yoda without prompting anyone to take notice. OK, she thought, lapsing into a recollection of any contact she had made with the young man who had called himself Justin.

She knew he had pretty much rubbed the front of his body against her bare skin – possibly a few body hairs could have attached themselves to him. Luckily, she was an extremely conscientious shaver in the summer, ignoring few places on her lower body where embarrassing bits of hair could work their way out from beneath a small bikini. Furthermore, if a stray had somehow found its way onto his sweats, the nearly white hair would stand out like a sore thumb on the black cotton. Head hair is much more probable. She kicked herself for the last-minute decision not to wear her Seahawks stocking cap. With her light chestnut-colored hair tucked neatly underneath, the cap would have greatly diminished the possibility that an observant CSI would find one somewhere on the victim's body. She knew she had discarded the idea because she thought it distracted from her allure.

I don't think it would have mattered much.

The irony of the understatement sickened her.

Next, she did a perfunctory check of her body to ensure she wasn't bleeding. Although the right side of her face was puffy and sore to the touch, there was no discernable trace of blood.

That's fortunate; I'm not going to have to try to sort out a minute splatter of my own blood from the pools around him.

She couldn't recall him scratching her during his attack and she examined the picnic table carefully, finding no trace of blood covering a splinter that had inadvertently wounded her while she had been thrust against it. She then ran her hands as far over her bare skin as she could reach, again finding no open wounds. She didn't have to physically examine her stomach, however. A quick look down revealed a mass of purple bruising, but no blood.

So far so good, she commended her efforts so far. She quietly began humming to herself, a rather annoying habit of hers when she was concentrating deeply. *I don't need to worry about his mouth. Thank God I learning that lesson last time. So,* she continued, *I need to complete a thorough check for hair from my head and what else? Come on girl, think!*

Perhaps her subconscious had somehow blocked the obvious but, as she looked toward the body, it became horrendously clear.

How could I be so stupid? His hands, of course! We held hands at the lighthouse, then he put his arms around me and felt my chest. She put her mind on re-wind to what had begun her appalling experience, recalling clearly that he had been very gentle up to that point. *OK, then he backhanded me,* mentally noting she would have to thoroughly scrub the knuckle region on his right hand especially well. *Then he pushed my shorts and underwear down, and then . . .* A nauseating feeling of revulsion overcame her, making her feel like throwing up again. *And then he stuck his fingers inside me,* tears welling up again as she realized he would always be the first man who had ever touched her there.

Come on, Alex, please, she pleaded with herself. *Please stay focused,* realizing that a total and immediate emotional meltdown was quite a viable possibility.

OK, she breathed deeply once again and continued. *I've got to do a complete scrub on his hands as well. Avoiding the blood was a given, the last thing she needed was to leave a perfectly-defined size five bloody footprint to be found.*

"No," she spoke softly, as if to the squad of forensic investigators that she knew would eventually comb the site, "you're not going to get me that easily."

Alex then got to work. She put on the gloves and walked purposefully to the body. She carefully scanned the front of the corpse and was very glad she did, as she plucked a single, long light brown hair from the front of his hoodie. She was not certain it was hers; however, as it seemed to have much too much body and waviness. Taking no chances though, she put it into one of the Ziploc bags.

I might have shed a few ectodermal cells as well, but there is no way I'll be able to recover those in a field situation, so c'est le vie about that one.

She turned her attention to his hands next. She stoically wiped the right one down thoroughly and vigorously with the bleach sponges, happy to note the skin had not been breached across his knuckles by its contact with her face. She then clipped his fingernails as closely as she was able to. This was standard procedure on crime programs; consequently, she logically inferred that any evidence contained under his nails was much better to be removed by her than the investigators. She then used the clipper's file to dig deeply under the nail, repeatedly wiping it with a bleach sponge to denigrate any possible remaining evidence beyond use. She repeated the procedure around each of his cuticles, then made a final scrub of the hand. As satisfied as she could be with her work, given her limited resources and still shaky state of mind, she moved to his left hand, duplicating her actions on the right. One additional step she took was to remove the U of W ring.

Not as some grisly memento, she reassured herself with a shudder, *but because the nooks and crannies of the ring would be a great place for a little bit of my DNA to hide. Besides, he doesn't deserve to wear it.*

Finished with his hands, Alex looked back at Justin's body. Despite her obvious distaste, Alex felt it best to obscure the evidence that he was about to have sex. She retrieved the condom from beside the man, where the combination of the loss of his erection and the voiding of his bladder had effectively removed it. She then pulled his sweat pants up, providing him with a dignity in death she felt he clearly did not deserve.

Flipping the body onto its side, she repeated her visual scan. She turned him again and again, methodically checking every facet to ensure no obvious evidence existing linking her to the dead man. Reasonably satisfied with her efforts surrounding the body, she turned her attention to the surrounding area. She picked up the condom wrapper he had thoughtlessly discarded thinking,

Fucking litterer on top of everything else!

She shook her head with disgust. She grinned despite herself, a faint return to her normal cheerful disposition somehow emerging despite the traumatic experience she had just endured.

Alex took one last, long perceptive scan of the clearing.

Is there anything I've left undone? she mused to herself. *I could check to see if he's carrying a wallet, maybe prompt some confusion among the police as to the crime's actual motivation. Yeah, just a robbery gone badly, then the perp slices the guy's throat from ear to ear. Sounds pretty damn improbable, doesn't it? Well, what have I got to lose? At the very worst they still think some psycho is murdering fine, upstanding male citizens for some as yet undiscernible purpose. At best, they come to the conclusion it's an uber-violent thief, probably some teenaged guy strung out on drugs, Red Bull, and twenty-four hours straight of Grand Theft Auto on the Xbox.*

Works for me, she decided.

Alex flipped the body onto its face once more and pushed her gloved hand into his right hoodie pocket, finding nothing but a set of keys and a couple more wrapped condoms.

How many did the bastard think he needed?

Hatred once again erupted within her. Moving on to his left pocket, however, she immediately discerned two rectangular shapes that, upon removal, proved to be a worn, brown leather wallet and his cell phone. She placed both of them into the Ziploc and arose once more.

Well, I can't spend all day here, can I?

She took off the gloves and put them inside the, by now, mostly full baggie. She again surveyed the site, totally aware that, once she left, she would never return to this spot of her own volition. Alex placed everything she had come with, as well as a few additional items she had not, into her hoodie pockets. Walking silently back to the trail, she listened carefully for the sounds of anyone approaching from either direction. Hearing nothing, she quickly emerged at full trot, hoping that, if anyone had spied her coming from the copse of trees, he or she would just surmise she had needed to tinkle. After that, she proceeded down the trail at the quickest pace her tired and sore body would take her.

Chapter 14

She cut across Loop Trail and up toward Texas Way, realizing there was no logical reason to continue the circuit back toward the Environmental Center. There was a good chance some other early morning joggers might be arriving there and even a casual wave might be enough to cement the memory of a young female jogger in a pink top in the mind of a prospective witness. Although the trip back to her car seemed to take ages, it was thankfully uneventful. For the most part, the few people she encountered seemed totally disinterested in her, wrapped up in their own problems and thoughts. One guy, however, did give her some attention. As she turned down 36th Avenue, her pace by now reduced to a slow trot, a young man in jeans and flannel shirt looked her up and down, appraising her lithe form appreciatively. She glared her best scowl at him, hopefully conveying her extreme lack of reciprocal interest, simultaneously sending him mind bullets to immediately succumb to a heart embolism. Passing him, she sensed he was checking her out from behind as well.

She waited expectantly for a wolf whistle or, "Hey baby, you're looking good this fine morning,'" but was greatly relieved neither was forthcoming.

Finally, her car was in sight. She placed her hand in the pocket of her hoodie, rummaging for the key. Her fingers moved increasingly frantically, unable to clasp on the key to her car.

Oh shit, have I dropped it? she thought hysterically, unable to even begin to conceive of retracing her route, including through the murder site. *Maybe I can call Britt to come and get me?* she thought, preferring to risk compromising her cover-up story by answering her friend's certain queries about why she was parked down some side street miles away from her home at an ungodly hour of the morning to another jog around the park.

Then, gazing randomly inside the car through her tearing eyes, she saw it. The key was still in the ignition. Hoping against hope, she prayed she hadn't locked the door. Pulling on the handle gently, the door swung open and she collapsed into the driver's seat. That's when it happened; tears started to run down her face like a Seattle in April rainstorm. Her chin quivered uncontrollably as her entire body became wracked with spasms from the force of her psychological release. There was no recollection of her harrowing earlier encounter, there was no conscious thought at all, just a complete outpouring of her pent-up emotions. After what seemed like hours, she began to bring her sobs under control, fearing the violence of her outburst could possibly cause some well-intentioned stranger to rap on her window, asking her what was the matter. She opened the glove compartment and retrieved her phone, which she had stashed there for safekeeping before leaving the car that morning.

Some precaution, you little idiot, she reproached herself, *you're lucky somebody isn't riding down the highway right now, telling his buddies about some dumb-shit who had not only left their phone in their unlocked car, but its keys in the ignition as well.*

She was dumbfounded to see the time on her phone, 7:26 a.m. It had seemed like days since she had left the car; yet, it had only been about three hours.

Well, time slows down when you're not having fun, she thought sarcastically, paraphrasing the old adage negatively.

She absent-mindedly wiped her eyes and blew her nose on a couple of Kleenex from the box in the console, placing them prissily into the small waste bag that dangled from the car's cigarette lighter. She then started the Toyota, slipped it into gear, checked her rearview mirror carefully, and pulled cautiously out into the street.

As she drove, Alex seriously considered whether she should at least put in an appearance at work, just to substantiate the story she had told her mother. She decided against it, however, primarily because she was just too damned tired and sore. She also realized her alibi wasn't airtight, as she couldn't have been at Discovery and Magnuson parks simultaneously.

Good, but not that good, honey, she told herself.

So, if her mom had decided to come by her work, she knew she was screwed, and checking by at mid-morning wasn't going to help that unless they just happen to get there at the same time.

Low probability of that.

No, she'd just have to tell her mother the truth, or at least a very select part of it. Your little girl is growing up, mommy, I've been with a boy. Hopefully, her mother wouldn't consider it "a teachable moment" to reiterate the story about the birds and the bees to her wayward, deceitful daughter.

I'm really not up for that one, considering the circumstances especially.

She made her first stop at Frank's Minit-Mart on Nickerson Street. Opening the trunk, she grabbed her athletic bag and headed straight for the ladies' room, locking the door behind her. She kicked off her running shoes and stripped off her shorts and hoodie, quickly replacing them with her uniform. She sat on the toilet, using it for its primary purpose before pulling on her boots, then tying their laces. She looked around for a contaminated waste receptacle, hoping once more to ditch the miscellaneous detritus she had collected from the crime scene in a place that probably wouldn't be gone through by human hands. Not finding one, she decided against dropping the baggies in the regular trashcan where, regardless of the unlikelihood, they could somehow be discovered. Instead, Alex placed them inside her bag, deferring their disposal until later in a much safer place.

She washed her hands and took a quick glance at her reflection in the mirror. A look of shock spread across her face, doing little to disguise the faint, yet still easily discernible green and purple bruise that mottled her lower right cheek. Combined with her disarrayed hair, rivulets of blue eyeshadow meandering down from her eyes, and miscellaneous smudges of dirt on her face, Alex felt like the spitting image of a crack whore.

God, time for some much-needed damage control.

She washed her face thoroughly, but gently, acutely aware of the ache that radiated out from the bruised area. She ran her fingers through her hair repeatedly, thanking her unintentional foresight in choosing a hairstyle that was very easy to maintain. Another look revealed her ghastly appearance had diminished considerably.

Still don't expect to be turning any heads, at least unless someone is holding auditions for a horror movie.

Then she thought about the guy who had looked her over on 36th Street and laughed at herself for thinking he thought she was hot.

Vanity, thy name is woman, she paraphrased - though well aware the quotation from Hamlet was actually "Frailty" instead. Somehow, she thought with a certain degree of returning self-esteem, that just doesn't seem appropriate.

Getting rid of the evidence in her possession was weighing heavily on her mind. She considered returning to the Arco station where she had dropped Tom Beach's stuff, but felt it too risky to develop a pattern. Inferring that, if one store had a contaminated waste bin, others in the chain were likely to have one also, she turned back in the direction of Discovery Park, driving towards 20th Avenue and the Arco she had passed by on one of her previous trips to the area.

A sudden thought occurred to her: should she just dump the wallet, or look inside first? This is a real moral dilemma, as Dr. Laura Schlessinger, her favorite radio talk show host, would often say to a caller. She chewed her lip absent-mindedly. There was absolutely no reason to see what was inside the wallet. Justin, or whatever his real name is, was dead and gone.

There is nothing to be gained from opening the wallet other than to satisfy a morbid curiosity as to what his name really was, or is, or whatever, she thought, *unsure of the proper verb tense to use in such a situation. What, then am I going to cruise past his house to*

- 153 -

see where he lived, maybe introduce myself to his girlfriend and tell her what a piece of crap he was and how much better off she is with him dead? Not very likely. Maybe I'd just like to take something from him without permission, the way he wanted to take to take something from me?

After turning this concept over in her mind for a few blocks, she discarded it, considering that acknowledging he had hurt her would be an admission of weakness.

Well, what if he's got some money? It would seem poetic justice to buy her White Mocha Latte as his treat. That's stealing, she thought, *and that's a sin,* she added for good measure. She actually felt somewhat better, having decided to leave the wallet unexplored.

Alex was much less torn between what to do about his phone.

It would be just too creepy to call one of his stored numbers, she shivered in revulsion at the thought. *I can't even imagine how horrible it would be to have his mother answer. What would I say? 'Oh, hello, how are you? No, I'm not trying to sell something, ma'am. I just wanted to inform you your son is a rapist son-of-a-bitch. Who's calling, you say? Oh, just the girl he was trying to stick it into, that's all. By the way, I left him with his throat cut in Discovery Park. Have a nice day.' No, I'll destroy the SIM card and dispose of the phone with the wallet, thank you very much.*

Pulling into the Arco station, Alex grabbed her bag, and walked inside. She went into the restroom, locked the door, and saw her logic had been faultless. Alex put the gloves back on her hands, opened the bin, and was happy to see it had been a while since it had been emptied. Wrapping the ring in a used sanitary pad brought on almost twenty seconds of uncontrollable gagging. Next, she took out the wallet. Despite her earlier decision, she was still unsure about dumping the wallet in the container. She had found a dirty diaper that would totally envelope it; yet, she was still hesitant. Her uncertainty bothered her quite a bit. She was not typically prone to indecision,

Maybe it's just fatigue clouding my reason?

"Shit!" she swore loudly, shoving it back into her bag. Alex dumped the rest of the items, replaced the lid, peeled the gloves off her hands and put them back into the bag.

As she exited the restroom, the attendant, an old guy, probably at least sixty, yelled at her from inside his Plexiglas booth, "Hey, ya gonna buy somethin', or what?"

Too weary to face even this minor of a confrontation, Alex turned to him and said, "Oh, yeah, twenty on number five, please."

She approached the checkout, took a twenty-dollar bill from her uniform pants pocket, slid it under the window, and flashed a weak parody of the Alex Tate' winning smile. The man took it, rang the sale up, and handed her a receipt without even a 'Thank You.'

She was beyond caring, however, and returned to the Toyota without giving a thought to the man's atrocious lack of customer service skills. She pumped the gas robotically.

For his part, he watched her drive away, shaking his head and muttering, "Damn kids. Always up to something no good."

Only one more stop, she promised herself wearily. She parked near the entrance to Bartell's Pharmacy and purposefully stepped inside, heading directly to the cosmetics section. She picked out a tube each of Trublend Fixstick Concealer and Cover Girl +Olay Tone Rehab 2-in-1 Foundation. She rarely used any face makeup at all, certainly not these products. She had to at least make a try at hiding the discoloration on her face, however, as her mom would positively freak out if she saw it.

No way am I facing an Inquisition today.

She went to the checkout and put the items on the counter. The fortyish, portly woman behind the till looked at the items, then fixed Alex with a hard look, before slowly passing the products over the scanner. Feeling increasing self-conscious, she handed the cashier her credit card. Running the card through the machine, the clerk again looked at Alex stonily. She placed the makeup in a small bag and handed it, the receipt, and the card across to Alex.

She then said in a low voice, "You don't have to take that crap, honey. Believe you me, I know. Best thing you can do is to leave the bastard."

Alex responded, "Thank you ma'am, but I hope to God I never have anything more to do with him."

"Bless you, young lady. I sure hope you mean it," the woman replied, reaching across her weathered hand to impulsively take Alex's, who gripped it tightly.

Feeling surprisingly rejuvenated by the woman's heartfelt concern, she returned to her car. She spent the next ten minutes making an attempt to repair her face. Satisfied she had done her best, she started the Toyota and returned to her homeward odyssey.

Alex glanced at the Bulova on her wrist, noticing it was now 9:25 a.m. Too early to put in an appearance at home, at least without some sort of involved explanation, she decided. A few minutes later, she turned into the Starbucks parking lot. She ordered her latte, adding vanilla and cocoa to the thick frothy top before sinking down into an upholstered couch. She idly watched CNN as she sipped the hot and delicious beverage.

So much misery, she observed sadly, as headlines relating to war, murder, and other miscellaneous outrages slowly streamed across the bottom of the screen. *So, are you really making a difference in the world, Alex?*

Yeah, she answered her own question emphatically after only a few seconds of consideration, *if I saved even one girl from experiencing what I did this morning, you're damned right.*

She drank off the last dregs of her coffee and walked resolutely out the door.

"Mom, are you home?" Alex pulled the door closed behind her.

Although her mother's car was parked outside, a brief check revealed she was clearly absent from the house. Alex sighed with relief.

Normally, she would have been somewhat disappointed if her mother was out, she loved seeing her beaming smile, hearing her, "Hi, honey, I missed you!" and feeling the almost tangible sense of being dearly loved.

Today was different, however. Not only was she too exhausted to endure even the briefest of conversations, she did not want to answer her mother's questions concerning her bruised face that, she was certain, would be immediately noticed, regardless of the amount of makeup she applied.

I've done enough lying for one day. Now, all I want to do is to clean myself up and hibernate in my bed for the next week, as a minimum.

She quickly penciled out a note, saying she was suffering from terrible stomach cramps and had gone to bed, posting it to the outside of her door. At least that's the truth. Alex then turned on the shower, adjusting the water to as hot as she could endure. She stripped off her uniform and underwear and tossed them into her dirty clothes hamper. She eased wearily into the shower and scrubbed her body vigorously in the near-scalding water, subconsciously seeking to rid herself from the invisible stain of his touch. Leaving her hair unbrushed, she crawled into bed naked, two things she would have never considered doing had she not been totally overcome by her profound exhaustion.

Alex awoke from her deep, yet restless, slumber to a heavy, persistent knocking at her door. She yelled out groggily, "Just a minute," before getting out from under her covers.

She walked unsteadily toward her door, then noticed with a shock she was nude.

She shouted, "Just a minute," again, simultaneously rushing to her closet to fetch a robe. Opening the door just a crack, Alex was surprised to find Britt, rather than her mother, peering through from the other side.

"Hey girl," Britt beamed, "Forget about me?" Seeing Alex's uncomprehending look, she continued, "Um duh, movie night, remember? Say, are you OK?" she asked, her nonchalant humor transitioning into concern at the sight of her friend's virtual insensibility.

"What? Um, yeah," Alex mumbled, glad that her door opened to the right, revealing only the left profile of her face to be exposed to her friend. She blinked her eyes a few times to clear her head. Now, more fully awake and with the revitalizing benefit of nearly eight hours' sleep, she felt almost like her old self.

"How could I possibly forget that I know the most beautiful girl in the world?"

Despite the jokingly outrageous exaggeration of Alex's comment, it still made Britt feel really good inside, like few people outside of her BFF could do.

Britt blew her a kiss and asked, "Do you really feel up to getting together tonight, Alex? Believe me, I know how shitty surfing the crimson wave can feel, pointing toward the note on the door."

"It's OK, really. Just give me a couple of minutes to make myself presentable and I'll be right down."

"No probs," Britt replied, although somewhat taken aback by Alex's insinuation she was not welcome in her room.

Despite her conscious effort to keep her look of hurt from showing, a slight frown creased her forehead as she turned and walked downstairs.

Probably just needing to attend to Mother Nature in private, she thought, reassuring herself their friendship was as solid as ever.

Alex sighed deeply as she turned from the door and began the process of getting dressed. Clearly, she had no problem with Britt seeing her bare butt, they had shared too much time in girls' locker rooms to even begin to worry about modesty.

I'm sure they'll swallow the story that I slipped on the dock reaching for some trash, then "boom," hit my clumsy big head on the pile, she thought, *but there's no way in hell they'll believe this happened too,* gesturing down to the two, fist-shaped bruises on her stomach.

Covered completely by her blue chambray button-down shirt and a pair of floral cut-off denim shorts from Guess, Alex went in her bathroom and brushed a quick dozen strokes through her auburn hair, promising it much more thorough attention later. She then used the concealer and foundation to complete a commendable job of camouflaging the blue, yellow, and black discolorations that peeked through the skin of the lower right side of her face.

Thanks for letting me help out at the theater, mom, but usually it's the other way around, she smiled, remembering creating gruesome wounds for the Gaslight's production of Sweeney Todd. Satisfied she had done everything she could do to make herself look human; she went downstairs.

Entering the den, Britt exclaimed, "Damn girl! You'd think you were getting ready for the f'in prom, or something. I could have watched one already!" holding up the three Blu-Ray cases for emphasis.

"Language, young lady!" admonished Alex's mother, sitting in the overstuffed chair across from the sofa where Britt lounged.

"Sorry, ma'am," Britt replied, trying to appear suitably contrite while also trying to refrain from giggling uncontrollably.

"I've got half a mind to turn you over my . . . what on earth happened to you, Alex?" Her mother sprinted across the more than twenty feet between her and her daughter, a look of utter shock on her face.

"Oh, mom, it's absolutely nothing," Alex replied, then launching into her prefabricated tale of on-the-job misadventure.

The telling took longer than it should have, however, as she had to stop three time to dissuade her mother from driving her to the emergency room for x-rays, "just in case."

Mollified at least temporarily that her daughter wasn't going to be permanently disfigured, she said, "I'm made a huge tray of nibbles for the two of you. If you need anything more, just let me know."

Alex realized she was completely ravenous. She took off at a trot for the kitchen, followed closely by the other two women. What she saw was a veritable feast that would have probably stuffed six lumberjacks. All of the foods the two girls liked best were laid out in abundance, both savory and sweet.

Alex turned to her mother and said, "Wow! This is like the greatest meal ever, mom. Thank you so much."

"Well," she replied, her eyes beginning to cloud, "this may be the last time the two of you ever sit down like this in our home again. I just wanted it to be special."

In a matter of seconds, all three of them were crying and hugging each other.

After a while, Britt broke away and said, "No way! Alex may be an ungrateful little snip, but I'll still be coming over to eat your food when I'm sixty! Starting right now!" She grabbed a plate and began piling it with smoked salmon and cream cheese finger sandwiches. Alex rushed to catch up and soon both girls were carrying their heavily laden plates into the den.

Alex yelled back to the kitchen, "Are you going to join us, mom?"

"No, honey," she responded. "I have some things I need to do. You two enjoy yourselves."

They leaned back and settled into the unforced repartee two lifelong friends can share so easily. After they finished their first plate, they returned to the kitchen for seconds. Back on the couch, Britt held up the three film cases, Alex choosing one with a young woman peering pensively out of her living room window at night. The garish yellow light of the room contrasting vividly with the utterly dark exterior. Popping their first selection into the Blu-Ray player, they were soon engrossed in the film, providing running commentary as to the myriad of mistakes, many of them fatal, the group of stalwart young actors were making in their attempt to survive the night.

"Oh my God, no!" screamed Britt, "Don't follow him into the woods, you stupid bimbo, are you crazy?"

Alex, however, was strangely silent, making no audible comment on her friend's critique of the representative example of cinematic nonsense. Instead, her thoughts had taken quite a different turn. She looked at Britt soberly.

Sometimes it's just not that easy to know what to do, babe.

The next morning, Alex sat in the pew at the Methodist Church, sandwiched between her mother and Britt. She felt largely recovered from the previous day's ordeal. Her face no longer ached and the purple discoloration was already starting to fade from her stomach. Emotionally, she felt rejuvenated as well, buoyed as she always was by the love she felt from those beside her as well as the spirituality of the service. Dressed in her modest, flowered knee-length dress, she looked no different than any of the other young women sprinkled throughout the congregation. In her mind, however, her thoughts had strayed from Reverend Roberts' reading on responsibility to consider her own, personal interpretation of the verse from Romans 13:4 that formed the basis of his sermon.

"For he is the minister of God to thee for good. But if thou do that which is evil, be afraid; for he beareth not the sword in vain: for he is the minister of God, a revenger to [execute] wrath upon him that doeth evil."

Was she indeed a minister of God, the' revenger?' She thought deeply.

Yesterday, she had been extremely fortunate, there was no doubt in her mind. She had blithely let herself be lured into a trap and, if her desperate kick had missed its intended target or been even partially deflected, she knew she would have suffered more than rape from the by then enraged young man. Yet, she had prevailed, exacting righteous punishment on an individual who was an abomination.

God was indeed watching over me, just as he always has.

She felt confident God had blessed her undertaking, that of freeing the community from the degenerate wolves seeking to prey upon its tender flocks. When the collection plate came around, Alex placed seventy-three dollars in it.

The money from Justin's, make that Robert Jackson's, wallet will be used for good works. Maybe that will at least gain him some small grace, she thought with satisfaction, her anger and hatred toward the man being somewhat supplanted by the innate sense of Christian charity and compassion she had learned from her church and her mother's constant example.

Later that afternoon, Alex went out on the patio and started the gas barbeque. With her father at work, her mother at the theater, and Britt caring for her mother, she felt confident no one would disturb her as she tied up the last few loose ends of her crime. Placing the credit cards and driver's license from the wallet, along with the SIM card from his phone, into an old, rather rusty, coffee can, she sat it on the grill. She watched as they slowly melded into one lump of indiscernible molten goo at the bottom. The acrid smell from the plastic assaulted her nose and mouth as she picked up the can and set it aside to cool. She went upstairs to retrieve the small plastic bag that held the pink hoodie, the only part of her previous day's ensemble she felt was distinctive enough to provide positive identification. She returned to the patio and picked up the wallet and the phone, placing them in the bag as well. Then, taking a hammer in her hand, she pounded in the sides of the can, eventually more or less producing a flat piece of metal in which no one would possibly suspect the remains of a man's life were entombed. She made a quick trip to a charity clothes receptacle across town, dumping the wallet, phone, and the hoodie inside. With that accomplished, she drove back home, hoping her final bit of business with Justin Hale, aka Robert Jackson, was now safely behind her.

Chapter 15

"Shut off that God-damned computer and get to bed, you've got summer school tomorrow!" Ed Buckley yelled up the stairs to his daughter's bedroom.

Alright, dad! You don't have to yell! In her mind, Shannon's answer was rendered in an equally loud and angry voice; however, no actual sound emitted from her lips. Her reply was typical for the introverted girl, who often responded to the statements and questions of others with avoided eye contact and stony silence.

She did as she was told, however, wishing at all cost to avoid another confrontation with her emotionally abusive father. Throughout her short life, he had always been there for her; telling her she was a disappointment as a daughter, an embarrassment, and the reason why her mother had walked out five years ago when she was fourteen.

Couldn't have possibly had anything to do with having an obnoxious, overbearing, failure of a husband, could it, dad? she thought for the millionth time. *How I wish I could tell him that, just once* – but she knew she never would. She'd just keep putting up with his crap, silently accusing him through her inscrutable, silent stares, which pissed him off even more; an endless, pointless, antagonistic ballet.

Shannon turned off her light and crawled into bed, resigned to the habitual insomnia that would permit her only four or five hours of sleep, at best.

At least tonight I've got something to think about besides how much I hate my life, she thought. *Just maybe for once in my life I've found someone who actually gives a damn about me.*

Awake since before five, Shannon finally decided to get up at 7:10 a.m. She went downstairs dressed only in the long-sleeved sweatshirt in which she had slept, well aware her father would have departed for work at least an hour before. She stopped off at the bathroom for a pee and then continued into the kitchen. She made herself a cup of green tea and popped a couple of pieces of toast. She then poured two Wellbutrin from the bottle into her hand, swallowing them with a quick chaser of water. She had been on the antidepressants for about three months now; however, they weren't working much better than the Zoloft she had previously been prescribed.

Just not too much to be happy about, she thought in stark self-appraisal. After her meager breakfast, she showered, then returned to her room to get dressed before leaving the house to go to her class.

She walked the three blocks to the bus stop in a manner that, by now, was habitually intended to draw the least amount of attention to herself. Head down and cowled within the hood of her worn grey sweatshirt, she appeared to be further isolated in a world of her own by the evidence of the white wire that led from her pocket upward, before branching in two and disappearing into the sides of the hood. Black leggings and brown leather ankle boots completed her nondescript ensemble.

Shannon strode at a quick pace, as if to further discourage any possibility of the company of friends, of which she had none in the very working-class neighborhood of the Beacon Hill district. Most of the houses on her street were built in the 1920s and had endured the enforced neglect brought on by the Great Depression. The economic boom that occurred in the war years and their aftermath had sucked the brightest and most motivated inhabitants away from the area in an almost vampiric manner, leaving mainly those too old or too discouraged by life to expend the effort to leave.

Like dad, she often thought bitterly.

Consequently, the untrimmed shrubbery, peeling house paint, and neglected maintenance of the faded pastel houses she passed was indicative of the general malaise that infected the area like a persistent, hacking cough that provided physical evidence of an ultimately terminal sickness.

Despite her outward silence, the turmoil of her inner thoughts hammered through her brain like a death metal amp, a repetitive howl of unbridled angst.

Step on a crack, break your mama's back, she recited to herself as she approached the bus stop, taking particular care to firmly plant her foot on every one of the fissures that irregularly divided the pavement as she neared the bus stop.

Her anger against her mother was at times almost overwhelming. Shannon had no illusion that theirs had been a perfect, loving little family prior to her mother's sudden exit. Too many shouted accusatory words, answered by angry, screamed denials had left little doubt as to the dysfunctional nature of her parents' relationship.

No, but it had at least been bearable.

Despite the venomous animosity she displayed toward her husband, Louise Buckley had always had time to talk to the shy, increasingly alienated little girl who was her daughter. Shannon's arrival at puberty had strained their relationship, which had been marked by progressively longer periods of silence and single word responses. There were times, however, when conversations had almost magically bloomed and they had spoken deep into the night about the meaning of life, love, and the future. At those times, Shannon thought, it was almost like we were one person, a single consciousness that shared everything.

The following day, however, the words between them did not come as easily and the emotional barriers somehow managed to reappear. Louise Buckley's place in the home was to serve as an abrasive foil to her husband, Ed; Shannon's was to fade into the background, unobtrusive and withdrawn.

That was how things were supposed to be, mom, that was the status quo we had all grown to accept. Why couldn't you just let it be?

Shannon remembered vividly the day she had returned from school to find the house empty. She had thought little of it, her mom was out somewhere and her dad was still at work. As six o'clock approached and her mother had still not returned, she knew there would be hell to pay when her dad got in and didn't find dinner ready. A niggling fear had started to take root in her mind as well, however.

Where are you, mom? Shannon had asked silently; *increasingly aware an answer would not be forthcoming.*

She went to the door of her parents' room and knocked for no apparent reason. She very tentatively turned the doorknob, as hesitant to invade her parents' privacy as she hoped they would be to violate hers. What she saw was now etched in her mind, a memory she couldn't erase no matter how hard she tried.

The closet was open and most of her mother's clothes were gone. Similarly, the drawers of her mother's side of the dresser were mostly ajar and emptied of their contents. Most horrible of all, however, was what Louise Buckley had left in the way of a goodbye note to her husband. Scrawled in red lipstick across the dresser mirror in big, bold letters was, "FUCK YOU, ED!"

That was it.

There was no long, consoling note addressed to Shannon and slipped into a pretty little envelope and slid under her door, providing an explanation and comfort. No words of guidance and encouragement to help shape her daughter into a strong, independent woman in the ensuing years.

Nothing.

Don't I even rate my own 'fuck you?' Shannon had thought as tears welled up in her eyes.

As if in partial answer to her question, Shannon suddenly heard, "What the hell?" spoken in a low voice from behind her. Her father pushed her roughly to the side, in the same way one would swat an annoying mosquito, while he surveyed the stark testimony of his wife's departure. After a few of what seemed interminable seconds, he turned to Shannon and bellowed, "Where is she? Where did she go?"

Shannon could only shake her head dumbly, unable to form, let alone verbalize a response. Her father, interpreting her silence as complicity rather than ignorance, slapped her hard across the face. She fell across her parents' bed, dazed. Her father looked down at her, a disgusted look setting hard on his face.

"This is all your fault," he spat between clenched teeth, a theme that would be recurrent throughout their subsequent relationship, both in word and in deed.

Later that night, the pain in her face inconsequential compared to the agony in her heart, she had ransacked her room, searching in vain for a nonexistent note written in her mother's barely legible handwriting, explaining why she had deserted her.

As Shannon's tears had dried that night, her heart had also hardened. Five months later, three days before her birthday, she had been surprised to find what appeared to be a card addressed to her in the mailbox, written in that familiar scrawl. She had taken the card in her shaking hands and carried it up to her room, placing it carefully on the top of her dresser. Shannon then went down both flights of stairs and into the basement. She found a scrap of board in the woodpile and inexpertly sawed a more or less six-inch square. Taking a large spike from her father's workbench, she hammered it through the middle of the board, leaving a good four inches protruding from the back. She returned to her room and, taking her mother's card in both hands, thrust it violently down on the spike, pushing the cardboard and paper all the way to the bottom.

Just like you did to my heart, you bitch! Shannon thought with hatred obliterating any vestiges of love left for her mother.

Over the years since that time, Shannon had received ten other cards and letters from her mother, each of which had been impaled on the spike, one after the other.

The sound of the expelling air of the city bus's brakes roused Shannon from the depths of her bitter reverie. She dug in her pocket for her ORCA bus pass, tapping it on the reader screen as the bus driver appraised her up and down, a diversion from the inherent boredom of spending hours each day driving a circular route like a fat hamster on a huge wheel. She mentally gave him the finger and turned down the aisle, scanning the array of faces that bobbed in their seats like corks in water. Each broadcast telepathic messages at her, ranging from overweight women who cherished the luxury of arraying their behinds across two seats to a couple of loser guys who were trying desperately to will her to sit beside them, strike up a deep conversation, and wind up the day fulfilling their most debauched sexual fantasies. Ignoring them all, she spotted two empty seats toward the rear of the bus and thankfully slid into the one nearest the window. Turning the volume of her MP3 player up, she let the haunting sounds of Sia's "Chandelier" at least temporarily obliterate the bleakness of her life.

Shannon got off the bus and walked up the pavement toward the entrance to the building where her summer class was held. Failing geometry had only served to further diminish Shannon's already pitiable sense of self-worth. Despite her problems at home and feelings of alienation, she had always been a good student, as evidenced by her 3.7 grade point average. Furthermore, she did not conform to the stereotypical mindset that girls were less able in mathematics and science. "What went wrong, Shannon?" she had been asked by everyone from her guidance counselor to the school psychologist to the principal. She had said nothing, however, knowing they wouldn't believe her if she told the truth.

What went wrong was Mr. Morell, that's what, she thought miserably. *It's not like I'm thin-skinned. A shy girl who doesn't say much, who dresses in blacks and grays to avoid attention, who listens to Evanescence, isn't going to fit in very well with the Barbs, is she?*

She had pretty well grown to accept the 'emo' label in the same way people had once referred to her as pretty, or blond. The other stuff, she just ignored. Becoming virtually wraith-like, the other students largely left her alone, too wrapped up in their own lives to care about such a nonentity. Not Mr. Morell, however. Since the first day she walked into his geometry class, he had seemingly taken great delight in not so subtly belittling and ridiculing her.

"What's that you say, Shannon? How can you be the only one in class who doesn't understand? Why don't you pay attention instead of daydreaming? OK class, time out while I go over the problem again, really slowly, for our special student!"

Just about everyone in class had laughed at that, making her close her eyes and wish she could somehow disappear. She became increasingly disengaged and stopped asking questions all together. Consequently, it was little wonder why she had failed.

Despite her regularly reinforced pessimism, however, for once the dark cloud had had a silver lining. Mr. Robertson, the summer school geometry teacher, was everything Mr. Morell was not. Within the first week, he had gotten her on-track and what had once been a confusing morass of lengths and angles had become a logical pattern of laws and formulas that she comprehended perfectly. Even more amazing, his kindness and support had caused her tentatively to feel somewhat better about herself. She had even started to consider starting community college in the fall.

The hour and a half class went well. Shannon had understood and completed the assigned homework, leaving her well prepared for the day's lesson. She had even answered two questions, albeit in a small voice that was barely discernable. When Mr. Robertson repeated her responses for the benefit of the rest of the students, it was accompanied by words of encouragement and praise. She inwardly shuddered at the thought of how Mr. Morell would have used her meek comments to viciously mock her.

After class, she caught the bus back to Beacon Hill, getting off three stops before the one next to her home. Walking a few hundred feet, she pushed open the door at Frank's Minit-Mart, waving a hand at the pimply-faced Asian boy behind the register as she passed through the aisle displaying Ramen noodles, chili, and other quick meals. Going into the small store room at the rear of the store, she took off her hoodie and hung it on a wall hook. Simultaneously, Shannon grabbed a lurid yellow, zippered vest from the adjacent hook. She shrugged into the garment, zipped it up, and looked in the small mirror hanging on the wall. She straightened the vest slightly, bringing the red oval patch over the left breast pocket, embroidered with the Frank's logo, parallel with the plain white nametag on the right where "Shannon" had been carefully written with a Sharpie. She ran her fingers through her shoulder-length blond hair, bringing it into the semblance of an actual hairdo. She then picked up a mop, bucket, and other cleaning supplies and exited the storeroom, well aware that Luke, the guy at the cash register, would have done nothing about the cleanliness of the customer restrooms.

Other than add to the pattern of yellow misfires accumulated on the toilet seat in the men's room, she thought, allowing herself a faint, wry smile.

Luke Zhao saw Shannon walk from the storeroom to the guy's toilet and sighed to himself. His adolescent imagination worked overtime, as he thought about how great it would be to lock the door to the store, follow her into the toilet, and have wild, monkey sex for the next hour. They could then get dressed, open the store back up, and no one would be any the wiser.

No chance in hell, he thought reluctantly. *No way a girl that gorgeous is gonna have anything to do with me. Nice hair, outrageous body, and a really beautiful face, what more could a guy ask for? Her choice of clothes and heavy eye makeup gives her a real sk8ter vibe too. She is so hot that . . .*

His appraisal was suddenly interrupted by an older woman entering the store, causing a buzzer hidden somewhere in the store's ceiling to noisily sound. Sighing again, this time aloud, he put a toothy smile on his face, the kind he knew old ladies loved, and began a half-hearted attempt to actually earn some of the money he was paid for the job.

If Shannon could have read his thoughts, the last part anyway, she would have understood.

"Hey, young lady, nobody gets a free lunch here, you understand?" her father had said. "If you're going to live under my roof, you're going to contribute. You got all summer, so you better find a job."

As always, it was far easier to just tell her dad 'OK' and do what he said. Surprisingly, she was hired by the first place she applied; for some reason, Big Frank had actually liked her. The work wasn't too bad either, as long as she didn't have to deal with the public too much.

That's why I like working with Luke. He'd rather work the register and talk to people, letting me do the cleaning, restocking the shelves, and other relatively boring stuff. It is kinda creepy, though, she contemplated. *Sometimes I catch him just looking at me. I wonder what he's thinking?*

After work, she re-boarded the bus and went home. Shannon knew her father would be out late tonight; Wednesdays were the nights he went to the local sports bar, watching baseball with his work cronies until around midnight.

Just as well, I won't have to put up with his crap tonight.

She brewed another cup of tea and made a tuna sandwich, carrying both with her to her room. Finished eating, she placed her dishes on the bedside table and grabbed her laptop computer.

God, what an argument it had been trying to convince dad to get WIFI, she remembered.

"What the hell do you need the Internet for anyway?" He had fumed. "Why can't you just go to the library?" he had countered to her meekly-voiced point that she needed access for schoolwork. It was only when she offered to pay the connection fee and monthly charge herself that he begrudgingly agreed.

Sitting down cross-legged on her bed, she placed the computer on her lap and pushed the 'on' button. A blank expression of concentration spread across her face as the boot sequence progressed. She went immediately to the chat site and typed in his user's name.

Her tentative "Hi?" was answered almost immediately by:

"OMG! I am so happy to hear from you, Shannon! I couldn't wait to talk to you again!"

A faint smile blossomed, replacing her habitual emotionlessness, a look that had been carefully groomed to keep people at a distance, to not let them see the hurt and anger that welled inside her like a festering sore. She had lived in such emotional pain she could hardly make it through the day without doubling-down on her meds.

The past few days, however, have actually been, well, bearable, she thought with a realization that surprised even her. *Don't get your hopes up, she cautioned herself. You've trusted people before and they've fucked you over – badly. Thanks, mom, you bitch. Maybe this is different though. God, not everybody can feel the way I do, or it would just be one worldwide mass suicide. Some good has to exist and maybe for once I've found it.*

"Hi," she typed, "I really wanted to talk to you too."

The next three plus hours passed swiftly, as thoughts, hopes, and dreams passed from one keyboard to the other. All too soon, it was time to say goodnight and Shannon disconnected, feeling an ache in her heart quite unlike the feeling that usually existed there as a dark, malevolent force. She stood up and stretched sinuously, placing the laptop on the top of her dresser. She kicked out of her leggings and pulled her sweatshirt over her head, dropping it to the floor at her side. She stood in front of her dresser in her bra and panties, looking at her door furtively. Opening the top drawer, she reached beneath the miscellaneous underwear and socks and grasped the small metal object in her hand. She unfolded the old towel she kept beside her bed for just this purpose and spread it conscientiously atop her bedspread.

She sat down.

Shannon looked down at her legs, at the thin tracery of lines that marred them like nearly decipherable hieroglyphics. Some were already white scar tissue, others were in various stages of the healing process, while some were still somewhat freshly scabbed. She clicked the blade of the box cutter into the open position, poising it closely over a relatively unscathed portion of her upper right thigh. She paused.

Just maybe I can get through tonight on my own, she thought reflectively.

It hadn't been such a bad day after all. She had avoided any confrontation with her father, class had gone alright, and work had been uneventful.

Oh, yeah, she added happily, an alien emotion she hadn't experienced in what seemed like forever. *And I just might have a boyfriend.*

Chapter 16

Haven't been up here since high school, he observed, gazing at the densely forested wood line as he parked at the end of the small dirt road already littered with a couple of black and whites, a K-9 unit, an ambulance, and other sundry official vehicles.

Exiting his unmarked car, he looked around to get his bearings.

Oh shit, he grumbled under his breath, *not up the goddam hill.*

Despite having driven as closely to the murder scene as his GPS could get him, the underarms, back, and neck of John Caldwell's crisp white shirt were wringing wet by the time he made it to the small clearing. He spotted Frank Chapman, who waved him over to a shady spot just outside the tape barricade.

"Christ, John, you decide to go swimming on your way over here?"

"Naw, shit Frank, this is supposed to be Seattle, not fucking Phoenix. It must be a hundred today and it's not even eleven o'clock yet."

"Quit your bitchin'. It wasn't even ninety on the First Sound Bank sign on the way over," Frank retorted. He continued more seriously, "John, you really have to get your ass in better shape. You gonna pass your physical?"

"Excuse me, but is there really a body here or are we shooting some fitness infomercial? Is there a hidden camera somewhere? If not, can we switch the fucking topic of conversation from my fat ass to something pertinent to the job we're actually getting paid to do?" John asked sarcastically, his patience wearing dangerously thin.

"Alright, it's your funeral, I guess," Frank replied with an air of resignation.

Hell, I'm no poster boy, but John's really let himself go, he thought. *Maybe I'll forget the donuts myself next time, bad for the ticker, my man.*

"OK, a guy out exercising his dog figured, what the hell, I'll let him off the leash for a while. Who's to know, right? Well, dog takes off like a bat out of hell and wouldn't come back. So, the owner goes to get him and, low and behold, he finds the buffet table open for business. Dog must have been barking at the seagulls, they had really done a number on the vic. Much of the face and hands stripped to the bone and they'd started to work on the neck. This one ain't gonna be an open casket funeral, that's for sure."

"Any ID?" John asked, now totally engrossed in his work.

"Nope, and not much chance of facial recognition either. All we know for sure is it's a young adult male, probably early twenties, tall and with dark hair."

"Not much at all," John repeated. "CSI have any clue as to how long he's been there."

"Could be about a week or two. They'll know a lot more after they analyze the entomological evidence."

"Interesting, but is there a reason why I'm here and not in my air-conditioned living room, sucking on a cold beer?"

Frank answered John's question with one of his own. "You haven't asked yet."

"What?" asked John, feeling too miserable to play guessing games.

"COD."

"Yeah?"

"Cause of death most likely resulting from a bilateral severing of the carotid arteries by a sharp instrument."

John let out a low whistle and muttered, "Son-of-a-bitch."

"Right, I know what you're thinking – just like the guy in Green Lake Park. If it was a stabbing, gunshot, hell, even blunt force trauma, I wouldn't have interrupted your day off. But this ain't normal, is it? I'm thinking same perp, how about you?" Frank asked, a grim look fixed on his face as he locked eyes with his friend.

"Yeah, I can't really see it any other way. And it's not the Woodsman/DIY Killer either. This is a whole new deal. Well, let's go up and see if the lab rats have found anything."

They lifted the tape and, bending over, passed through to the other side. John was happy to note the senior pathologist on site was Megan James. He had worked a few cases with her in the past and knew she knew her business. He felt assured that, if there was any evidence present, she would find it.

"Hey, Megan. How you doing?" he asked hopefully.

"Hello, John," she replied in a not-unfriendly, yet consummately professional voice. "This one of yours?" she asked, leaving him to make sense of her verbal shorthand.

"Could be. Frank and I are working the Green Lake Park murder and he thought the cause of death could be the same MO. What do you think, scalpel or box cutter?"

Megan gave John a thoughtful look and said, "I really hate to give an opinion without the lab work to back it up. It's a bad habit to get into."

John's hopeful, silent stare was convincingly imploring.

She sighed.

"Box cutter. Way too much force for as delicate of an instrument as a scalpel. The murderer got the jugulars as well as just about severing the trachea. Either he didn't know his own strength or he was mighty pissed off."

"Thanks," John said, then continued, "What else do you have for us, Megan?"

Well, I'm pretty sure the murder took place on site, judging from the width of the area of blood seepage into the soil. I figure the body's been here for between a week and nine days, seeing as how the rainstorm a week ago last Wednesday would have denigrated the blood residue considerably more. Victim was probably in his early to mid-twenties and pretty well-off, considering his running gear and Tag Heuer sports watch. Some evidence of a struggle perhaps, but the ground could have just as likely been disturbed pre- or post-mortem. One interesting thing is the body has obviously been rolled. t could have occurred during the death throes, but highly unlikely that he would have turned both directions. Might have happened pursuant to robbery of the body, but I don't think so. We already talked about COD, so that's about all I have for now, I'm afraid."

"Why do you think the perp didn't just turn him over to check his pockets?" Frank asked immediately.

"Well, a new Tag Heuer costs somewhere in four figures, while those Adidas Tech Runners are definitely over five hundred new. I know, because my teenaged son has been panting over a pair like them on E-bay. No self-respecting crim would take a wallet and leave a couple of grand's worth of bonus items."

"Thanks a lot, Megan," John said, "Let us know if you get anything else for us at the autopsy or in the lab, OK?"

"Certainly will, gentlemen. Now, if you don't mind . . .?" She gestured vaguely toward the body and, seeing both detectives shake their heads simultaneously, turned back to finish her examination of the crime scene.

The two men moved back to the other side of the tape to give the CSI unencumbered room to work.

"I guess not much hope of turning up anything on the door-to-door, seeing as how there really aren't any, doors I mean," John asked Frank rhetorically.

"Well, I got a couple of uniforms talking to the morning shift down at the wastewater treatment plant. Afterwards, I'll send 'em over to the Indian Cultural Center and Discovery Center. By that time, maybe the second shift will be on at the treatment plant. We'll also put it out on CrimeStoppers. Maybe we'll get lucky, I don't know."

As if in answer to John's question, a rather short, Hispanic uniformed officer appeared from the direction of where everyone was parked, walking purposefully toward him and Frank. With him was a middle-aged man in coveralls.

"Murphy, sir," said the officer, pausing briefly for the almost obligatory comment about his heritage. When the two detectives failed to ask, he continued, "This is Mr. Tomlinson. He's maybe got some information about the case."

"Please go ahead, sir," said Frank reassuringly, trying to hide his eagerness and doing a poor job of it.

"I was taking a smoke break outside the plant door early last Saturday morning, must have been about five or six, seeing as how they don't let you smoke inside anymore. Funny, they don't mind you smelling shit for eight hours, but a few minutes of smoke is gonna kill ya, right?"

The mention of a cigarette made John realize suddenly how much he wanted one.

"Well," the plant worker continued, "I was just about to go back inside when I see this couple of kids jog down the trail at a hell of a clip. I remember thinking to myself how nice it would be to be young and in shape again."

Nodding his head encouragingly to the man, Frank poked John in the ribs, all the while never taking his eyes off the speaker. To his credit, John remained expressionless, saving his retribution for later.

"The fella was tall, wearing a black running suit."

Now John and Frank looked at each other, all thoughts of horseplay forgotten. Frank said, "Go on please."

"That's about all I can think of about him. The girl was the one I remember more."

"Why is that?" John took a turn at prompting Tomlinson.

"Well, she must have been really hardcore, I was thinking. It was colder than hell that morning, and all she was wearing was a little pair of shorts. Well, a pink hooded sweatshirt and shoes too, of course. Hard to take my eyes off the shorts though," he said, a bit ashamed of his lechery.

"Do you remember anything more about her, Mr. Tomlinson?" queried Frank.

"No, it was still kind of shadowy out and I wasn't really paying much attention, really. Sorry."

"No problem at all, sir. If you think of anything else, will you please give me a call?" asked Frank, handing the man one of his cards.

Tomlinson looked at it and then at Frank. He said, "Chapman, eh? Aren't you the one that's working on the Woodsman case? Hey, do ya think it's him what did this?"

"I really couldn't say at this point, sir. Not enough evidence either way. Well, thanks again."

Frank's look of appreciation couldn't help but being pretty plainly an act of dismissal as well. Tomlinson took the hint, turning and walking to the edge of the clearing. He briefly paused and turned back and waved before disappearing behind the trees.

"Well, that fits in with Megan's estimate of TOD," Frank said, not trying to conceal the excitement in his voice.

Maybe we're actually going to catch some breaks in this case, he thought. *About damn time, too.*

"OK," summarized John. "So last Saturday Susie Sweet-cheeks and her boyfriend Jack-O are out for an early morning run. Both are athletic and in good shape. Along the way, the jock gets whacked. But what happens to Susie? Does she just finish her run, oblivious to or not caring about what happened to her guy? They probably would have still been together up to this point, since the trail doesn't branch until after the clearing."

"Hey, maybe she just left him in the dust and he was so embarrassed he walked off the trail and slit his own throat. Case solved, let's go get a beer!" Frank said, somewhat less than helpfully.

"Fuck off, can't you see I'm on a roll here?" John continued, "On the other hand, she could have been killed too and there's another body festering somewhere deeper in the woods. Damn, you better arrange to have the rest of the area checked as well, just in case."

Frank nodded, motioning with his hand for John to continue.

"Or . . ."

"Or what, for Christ's sake?" Frank said impatiently.

"She's been grabbed. Maybe by our friend."

"Yeah, but I thought we agreed it wasn't the DIY killer." Frank countered.

- 181 -

"Well, that's before we thought there might be a young girl missing."

"Goddammit," Frank swore viciously. "I am so fucking sick and tired of going around and around on this. I guess we just have to leave all options open and see if anything comes up to help us narrow things down. Until then, I'm going to put out an APB to haul in every girl with a pink sweatshirt and a nice ass for questioning!"

"Well, that should narrow it down to about a thousand or so in Seattle metro alone. You want to expand the search to include the entire Pacific Northwest?" John jokingly replied, but sharing the frustration of his friend equally.

"Let's get the hell out of here, OK?" Frank said. "You got time to go back to the office?"

"Yeah, sure. Claire's out and the Mariners are playing the Rangers later on tonight, so not much happening there either way," replied John.

A half hour later they were walking down the sparsely populated hallway to Frank's office. Both men collapsed into chairs, taking a moment to relax in the air-conditioning.

Finally, Frank began again, asking, "So what do you think we've got here, John?"

"I don't know, really. Why don't you call up the current missing persons' report while I go take a leak? Maybe it's best to start with the more straight-forward end of the deal. Somebody's going to be missing a kid like that."

"Makes sense," Frank replied. "I'll contact MUPU and ask them to email over any likely reports."

The Missing and Unidentified Persons Unit (MUPU) of the Washington State Police had been established to serve as a clearinghouse for missing person reports.

Yeah, seems likely someone would have reported Jack-O by now as well, he thought as he dialed the phone.

By the time John returned, Frank was already scrutinizing three reports that had been sent as enclosures to an email response from MUPU. He distractedly motioned for John to sit back down without breaking eye contact with his computer screen.

"Damn, that was quick. Must be a really slow day over at MUPU," John commented.

"Naw, just got a bit of pull, that's all. My cousin Marsha is a shift supervisor over there," Frank replied, then abruptly followed with, "Hey, this just might be our guy. Brandon Whitehurst, age 21. He's a student at Seattle University, member of the Redhawk basketball team. 6'2" and about 185. Black hair and brown eyes. No distinguishing marks or tattoos. Last seen late last Friday night. Report filed by his father, Brandon senior."

Frank picked up his phone and dialed the contact number on the report. After a couple of rings, he heard a female voice say, "Hello. Whitehurst residence. Emma Whitehurst speaking."

Frank put the phone on speaker for John's benefit, simultaneously answering, "Hello, Mrs. Whitehurst. This is Detective Frank Chapman with the Seattle Police Department."

"Yes. Is this about my boy, Brandon?"

"It is, ma'am . . ."

Before Frank could continue, Mrs. Whitehurst began to pummel him in a near-hysterical voice with a series of questions about the whereabouts of her son. He gently interrupted her.

"There's really nothing certain right now," he felt guilty about what he felt in his gut was a lie. "Ma'am, could you perhaps tell me what type of watch your son wears?"

- 183 -

"My husband and I bought him a Tag Heuer Aquaracer for a graduation present three years ago. That's the only watch that I'd know anything about. Tell me, Detective Chapman, is my son dead?"

At that, Frank and John exchanged a grimace, simultaneously thinking that, regardless of an officer's time on the force, this part just doesn't get any easier. In a carefully crafted, neutral voice, Frank replied, "Like I said, ma'am, there's nothing I can say at this point."

Quickly wishing to change the subject, he asked, "How did you determine your son was missing, ma'am? Could it be possible he just left town on the spur of the moment with some friends? Hiking in the Cascades, maybe?"

He kicked himself for offering what, his senses guiltily told him, was false hope.

"Well," she replied. "It was really his fiancé, Jacqueline, who called us, Jacqueline Eaton. She and Brandon share an apartment in North Delridge, on 26th Street. It was about three o'clock last Saturday afternoon. She said she had woken up at about ten and he was gone. She tried calling him several times throughout the day, but all she got was his voice mail. She said she left message after message, up until his mailbox filled up, but still no answer. In answer to your second question, detective, Brandon would have never left for more than an hour or two without telling Jackie where he was going. Our son is a nice boy who is very kind and considerate, especially where Jacqueline is concerned. He is utterly in love with her, they're planning on getting married later in the autumn."

At that she broke down into heart-wrenching sobs. Frank let her cry into the phone uninterrupted.

After a minute, she continued, "I'm so sorry about that, Detective Chapman, you must think I'm terribly silly."

"No, ma'am, absolutely not," he responded truthfully. "Um, one more thing if it's not too much bother. Would you please verify the address of your son and his fiancé? I'd like to speak with her."

Mrs. Whitehurst replied, "Certainly, but she's not there. She's staying with her parents right now."

She provided Frank with the address of Jaqueline's parents.

She then asked, "Please, detective, please let me know as soon as you find anything out about my son."

"Of course, Mrs. Whitehurst," he answered, knowing full well in his heart another phone call would not be long in coming. "If you think of anything else, please let us know, ma'am. Goodbye."

Frank hung up the phone and looked at John, who stated, "Makes you feel like a real jerk, doesn't it?"

"Yeah, it really does. I'd say it's about a 99.9% chance it's her son laying in the morgue. Want to take a ride up north? I'd really like to know if Ms. Eaton likes pink."

"Let's go," John answered immediately and was already heading for the door, feeling that, for once, things were actually moving fast.

It didn't take long for John's initial optimism to deflate like a popped birthday balloon. The two detectives drove to the address Mrs. Whitehurst had provided, a spacious home in the city's posh Magnolia district. They stopped in front of wide ornamental wrought iron gates. Frank exited the vehicle and spoke briefly into the small call box located on one of the massive pillars that supported the gates. As he returned to the car, the gates began to slide open automatically and the car proceeded slowly up the sweeping red block pavement drive. By the time the two men had shut their car doors, a middle-aged man had opened the entrance door to the house. Tall and athletically built, he introduced himself to Frank and John as Robert Eaton.

After showing their badges, introducing themselves, and shaking hands, Frank said, "Pleased to meet you, Mr. Eaton. May we go inside please? We just have a few questions relating to the disappearance of your daughter's fiancé, Brandon Whitehurst."

"Of course," replied the man. "Please follow me. Jaqueline is upstairs, I'll call her." Entering the spacious marble-floored foyer, Mr. Eaton motioned for the men to have a seat while he ascended the adjacent stairway. Frank and John looked idly about the richly furnished interior of the room as they waited. Within a couple of minutes, they heard sharp steps from what had to be a tiled upstairs landing, followed by the appearance of Mr. Eaton and his daughter descending the stairs.

The two detectives shared a quick look of abject disappointment, then rose to be introduced by Bob Eaton to his daughter. They posed a short battery of questions to the young woman, who answered them to the best of her ability, all the while fear and dread creeping in and out of her responses like the ocean tide. Within a few minutes, Frank thanked her for her assistance, promised to let her know if there were any updates to the case, and said goodbye.

As soon as they pulled back out onto the city street, John commented, "Damn."

"Damn," echoed Frank.

"There's no way that woman would have been running that morning, let alone have some guy checking out her butt," John stated the obvious. "Just as soon as I saw her dad helping her down the stairs, I knew she wasn't going to be the girl in pink. The only pink she is probably interested in is if it's the right color to paint the nursery. She has to be at least eight months along."

"Yep, I agree," said Frank. "OK, so what have we got now? The Whitehurst boy sneaks out of bed with his pregnant girlfriend for an early morning rendezvous with a hot little number in short-shorts and a pink sweatshirt. Could be completely platonic, but why didn't he let the girlfriend know where he was going? Obviously because she wouldn't have taken it too well. So, either he was just trying to

- 186 -

avoid an early morning argument or Mrs. Whitehurst's "nice boy" isn't so nice after all. What do you think?"

"Call me jaded, but I'm more for the latter than the former. There's a lot of places closer to their apartment where he could have went running, especially that early in the morning. Speaking of which, why was he out at that time? Jackie Eaton said it wasn't part of Brandon's normal routine, he normally liked to sleep late if he didn't need to get up. Sounds really fishy to me too, Frank."

"Yeah, so Brandon boy thinks he's got all the bases covered. Leaves the house while Jackie's still sleeping, probably hoping to get back while she's still in bed. Sees Susie Sweet-Cheeks, maybe even gets some on the side. Even if the girlfriend is awake, he's coming back in his jogging suit, for God's sake. Pretty damn well thought out, if you ask me."

"OK, so what goes wrong?" John asked.

"Well, what if they do run into someone on the trail? He gets the drop on Brandon, but Susie just kicks it into overdrive and gets the hell out of there. She's afraid to say anything because she wasn't supposed to be with him anyway. Could he have been cheating on his girlfriend with someone they both know? Might not be a bad idea to ask Jackie a few innocent questions about their mutual friends, those of the female persuasion," suggested John.

"A long shot," replied Frank," but it certainly couldn't hurt."

"Otherwise, we're left with the scenario that another body is waiting to be discovered, the girl's been snatched, or . . .," John hesitated before continuing, "she's is in on the murder herself."

"If that's so, I don't figure it for a crime of opportunity," answered Frank. "The kid wouldn't have driven all the way out to Discovery Park on a whim, met a girl who just happened to be waiting for a mark, jogged a few miles with her, and then let her persuade him to go into the bushes to get his throat cut. No, he went there specifically to meet her, it was definitely pre-arranged. I'll get a court order to check his phone records and email accounts to see if we can get a fix on her there."

"Yeah, makes good sense," John agreed, "But can we tie the murder of Brandon Whitehurst to that of Tom Beach? Besides the same or similar COD, what have we got? First, both murders involve solitary males in a somewhat secluded wooded setting. The killing was done up close and personal and robbery doesn't seem to be the primary cause. For some reason, our perp just thinks there's reason enough for these guys to die."

"So, what do you think they have in common? Or does the killer have a top ten list of reasons to murder people?"

"Well, if so, we're back at the starting line again. Let's just assume there is a specific connection," continued John. "We know Beach was a sexual offender. On the other hand, the only dirt we have right now on Brandon Whitehurst is that he could have a wandering dick. If you ask me, that might point at the girl as a possible suspect, or a relative of someone whose been hurt by both of the two men. I'll see if I can get any information about the kids Beach molested."

Frank thought a few seconds before saying, "Yeah, it's definitely possible; however, I'm still leaning toward the girl getting nabbed, maybe by the Woodsman. We know he's got to be getting his victims somewhere, what's easier than on a secluded trail in the wee hours of the morning? He just waits for the two kids to come running up the trail and then gets the bead on them with a weapon of some kind. Marches them off into the clearing, has Brandon tie the girl up like a Thanksgiving turkey, then kills the boy. Now he forces the girl through the trees and to his car. Did I mention this all takes place in the woods?"

"Well," said John, "The scenarios couldn't be any more different, except for one dead Whitehurst boy in both of them." As they pulled into the North Precinct parking lot, he asked, "Unless you have something else, I'm going to go on home, OK? I'll try to run down the info on Beach tomorrow morning."

"Might as well, John. I can't see anything happening until we start getting lab reports back. Give my love to Claire, OK?"

"Yep, see ya," John replied.

On the trip back home, he stopped at a service station and bought a pack of Camels. He then drove to Green Lake Park and re-examined the scene of the killing of Tom Beach. He absent-mindedly chain-smoked a half a pack while he surveyed the bench from different angles. Park maintenance had eradicated all traces of the man's blood from around the bench area; yet, in his mind's eye, John could envision the crime scene as he had first seen it.

What the hell is not making sense here? He kept thinking. *What am I missing, dammit?*

Frustrated both at his inability to make progress in any of the cases that were now beginning to stack up, as well as his surrender to full nicotine addiction, he returned to his car and drove home. He hoped that Claire had not yet returned, giving him a chance to take a long shower, brush his teeth, and down some Listerine to mask the cigarette smell on his breath.

Even in this modest wish, John Caldwell was not able to catch a break.

Chapter 17

"It's really great that you're thinking about going to college," he typed.

"Yeah, I'd really kinda given up on the idea, what with the crap at high school and all. But I guess I've gotta do something besides hang out around the house feeling sorry for myself the rest of my life," she replied.

"Good for you, girl. Glad to see you've got the strength to get beyond things."

During the few seconds of hesitation prior to her reply, he imagined her chewing her bottom lip.

"Um, so like Jason, do you want to get together, or something?"

"Wow, do I! I'd love to actually meet up with you and see if you're as great in person as you are online!"

Maybe that was a little over the top; I certainly don't want to scare her off now.

"You are so full of crap!!!" Her reply was immediate.

Oh, shit, what should I do now?

Her next response alleviated his concern, however.

"I mean, you really don't know me at all, other than online. I could be a perv or something in real life, just posing as some messed up chick to make you feel sorry for me. All kidding aside, I'm just kind of nobody actually – definitely not 'great' material."

He typed furiously.

"Stop putting yourself down! Just because other people underestimate you, it doesn't mean you have to agree with them. You seem really intelligent and actually kind of sweet in a bizarrely strange sort of way." He imagined her smiling as she read that last bit. "Besides, unless you sent me someone else's photo, you're like crazy beautiful!"

Her response was brief and seemingly heartfelt. "I think you're beautiful too, Jason."

Somewhat embarrassed by her surprising frankness, he hurriedly continued, "So where would you like to meet up? How about Northgate Mall?"

"Um, I'm not much of a mall person really. You said you had a car, right? Couldn't you just pick me up and we could just go riding around somewhere and talk? Promise I won't bite."

This is going even better than I thought it would, he thought.

"No problem, if that's what you want to do. Where do you want me to pick you up and when?"

They quickly settled on a time and place.

"So, like I've gotta go, OK?" she asked, then added, "I really can't wait to go out with you."

"Yeah, I know what you mean. I'm really happy we're getting together at last."

"Me to," she responded. "Bye."

"Bye yourself, Shannon."

Walter logged off and shut down the computer.

This one is really different, my man, he said to himself as he made his way into the kitchen. *Thirsty work,* he thought with a grin, taking a long drink from the bottle of Budweiser he had just opened.

He looked at the clock over the door and saw it was just after eleven p.m.

God, have I really been talking to her for over three hours?

He opened the patio doors, letting his Labrador retriever bound about for a few minutes while he finished his beer. Walter felt quite pleased with himself, feeling he had made a very good impression on the girl. Not only had it taken only four sessions to get her to suggest they get together, but she had also freely given him her address. The bus stop where they had agreed to meet was only a few blocks away from her house, but the route provided an extended window of opportunity to grab her that he had not enjoyed with any of his other dates. Not only could he pick her up anywhere between her house and the bus stop, but he could also do it some other time, if there was a chance someone would see him take her.

Sweet.

He let Mike back into the house and locked the door behind him.

Can't be too careful, he mused.

He shut off the lights in the house and went to bed.

Tomorrow's going to be a busy day.

Walter was already awake when his alarm went off at seven a.m. He went to the kitchen and let Mike out, then started a pot of coffee. While it was brewing, he showered and got ready for work. He looked in the mirror and was happy with what he saw. The crisply ironed button-down white shirt made an excellent backdrop for his Essex Check navy and blue silk tie. He shrugged into his grey pinstripe jacket, which nicely complimented the rest of his attire. After a bit of breakfast for both himself and the dog, he left for work.

His day at the office was mentally stimulating, leaving him little time to think about his date later that evening with Shannon. Throughout the morning, Marianne passed in and out of his office efficiently, providing scant distraction from his work. Close to noon, however, he called her on the office intercom.

"Yes, Mr. Harrison?"

"Um, Marianne, are you going out for lunch?"

"Yes, sir, I was just going to grab a tofu salad from the Thai takeout and bring it back to my desk."

Walter inwardly groaned at the thought of tofu, but then replied, "Honey, would you mind picking me up some Moo Yang grilled pork please? I'm kind of tied up in the middle of this report."

"Of course, Mr. Harrison, would you like fried rice with that?" she asked, familiar enough with his eating habits to know the question was rhetorical.

She inwardly flushed with pleasure at his familiarity, although she realized it had no real significance.

"Sure, that would be great," he replied. "Sometimes I think you know me better than I know myself, Marianne. Come get the money."

The secretary went into Walter's office and he handed her thirty dollars.

"That ought to cover it. My treat, OK? I buy and you fly?"

"Why thank you Mr. Harrison," she beamed at him with a smile as bright as an August sunrise. "How very kind of you."

As she left his office, Marianne Peters wondered if she should reconsider her decision not to actively pursue an other-than-business relationship with her boss.

Watching her leave his office, Walter thought admiringly, *really nice girl. I wonder if . . .?*

No way, he warned himself. *Definitely bad to mix business and pleasure. Besides, right now I'm already taken.*

If Marianne would have suddenly turned around, she probably would have misconstrued the toothy grin on her boss' face, which in actuality had nothing to do with her shapely derriere.

Twenty minutes later, he began to wolf down his lunch, interspersing bites of succulent pork and fried rice with examining the intricacies of the office's monthly costings report. Finishing his meal and his analysis more or less simultaneously, he placed the report neatly within its labeled folder and the Styrofoam residue from his meal into his wastepaper basket. Having worked the morning and most of the afternoon more or less steadily, Walter didn't feel guilty about taking a few minutes to plan out his anticipated rendezvous with Shannon Buckley.

As he reviewed his evening's upcoming activities, his satisfaction with his plan grew. He had agreed to meet the girl at the bus stop at seven o'clock. That left him sufficient time to go home after work, feed Mike and change clothes.

Eat or not to eat? he thought, carefully considering his choices.

Eating lunch this late, I'd better put dinner off until after I picked her up, he decided, smiling to himself. *Need to watch the weight, don't want to start wearing a middle age spread quite yet.*

He patted his trim stomach for emphasis.

What else? he continued his self-examination. *Obviously, need to get the 'pick-up kit.'*

He had purchased the small Rubbermaid container years ago from Walmart, but had assigned it its current purpose only a few years ago. The contents had evolved over that time. Now it contained his homemade blackjack, a roll of gray duct tape, a box cutter, and a few heavy-duty cable ties.

Everything I should need in one tidy place, Dad would be proud, he thought with satisfaction.

Don't forget to change the plates, he warned himself. He had got the idea of changing his Kia's plates from a TV crime drama, he didn't remember which one. The bad guy had furtively looked around a parking garage before lifting the license plate from one of the cars. At the time, he had wondered why the man had taken the chance of stealing the plates from someone's car.

What if the owner had returned and saw someone fiddling with his car? he had mused at the time.

Although he readily admitted the advantage of not letting some passerby with a photographic memory being able to provide the license number to the police, it seemed like an unnecessary risk to take them from a car someone cared about. A subsequent trip to an out-of-town junkyard had netted him a haul of six sets of current plates, efficiently collected while the disabled vet who owned the yard gratefully waited in the office. He also found a couple of serviceable floor mats that looked like they would fit his SUV. He slipped the license plates up the back of his jacket and carried the mats into the office, giving the man ten dollars. Need to replenish my stock soon, he noted, wouldn't pay to run out.

So, I'll leave about six, that should give me plenty of time to get there, he continued his analysis. *That'll also allow me to look things over before the grab.*

The grab was always the dicey part. It looks so easy on TV; you just cover their mouth with a rag dipped in chloroform or else inject some instantaneously acting tranquillizer into their neck;

either way, the victim just collapses like a sack of potatoes into your arms.

He had found out that, although it is possible to buy chloroform from a chemical supplier, they ask a lot of questions, too many to risk it, he had decided. Ditto for the tranquilizers, he had discovered. So, unless a guy has a connection at a medical facility that he trusts completely, which he did not, using chemicals or drugs was out.

A quick wrap to the back of the head with the blackjack may be low tech, but it definitely doesn't complicate things.

He looked at the clock and was surprised to see he had spent the last forty minutes contemplating his evening's activities. Somewhat guiltily, he threw himself back into his work, finishing two policy reviews before five o'clock. He arose from his desk and, putting on his jacket, walked into the reception area.

"Marianne," he said, "I'm calling it a day. I finished those two reviews, they're in my out box. Make sure you get out of here on time yourself, OK"

"Sure, Mr. Harrison. By the way, thanks again for lunch. Um . . ." She looked at him as she hesitated.

"Yes?"

"Uh, well, nothing really. Have a good evening."

As he turned and walked away, Marianne felt her face redden. She had almost asked him if he wanted to go grab a drink on the way home; however, she had worked for her boss long enough to know that, if he was leaving the office at five o'clock on the dot, he had definite plans for the evening. It would have been even more embarrassing to have him turn down her somewhat forward offer than to look like the stammering idiot she felt she had in their conversation a few minutes prior.

Even if he did agree, she thought, *it would only be for one, and that out of pity or a sense of obligation. What I've got in mind needs a whole evening to unfold, better to wait for a time when I can get his undivided attention.*

She sighed and went back to finishing up her work for the evening, at the same time hoping some other woman wasn't going to be getting the kind of attention she was starting to realize she increasingly desired from Walter Harrison.

His drive home was completely uneventful. He gave Mike his can of Alpo, leaving him to happily slurp it down while he went to shower and change clothes. He put on jeans and a purple University of Washington t-shirt.

She told me it's her favorite color, he recalled as he finished dressing, *I hope she realizes I chose it for her. I think we're really going to hit it off together. That is, if everything goes right.*

But why shouldn't it?

The sense of excited anticipation he always felt about this time was mounting. Despite the very real danger involved, he absolutely loved meeting one of his dates for the first time. Sure, it was a little rough at first, but most of the girls learned very quickly to behave correctly.

Got to keep a woman in line, dad had said; otherwise, she thinks she wears the pants in the family. Can't have that happen, can you?

No sir, he had answered, a twelve-year-old boy looking up at the man he idolized.

Yep, that was just one of the valuable lessons I learned from dad, an important one.

He coaxed Mike back outside with a treat, promising the dog he would have time to play with him later that evening. He then went into the garage and removed the license plates on his Sorento. He gazed thoughtfully at the two sets of stolen plates he had remaining, selecting the ones with the "Volunteer Firefighter" logo. He quickly attached them to his vehicle, front and back. Walter placed his pick-up kit and the morning newspaper in the passenger seat of the car and dug in his pocket for the post-It note on which he had written Shannon's address.   Confident he had completed all of his preparatory tasks; he got in his Kia and started the engine. The automatic garage door was opening slowly to his rear. Carefully, he backed out of his driveway and completed a three-point turn onto the street.

Get ready, honey, he paraphrased the old Motown song, *cause here I come.*

In a short time, he was cruising warily down Shannon's street.

Not too fast, not too slow, he cautioned himself. D*on't want to draw anyone's attention, especially not hers.*

He looked to the right and saw her house, no lights showing in the windows and apparently lifeless.

Not to worry, he thought, she said her bedroom is on the back side of the house. *I wonder what she's doing right now; maybe taking a shower, maybe trying to pick out just the right clothes to make a great first impression on the guy of her dreams.*

His sense of anticipation grew as he imagined seeing her in real life for the first time, talking with her, touching her.

Hold on, big guy, he bridled his daydream. *Got a lot to do before we get to the good parts.*

As he proceeded up the street, he noted with elated surprise a series of traffic cones blocked the sidewalk on the right side of the street for almost a half of a block. He logically inferred the girl would have to cross over the street at that point or before to avoid the water main work that was obviously taking place.

Well, avoids flipping a coin as to which side of the street to park on.

He drove past the bus stop where he was supposed to meet Shannon, going three streets beyond before turning to the left to make his way around the block to execute a change direction. He eased the Sorento into a curbside parking place across from a somewhat derelict house that was evidently vacant, judging from the "For Rent or Lease" sign in the overgrown grass of the front yard. The spot was approximately halfway between the Buckley's house and the bus stop and its value to Walter was further enhanced by the mature red oak that grew between the cracked sidewalk and the street. A thick, raggedly trimmed hedge ran between the unoccupied house and its neighbor, further enhancing the location's value to Walter's intention.

This would be his first grab without the diversion offered by Mike. When he had deftly worked the topic of dogs into one of his chats with Shannon, he had been quite surprised when she had confessed that, not only did she not like dogs, but she was deathly afraid of them.

That would have been a laugh, he thought with a grin, letting out Mike to get her attention, only to have her run off screaming the other direction.

Really glad I asked.

He had decided against waiting in the car, thinking it might seem noteworthy to an observer to see a man sitting in a parked car for an extended period of time, especially just down the street from the house where a young girl was abducted. He had also discarded the idea of loitering on the street, all the while keeping her house in sight.

All it takes is one busybody, and then the police know much more about me than I want them to.

In the end, he had decided the best thing to do was to hide in plain sight. He grabbed the newspaper and exited his vehicle, walking briskly toward the bus stop. He sat down, opened the paper, and began to appear to read, using it as a psychological as well as a physical barrier to human interaction.

Not much chance of that though, this is definitely the type of neighborhood where you don't strike up casual conversations with strangers.

All the while, his eyes grazed over the top of the newspaper, silently scanning for sight of his target approaching.

Suddenly, he saw an obviously female figure dressed in jeans and a t-shirt cross the street from the direction of the Buckley house. As she got nearer, his certainty grew that it was Shannon; her tall frame, blond hair, and pretty face unmistakably those of the girl whose picture he had been infatuated with over the past few days.

Trying hard to control his eagerness, Walter forced himself to casually rise, fold his paper, and walk toward the approaching girl. When they were approximately twenty feet apart, she briefly raised her eyes to meet his. Recognizing he was not Justin, or at least the young man whose picture she had been led to believe was Justin, she dropped her gaze back to the pavement in front of her, using her MP-3 player to avoid contact with Walter in a similar manner to how he had used his newspaper. Then she was past him. He successfully resisted the urge to turn and look in her direction. He was left with the whisper of her perfume; however, probably from an inexpensive, drugstore special set, maybe a Christmas present, he surmised.

I wonder how long she's going to wait, he asked himself, realizing he could have quite a bit of time on his hands.

He had just assumed she would return home when it eventually dawned on her Justin was going to be a no-show.

What if she decides to go over to a friend's house for a good cry?

Relax, he told himself, *if I don't pick her up today, I can always try for tomorrow, or any other time really. You know where she lives, Walter, so just chill out.*

Despite the logic of his rationalizations, Walter realized he did not possess the patience to delay taking the girl. He had to have her tonight. Sooner or later, the odds were good she would return home.

What to do until then?

He looked up to the second floor of the vacant house, noticing one of the windows appeared to have an unfettered view down the street.

Today must be my lucky day, he mumbled softly under his breath.

A quick trip down the side of the building, a rock thrown through the window on the back porch and, before he knew it, he was ensconced in an upstairs bedroom, scanning the street for the return of the jilted young girl.

Man, I wish I would have brought the newspaper, he complained after almost two hours. He knew, however, that, even if he had brought the paper to his observation perch, he wouldn't have taken the chance of getting immersed in the sports section, only to have her walk right past him undetected.

That just wouldn't do, would it?

Instead, he kept steady watch, his mind occasionally slipping into fantasies of his upcoming evenings to be spent in such stimulating company.

Darkness was beginning to seriously impede his surveillance when he saw her appear at the limits of his vision, slowly trudging back toward her house. He didn't know if it was his imagination, prompted by vanity, or was her head even further bowed toward the ground as she walked.

Poor girl, he commiserated, *I can understand your dejection, being stood up and all. Things aren't as bad as they seem though, you've got a really good surprise coming, honey.*

Walter left the room and made his way through the murky halls of the house, exiting the way he had entered. He walked swiftly toward the street. He halted just behind the front edge of the hedge, fully obscured from the notice of anyone walking southward, especially a despondent girl too caught up in her problems to be cautious. She was probably still wearing her earbuds as well, further diminishing her sensory warning system.

He waited, adrenalin coursing throughout his body, as the first of her footfalls became discernible. They became louder as she neared.

So close, he thought, but not quite yet.

His fingertips tingled with an almost electric intensity at the delicious thought of touching her young, pale skin for the first time. Then, she appeared, rounding the head of the hedgerow; not looking at anything other than the sidewalk in front of her, oblivious to the danger that was quickly overtaking her from behind.

Chapter 18

What should I have expected? she thought bitterly, *some Prince Charming to come galloping in on a white charger to take me away from all this?*

She made a vague, small sweeping gesture with her right hand.

Out of this fucking shithole of a neighborhood, away from my asshole father, even the memory of a bitch mother who deserted me.

Hot tears fought through, coursing down the swell of her cheeks. She swiped at them angrily.

How could I have been so stupid? You waited there for almost two hours before you got up enough courage to call him, you dumb cow. Then you find out that he hadn't even given you his real number! Why did he do this, why does he hate me so much that he wants to hurt me so badly?

Shannon knew there was no answer to her questions, it was what it was; just another stab in the heart like so many she had experienced before.

What to do now? she wondered.

She left the bus stop and started walking automatically back toward her house. She felt lifeless, as if her body had been sucked dry of its already depleted energy. She thought of a return to the dismal routine of her life with horror.

Home, school, work, which one is the worst?

Imagining an endless cycle of days trapped in the hopelessness of that routine appalled her. She felt she could swallow her entire bottle of antidepressants and it wouldn't make any difference. Shannon turned her music up to full volume, hoping desperately that the pain in Amy Lee's voice would somehow drown out that of her own.

The depth of her despair consumed her. She sensed nothing until she felt the sharp pain to the back of her skull. Although she experienced fear in the instant before consciousness left her; paradoxically, she also felt gratitude at the blessed darkness that obliterated her emotional agony.

Shannon awoke with a sense of disorientation in her brain and a dull, throbbing ache in the back of her skull. As her eyes came into focus, she became aware of the utter unfamiliarity of her surroundings. She appeared to be in some sort of cage.

No, a cell.

Although she had never been arrested, it was clearly evident to her she was not in jail. Through the bars she saw what appeared to be a combination workshop and do-it-yourself den, like some sort of basement or garage conversion. A large, but old television stood diagonally in one corner with an overstuffed chair and sofa approximately six feet to its front oriented to face it. A wooden table with two chairs occupied the opposing corner. The workbench with a huge array of neatly organized tools was directly across from where Shannon stood. That left only one corner unexamined, the one in which she was imprisoned.

Quite a bit of the enclosure was taken up by the large cot on which she had awakened, an obscenely festive, floral bedspread arrayed across the top. A toilet and a sink were installed on the wall to her left. Incongruously, a large white princess vanity, complete with an ornate mirror, stood tightly against the bars to her right. Near the dressing table, a large steel eyebolt protruded from the floor, a length of substantial chain threaded through and ending in a metal manacle. She pushed and pulled on the door to the cell in the absurd hope that it had somehow been left unsecured. It hadn't been. She began to tremble uncontrollably, the magnitude of her dilemma becoming increasingly evident.

After a short while, the intensity of her terror became somewhat mitigated by a growing awareness she had to use the toilet. Absurdly, she felt embarrassed to take her jeans down in the exposure of the cell. As she did, however, her humiliation became compounded by the realization that, sometime during her unconsciousness, she had peed herself. Sobbing with equal measures of fear and shame, she took off her jeans and panties, figuring that getting caught half-naked by her abductor was really the least of her problems. She rinsed the garments under the tap, wringing them dry in her hands as best she could. Although they were still wet, she put them back on, seeing no alternative.

Having nothing else to do, she went to the vanity and opened the drawers one by one. In the bottom right one, she found a variety of lingerie. Choosing a black cotton brief, she again took off her jeans, replacing her own underwear with what she had found.

Just the feeling of having clean, dry underwear somehow helps, she thought almost absurdly as she pulled on her jeans.

She went back to the dressing table and examined the variety of makeup and nail polish that littered its top. She picked up a hairbrush and found several long, blond hairs stuck in the bristles. Although it was frighteningly obvious to Shannon other girls had preceded her in the cell, the physical evidence of the hair of one or more of those others numbed her.

He's the Woodsman, her brain came to an obvious conclusion with a sense of certainty.

Her thought processes disengaging from the new horror that now permeated her predicament. She sat down on the edge of the cot, staring dumbly at the extent of her new universe.

Shannon was shaken from her near catatonia by a sudden light that permeated the gloomy chamber. She heard the unmistakable gait of a person descending a flight of stairs, accompanied by what sounded like the barking of a large dog. Feet became legs, legs became a body and, finally, body became head as she gazed with foreboding at what could only be her captor. Her brain could only register he was middle-aged, with dark hair and a slender build. She waited for him to speak, to explain himself and what intentions he had in mind for her. She was afraid she already knew, however.

He approached the cell and said, "Hi, sleepy-head. How are you doing?

The grotesqueness of the apparent concern in his voice shocked her to such a degree she could only softly reply, "OK, I guess."

"Glad to hear that, honey, really glad to hear that. Are you hungry?" he continued not pausing for a response. "I hope so, because I've got some really nice lasagna in the oven – should be ready in . . ." he paused while looking at his wristwatch, ". . . about forty-five minutes. If it's alright with you, I'll mosey back upstairs, grab a shower, and change clothes. Then I'll be back down with dinner. Red wine, OK?"

She just stared at him, dumbfounded that the man could engage in such mundane conversation after knocking her unconscious and abducting her. After a few seconds, she saw his expression begin to darken.

With escalating anger in his voice, Walter said, "Goddammit, I asked you a question! Don't make me ask you again!"

Finally, an unbidden thought passed through Shannon's consciousness.

There's something I understand about all of this. Years of living with her father's emotional abuse had prepared her well for this moment.

She replied meekly, "Yes, red wine is fine, thank you."

A smile replaced his scowl as he said, "Well, you're most welcome. Remember, mutual respect is very important in a relationship. By the way, my name is Walter," he extended his hand through the bars.

She shook it weakly.

"I'm Shannon, Shannon Buckley," she said in a small voice, then let her hand fall back to her side.

"I know," he replied lightly, then, "Well, I've got to get back upstairs or we're going to be eating burnt lasagna. See you in a bit!"

He turned and crossed the room quickly, bounding up the steps to the floor above two at a time.

Later that night and finally alone once more, Shannon sat on the cot, considering the surreal situation in which she was trapped. As promised, Walter had reappeared with dinner for two and a bottle of Cabernet. He told her to attach the metal shackle to her leg, which she did. He then opened the cell door and, with an exaggerated flourish that might have been comical under other circumstances, motioned her toward the table. He pulled her chair out and she sat as directed.

The plate before her was filled with a generous portion of lasagna, a slice of garlic bread, and a helping of Caesar salad. Although she'd had nothing to eat for what she estimated to be nearly twenty-four hours, she felt her gorge begin to rise at the thought of food going into her mouth.

She began to protest, "Uh, thanks for the food and everything, but I really can't eat anything now . . ."

His retribution had been swift, his backhand nearly knocking her from her seat.

"Listen, I paid good money for this food and you're not going to waste it," he cautioned calmly.

She could feel tears forming and knew she was within seconds of breaking into full-blown hysterics. She realized, however, that any emotional outburst would only make the situation worse.

Expending tremendous effort to maintain control, she replied, "I understand, I'm really sorry, OK?"

The rest of the meal passed without further incident. Shannon fell into the routine she had learned through countless meals sitting across from her father: speaking when spoken to, refraining from saying anything that could cause a disagreement, appearing interested in everything her eating companion said, and always in a soft, non-confrontational voice.

After that came the rape. Inexperienced as she was, Shannon didn't realize that her tense, inert body would throw the man into another rage. This time, however, the punishment wasn't inflicted with his hands; in fact, it wasn't punishment at all, it was torture. She didn't know what the tool was called that he used to inflict livid red welts on her body; only that it hurt so badly she nearly fainted. In her mind, she begged for the exquisite, precise pain of the box cutter slicing through her skin to replace the agony to which she was currently being subjected. Eventually, his anger subsided and he ordered her back into her cell. She complied immediately, although every step caused her aching body to protest. She was told to stick her foot through the bars, which she did, allowing him to fit a key into the shackle on her leg, removing it.

He then returned to the stairs. Turning before ascending, he looked at her and flashed the semblance of a smile.

"Sweet dreams," he said with a warmth that somehow chilled Shannon to the very essence of her soul, "See you tomorrow, OK?"

"OK," she replied, fearing another vicious reprisal if she failed to respond.

In her mind, however, she knew she would not be able to endure too many tomorrows like today.

He mounted the stairs, shut the door, and turned off the light. Shannon was left in the hellish red glow of charging lights from the power tools at the workbench.

How appropriate.

Now that she no longer feared his retribution, sobs began to wrack her body as she confronted the hopelessness of her situation. Sometime in the long, lonely night, her mental and physical exhaustion impelled her into a deep, and mercifully, dreamless sleep.

She was awakened by Walter's energetic, "Good morning, babe. How are you feeling this morning?"

A sudden compulsion to respond with, "Like I've been tortured and sexually assaulted, you sick fuck! How do you think I'm supposed to feel?" was successfully resisted, replaced with a submissive, "All right. How are you?"

"Great, thanks. I've got to get to work, though. By the way, I've made you some stuff for breakfast and lunch. Sorry it's not eggs and bacon, but I'll make that for this weekend, promise. He placed a tray with a number of sandwiches in Ziploc bags, a six-pack of Coke, and a few candy bars on the floor just outside the bars of the cell door.

"See you tonight," he said, turning and beginning to return upstairs.

"Bye," she called after him.

He turned and smiled.

"That's my girl," he said just before disappearing from her view.

After his departure, Shannon collapsed in a heap on the floor.

I just don't have the strength for this, she thought, tears again fountaining down her cheeks.

The food outside of the cell door held no appeal; yet, she knew it would have to be gone by the time Walter returned.

Otherwise, there will be hell to pay.

She knew the consequences for displeasing the man who now had her under his complete domination. She felt the results of his wrath throughout her body.

No, she vowed, *the God damned food will be gone by the time he gets back, even if I have to flush it down the toilet.*

Her mind drifted back to when she was growing up.

See Daddy, it's all gone, she had told her father, opening her mouth wide to verify that whatever was on her plate had been consumed and not wasted.

Later, she would stick her finger down her throat, regurgitating the offending morsels into the toilet. She had learned that, despite the fact you can never really win, sometimes you can fight back.

Small victories, sometimes make life bearable.

Shannon arose from the floor and attempted to consider her situation dispassionately. he figured she was being kept in a basement with, as far as she could determine, only one exit, that being up the stairs.

OK, I've got two choices if I want to get out of here, she considered. *Either I've got to get out of this cage and out that door or else I've got to attract someone's attention to come to me. Well, let's get on with it then.*

On television it always looks so damned easy, she swore to herself in frustration.

She had been moving the bobby pin around in the cell's lock for almost an hour without even a glimmer of success. She had been elated to find the pin among the grooming paraphernalia on the dressing table; yet, it had ultimately led to nothing other than a cramped and aching hand. Shannon then tried screaming at the top of her lungs for as long as her voice held out, another fruitless attempt to gain her freedom. She hadn't even been able to rouse an answering bark out of his dog.

She sat back down, totally defeated. She did not even consider overpowering the man; there was no violence in her psyche. Similarly, she dismissed the chance that he would eventually tire of her and set her free unharmed. She was enough of a realist to know what the Woodsman did with his victims.

Her depression progressively deepened over the course of the day, fueled both by the bleakness of her situation and the diminishing Wellbutrin in her body. She gave up any hope of rescue, her only wish was that she could somehow strike back at the man who had destroyed her life, pitiful though it was.

How long she remained in her semi-comatose state, she had no way of knowing. She sensed; however, it had been several hours. She tried eating one of the sandwiches, only to have it trigger a gag reflex that sent the limited contents of her belly spewing down into the toilet. After her belly ceased its spasms, she tore the remainder of the food into bits and flushed them down the toilet as well. A can of Coke fared better on her stomach, as her dehydrated state prompted a desperate need to replenish her body's fluids. Realizing that Walter would be on his way back to the house soon, she cleaned herself as best she could, knowing he would punish her should he find her not to his liking.

Similar to the day prior, Walter arrived in a happy and buoyant mood. He greeting Shannon with, "Hello, honey, I'm home! Have a good day?"

The ludicrousness of his question almost caused her to laugh, although she was not willing to risk the potential consequences of such a response. Instead, she answered with a response ingrained from countless such daily reunions with her father. "OK, how was yours?"

The evening passed in a bizarre caricature of normality. Shannon's ingrained passivity seemed to somehow please her abductor; however, it only made her despise herself even more. After it was finally over, she sat on the cot and wept, overcome with hatred for the man, her situation, but most of all herself.

In the morning, she was again awakened by his turning on of the light.

At least I think it's the morning. What if he works nights and it's really eleven p.m.? Somehow, it seems to make a difference, knowing the time of day. I must remember to ask him about that, she noted groggily.

Shannon groaned as her body began to recognize the ache of the pains he had inflicted, both old and new. Almost simultaneously, she heard the door open as well as his now familiar footsteps beginning to descend the stairs. Suddenly, a telephone ringtone approximating some golden oldies rock anthem sounded and she heard his progress on the stairs immediately halt.

"Hey, Pete. What's up, my man?" she heard Walter greet the caller.

"Fresh lobster, right off the boat? Hell yeah! Save me a couple, will ya? I'll be in after work to pick them up. Yeah, I know that's why yours is the best deli in Seattle, you conceited son-of-a-bitch. OK. Hey, thanks again. Yeah. See you later, Pete."

The conversation had obviously ended as he returned to his descent of the stairs. Shannon, however, paid only scant attention as the germ of an idea began to coalesce in her mind.

"Good morning," he said cheerfully, "and good news too. Do you like lobster?"

"Sure," she replied, seeking to prolong his jovial mood.

"Well, that's what we're having for dinner tonight, love. What do you think about that?"

"How exciting," she responded. Then, seeing his eyes narrow as if to weigh the inflection of sarcasm in her voice, she hurriedly continued. "I mean, lobster is my favorite food of all time. Thanks for being so thoughtful and all."

His face burst into a happy grin.

"Um, Walter, would you please tell me what time it is?"

He glanced at his wristwatch and replied, "Seven thirty-five a.m. on the dot."

"Thank you," she said, "Like, I don't mean to be a bother, but do you have a book I could read? There's not really much to do all day, that is until I have to get ready for you to come home," she added the last part to not seem unappreciative in his eyes. She knew any negativity or scent of criticism on her part could trigger his rage.

And right now, I really have to keep you in a good mood, don't I, you mother fucker, she thought, roiling anger permeating her entire being.

"Sure. Let me run upstairs and I'll bring a couple down for you. Anything in particular?"

"No," she said, "anything you like is OK with me."

A few minutes later, he reappeared with a couple of paperbacks, a John Grisham and a Tom Clancy.

Figures, doesn't it? She said to herself.

"Thanks a lot," she told him, "These are great."

"Good. Well, have a nice day reading. We can talk about it later, over lobster. I can hardly wait, honey!"

- 213 -

"Me too. I can hardly wait until you come home either, Walter," she replied, her response more truthful than anything she had told the man during her time in captivity.

He smiled and left, unaware of the ironic meaning of her words. She was alone. She knew what she had to do. There were no alternatives.

Shannon walked to the vanity and sat down, carefully clearing some of the clutter to the side to give her room to work. Opening the Clancy novel to a blank page next to the rear cover, she carefully tore it out of the binding. She then searched through the assorted makeup for what she needed, a liquid eye liner applicator. She found a Maybelline Ultra Liner almost immediately; coincidently, it was the kind she used herself. Although that unbidden realization again brought tears to her eyes, she rebuked herself sharply, knowing she would have to be strong if she was to do what she planned.

Slowly and carefully, she used the precision brush of the liner to write.

Walter _____ is the Woodsman. I was kept in a cage in the basement of an old house. I don't know where it is. He is tall. Dark hair. Brown eyes. Thirty some years old maybe. He has a dog named Mike. Orders fresh lobster from a deli – "Best in Seattle," he said. Friends with a man who works there named Pete.

Please catch him!

Shannon Buckley

She wondered if she should add a message to someone.

But who? She thought.

Her dad, who never had a good word to say to her, who reminded her a lot of Walter, except for the sexual assaults? Her mother, who had left her without even a goodbye? How about Mr. Morrell? He'd certainly made a great impression, taking away the

- 214 -

one part of her life she had at one time felt good about herself. She realized she had nothing to say to any of them, other than to curse them for the irreparable harm they had done to a shy, sensitive young girl who had been entrusted into their care.

There isn't enough room on the paper is I was going to do that, she thought cynically.

As horrible as the thought was, the only person who seemed to really give a damn about her was Walter, or Justin, or whatever he chose to call himself.

Even though he kidnapped me, tortures me, rapes me, and will probably murder me like the girls he's taken before, he actually seems to care about me. And that's just sick, Shannon, she thought to herself with self-loathing. *Is this the Stockholm Syndrome kicking in, am I starting to sympathize with my captor, to fall in love with him even? No way is that going to happen to me. This ends now.*

Last night, she had come to the realization that, as horrible as the situation was in which she now found herself, her previous life hadn't really been any better. She had only been able to face each day through a combination of the Wellbutrin and self-mutilation. She had no reason to live, was her sad appraisal, but what had been lacking was a reason to die.

Up until this morning, she had felt she had been denied even this. Yet, when she had overheard the conversation between Walter and the guy at the deli, it had dawned upon her that maybe she had one chance to make meaning out of her hitherto worthless life. If she could help other lonely girls like herself from being seduced by Walter, by the Woodsman, maybe they could somehow find happiness in their lives, an emotion she had been denied for so long.

At last, she had a purpose.

She folded the note she had written over and over, making it as small as possible. She took one of the bagged sandwiches Walter had considerately left on the tray outside the cell door out of the Ziploc and sat it carefully to the side. Shannon took the note she had written and placed it inside the bag. The baggie was then folded until it too could not be made any smaller. Then, picking up a small, red rubber band from the top of the vanity, she wrapped it around and around the plastic, eventually forming a tightly wound pellet shape.

God, it looks huge, she fretted, fearing she would not be able to complete the next part of her task successfully.

She reached through the bars and grabbed one of the Cokes.

Opening it, she said to herself, *OK, here goes.*

She placed her homemade capsule into her mouth and swallowed, following it with a large gulp of the effervescent beverage. Immediately, it caught in her throat, refusing to go any further into her digestive system. She gagged, returning it into her hand.

Well, that didn't work very well, she observed in understatement.

Spotting the sandwich on the vanity, she picked it up. Separating the two slices of bread, she saw they and the ham and cheese they contained had been liberally spread with mayonnaise. She rubbed her capsule over the sandwich interior, coating it liberally with the white, greasy substance. She then attempted to swallow the bolus again.

On the fourth try, she was successful.

Message in a bottle, she hummed to herself, having no idea where or when she had heard the song snippet.

Pleased with herself so far, Shannon now moved on to the second, more problematic, part of her plan.

She gazed at the rear of the dressing table, seeing the eyebrow pencil sharpener she had found while going through the makeup the day before.

How pitifully small, she thought sadly as she took it into her hand.

She got onto her knees and, with one hand, raised the corner of the cot, and with the other placed the sharpener on its side beneath the metal leg. She had to drop the cot four times before the tiny blade had been broken away from its surrounding plastic. She looked at it with satisfaction and a tremendous sense of longing. To her, the tiny piece of metal represented escape on so many levels.

She took a long, unhurried sip of Coke, savoring its fizziness and sweetness as it traveled down her throat to join her final communication to the world. She sat back on the cot, making herself comfortable by propping the pillows and blankets behind her. Drawing the tiny blade across the vein in her right wrist, she was gratified to see the release of a few droplets of blood. She sawed back and forth until a steady stream erupted down her arm.

Remember to trace up the vein, Shan, she admonished herself, *cutting across is for wimps who want to be found before it's too late.*

Not me.

She smiled wanly at the thought of the demons that had haunted her fading from her life just as quickly as the claret-colored current flowing down her arm. She thought about repeating her actions with her left arm, but reconsidered.

Not enough energy for all of that, she thought, weakness already beginning to pervade her body.

Am I going to Hell? the random thought flashing into her mind.

It had been so long since she had had a religious thought of any kind, back before her mother had left actually.

She hoped not.

Haven't I already suffered enough for one person?

Maybe what she was doing wouldn't count as suicide, since she was doing it to save others.

Don't lie to God, she chided herself. *He'll definitely know 'cause he's God, right?*

She also knew she had mainly done it for herself. Her mother had told her God loves everybody, she remembered. Of everything, she wished she could be little again, back in her mother's arms, feeling warm, loved, and protected.

I love you, Mom, she whispered, perhaps aloud and perhaps just in her mind, as she lost consciousness.

"So, would you like to go get a drink?" Marianne asked, finally resorting to the direct approach in seeking the attention of her boss.

"I'm really sorry, Marianne, I really am, but I've already got a date tonight."

She wanted to say, "How about another night then? Tomorrow, next week, two months from now? Just when do you think you could fit me into your busy social calendar, Walter?"

She realized, however, that desperation was not a quality that people admired, probably not Walter Harrison especially.

Instead, she just smiled and said, "No problem."

"Thanks, can I get a rain check though? I'd really like to, but . . ." his accompanying hand gesture was intended to imply he was stuck with his other commitment, but he'd really rather take her up on her offer.

To Marianne, however, it just seemed contrived. Probably what everyone has said about the guy is true, her animosity gradually surmounting her sense of humiliation at being turned down.

It will be a cold day in hell when I suggest getting together with you again, you prick.

His smile melted her resolve as swiftly as ice on the burning pavement outside.

"Sure," she replied, knowing that, if he ever did go out with her, she would be game for whatever he had in mind.

"OK, see you on Monday. Have a great weekend," he said, turning and departing the office and heading out into the street.

He stopped at Wolf's, engaging in the obligatory banter with Pete before continuing on his way with the lobsters and a pound of coleslaw in tow. A few minutes later, he started his car, the engine noise of the big SUV insignificant besides that of the air conditioner on full blast.

What a scorcher, he thought, *I really hope it's not too warm in the basement. Maybe have to pick up a fan or something.*

A look of actual concern clouded his face. In the short time he had been dating the girl, he had really grown to like her.

She really has a lot going for her. She's so different from the other girls I've dated. She's quiet and respectful, and really seems to take an interest in what I have to say. She also takes care of herself, not like some of the pigs I've dated in the past who didn't know the difference between their underwear and toilet paper.

He shuddered, remembering Amy Reiss.

Even the sex is getting better. Walter, are you falling in love? he asked himself, perhaps more seriously than he cared to admit.

He felt badly about turning down Marianne's suggestion that they go for a drink. Even though she put on a brave face, he knew his refusal had hurt her.

I'll make it up to her, he promised himself. *I wonder how she'd feel about a bouquet of flowers. Not roses or anything that might be misconstrued. Just a nice bunch of flowers letting her know her boss really appreciates her.*

Don't want to mix business with pleasure, his father had always said and Walter agreed, just as he did with everything his father had told him. He made a mental note to pick the flowers up on his way to work Monday.

He had also hated turning down Pete's suggestion they go to Finnegan's later that evening.

Sure, I could cut my time with her short, then head out at nine or something, considering, then discarding the idea. *It would be almost like cheating on her and I respect her too much to do that. Yes, this girl is definitely something special.*

He pulled into the garage and stopped the car. He put the lobster container on the center of the kitchen counter, ensuring Mike wouldn't knock it to the floor by his inquisitive investigation. Walter let the dog into the house, watching it happily run about before standing on his hind legs, placing his front paws firmly into Walter's chest, and liberally washing the man's face with his wet tongue.

Maybe I should introduce her to Mike. I know she said she was afraid of dogs, but maybe if she gets to know him, she'll like him, he thought hopefully.

He put the coleslaw into the refrigerator and put a large cooking pot onto the stove. Although he really loved the taste of lobster, he was always a bit squeamish about boiling them alive.

Hope they don't feel anything, he thought, not for the first time.

He reached into the refrigerator and got himself a beer then, reconsidering, he fetched another. He didn't know if she liked beer, but it would be impolite not to offer her one as well. Besides, the Coke must be pretty tepid by now.

With the necks of both beers in one hand, he turned on the basement light and opened the door. Descending the steps, he called out, "Hey, honey, I'm home. How's my best girl?"

Instead of the immediate, albeit, brief reply he had been expecting, he was instead met by utter silence.

Maybe she's sleeping, he hoped, despite a growing sense of concern beginning to gnaw at his mind.

He crossed the room and, to his horror, saw the reason why he had not received her anticipated response. Her head lolled against the wall, while a lake of blood marred the gaily colored bedspread before cascading to the floor like a ruby waterfall.

"Oh, God, no!" He cried in horror, hastily unlocking the cell door and rushing to the girl.

He checked for a pulse on her unmarred left wrist, but the feel of her cool skin had already alluded to his inevitable conclusion. Unbridled sobs wracked his body as he held her lifeless corpse close, beseeching her as to why she had left him, why she had chosen to end her own life.

After a few minutes, his mourning abruptly ceased, transformed into a cold detachment that would have startled even the most experienced of medical observers.

"Can't leave the job half finished, can I dad?" he asked aloud, as if the father who had been executed over twenty years previously for the brutal murder of Walter's mother had been standing by his side.

First things first, change clothes. Then start the water to boil. God, I'm starved, but it looks like I get seconds for dinner tonight, he thought happily, relishing the idea of polishing off over a pound of succulent lobster. Later, he'd maybe go down to Finnegan's in the hope of running in to Pete for a couple of beers.

And after that? He asked himself, already knowing the answer. *And after that, I have 'miles to go before I sleep.'*

Chapter 19

It had been over a week after she killed Robert Jackson before the police had found his body. Alex had been taken aback by the amount of media coverage given to the murder.

Yep, I guess they pull out all the stops when a rich kid dies, she thought.

She was especially upset by the television interview of his fiancé, the swell of her pregnant stomach clearly visible, as she broke down into hysterical sobbing on camera.

If you only knew what he had been up to that morning, Jackie, you'd probably have a lot less tears for him, she shook her head sadly.

She felt so sorry for Jacqueline Eaton, as well as the young man's parents. They had done nothing wrong; yet, even from the grave, Justin Hale continued to hurt people who trusted him.

Like he hurt me, Alex remembered soberly. *It's funny but, even though I know his real name, I'll always remember him as Justin. It's like he had two sides to his life. One good, the Robert Jackson memorialized by his loved ones and friends, and one the epitome of evil, the Justin Hale I knew. I guess everyone has their secrets; God knows I have mine.*

The fact a reward was being offered for information concerning a female jogger in a pink top who had last been seen in the company of Robert Jackson the morning he had died chilled her to the bone. She had not noticed anyone during her run that morning, only afterwards.

What if the guy who had checked me out on 36th Street that morning remembered me? What if he called the police, providing a much more definitive description of the girl now only identified by a pink top? Even now, the police could be putting together a composite that would eventually prompt them to ring our front doorbell, she had thought with extreme trepidation. How embarrassing would that be, especially for Dad?

As the weeks passed, however, no leads had had been reported and the murder became old news, supplanted by more current, equally shocking, occurrences both in the Seattle metro area and beyond.

As for Alex, the last part of August had passed like a blur. Her job with the City Parks and Recreations Department was winding to a close, scheduled to end right after the Labor Day weekend. Until then, however, she had volunteered to work as many hours as possible, building her nest egg for Stanford. Coupled with the three days she had taken off to visit the University campus with her mother, she had had little time for socializing with her friends, even her bestie.

Consequently, it came as a bit of a surprise to Britt Stevens when her phone rang, the ring tone readily identifying the caller as Alex.

"Oh my God, girl! I thought you'd been abducted by an Arab sheik and been carried off to join his harem!" Britt said, laughing at the joy of talking to her friend.

"Yep," Alex replied, "I'm wife number sixty-three right now, but I'm working my way to the top!"

"You little ho, what are you?"

"Prostitute!" Alex retorted.

"Streetwalker!"

"Slut!"

"Am not!"

"Are too!" Britt collapsed onto her bed, overwhelmed with giggles. "OK. You win! So, did you call me up just to insult me, or for some other reason?"

"Oh, honey, it's just been too long!" answered Alex, wiping tears of laughter from her eyes before continuing. "I'm so sorry I haven't called you lately, but I've just been so busy, what with work and everything. Plus, I just got back from Stanford yesterday. Would you like to get together? I'd really love to tell you all about it."

"Absolutely! You say when and I'm there!"

"Uh, how's your mom doing?"

"OK, but, like random!" Britt replied, somewhat puzzled by Alex's quick change of subject.

"I mean, is she getting around on her own, or do you still have to help her out?"

"Old news, girl," said Britt. "She got the cast off last week and is doing fine. Why?"

"Well, remember how my parents were going to spend the 4th of July up in the Straits and my dad got all kinds of pissed off because I wouldn't cut work to go with them?"

"Yeah."

"It turns out, he couldn't even go himself, big deal at work it seems. Well, they're going this weekend and their little romantic getaway doesn't include little old me. So, I was wondering if you'd like to stay over, just the two of us?" Alex asked.

"Are you asking me to shack up with you? Why Alex Tate, what kind of a girl do you think I am?" Britt replied in an overly dramatic, saccharin voice. Then she continued excitedly, "Bet your sweet ass I do!"

"Fantastic! So, they're leaving Friday afternoon and coming back Monday morning. I've got to work on Friday and Monday, but the rest of the time, you'll have my undivided attention. See you about four-ish?"

The rest of their conversation was spent working out the logistics for their upcoming time together; food to buy, films to see, and shops to visit at the mall on Friday. Neither girl mentioned it would probably be the last time they would have a chance to be together for quite a while, since Alex's departure for California was scheduled for September 12th. Both realized it made no sense to ruin their shared happiness with a sense of impending melancholy. Soon the two girls, who had grown so close over the past seven years, would be separated by the irresistible allure of adulthood.

By the time Alex pulled her Toyota into her driveway Friday, Britt was standing on the lawn with her thumb out, jokingly bumming a ride. Alex exited the car and yelled to her, "Sorry little lady, but my mama warned me against pickin' up strange wimmin! And girlfriend, there ain't any of 'em stranger than you!"

Britt giggled and raced over to her friend, enveloping her friend in one of her vise-like hugs. "Oh, Alex, I just love you so much!"

Alex put her arms around her, attempting to squeeze her friend with near-equal force. "Right back at ya," she said, tears unexpectantly beginning to cloud her vision. "Well, look at you, beautiful. What a knockout!"

Even to the most critical of observers, Britt looked absolutely gorgeous about 99.9% of the time. In addition to immaculately applied makeup and hair that looked as though she had just stepped from the salon, today she wore a rose on ivory floral print sundress. Coupled with a pair of white suede lace-up heels, she stood in stark contrast to Alex, who still wore her uniform.

Somewhat self-consciously, Alex said, "You better get off from me or else you're going to ruin your outfit. I am what you call one stanky girl."

"Oh my God, yes, girl," Britt retreated in mock horror, wrinkling her nose with exaggerated disgust. "You get right up those stairs and wash your nasty self, or else momma's gonna give you a whuppin!'"

"Yes, ma'am," Alex replied. Both girls ran into the house, Britt to the living room to turn on the TV to catch some of the afternoon soaps, Alex upstairs to shower and change. Less than an hour later, Alex reappeared, quite transformed. Her unisex look had been replaced by one of unmistakable femininity. She wore an off-the-shoulder wine red skater dress that contrasted attractively with her auburn hair, now falling casually in rings of curls. Although not quite matching the sheer perfection of Britt's flawless beauty and fashion sense, Alex would certainly draw an admiring look from any man with even the slightest semblance of a pulse.

The evening passed in an air of retail bliss, each girl purchasing several items that met with the discerning approval of the other. Interspaced with their shopping, they shared a pretzel and gorged on hot fudge sundaes. Before leaving the mall, they decided to have some Thai food in the food court, both girls too exhausted from trying on clothes to even think about throwing together something for dinner at Alex's house.

Selecting two sampler boxes, they searched for somewhere to sit down. Britt nudged Alex and pointed excitedly toward a table near the center of the seating area. Alex looked in the direction in which Britt was indicating, then recognized her friend's intent. They moved through the seating maze, finally arriving at their selected destination.

"Looking for some company, boys?" Alex asked languidly, simulating the speech of a 1950s Hollywood vixen.

Startled from their conversation, Tom Reynolds and Bobby Parker turned their heads in the direction of the unexpected voice, looking up to see the faces of their high school friends.

"Holy shit," Tom said, unabashedly impressed by the appearance of the two stunning young women. "Wow, I mean, sure. You guys look great!"

Britt and Alex each gave the two young men a smile that caused their hearts to flutter, then sat down. As the girls shared the contents of their samplers, they kept up a steady stream of conversation. For their part, Tom and Bobby were mainly content to listen, although interjecting a comment or question of their own here and there.

Gosh, this feels, like, so normal. No worrying about trying to arrange a meeting with some perv, or trying to figure out how best to take him out, she grimaced at the cinematic euphemism. *It's just great hanging with my friends for once.*

Although she had not given up on her calling, she had decided to defer trying to groom any other likely candidates for the foreseeable future. She was simply too busy trying to finish work and get ready for Stanford. Although she wouldn't admit it to herself, Alex had also been frightened, very badly frightened actually, by the knowledge she had been partially identified after the Robert Jackson murder.

No, I just need to take a little break right now.

Lost in her own contemplations, Alex was surprised to see Bobby staring at her, as if expecting a response. Breaking out of her reverie, she said, "Oh, sorry, Bobby. I didn't hear what you said."

He repeated, "I was just saying it was really nice seeing the two of you again," echoing her own previous thoughts.

She nodded in agreement with his sentiments.

Feeling bolstered by Alex's affirmation, he continued hopefully, "Um, we were going to head on out to Discovery Park and watch the sunset from the lighthouse. Would you and Britt like to come too? I mean, with everyone going away to college and all, it will probably be the last time ever we're together."

Knowing Discovery Park was the absolutely last place she wanted to go, Alex began to formulate a polite, but adamant, refusal.

Before she could speak, however, Britt said, "Oh, wow. Sorry guys, we'd really like to go, but Alex and I already have plans."

His temporary courage deflated, Bobby said, "Sure, no problem. We haven't really made our minds up anyway."

He looked to Tom for moral support, but his friend simply wasn't up to putting himself on the hot seat to get him off the hook.

"Well, we have to go anyway. It was really great seeing you."

Somewhat in atonement for her brusque dismissal of Bobby's offer, Britt stood up and, throwing her arms around Bobby's neck, gave him a loud, firm, kiss on the cheek. Not to be outdone, Alex did the same to Tom. Despite being turned down, both boys left the food court with grins on their faces, poking and jabbing at each other in shared delight.

"God, boys!" said Britt, turning her eyes toward heaven as if seeking an explanation for what was obviously in her mind an inferior species.

"Amen!" laughed Alex, then, "Uh, were you just making an excuse or do you really have something else planned?"

A sudden look of guilt passed over Britt's face as she said, "I just need to do something online. I'll tell you later, OK?" making it clear that it was neither the time nor the place to discuss the matter further.

Although she was intrigued by her friend's unaccustomed evasiveness, Alex knew Britt well enough to know that she didn't want to be pressed about the matter. She let it drop for now, but made a mental note to question her about it later that evening.

On their way back to the car, the girls' window shopping restored the buoyant mood they had enjoyed for most of the evening. An on-sale, white silk blouse for Britt proved to be their final purchase of the day. They shoved the Toyota full of their packages, boxes, and bags and made their way back to Alex's house.

After they dropped their bags in the corner of the dining room, Alex made them each a tall glass of iced tea.

"You first, or me?" she asked, their verbal shorthand completely understood from years of practice.

"You," Britt replied, punctuating her response with a most unladylike belch stemming from the huge gulp of tea she had just consumed. "I can't wait to see you in that red hootchie skirt. The looks of you in that should get you an 'A' from any male professor under eighty years old."

Alex complied, performing an impromptu fashion show, modeling each of her day's purchases for her friend. They then switched, with Britt walking with an exaggerated hip swing down the living room carpet runner that had served as their runway since they were in middle school. Changing out of her last new ensemble, Britt excused herself and, grabbing her bag, went into the downstairs bathroom. Realizing her friend's purpose, Alex went to her room and changed her clothes as well. Reunited in the living room, now dressed in comfortable shorts and sweatshirts, the two girls sat down on the couch, browsing through the Blu-rays Britt had picked up on her way to Alex's house.

Britt glanced surreptitiously at her watch. Alex realized this was the third time in about the last half-hour. Time to find out what's up, she thought.

"OK, little missy, that was then and this is now. What's up with all the time checks?"

"Um, I need to be online at eleven," Britt said, still somewhat elusively.

"A guy." Alex's inference was immediately voiced.

"Yep," Britt replied with unaccustomed bashfulness.

"Shut up!"

"Yeah, really," Britt's smile was radiant, overjoyed now to be sharing her secret with her BFF.

Alex hugged her friend, pleased for her happiness.

"So, tell me all about him!"

"Well, his name is Andy and he is just absolutely gorgeous. We've been talking now for about three weeks, but it seems like I've known him all my life. He's a freshman at UW, so I'll only be a year behind him. . ."

Alex dreaded what was coming next. She sent a sudden, silent prayer to heaven, begging that it wouldn't be true. For once, God turned his back on Alex Tate.

". . . So, we met online, at the new student chat room and . . ."

"What the fuck?" Alex screamed, causing Britt to jump up in alarm.

Alex went to her, taking her by the arms and moving her forcibly back to her seat.

Looking straight into her eyes, Alex said in slow measured tones, "Britt, you've got to stop talking to this guy, and I mean right now. Don't you know how much trouble you can get into?"

"Come on, Alex, you know I'm not stupid. I can take care of myself."

"Britt, you've seen the papers, the Woodsman is out there, still raping and murdering girls who probably thought nothing would happen, just like you. He's not the only one either."

Like Justin Hale, she thought, without adding his name to her warning.

"Take it easy," Britt tried to calm her friend, shocked at her unexpectedly violent reaction. "Yeah, I know there are creeps everywhere, but you can't let the possibility of one bogeyman ruin your life for you, can you? I mean, I know in the movies . . ."

Alex brusquely interrupted her friend. "Britt, this isn't a movie and these guys don't work from a script. And, at the end of the day, the murdered coed doesn't wipe away the fake blood and go home to her mansion. This is real life. You've been my rock for so many years, I couldn't go on if something happened to you," Alex pleaded, emotion flooding through her voice.

"Look, I appreciate your concern and all but, frankly Alex, this is none of your business."

They stared at each other with rare hostility. Conflicting emotions fought for control of Alex's subsequent actions. She wanted to shake Britt, slap her even, until she came to her senses. She was so sad to be quarrelling with her friend, the first argument they had had in years. Realizing, however, that Britt Stevens, once she had her mind made up, was as stubborn as a Missouri mule, Alex tried a different tact.

Taking a deep breath and letting it out slowly to calm herself, Alex spoke in an even voice, "OK, I get it. I'm probably just psycho and there's about as much chance of you getting hurt by some guy you met on the Internet as you have of getting hit by an asteroid."

"But . . ." interjected Britt in a brittle voice, "Come on, spit it out. I know there's a 'but' coming. What is it?"

"Have you made plans to meet up yet?" Alex evaded her question, posing one of her own instead.

"Um, yeah. Next Tuesday, actually."

Alex's heart leapt. She had dreaded the thought of Britt's first meeting with the man to occur after she had left for California, leaving her unable to provide any sort of assistance whatsoever.

"OK, Britt, for the love of our friendship, I want you to listen closely to what I have to tell you."

For the next fifteen minutes, Alex gave Britt an abridged version of everything she had learned about the older men who pose as young, university types online.

"God, so do you have like an obsession or something?" Britt asked somewhat awestruck. Alex was relieved some humor had returned to her friend's voice.

"Um, no," Alex felt guilty about lying. "I had to do a lot of research for my college psychology class, that's all. So, like I know it would be a real invasion of privacy . . ."

Britt cut her off before she could ask the obvious question. "Yeah, a real invasion of privacy, and super weird besides. I'll do my chatting by myself, thank you very much. But, Alex, I truly appreciate you trying to look out for me, I really do. I promise I'll tell you everything afterwards, pinkie swear."

They linked their right pinkie fingers to seal the vow, just as they had been doing for years when agreeing to anything of importance.

Alex said, "Thanks, babe. Love ya lots. Um, so do you want to do your dirty talking here, or would you rather use my bedroom?"

"I can just go up to your room, if that's alright. That leaves you run of the house, OK?"

Alex agreed and Britt ascended to Alex's room, taking her IPAD with her. For over an hour, Alex fretted, unable to read, watch television, or even sit still without transitioning into worrying about her friend. Finally, she decided to bake a batch of banana-walnut muffins, hoping the task would occupy her mind, diverting it from thoughts of Britt blithely going to meet the likes of a Tom Beach or Justin Hale.

At least I've somewhat bettered the odds against that happening, she thought grimly.

After what seemed like forever, Britt came down the stairs. Alex brought the plate of muffins and two tall glasses of skim milk into the living room and they both sat down on the couch.

As nonchalantly as possible, Alex asked, "So, everything OK?"

Britt turned to her and replied, "Yeah, I think it really is, Alex. I've never really met anyone like Andy, he just seems so different than James." James Logan had been Britt's steady boyfriend throughout most of their high school years. It wasn't until midway through their senior year that they had broken up. The gulf between them had been steadily widening for the year before that until, finally, the relationship just collapsed of its own accord. Even though she had seen it coming, it had devastated Britt, and it was only through the love and support of Alex and a couple of other good friends that she had been able to recover relatively unscathed.

Britt is like that, Alex thought, her concern unabated. *She is definitely a one guy girl and, once she's given her heart to someone, she'd rather go down with the sinking ship than jump off.*

"So, it's good, yeah?" Alex asked, not knowing what else to say.

"Yeah, really good."

"So, compromise, OK?" Alex asked, determined to help her friend in any way she could. "Where are you guys going to meet up?"

"The food court at Northgate."

At least it's not for an early morning jog, thought Alex, chilled by her own nearly devastating experience.

"So, how about this? You go to meet Andy, exactly as you two have planned. Meanwhile, I'll just take my own little trip to the food court. I can have some sushi; meanwhile, at the same time, I can be watching over my bestie to make sure nothing bad happens to her. If Andy shows up, and he's who he makes himself out to be, great, I'll go over to Cinderella Boutique and start picking out my bridesmaid's dress. If he doesn't show or you two don't hit it off in real life, its big sister to the rescue, reminding you it's time to go to grandpa's birthday party over at the retirement home. Great plan, n'est-ce pas?"

"I . . . I don't know, Alex. It just seems like something out of a spy movie," Britt said hesitantly.

"Look, Britt," Alex was working hard to convince her. "If he turns out to be the dreamboat you're expecting, then I'll let you dye my hair blonde again, OK?" The hair dying incident had occurred when they were both eleven and had been an unmitigated disaster. Ever since that time it had been part of Alex and Britt folklore, often referred to in jest, but never repeated.

"Alright, Mata Hari," Britt agreed, though Alex could tell she was far from actually convinced. "You're going to look too cute as a blonde."

"But what if I'm right?" Alex replied soberly.

"Well, then, I guess I'll be one of those bimbos from a slasher flick, running around doing stupid stuff until I'm saved by the intrepid hero, um heroine, in this case."

"Don't flatter yourself, honey," Alex said, trying to recapture the carefree mood that had characterized their earlier evening. "Your boobs ain't nearly big enough."

Britt punched her lightly on the arm, then gave her a hug. Even though she was sure she had nothing to worry about in her anticipated meeting with Andy, it was reassuring to know she had such a great friend to watch her back. Then she remembered.

"Um, Alex?"

"Yeah?"

"I forgot to tell you. Andy wants to meet up tomorrow, rather than Tuesday."

Well, that's strange, Alex thought.

According to her research, the profiles of these criminals revealed them to take painstaking care in planning their abductions. A spur of the moment change in plans just didn't seem very likely.

Unless . . . unless he really was just some guy lucky enough to get the attention of the most desirable girl in Seattle.

She decided to take the 'cup's half full' approach.

"No probs," Alex replied. "Hey, do you think he's got an equally gorgeous friend for me?"

Although the weather report had called for rain, Alex was not prepared for the deluge that greeted her the next morning. Britt had originally suggested they spend Saturday at the beach but, as the weekend approached, the forecast had solidified into a definite call for precipitation. As she made a pot of coffee, Alex was glad they had gone with plan B; fortuitously, a primarily indoor activity. Neither girl had been up in the Space Needle for years, as viewing Seattle from a dizzying 600 feet above street level had become quite passé as they entered their teenaged years.

Today, however, it just seems right, kind of a final farewell to the city in which I've been born and raised before moving to California, Alex thought philosophically.

Then, a few hours at the EMP Museum, a favorite from their middle school field trip days, would round out a pretty full afternoon.

Pouring herself a steaming cup of her favorite beverage, Alex sat down at the kitchen table, somewhat mesmerized by the sound of the heavily falling rain on the patio. Although it was still quite gloomy outside, she could discern the slight brightening in the eastern sky that signaled the approaching dawn.

Problem with going to work at the crack of dawn is getting up at an ungodly hour becomes a habit, she mused to herself.

She knew Britt wouldn't be awake for hours, a concrete fact that had been confirmed during countless sleepovers.

What to do until Britt woke up plagued Alex, as her thoughts invariably turned to what was on their agenda for after their time in downtown Seattle. Alex was worried; for once, definitely outside of her comfort zone.

If this guy is on the level, I come across like an overprotective grandmother, not to mention a very blonde one, she almost giggled at the image of an old lady in a blond glamour wig.

But, what if I'm wrong? she countered. *What's the best way to play it? I obviously can't just go over and slit his throat with Britt watching, can I?*

She spent the next hour formulating and discarding eventualities, trying to determine how best to protect her friend from any harm that might potentially befall her. Finally, overcome by sheer mental exhaustion, she moved to the living room and snuggled up on the couch, vowing to just rest her eyes for a few minutes and then move on to something a lot more practical, and considerably less frustrating.

After several short dream vignettes, thematically linked by situations of vague peril, she awoke with a fit of sneezing. A fully clothed Britt stood over her, laughing hilariously and holding a sprig of feather-like reedgrass she had pulled from a nearby flower arrangement. Alex looked at her in mock anger, then stuck her tongue out. Both girls giggled in unison.

"You are so lucky I didn't put your fingers in a bowl of warm water instead," Britt wiped tears of laughter from her eyes. "I would have too, except your mom would have killed me for making you pee on her couch!"

"Just remember, young lady," Alex shook her finger sternly at her friend, "payback is a bitch!"

Alex looked at her watch and saw it was already half past ten.

My God, did I really conk out here for four hours? she thought in amazement. I must have really been more exhausted than I thought.

Leaving Britt to rustle up her own breakfast in the kitchen, Alex returned to her bedroom to get ready for their day out.

They left the house approximately an hour later, running through the still-pelting rain to Alex's Yoda and splashing in the puddles like two young children. The afternoon passed quite enjoyably. The trip to the observation deck of the Space Needle was not quite as lame as they once thought. The EMP Museum, as always, absolutely enthralled the girls. They both took a turn at the karaoke exhibit, before recording a video performance as a duo. Afterwards, Alex begged Britt to go into the Star Wars exhibit.

"You are such a geek," Britt shrieked, "How can I hang out with someone so embarrassing?"

In the end, however, she relented, enjoying the exhibition just as much as Alex, although she would never admit it. Before they knew it, it was four o'clock and they realized they would have to get back to Alex's house soon to have sufficient time to get ready for Britt's rendezvous with Andy later on that evening.

The two girls' return to Alex's house was characterized by a flurry of activity as clothing was tried on and discarded and makeup applied and reapplied to correct barely perceived imperfections. Finally, they were both satisfied with their own, and each other's', appearances. By the time they left the house for the second time that day, the sky had cleared and a spectacular rainbow dominated the westward sky.

"Good omen, honey. Maybe Andy is your pot of gold," Alex said hopefully.

"As long as he isn't a three-foot tall, evil, crusty leprechaun, like the one in the movies," Britt retorted, sniggering.

They arrived at the mall a good half hour prior to Britt's agreed upon meeting time.

"Don't want to seem needy, girl. Let's look around a bit before going to the food court. Getting there five minutes late, will do," Alex said. "It doesn't imply you're desperate, but it also doesn't show you're inconsiderate."

"Perfect. Couldn't have planned it better myself," Britt complimented her friend, although she had made the same decision herself the night before.

After visiting a couple of their favorite stores, they began to stroll toward the assortment of fast-food kiosks that constituted Northgate Mall food court. Alex repeated her plan to Britt, just to make sure she understood.

"OK, so I'm going to let you walk ahead now and I'll like totally ignore you, as if I've never met you before in my life. You sit down and wait for your beau to appear. As for me, I'll browse around, grazing on free samples and keeping a sharp eye on my bestie. If he shows, I'll come over and say, "Why, my word, Miss Stevens, fancy meeting you here." You can then decide to give me the high sign, she stuck her finger deep into her nostril, and we can high-tale it out of there, or you can just tell me to piss off. Now, go get him, tiger!"

Britt gave Alex a mock salute, spun on her heel, and began walking briskly toward the food court. She bought herself a large Coke, and proceeded to find a free table. She took out her phone and idly checked and sent messages, trying to appear both nonchalant and alluring simultaneously.

Conversely, Alex sought to avoid drawing attention to herself. She appeared to intently peruse the menu boards of each of the eateries that formed a horseshoe shape around the central seating plaza, despite the fact frequent visits had imprinted each indelibly on her brain. Periodically, she would cast a casual glance in the direction of her friend, who remained the solitary occupant of the table at which she sat. As time passed, Alex became increasingly worried. It was now almost ten minutes after the time Britt and Andy had agreed upon, and it definitely was not proper dating etiquette for a guy to be late, fashionably or otherwise.

Actually, it's pretty fucked up, Alex thought primly.

The fact that Andy was maybe proving to be a thoughtless jerk was really the least of her problems, however. She began scanning the other diners in the seating area, seeking to identify any guy who was trying to unobtrusively observe her friend.

This is freaking hard! Alex thought to herself in frustration. *Of course, guys are going to be checking out Britt, she looks totally amazing. How am I supposed to tell if it's just some man who's surrendering to an irresistible hormonal urge, or a perv trying to figure out how to abduct her?*

Although she now recognized her methodology wasn't exactly foolproof, Alex decided to concentrate her surveillance on middle-aged men seated by themselves. *That cuts the suspect list down to six.* She watched each of them in turn. Ten minutes later, three of them had departed the area, while two more likely candidates had entered.

Does that mean I can discard the guys who left? she thought, unsure of herself. When the last of the three remaining original solitary, male diners had departed, Alex looked toward Britt, only to be met with a face that obviously was having a hard time holding back tears. Alex walked over to her table and sat down.

"Fucking men, I hate them all!" Britt blurted out angrily. "God, how could he be such an asshole?"

Alex could only commiserate with her friend. She knew Britt had really been taken in by Andy, or whatever his name really was. Although they had only been talking for a short while, Britt had told her she had spent hours each session, discussing her likes and dislikes, hopes and dreams, with the guy.

Big investment, no return, Alex thought sadly, reaching out to hold the hand of her devastated friend in silent support.

"Maybe something happened to him," Britt started hopefully, "like he got into an accident or something?"

She gazed at Alex's carefully composed neutral expression.

"He could only be so lucky, I guess. The fact he didn't call makes it even worse. I tried calling him a couple of times, but I only got switched to voicemail. Not even a text, damn it!"

"Look, Britt, if you didn't know it already, at least a dozen guys here were checking you out, fantasizing how great it would be to grovel at your feet. There's too many fish in the sea to spend your time moping over some little flounder!"

"Yep, that's me, Ariel from The Little Mermaid, waiting patiently for Prince Eric to show up," she pronounced sadly, then, "I hope the sharks got the lying son-of-a-bitch!"

"That's the girl I know and love," Alex laughed. "How 'bout mama buys baby girl some ice cream to make it all better?"

"Uh, huh," Britt's face took on a seriously pouty, little girl expression, slowly nodding her head affirmatively.

Glad that her friend was recovering from the bitter disappointment of being stood up, Alex went to the Baskin Robbins counter, returning with two massive sundaes. For the next half hour, they ate ice cream and discussed their plans for the remainder of the weekend, their conversation periodically peppered with Britt's venomous invectives against the guy who had callously left her hanging. Finished, they departed, returning to Alex's house for a night of B movie viewing.

A couple of minutes later, the dark-haired man who had been working diligently on several folders of paperwork, placed them into his briefcase, excused himself from the stranger sitting across from him, and departed as well.

Chapter 20

Walter kept well back of the two girls, just making sure he kept them in his line of vision. Although he had at first feared he might lose them in the scant seconds between their leaving and his own, he was relieved to find they moved at an unhurried pace, stopping frequently to peer into shop windows and discuss what caught their fancy. When they exited into the parking lot, it was obvious they were departing the mall.

Here goes, he thought, taking a deep breath.

He called the number Britt had given him, simultaneously walking quickly toward his Kia. He was hoping fervently she wouldn't just hang up on him, at least not until he had the time to get his car and get them back into his sight. From what he had overheard at the food court, Britt was the kind of girl who wouldn't give him the brush off without first giving him a piece of her mind.

Gotta keep her talking, he cautioned himself, hoping she wouldn't choose to walk and talk at the same time.

"Hi?" he heard one of the female voices he had been eavesdropping upon for the past hour.

"Um, Britt, uh, hi. This is Andy," he steeled himself for her verbal onslaught. He was not disappointed.

"Where the hell have you been? You left me waiting there like I was some kind of a pathetic loser – which I am not, thank you very much!"

"I am so sorry, but I had an accident, a really bad one, out on I-5. A truck sideswiped me and my car is like totaled."

He turned the corner at J.C. Penny's and continued toward where he was parked.

"Really, and you expect me to believe that? Uh, were you hurt?" Her innate compassion began to surmount her anger.

"Uh, yeah. I'm just leaving the hospital now. I had to get twelve stiches," he replied, spinning his story freestyle.

God, I hope twelve was a good number – serious, but not overly so, he thought as he unlocked his car door and immediately started his engine.

"So where are you now? It sounded like a car engine just started?"

As he drove hopefully toward the girls' last position, he said, "Uh, yeah, my dad had to come pick me up from the hospital – can you say embarrassing? We're heading to the house now. I asked him if we could go to the mall instead, but he told me he's taking me straight home. Besides, you're probably long gone by now, right?"

"Um, yeah."

Liar, liar, pants on fire, he thought, now grinning as he saw the two girls standing roughly where he had last seen them.

"Um, hey," he continued, "sorry, but the pain relievers they gave me are really starting to kick in. Look, can I call you in a couple of days, that's if you forgive me that is. I'd still really like to get together with you."

Suspicion clearly evident in her voice, Britt said, "OK, I guess so, but first let me talk to your dad. I'd like to make sure you're really alright and not just downplaying your injuries. Totaling a car is nothing to be taken lightly."

Caught off guard, all he could think of to say was, "Alright then. Thanks for being so understanding, Britt. Talk to you later," as if he had not heard what she said.

He then hung up the phone, a bit shaken.

Walter watched the girls through his windshield, his anger building as he saw them giggling hysterically, obviously at his ill-concealed lie.

It doesn't really matter if you believe me or not, he thought. *I've got what I want. Now, just a little drive to see where you live. Go ahead and have your fun now, but we'll see who's laughing later, won't we?*

The two girls then walked to a red Toyota, still talking and occasionally laughing. The brunette got into the driver's seat.

Probably the owner of the car, he logically assumed.

As they began to pull out of the parking lot, Walter kept well back, despite the belief they had no idea they were being followed.

As he drove, Walter reviewed his plan for Britt's abduction. It had been much the same as it had been for most of the previous girls. The food court was an innocuous locale, the girl had felt safe and protected in the crowded area. He had found a table near where she sat, very politely asking the preoccupied older gentleman already seated if he could sit there as well to finish up some work.

"Good manners get you a long way in life, son," his father had said.

As always, his father had been right. The man had looked up from his newspaper and vaguely gestured toward the facing chair. He now felt he could covertly watch her without drawing undue attention to himself, he enjoyed watching the look on the girls' faces turn from eager anticipation to gloomy dejection.

Later, I'll make it up to you, honey, he always thought.

He would then follow her home. If the opportunity presented itself to grab her along the way, so much the better. If not, he would make plans to take her later.

Yeah, a great plan, too bad the other girl ruined it.

He had been very surprised when the girl named Alex joined Britt at the table.

Well, it really makes sense, doesn't it? He asked himself. *Come to think of it, he wondered why none of the others had thought of creating a safety net. I thought we'd have time to get to know each other better later on; but this has certainly spoiled my plans for tonight, hasn't it?*

Since Shannon Buckley's abrupt decision to end their relationship, he had been eager to find someone new to date, someone who wouldn't betray him as Shannon had. Britt had seemed perfect, both beautiful and intelligent, and they had hit it off really well right from the beginning. Now, however, he wasn't so sure, still stinging from the sight of her laughing at him. There was something else bothering him as well, the other girl, Alex. She definitely complicated things, but something he had overheard in their conversation would simplify that. As he drove, he mulled over various ideas as to how to accomplish his task. Walter's musings were suddenly interrupted as the Toyota pulled into a suburban driveway in a well-to-do neighborhood. He didn't wait for them to exit; he drove past at the same steady speed he had been maintaining.

He turned left at the end of her street, beginning his lengthy drive across town to his own house. Suddenly, his frown of concentration eased into a slight smile. He began to whistle tunelessly to himself, happy in the fact he now knew exactly what he was going to do.

Chapter 21

The call to Frank Chapman's home came at 9:42 a.m. on Sunday morning. Normally, it would have been forwarded to his cell after the fourth ring, as he would already be on the back nine at Jefferson Park Golf Course. Today, however, he picked it up almost immediately, the lashing rainstorm outside having dissuaded him from his customary weekend pursuit.

"Hello, Chapman," his greeting terse and to the point.

Frank's years on the police force had shaped many of his habits, including his manner of answering the phone.

Besides, he thought, *a Saturday morning call usually means bad news: for me, as it was probably a summons to work, as well as for some poor soul who had somehow wound up very much dead.*

"Frank? This is Megan, Megan James. Sorry to bother you on a day off, but I've got something I think you'd like to see?"

"Uh, you on site or in the office?" Frank asked, hoping to hell he'd luck out and be able to stay out of the raging downpour going on outside.

"On site, Frank." His groan was audible. "Sorry, I really wouldn't normally involve you on an apparent suicide . . ."

He interrupted; his growing anger evident. "Suicide? Dr. James, did John put you up to this as some kind of a damned joke? I've worked seventy-two hours this past week, and now you want me to go out and get drenched, just to take a look at some stiff you're already calling a suicide. The nameplate says, 'Frank Chapman, Homicide,' not 'Frank Chapman, Nothing Better to Do with My Life.'"

Despite some irritation at his sarcastic tone, Megan's voice remained professional and dispassionate. "Frank, her body shows definite signs of heavy abuse. It looks like an instrument with a multitude of sharp metal teeth has been pulled across her back, buttocks, and thighs. The only thing I can think of that would make marks like that is a cabinetmaker's rasp."

"Shit, the DIY Killer."

"Who?" she asked.

"Uh, sorry, it's the name John and I gave to the Woodsman, seemed more appropriate to us."

"Well," she said slowly, obviously mulling the nickname over in her mind. "I would tend to agree with you, given each of the girls we can attribute to him displayed evidence of physical abuse caused by ordinary tools. Oh, and one other thing of interest as well."

"What's that?"

"The body's fresh, Frank. She couldn't have been dead over twenty-four hours."

"So, where you at?" he asked, his earlier reticence overcome by a mounting sense of excitement.

It took him less than an hour to reach Bainbridge Island, having caught the ferry almost ready to depart. A few minutes later he parked, only a few hundred yards from Bainbridge Island Transfer Station. He reached over to the passenger seat and grabbed a black rain slicker, struggling into it prior to departing from the vehicle. A King's County Sheriff's Department deputy directed him to the crime scene. He spotted Megan James and walked briskly toward her, the rain already beginning to drench his jeans.

"Thanks for calling, Dr. James," Frank began then, hoping to make amends, "Sorry about the bad attitude, OK?"

"No need to apologize," she replied. "Believe me, I know what it's like to get called in on a day off."

"Yeah, so what have we got?"

Hikers found her earlier this morning. Female, late teens or early twenties. Blond and green eyes, probably 5'10" and about 120. Pretty girl, really,"

The Medical Examiner's pity for the young life that had been tragically ended was evident. Despite her best efforts, sometimes Megan's detached demeanor momentarily slipped.

Recovering, she continued, "Black t-shirt, with a large yellow wig emblem on the front. Black bra, panties, and athletic socks sum up the rest of her clothing. No ID whatsoever."

"Naturally. Why can't it ever be easy," he asked, rhetorically. "Tats, piercings?"

"Just a couple of holes in each ear, but she was obviously a cutter, primarily upper thighs. Probable cause of death was exsanguination, occurring from an approximately four-inch-long incision stripping the ulnar vein of the right forearm."

"Jesus," he said, thinking the girl definitely knew what she was doing. "Any signs of forced sexual activity?"

"Well, she's definitely had intercourse, but I can't really be more definite as to whether it was coerced or consensual until the post mortem."

"Anything else?"

"Well, she definitely didn't die here, there would have been some evidence of blood, even with the rain. Nothing, though. She was drained pretty much dry before she got here."

"Thanks, Megan. Can I ask a favor?"

"Certainly," she said, her eyes narrowing somewhat in puzzlement, however.

"Could you do the p.m. ASAP, please? I can't help thinking he may have another girl lined up already. Anything you find out might be the straw that the breaks the camel's back in helping us to catch this bastard."

"I'll try to move it to the top of the list, Frank. I want this madman off the streets just as much as you."

As he drove back home, Frank wondered whether he should call John Chapman to share the news about the discovery of the young girl's body.

God, Claire would skin me alive, he thought, shaking his head. *No, if anything, John's put in more hours the past few months than I have. The guy deserves a few days' break; plus, he's a walking heart attack waiting to happen. I know the doctor's going to have a shit fit when he goes in for his physical. Overweight, high blood pressure, eats and drinks too much, no exercise, and now he's back on the smokes. He'll be lucky if he doesn't get his ass suspended. The only way I'm calling him is if I hear back something definite from the M.E., and I mean a real break in the case, not just incidental bullshit.*

Although the rain had let up a bit, it was still falling in heavy sheets as Frank pulled into his driveway. He ran to his front door, fumbling with his key in his haste to get out of the horrid weather. He went inside, stripping off his wet clothes in the foyer to keep from leaving a wet trail into the bathroom. He took a long shower, the hot jets of water feeling like needles on his skin before drying himself vigorously with a thick towel and re-dressing. Feeling much more human, he grabbed up his wet clothes and tossed them directly into the washer. The next few hours were spent in a vain attempt to divert his thoughts from the body on Bainbridge Island, just the latest in a string of dead, young girls he had been unable to help keep alive.

"Shit," he mumbled to himself, turning on his computer.

Although King County Sheriff's Office held jurisdiction in the case, he still wanted to see if he could identify her from the MUPU database. After an hour spent reviewing the file of persons recently reported missing, he still had not come up with a likely match for the Jane Doe on Bainbridge Island.

Well, he contemplated, *that could mean one of a couple of things. She might be from out of state, but that's not likely since the Woodsman seems to have a thing for local girls. It's also possible she was just grabbed, and no one's reported her missing yet. Hell, it might even be that her report just hasn't been entered into the system yet.*

Realizing there was nothing he could do about the first two alternatives, he decided to follow up on the third. A quick call to the administrative department of MUPU revealed that, because of their chronic administrative staffing shortages, a backlog of reports did exist. A quick discussion led to a possible identification, as only one file matched the description Frank had provided to the clerk. Her name was Shannon Buckley, aged nineteen. Physical features seemed to match perfectly. She had only been reported missing yesterday, but the person who filed the report, her father, said she could have been gone for several days.

What the hell's up with that? Fucking father doesn't even know where his daughter's been for days. It's a pity they let people like that have kids, he thought to himself grimly, identifying another target for his pent-up anger. *I wonder if it's really her, or if I've missed something? One thing for sure, I bet the Woodsman was mucho pissed off when he discovered his little sweetheart had preferred offing herself to letting him have his way with her. Kind of takes all the fun out of it, doesn't it, you son-of-a-bitch?*

The possibility of knowing her identity really didn't get him any closer to solving the crime but, psychologically, it felt like he was making some kind of progress. He called the Sheriff's Office and relayed the information about a possible ID on the girl. After that, there really was nothing to do except wait, hoping against hope something would happen to provide him with the one big break he would need to find the Woodsman.

The rest of Frank's day passed uneventfully. He read the Sunday paper, did a load of laundry, watched a Royals-Rangers day game, all the while distracted in varying degrees by the mental image of the girl lying dead out on Bainbridge Island. He couldn't help but worry the Woodsman's plan had been disrupted by the apparent suicide of his victim. What was it Agent Rhodes, the FBI profiler, had said? These guys are creatures of habit, their actions become an ingrained, set sequence, almost like a ritual. Now, with his pattern interrupted, there was only one logical conclusion as to what he intended to do next: kidnap another girl and get the train back onto the tracks.

It's hard to take that, while I'm sitting here on my ass, that bastard could already have snatched another girl.

He awoke with a start, awakened by the incessant ring of his cell phone. Groggily gaining his bearings, he arose from his leather recliner and walked a bit unsteadily to the end table where he had left the phone. On what must have been the tenth ring, he answered.

"Chapman," he mumbled into the phone.

"Detective Chapman?" The voice on the other end of the line was just too chipper for the drowsy police officer's liking.

"Yeah, that's what I said. Who are you and what do you want?" He replied, growing surlier by the minute.

"This is Dr. Weller, at King County morgue. Megan, uh, Dr. James, asked for me to let you know if we found anything important during the autopsy of the Jane Doe from Bainbridge Island. Detective Chapman," he said, barely able to conceal the excitement in his voice, "Can you please come down here right now?"

Frank looked at his watch and groaned, it was after 11:00 p.m. Knowing the M.E.'s office, it was probably a trace of DNA they couldn't attribute to the girl, important evidence admittedly, but nothing that he could do anything about right now.

A fucking guy has got to sleep, doesn't he? he asked himself rhetorically.

To Dr. Weller, he replied, "Look, I really appreciate the call, but can I just drop by in the morning . . ."

"Detective Chapman, we've found a note."

"What the hell did you say?" Frank was jolted fully awake and attentive in an instant, hardly believing what he had heard.

"I said the body contained a note. What's more, it provides detailed information as to the identity of her abductor. She refers to him as the Woodsman, detective."

"I'll be there in twenty minutes. Hey, thanks, alright?" Frank hung up, not waiting for the man's reply. In less than five minutes, he had taken a leak; put on his shoes; grabbed his weapon, coat, and badge; and exited his house. He was determined to make it to the morgue faster than his self-imposed time limit.

Driving swiftly through the darkened streets of the city, Frank thumbed his phone to speed dial John Caldwell's number.

Come on, damn it, answer your fucking phone, Frank cursed, urging his fellow officer to pick up.

After what seemed like forever, he heard a sleepy voice say. "This better be important, Frank Chapman.

"Put John on the phone, Claire, please."

"Look Frank," Claire Caldwell's ire was easily detectable from the other end of the line. "John works himself to death and, when we just for once get a chance to get away . . ."

"God damn it, Claire, put him on the phone now!" Frank knew that swearing at Claire Caldwell was something no sane person would do of his own volition, but he had to get through to her the importance of speaking with her husband right away.

"Fine," she replied evenly, though with an undertone of pure venom clear in her voice.

Even though she didn't like it, she had been a cop's wife for long enough to respect the urgency in Frank's voice.

"Uh, what?" John's response was semi-coherent.

Clearly, he had been shaken awake out of a deep sleep.

"Listen, John, get your shit together right now and get to here as fast as you can. We may have him!"

"What?" John repeated, only slightly more aroused from his sleep-induced stupor.

"God damn it, John, just listen to me! We may have a huge break in the DIY Killer case. M.E. found a note in the body of a victim, a girl they just found yesterday. It's supposedly got a bunch of details about her abductor written on it. I'm in the car, going to get it right now."

"What?" the other detective asked for the third time, only now completely alert. "You're kidding, right?"

"No shit," Frank said." Now, are you in or out?"

"Definitely in, "John answered emphatically. "I can be there in about two hours. I'll meet you at the office, OK?"

"Great! Tell Claire I'm sorry to ruin her time alone with you. She was probably bored as hell with your sorry ass by now anyway. See you in a couple of hours."

"Yep" was John's terse reply, failing to rise to his friend's jibe.

Then the line went dead.

Assholes and elbows, Frank thought to himself, recalling the term they had used when he was in the Army to describe getting ready in a real hurry, which he imagined John to be doing this instant.

Happy he would soon add John's years of experience and deductive reasoning ability to augment his own, he went back to focusing on his immediate task, which was to get to the county morgue as quickly as possible.

When Frank opened the door into the examination suite, he recognized the girl he had seen at Gazzam Lake earlier that morning on an autopsy table. The Y-Incision had been completed and her internal organs had been removed, leaving her resembling an empty husk.

I'm really sorry, Shannon, or whoever you really are, no damn way any young girl deserves this, he thought sadly, despite having witnessed several others before her in even a grislier state.

A gray-haired man approached from the back of the room. He held out his hand and introduced himself.

"Dr. Weller. Detective Chapman, I presume?"

Frank shook his hand and cut to the chase immediately. "So, what have you got for me, doctor?"

The physician motioned Frank to a nearby table, relating, "I had opened the stomach to survey its contents. It was largely empty, except for this." He produced a metal tray containing a rubber band, a plastic sandwich bag, and a note. Written in a large elegant hand, the message from beyond the grave read:

Walter _____ is the Woodsman. I was kept in a cage in the basement of an old house. I don't know where it is. He is tall. Dark hair. Brown eyes. Thirty some years old maybe. He has a

- 255 -

dog named Mike. Orders fresh lobster from a deli – "Best in Seattle," he said. Friends with a man who works there named Pete.

Please catch him!

Shannon Buckley

So, it was the Buckley girl after all, Frank thought, shaking his head in silent admiration for the terrified young girl who, in her last moments, had tried to save other girls from suffering the horrors she had endured. *Girl should get a God damned medal.*

Although fifteen years on the force had hardened him in ways that he had thought not possible, tears suddenly welled in his eyes.

I swear to you Shannon, I'll nail this bastard before he has a chance to hurt another girl.

Frank thanked the doctor profusely for calling him and proceeded to copy the information from the slip of paper into his notebook. He quickly departed, ringing his captain simultaneously. By the time he arrived at the North Precinct building, Captain Phillips was nervously pacing the hallway outside of Frank's office.

Quickly greeting each other, they went inside and sat down.

Frank's superior asked, "Just tell me what you need, Frank."

"OK, we've got to start by identifying delicatessens with someone named Pete who would take an order over the phone."

"Damn. There must be hundreds of delis in Seattle metro alone," Captain Phillips said with consternation clear in his voice. "Any way we can cut that down?"

"Well," began Frank, "There's probably no more than twenty or thirty that would be selling fresh lobster. I'd also start with the big, trendy places, ones that might make a claim like 'Best in Seattle.' That would be my starting point, then work down from there until we've checked every mom-and-pop operation that can throw together a ham sandwich. We're getting this guy, Captain, no two ways about it."

"You better believe it," the senior officer agreed, then reiterating his previous offer. "What do you need right now?"

"Nothing, for the moment at least. It's better to get organized than go off half-cocked. I'll get started on going through the phone book, identifying the most likely places to check first. I'd thought about starting to call around immediately, but it's . . ." He checked his watch. ". . . almost one now. No deli that stocks lobsters is going to be open this time of night. Trying to get somebody in at Public Records to start researching business licenses isn't going to speed things up either. As much as I hate to say so, we really can't get things underway until probably roll call. By then, I'll have everything planned out and I'll need as much manpower as you can give me to contact the delis. Any we find that take fresh lobster deliveries and have a Pete working for them, and there can't be many, will get a visit. If Pete identifies our guy, we'll have to play it by ear depending on what info they have on this guy, Walter."

"Yeah, can't find fault with that, good thinking, Frank," said Phillips, still wishing there was more he could do to get things moving right away.

God, things will sure be easier around here if I can get the mayor, city council, and everyone else off my back by putting this son-of-a-bitch behind bars.

His reverie was broken by John Caldwell's straight to the point comment, "So what have I missed?"

"Caldwell," said Captain Phillips, "What the hell are you doing here? You're supposed to be off on vacation up north, right?"

"I was, but Frank called me. You didn't think I'd let him grab all the glory for himself, did you, Captain?"

"OK," Phillips said, "I'll make it up to you later." He turned to Frank and asked, "You alright with this?"

Frank nodded his assent and said, "Yeah, I can definitely get through the phone book quicker with John's help. Plus, we can work out what to do once we've identified the perp."

The captain agreed and left, vowing to put all available manpower at the detectives' disposal.

Frank looked at John and gave him a wink, all fatigue drained from his body by an overload of adrenalin.

He said, "You ready to start earning your paycheck partner?"

John smiled in return and said, "You damned right. You have the coffee on?" Frank's negative shake of the head elicited a further, "Shit, how'd you get along the past couple of days without me?"

John went to fill the pot with water, while Frank grabbed a couple of municipal phone books. It was going to be a long night.

Chapter 22

By six-thirty a.m., Frank and John had categorized the city's delis into three categories; probable, maybe, and not very likely. There were over sixty among those that were probable, the portion of the list on which their efforts would initially focus. As officers arrived who had been detailed to the case, one of the two detectives handed them an annotated copy of an EXCEL spreadsheet, indicating the calls they were to make.

Within fifteen minutes, they had their first full hit, Faccio's Delicatessen on Queen Anne Avenue. The officer making the call relayed that the manager, Mr. Dale Simpson, confirmed they do indeed sell live lobster. Furthermore, they do have a counter man named Pete Campbell, who routinely takes phone orders. He wouldn't be in until 10:00 a.m., however. Finally, the officer said that, when he asked if people said they were the best deli in Seattle, Simpson had said, "You're damned right."

Excitedly, the two detectives got out of their seats, determined to be standing in Faccio's when Pete Campbell reported to work. Just as they were about to depart, however, Pam O'Rourke, another of the officer working on the deli list, yelled from down the hallway, "Detectives, I've got a match!"

John turned to Frank and said, "I'll take this one, OK? You head on over to Faccio's." The homicide detective nodded in agreement and went out the door.

John walked over to the female officer and said, "Tell me what you've got."

"Wolf's Deli, on South Stacy, sir. The guy I talked to said the owner's son, Pete, is the manager. What's more, they just got in a shipment of live lobsters last Tuesday."

"Hey, thanks for the good work, Officer O'Rourke. Pam, isn't it? Hey, can you hold down the fort here, please? Detective Chapman is already gone and I want to get up to Wolf's right now. This is the second lead in the last few minutes, who knows how many more will turn up. God, who knew Pete was such a popular name in the deli business, eh? Give one of us a call ASAP if anything else turns up."

She flashed him an appreciative smile for the compliment toward her work and the opportunity to pinch hit as a detective.

A real up-and-comer, John thought, satisfied he had left the coordination of their efforts in capable hands.

John knew Wolf's Deli, just about everyone in town who liked good food did.

As a matter of fact, he thought, *I may even remember a guy named Pete. Big fella, liked to talk. Well, I sure as hell hope he's got a lot to say about a guy named Walter.*

Before leaving, he gave a quick call to Captain Phillips, providing him with an update on their progress with the case. Then, after making sure the young officer behind Frank's desk had both his and his fellow detective's cell number, he departed on his way to South Stacey.

John arrived at Wolf's Deli less than twenty minutes later. Even before going through the front door, he was assailed by a multitude of delicious smells that acutely reminded him he had missed breakfast. Approaching the counter, he guiltily glanced at the assorted meats, cheeses, and other scrumptious tidbits in the refrigerator case. While he was somewhat distracted, a young woman approached unnoticed.

He was surprised, therefore, when a pleasant voice asked, "Good morning, I'm Lynn. Can I help you with something?"

Jolted from his gastronomic wet dream, John replied, "Uh, yeah. I'm Detective Chapman, Seattle P.D." He flashed his badge. "Is Pete here?"

"I'm sorry, but Pete isn't in today. Would you like to talk to his father, Gunther?

It's never simple, is it? He thought to himself ruefully.

Then, smiling at the woman, he said, "Yeah, that would be great."

She disappeared through a door and returned seconds later with an elderly man who was visibly nervous.

He approached John and asked, "Detective, has something happened to my boy, Pete?"

John assured him nothing had happened to his son, nor was he in any kind of trouble; he only needed to ask him some questions.

The man's anxiety drained from his face as he said, "That's a relief, thanks. A parent is always afraid of having a policeman show up, saying that something has happened to your kid."

John agreed, having had the same thought hundreds of times himself as his daughters had grown up.

He then said, "Sorry to give you a fright, Mr. Wolf, but I really need to talk to your son about one of your customers he had contact with named Walter."

"Sorry, but he's not working the rest of the week. He and a couple of his buddies went sailing up in the Straits, won't be back until Friday."

Lucky bastard, John thought jealously. *I should still be up there myself, instead of on this wild goose chase.*

"I see. Can I get his cell number from you at least?"

The elder Wolf recited his son's number to John, who immediately put it into his own phone and hit 'call.' As bad luck would have it, the call switched to voice mail after a couple of rings. Cursing silently to himself, John thanked the older man and gave him his card, requesting he have his son contact him, day or night, as soon as he heard from him. Gunther Wolf readily agreed, assuring the detective he would try to call his son throughout the day to give him the message. He then returned to the back room of the deli.

Frustrated, John turned to go, but then reconsidered. As long as I'm here, I might as well pick something up for breakfast, maybe lunch too, while I'm at it. Got to be better than fast food.

Turning back to the refrigerated display, he was savoring his options when the woman who had introduced herself as Lynn said, "Excuse me, officer, I really wasn't trying to eavesdrop, but did you say you wanted to know about a customer named Walter?"

All hunger forgotten, at least for the moment, John asked, "Yes, yes I did, please go on."

Encouraged, she continued, "We do have a regular customer named Walter, Walter Harrison." The look of admiration in her eyes was unmistakable, it was evident Lynn had a bit of a crush on the man.

Finding it hard to conceal his excitement, John asked, "Can you describe him please, miss?"

"Oh, yes. Tall and very athletically built. Brown eyes and hair and always well dressed. He must be about thirty, but he certainly could pass for his late twenties. When he smiles . . . "

John interrupted the woman, realizing she could probably go on for hours about every detail of the man's appearance. Description certainly fits, though – things were definitely warming up. "You don't happen to have a record of his address, do you, like for deliveries?"

"No," she replied, "we don't deliver."

"Well, how about a credit card receipt?"

"Oh, no. Mr. Harrison always pays cash. He even gives me a tip when I fill his order."

Smooth son-of-a-bitch, John thought, realizing Lynn was completely captivated by the guy. *Well, this seems to be going nowhere.*

"Um, I do know where he works, Detective, if that would be helpful."

John had to work hard to keep from yelling at her.

What the hell do you think? he thought angrily.

Instead, he replied in an even tone, "Yes, miss, that would be most helpful."

"Well, he works at International Underwriters Insurance Company, just over on 8th Avenue, you know. He's a very important man, like a vice-president or something. My friend, Marianne Peters, is his secretary. Does that help?" she asked hopefully.

"Yes, yes it does. Thank you so much, Lynn. I'm going over there right now, as a matter of fact. Oh, and will you please not let them know I'm coming?" he asked, knowing that a heads up from Lynn could cause Walter Harrison to flee the premises before he got there.

"Oh, yes. Certainly." She had seen enough crime dramas on television to surmise the reason for the detective's request. Still, she was bubbling over, hardly able to contain herself until she got a chance to discuss this bit of gossip with Marianne. As the police officer turned to go, she said, "Say 'hi' to Marianne for me, will you?" He waved, an action she took to mean that he certainly would do as she asked.

John walked to the offices of International Underwriters Insurance at a pace he was finding hard to maintain. By the time he reached the company's entrance, he was almost gasping for breath. He took a minute to compose himself before attacking the set of stairs leading to the reception area, running his fingers through his sweaty hair before ashamedly wiping his hands on the side of his trousers.

Gamely mounting the stairs, John was greeted by yet another attractive young woman asking if she could be of assistance. He presented his police credentials and said, "Detective Chapman. You wouldn't happen to be Marianne Peters, would you?"

The young woman's face flushed red as a series of past minor transgressions raced across her mind. Realizing her discomfort, John said, "I was just talking to your friend Lynn at Wolf' Deli, she said to say hello."

Marianne immediately felt relieved, but suspected the fat police officer in front of her desk had not climbed the stairs to her office just to pass along Lynn's greeting.

Her notion was confirmed when he continued, asking, "Is Mr. Harrison available?"

"No, I'm afraid he isn't. Mr. Harrison isn't in the office today; he's taking a day off. Can someone else help you?"

"No, I really need to talk to Mr. Harrison about a private matter; well, to see him, actually. Can I get his home address and phone number, please?"

Marianne quickly surmised the detective's inquiries may have nothing to do with insurance. When in doubt, she recalled her early training in her job, follow Company standard procedure.

She quoted almost verbatim, "It's corporation policy that we do not disclose our employees' personal information. I'm sorry, but you'd have to contact our headquarters in Connecticut to find out that data."

Passing the buck works well too, she thought, a bit smugly.

Besides, the last thing she wanted to do was to get her boss in any trouble.

Getting a bit pissed off at the young woman's officious attitude, John decided to lean on her a bit.

"Look, Ms. Peters, I need this information in conjunction with an official police investigation, and I need it now, not after you finish jerking me around. Mr. Harrison may have information involving a serious crime, a matter of life and death actually. Do you know what it means to be an accessory to murder, Ms. Peters?"

Marianne blanched at the not so veiled threat. She felt she was now getting in over her head. She wanted to protect Mr. Harrison, but her desire to keep in the good graces of her boss was fast being overcome by her aversion into getting into trouble with the police.

"Wait just a minute, Detective Caldwell, let me get the information you need off the computer."

She efficiently accessed Walter's contact details and copied them down on a large post-It. She removed the note from the pack and handed it to John.

"There you are, Detective. Will there be anything else I can help you with?" She hoped he could detect the icy coldness she was trying to instill in her voice.

"Yeah. Make sure you don't contact Mr. Harrison to let him know we're looking for him. It would not be in your best interests if we miss him because of you. Well, thank you very much for your assistance, miss."

John hoped she recognized the saccharine sarcasm in his voice as well.

Before she could retort, he turned on his heel and left her office. Fuming, she prayed he would slip and fall down the stairs on his way out. She heard the vestibule door close behind him, her curse left unfulfilled.

Well, one thing for sure, she thought, reaching into her purse for her personal phone. *I'm going to let Walter know the police are searching for him. I just hope he's not angry with me when he finds out I gave them his address and phone number.*

She hoped her impulsive assistance to the police detective wouldn't diminish her boss's estimation of her, either personally or professionally.

John headed quickly to his car, calling Frank on the way to give him an update on his progress at Wolf's and the insurance agency. Begrudgingly acknowledging his friend's headway, Chapman himself was absolutely livid with the lack of success he was having with his own investigation. Arriving at Faccio's Deli, he was immediately informed by Pete Campbell he knew of no customers by the name of Walt or Walter. Before he could leave, however, Pam O'Rourke had called, providing two more leads. The first had proven as fruitless as Faccio's and he was on his way to the second.

Does every fucking deli have to have a guy named Pete working there? Is it like a licensing requirement or something?" Frank groused.

Having known his fellow detective for years, John knew it was better to ignore Frank's bad mood than to comment on it. "Hey look, check the other lead out and, if it's nothing, come join me over at 107 Locust Lane."

"So, are you going to wait for me to show up before knocking on the door?"

"You want to hold my hand, or something? Naw, I got a bad feeling about this one, partner. I really want to see what's up with this guy sooner, rather than later," John replied.

"Shit, you know that's bad business, John. At least call for a couple of uniforms for backup," concern clearly etched itself into Frank's voice.

"Yeah, right. That's exactly what you'd do, right?"

The last thing I need is for a rookie patrolman to screw things up.

Besides, he told himself, I'm going to take this one easy, really easy.

Chapter 23

Alex got out of her bed gingerly, hoping to keep from awakening Britt, whose heavy, regular breathing indicated she was still deep in her slumbers. She had already pre-positioned her clothes in her parents' room, ready to put on after she'd gotten ready for work in their bathroom.

Well planned, girl, she congratulated herself, pulling the bedroom door silently closed behind her.

Still in her pajamas, Alex descended the stairs and padded through the semi-darkness toward the kitchen. Starting the obligatory morning pot of coffee, she looked out the window to see the sun beginning to rise above the horizon.

Another beautiful day, she observed happily.

This was her final week of work and she hoped the weather each day was going to be gorgeous.

She placed two slices of wheat bread into the toaster and returned to the percolator, pulling a cup of extra-strength java from the, as yet, unfinished brewing cycle. She added creamer to her cup and spread butter and jam on her toast. Although her breakfast was, by Alex's normal standards, rather Spartan, she knew she would make up for it at lunch. Britt had informed her she would make a picnic lunch and bring it to Magnuson Park at 1:00 p.m., the usual time for Alex's meal break. She then planned to lie out, stealing the last few nice summer days to work on her already gorgeous tan. Then, after Alex's shift was over, they would head over to the beach for perhaps the final time this year.

Maybe forever, Alex thought glumly.

I'll miss you so much, Britt, she thought, her melancholic mood deepening.

With superlative grades and almost 2300 on her SAT, Alex would have been gladly accepted by any university in the country. She had chosen Stanford primarily for its reputation in the sciences, but also to expand her horizons. Repeatedly, she guiltily regretted not accompanying Britt to UW. They had vowed, however, to never lose contact with each other, a promise she sincerely hoped to keep.

Munching on her toast, Alex's mind wandered to a recollection of their time together the past couple of days.

The whole Andy thing was just too bizarre, she grinned, her mood somewhat lightening at the thought of the absurd chain of events.

She was relieved her friend had sworn off all contact with the guy who had stood her up, a promise she knew, from experience, her friend would surely keep.

Hell hath no fury like Britt Stevens scorned, she paraphrased.

Regardless of whatever the guy's game was, he wasn't going to be playing it with Britt. For that she was truly thankful.

She had offered up a special prayer in church the day before to that fact. Whereas most of her friends would have been happy to avoid attending services if not forced to go by their parents, Alex loved sitting in the solid, oaken pew, polished smooth by the comings and goings of countless parishioners before her over the past seven decades. The choir's hymns always brought her a sense of peace, a feeling she was safe and protected. Pastor Roberts' sermons, though at times a bit lengthy, provided lessons for the living of one's life, shaping her into a firm follower of God's Commandments.

Afterwards, she and Britt had just hung out at the house, comfortable in the easy companionship of each other's company. Alex had fired up the gas barbeque about five, quickly grilling a pair of mouthwatering lemon butter swordfish steaks. The rest of the evening had been a continuation of their movie marathon until, well after midnight,

Alex had finally said, "No more, honey. Some of us have to get up in the morning. Remember, I'm just a simple working girl."

Britt looked down her nose imperiously, a look of mock disdain fixed on her face.

"Yes, I must remember how the peasantry must toil." She then ducked as Alex sent a throw pillow whizzing at her head in quick succession.

Wow, Alex thought as her gaze randomly brushed the kitchen clock. *Am I going to sit here reminiscing about good times all morning or what? Get a move on, Alex, or you're going to be late!*

Thirty-three minutes later, she emerged from her parents' room, dressed and ready to face the world. As she passed by her own door, she opened it partway, looking in on her friend. Britt was still asleep, her breathing now characterized by low, sonorous snoring.

Thank goodness she wasn't doing that last night, Alex thought, sniggering to herself as she pulled the door shut quietly. *She would have woken up with a set of sore ribs from getting jabbed by my elbow! Oh well, sweet dreams, Sleeping Beauty. Mama has got to go make some money.*

Still giggling, Alex exited the front door and got into her car.

As she pulled out of the driveway, she thought to herself, *did I lock the door?*

Always before, her mother had still been in the house when Alex left for work, making setting the lock unnecessary. Now on the street, she discarded the idea of going back to check.

Must be going senile in my old age, she chided herself.

As she was driving, she suddenly thought, *can you believe it? This is my last Monday going to work!*

Although originally unsure as to how much she was going to like holding down a steady summer job, she soon grew to love her time spent each day at the park. Despite the fact the tasks were more or less redundant, she never found her work boring.

Besides, having your own money is great.

She soon pulled into the parking lot, pulling the Toyota into the spot under the big spruce where she knew it would be shaded from the afternoon sun. She relieved Dmitri, who left to catch his bus immediately.

"Large and in charge," she declared aloud, although there was no one else in the park to hear her declaration.

Over the next couple of hours, a few boat owners came by, paying their fees and more or less immediately undertaking the launching of their vessels. In between, Alex occupied herself with tidying up, placing several bits of loose trash into the waste receptacles to maintain her workplace's pristine appearance. She suddenly looked up, attracted by the sound of a car door slamming in the far parking area, accompanied by a few mild curses. Her forehead crinkled into a frown as she saw something she felt she was obliged to investigate.

Back at Alex's house, Britt was also disturbed from the task before her by an unexpected sound. In her case, however, it was the front door chime. She placed the knife she had been using to cut the sandwiches she had made into triangles carefully down on the counter and wiped her hands conscientiously on a towel.

She unconsciously reviewed her appearance and found it to be at least semi-presentable. She was wearing an emerald green crop-top and a pair of Levis cut-offs. The nails of her bare feet were a meticulously painted cherry red, thanks to Alex, who had painted them the day before as part of their shared routine. No makeup, regrettably, but I've at least brushed my hair, she thought. Satisfied she was in a fit state to answer the door, she walked into the foyer, peeking through the peephole to ascertain the visitor's identity.

She saw a younger looking man with dark hair, holding what looked to be a couple of large boxes in his hands. She opened the door, saying, "Yes?"

He replied, "UPS, ma'am. I have a delivery. It's kind of heavy, would you like me to put it inside for you?" She motioned for him to come in and gestured for him to put it down beside the library table. As he did, she barely stifled a giggle.

'Ma'am?' Do I really look that old?

She suddenly sobered, promising herself that, in the future, she would definitely put on some makeup before letting strange men into the house.

She signed the man's electronic signature pad where he indicated with a flourish, feeling suddenly quite grown up. She smiled at him as he departed, thinking he was rather cute.

Woman of the house, that's me, she thought humorously, before returning to the kitchen to finish preparing her picnic feast.

As Alex approached the black SUV, the source of the driver's consternation became readily apparent. The left rear tire was completely flat. The dark-haired man stood behind the open back hatch, looking inside with a visible look of frustration on his face. He tried to move his crutches into his left hand while reaching for something with his right, only to erupt into a yelp of obvious pain.

Now within speaking distance, Alex said loudly, "Sir, can I help you with something?"

The man turned awkwardly toward her, wiped a sheen of sweat from his forehead and replied, "Oh, hi. Well, as you can see, I've got a tire that's pretty well totally flat. I was just trying to get my spare out, but I'm having the devil's own time trying to manage it on these."

He lifted the crutches to indicate his reference.

"Um, I really hate to impose on you, but do you think you could give me a hand with at least getting the spare out? I'll gladly pay you for the help."

He flashed her an encouraging smile.

Well, this isn't in the job description, she thought humorously, *but I just can't let the guy try to change the tire by himself, he might injure his leg even more.*

She took a quick glance back to the boat landing area; luckily, there was no one that needed any assistance.

Flashing the man a friendly smile, she said, "No problem at all, sir. Don't worry about paying me, either, it's all in a day's work."

He thanked her and stood aside so she could get at the tire and jack stored in the rear of the vehicle. Looking inside, Alex saw he had already removed the mat that concealed the storage compartment. She leaned into the interior of the Kia Sorento and started to unscrew the wing nut that held the spare in place. Suddenly, she felt a sharp pain in the back of her skull. Immediately, her senses dulled and the bright summer day began to fade into shadow. Just before she lost awareness, she felt herself being lifted and deposited into the back of the SUV. Then there was nothing.

A spark of consciousness appeared, flickered piteously, and then went out. In a few seconds, it reappeared, stronger this time. Alex would have moaned aloud, but the material tightly covering her mouth prevented that. She sought to remove it, then realized her hands were tightly bound behind her back. She attempted to look downward, toward her legs, but everything was still a blur. Another few seconds and her eyes found their focus and she saw her legs were tightly bound with gray duct tape. Realizing the terrible enormity of her situation, she began to panic. She felt her stomach lurch, the morning's toast and coffee struggling to expel itself. She fought the urge desperately, knowing the vomit would be dammed behind what she inferred to be the duct tape that held her mouth closed. The liquid would then be inhaled into her lungs.

Don't want to die choking on my own puke.

Now fully alert, but mentally impaired by what she felt was the worst headache she had ever experienced in her life, Alex began to breathe deeply, using years of yoga training to calm herself so she could objectively assess her situation. She realized she was laying on her right side in the cargo area of a car, undoubtedly the large black SUV from the park. The side of her face rubbed roughly on random bits of gravel on the floor any time the car hit a bump in the road. She ignored this pain; however, as it paled in comparison to that which she felt in her head.

Alex noted they were still moving, they had yet to reach the driver's intended destination.

Which is where? She suddenly wondered, hysteria seeking to overcome coherent thought.

Doesn't matter, she told herself, *we'll cross that bridge when we get to it. As for now, it's a foregone conclusion that I'm in a pretty desperate situation. The best thing I can do is keep my wits about me, stay ready to capitalize on any break that comes my way.*

She made herself believe that an opportunity to escape would come about, the alternative would have been to simply sink into a morass of despair.

Remember, she told herself, *you're a 'cup half full' sort of girl, Alex.*

Suddenly, the car slowed drastically, turned, and then halt. She heard the sound of an electric motor and the clanking of moving metal. The car moved forward slowly, the light diminishing noticeably as they passed the line of demarcation into what Alex concluded was a garage. The car stopped and the sound of its motor abruptly ceased, although that of the garage door continued as it closed, increasing the depth of the gloom that surrounded her. She heard a car door at the front of the vehicle open and close, then footsteps become increasingly louder.

Have to pretend I'm still knocked out, she thought, *it might give me a bit of an advantage. He'll have no way of knowing if I'm conscious or not. Knocking people over the head can't be an exact science, can it?*

With her eyes closed, Alex heard rather than saw the back hatch open. Without warning she felt a sharp, new pain permeate her body, rivaling the one that still wracked her head. Her eyes flew open involuntary, the tape stifling her scream. She recognized the man who had been on crutches the last time she saw him, now miraculously healed and standing unaided. He smiled at her and wiped blood, her blood, onto her uniform trousers from the tip of a small knife; undoubtedly the source of the acute agony she had felt in her upper thigh.

"Good morning, Alex," he said in a surprisingly even, conversational tone. "Sorry about the little tweak," he gestured toward her slightly with the knife, "but I thought you were just playing possum. Quite the little actress, aren't you? Oh, by the way, thanks again for offering to help change the tire but, as you can see, I was able to do it by myself."

She said nothing, her outward silence contradicting the myriad of thoughts that raced through her mind.

How the hell does he know my name? Then she thought, *stupid, you're wearing a nametag, aren't you?* Yet something about him did seem familiar now, almost as if she had seen him sometime previously.

He looked at her intensely, almost as if he was trying to peer into her soul.

Then he slowly said, "God, you really are beautiful, aren't you? I was really interested in Britt at first; honestly, I was, but as soon as I saw you, I knew you were the one for me. You should take that as a real compliment, Alex."

She realized immediately where she had seen the man before, he had been seated near them at the food court on Saturday. Alex had dismissed him as a possible alter ego for Britt's Andy, since he had been seated with someone else. She groaned inwardly, kicking herself for not recognizing the man at the park.

If I had, I sure as hell wouldn't have got anywhere near his car, she thought remorsefully.

"By the way, I'm Walter. Pleased to meet you." She absurdly expected him to extend his hand, even though hers were still bound firmly behind her back. "Listen very carefully, please. I've got to get you into the house, so what I'm going to do is put my hands under your armpits and kind of drag you backwards. Don't worry, you'll be in good hands," he chuckled at his pun. "Now, there's an easy way and a hard way to do this. Your best option is to cooperate, keeping your body stiff and letting me pull you along just like a little choo choo train. On the other hand, if you try to struggle, I'll just have to knock your ass out again and drag you like a dead weight. Harder on both of us; plus, I'll be all sorts of pissed off at you. And one thing you're going to learn, Alex, is you really don't want me mad at you, understand?"

She shook her head in the affirmative, seeing no real advantage in antagonizing the man unnecessarily at this point. He pulled her out of the car and stood her on her feet. She experienced a sudden bout of vertigo and would have collapsed if the man had not caught her as he had outlined. From inside the car, a phone ringtone began to play insistently. He looked toward the direction of the noise, a mild look of irritation forming on his face.

"Work," he said, "Can't have a day off without some crisis happening." He suddenly grinned. "Well, they're just going to have to figure it out for themselves. Right now, I've got something more important to do!"

He winked at her for emphasis.

As he pulled her along, she could smell his cinnamon-scented breath rustling through her hair, her revulsion triggering a renewed feeling of nausea to course through her body. He stood her upright once more as they reached a doorway. He opened the door and dragged her past a large laundry room located opposite a closed door and through into a kitchen.

He sat her in a chair and wiped his hand across his forehead again, saying, "This is hard work, isn't it? Thought about going on a diet? No, just joking, babe. You are absolutely perfect just the way you are. By the way, if I take the tape off your mouth, do you promise to behave?"

She nodded her head vigorously in assent, gauging even something this trite could possibly be her first step toward regaining her freedom.

He said, "Sorry, but this is going to hurt a bit."

In one swift movement, he tore the tape from one side of her mouth, leaving it dangling from the other. Alex gasped, both from the sting of the sensitive flesh around her mouth as well as the taste of fresh, clean air. Despite now having the freedom to speak to her captor, she could think of nothing to say that would help her situation. Consequently, she remained silent.

Suddenly, a dog began to bark from somewhere outside.

Walter said, "That's Mike. Would you like me to introduce you to him later? By now, most of the others had already met him in one way or another."

His face began to change, metamorphosing into a look of cold, harsh dispassion. To Alex, it appeared as though his thoughts had drifted far away from what he was doing right now. Then it passed, and his appearance returned to what it had been, that of a nice, good-natured middle-aged man.

Yeah, a great guy, Alex thought, *one who's planning on raping me, and worse.*

The man's casual comment had revealed Alex was not his first victim. He had taken other girls before her, honing his sick craft until he had so easily ensnared her. There was little doubt in her mind now as to her abductor's real identity, he was the man the newspapers had dubbed 'The Woodsman,' she felt with a ghastly certainty. And in all the time she had been following his spree in the paper and on television, reporters had only referred to his victims, never his escapees. Alex realized she may only get one opportunity to get away and that she had to be ready to capitalize on it.

With a heavy sigh, Walter picked her back up and moved her through the kitchen to where they were in front of another door. He leaned her back against the opposite wall and, just as he was reaching for the doorknob, a chime sounded from somewhere further in the house. Alex saw him turn around in alarm, looking immediately toward the opposite end of the hallway. It was evident he was confused as to what to do next. Suddenly deciding on a course of action, he immediately replaced the tape across her mouth. He then turned away from the door he was about to open and moved to drag Alex back toward the garage. Sensing a faint hope, she began to struggle vigorously, although her tightly bound hands and legs reduced her range of motion considerably. She fought against the tape across her mouth, which effectively diminished her screams into muffled mutterings. He hit her hard then, three quick, hard slaps to the sides of her face. Stunned, she sagged in his arms. He dumped her callously on the floor of the laundry room. She hit the poured concrete floor sharply with her left knee, adding another source of pain to her growing inventory. On the positive side, however, it did lessen the shock of her head bouncing on the floor, allowing her to maintain consciousness. He looked down at her, his face once again fixed in that terrible, blank stare.

Through tight lips, he said, "Make any sound whatsoever and I will teach you a lesson you'll never forget as long as you live."

With that he shut the door, leaving her alone for the time being. She cared nothing about his threat, she realized the chances of this man letting her survive their time together was absolutely zero. She tried to get to her feet, only to fall back down in pain as soon as she put her weight on her injured knee.

Come on, you bitch! She thought to herself in anger, *are you just going to lay here and die?*

Disregarding the ache of her various injuries, Alex began to excruciatingly find her way back to her feet.

Chapter 24

Regaining his composure somewhat, Walter walked swiftly toward his front door. He had seriously considered leaving the bell unanswered, but an almost immediate second, and then a third, chime had caused him to believe that, whoever the visitor at the door was, he had almost certainly seen Walter arrive less than five minutes prior. It would look pretty strange not to see who was at the door. The last thing he wanted was to pique someone's curiosity, prompting him or her to pay more attention to his comings and goings.

Besides, it's probably just one of the neighbors wanting to borrow a tool or something, he rationalized. *Well, the sooner I get rid of them, the sooner I can get onto things with the girl.*

That thought made him very happy, he began to whistle softly as he went to the door.

Wish I had one of those little peepholes in the door, he thought, making a mental note that it would probably be a good thing to install. *Dad always used to say, "Can't think of everything," especially when mom was harping on him about something he'd forgotten to fix. Well, at least until he fixed her instead.*

Walter opened the door and stepped forward to the sill. Confronting him was an overtly overweight middle-aged man, dressed in a rumpled suit.

People sure should take better care of themselves flashed through Walter's mind as he tried to place the man from among the sketchy lineup of those neighbors he recognized by sight.

Failing to readily identify his visitor, he asked, "Can I help you?"

To his utter surprise, the man reached into his pocket and produced a badge wallet, identifying himself as a member of the Seattle police force.

At the same time, he said, "Afternoon. I'm Detective Caldwell, Seattle P.D. Are you Mr. Walter Harrison?"

Walter's mind exploded into a cacophony of panicked thoughts. He was struck speechless, unable to respond. The detective repeated his question, again Walter couldn't form a coherent response to the simple yes or no question.

Caldwell said, "Sir, are you alright?"

Finally regaining control of his power of speech, Walter replied, "Yes. Um, yes I'm all right and, yes, I am Walter Harrison."

"Would you mind if we went inside, Mr. Harrison?"

"Can I ask what this is about, please?"

By now, the synapses in Walter's brain were once again functioning properly, more or less.

With a little bit of luck, a whole shit load of luck, he corrected himself, *the detective would be investigating something other than what was, to Walter, the obvious.*

"It's probably better discussing it inside, don't you think? Don't want the neighbors knowing your business, do you?" the detective replied smoothly.

Growing impatient at Caldwell's polite, yet firm insistence, Walter said, "We're not going anywhere until you tell me exactly what you're doing here."

"I have rights you know," He added for good measure.

The detective looked at Walter and a thin smile appeared on his face. "OK, Mr. Harrison, have it your way. I'm investigating a lead concerning the abduction, rape, and murder of a young girl. Now, we can both go inside and discuss it like two civilized gentlemen or we can sit out here on your doorstep until my partner arrives in about forty-five minutes with a search warrant. I will then handcuff your ass to that maple tree over there and I'll go inside anyway. Now, got a preference?"

A sick feeling nearly overcame Walter, who realized he had received no fortunate reprieve from his worst fears. In considering the two alternatives presented by Caldwell, he knew a thorough search of the house would inevitably prove disastrous for him. On the other hand, although the last thing in the world he needed was a Seattle police detective wandering about his house, he might just be able to bluff his way through. He hoped the man would interpret his sudden change of heart as concern for the girl in question, rather than cowing to his threat.

"Oh, my God!" he said, eager to instill a sense of worry in his words. "Why didn't you say so earlier? That poor girl! Of course, I'll be of any assistance I can. Please do come in."

He held the door open for the policeman to enter.

Walter stood aside as the detective walked into the wide reception room of the house, noticing the man moved to maintain at least ten feet of distance between them.

Guy's a veteran, he thought, *wants to keep space between us in case he needs to go for his gun. If the shit hits the fan, I'm going to have to find a way to get closer. Hopefully, it won't come to that though.*

He invited the other man through to the front parlor and motioned to him to have a seat.

Caldwell smiled and said, "After you, please, Mr. Harrison."

- 282 -

Fully cognizant of the detective's rationale, Walter did as he was requested. He selected his favorite piece of furniture in the room, an antique oak Morris armchair, in which to sit. Caldwell then chose an overstuffed leather recliner directly across the room, unbuttoned his jacket, and sank gratefully into its comfortable seat.

Caldwell began. "Thank you, Mr. Harrison, for being so helpful. I just need to ask you a few questions and then I'll be out of your hair, OK?"

"Sure," replied Walter, feeling increasingly at ease with the situation, "Fire away."

"All right," said the detective as he stared into Walter's eyes. "First, do you know a young woman by the name of Shannon Buckley?"

Although he tried hard to maintain a poker face, Walter felt certain Caldwell perceived his slip in composure.

Well, what the hell did you think he was going to ask? he thought, angry with himself.

After what he considered to be an appropriately pregnant pause, one in which he hoped the detective inferred he was thinking deeply, Walter replied, "No, I can honestly say the name doesn't ring a bell."

"Well, how about an easier one. Do you know a fella named Pete Wolf?"

No harm in answering this one, Walter thought.

"Sure, he's a buddy of mine. His dad owns Wolf's Deli downtown, near where I work."

Caldwell's piercing stare was making Walter nervous in spite of himself.

He was just about to ask what did this all have to do with him when the detective said, "Well, it seems Ms. Buckley overheard you ordering some lobsters from Mr. Wolf."

Again, a wave of panic coursed through Walter's body like an electrical charge.

What the hell? How in the hell could he know that? Could she have somehow had a phone on her that he didn't find? No way, he thought, *No fucking way!*

Despite his growing apprehension, he managed a rather sickly grin before answering, "OK, so I bought a couple of lobsters. What, were they stolen or something?"

His pitiful attempt at humor left his listener unfazed, who continued with his questioning relentlessly.

"Well, it seems she was a guest of yours, Walter, may I call you Walter?"

There was no friendliness in the detective's eyes, despite his polite request. His next question was more to the point and constituted a line of questioning Walter was dreading.

"Do you have a basement, Walter?"

Well, that tears it, Walter thought. *However that little bitch communicated with the cops, it's a damn certainty Caldwell wasn't here on a fishing trip. Well, I've got one more little trick up my sleeve before we go to Plan B.*

"Sure do, Detective Caldwell, would you like to see it?" The detective's surprise at Walter's ready offer was obvious.

Didn't see that one coming, did you, you fat fuck?

Caldwell replied, "Yeah, Walter that would be really interesting."

"Alright then, follow me. By the way, since it seems we're on a friendly basis here, may I call you, John?"

Caldwell made no reply. Walter arose and, followed a few steps behind by Caldwell, walked from the parlor into the central hallway of the house. He paused in front of a door and, flipping an adjacent light switch, turned to look inquiringly at the detective, who said nothing in response. Shrugging his shoulders, Walter turned the knob, opened the door, and began to walk down a set of stairs.

After Walter had descended the first three steps, Caldwell began his own, cautious descent. Reaching the floor of the basement room, Walter moved to the opposite wall, his hands were folded across his chest and a disarming look of patient innocence dominated his facial features. In a few seconds, the detective joined him on the floor of the room. Walter said nothing as the detective slowly scanned each wall in turn. A layer of dust rested uniformly on every surface, giving the impression that no one had disturbed it in years. The only exceptions were near the stairs, where a large wine rack held a few bottles and a couple of cases of beer laid open. Other than that, there was no place where a mouse could have concealed itself without leaving telltale tracks in the dust to indicate its hiding place. Obviously, there was even less evidence of a succession of traumatized girls being imprisoned. The frustration on the detective's face somewhat compensated Walter for his earlier anxiety.

Rather sarcastically, he asked, "Seen enough, John? Would make a pretty shitty guest room, don't you think?"

Caldwell looked like he wanted to tell Walter to shut his smartass mouth, but instead said, "Yeah, sorry about that. Definitely nothing down here like what I was led to believe."

Magnanimously, Walter replied, "It's OK, I really do understand. You're just following a lead, that's all. Even though, you probably need to put the fear of God into this Buckley girl for wasting your time on a wild goose chase, if you don't mind me saying. Damned kid is probably laughing her ass off right now."

Or not, he thought with satisfaction.

Walter ascended the stairs with Caldwell following behind. Reaching the hallway, Walter waited for the other man, then shut the door. He led the detective back into the parlor, where they returned to their previously chosen seats.

Feeling immeasurably relieved he had apparently deflected the police officer's interest, he asked, "So, John, is there anything else? If not, I've got some work I brought home to catch up on and I'm sure you have other things to do as well."

His air of dismissal was obvious.

Caldwell looked confused, like there was some part of a puzzle he just wasn't understanding.

You thought it all was going to be so easy, didn't you? Walter thought cockily. *You'd just waltz on in here, I'd take you down to the basement, and there would be the cell with a nubile little honey in it crying her eyes out. You'd pull your gun, throw me your handcuffs and I'd slip 'em on, confessing to everything. Hell, maybe I'd even write your report for you. That way, you'd have more time to play the big hero for the television cameras. Who knows, maybe they'd even give you a lifetime free pass to the all-you-can- eat buffet. Well, sorry to break your heart, John, but life just ain't that easy. As Dad always used to say, "Hope doesn't just come to you, you've got to work for it."*

Suddenly, the sound of barking came from the backyard. Seemingly making idle conversation, Caldwell asked, "Have a dog, Walter?"

"Yeah, a Labrador. His name's Mike. Usually he doesn't make a fuss, don't know what's gotten in to him. Say, you're not going to arrest me for disturbing the peace, are you, John?"

He smiled at his own little joke.

Looking at the detective, Walter was a bit alarmed to notice he was now smiling as well, as if he knew a joke of his own, he was about to share.

Caldwell said, "Mighty large house you have here. What is it four or five thousand square feet?"

"Yeah, forty-three hundred and ten, to be exact."

"Seems pretty strange, doesn't it, that a house this large would only have one small room for a basement? Peculiar thing about these houses, some of them have two separate basements. Yours have two separate basements, Walter?"

An extraordinary wave of calm seemed to wash over Walter like a warm, tropical tide. His feelings of fear and uncertainty became stilled as he realized exactly what he now had to do.

There's only one possible way out of this, he thought logically now, his earlier near-hysteria having passed, *and that's to leave this bastard laying somewhere in a pool of his own blood. No more bullshitting around. If I can't take this guy out, I deserve to get caught. You just have to pick the right spot, Walter, my man.*

"Oh, yeah. You know you're absolutely right, John. I'd actually forgotten about it. At least the beer gives me a reason to go down into the other one every now and then. I can't remember the last time I was in the one at the back of the house. Suppose you'd like to see that one too?"

The detective looked at him and, in that instant, Walter knew that Caldwell knew their relationship had somehow changed. In a slow voice, he said, "Yes, Walter, yes I would."

Repeating their trip into the central hallway of the house, they proceeded further this time, into the kitchen. Again, Walter turned on the light and opened the door, stepping through onto the small landing at the top of the stairway. Suddenly, he heard the sound of another door opening somewhere nearby. He peered back around the door and, as if in slow motion, he saw the laundry room door abruptly open. Without warning, a bound figure hopped into the hallway and crashed into the opposite wall. Walter quickly turned to look at the detective who stood transfixed in shock.

"Alex?" Caldwell asked incredulously, completely oblivious to the swift approach of the younger, more athletic man.

The girl looked wide-eyed toward John Caldwell, working frantically to free the tape from her mouth so she could speak.

Still completely stunned by the unexpected appearance of the girl, the detective offered little resistance as Walter grabbed him by the lapels of his jacket and jerked him violently toward the gaping maw of the cellar door. Walter pivoted to throw the man down the long flight of steep stairs. Caldwell, however, had regained his wits somewhat and, as he began to fall, reached out and grabbed the other man by the top of the belt buckle. In an instant, both men were falling, struggling to gain an advantage in what they knew would be an encounter that would inevitably end in the death of one of them. The next few seconds were characterized by the sound of flesh impacting on unyielding wood and concrete, a yell, a gunshot, and a cry of intense pain.

As Walter lost consciousness, he imagined he heard one more sound, a young, female voice screaming, "Daddy!"

Chapter 25

Alex stared at the unfolding tableau before her in utter disbelief. After thudding into the wall outside the laundry room, she found herself staring into the eyes of John Caldwell, detective in the Seattle police department but, more importantly, her father. Or at least the only man she had known by that name since she was ten years old. She could say nothing, both because of the duct tape that covered her mouth as well as the shock that immobilized her. Abruptly, she saw a head peer around the corner of the doorway in front of her step-father, fixing her with a cold-blooded stare that, despite lasting no more than a second, penetrated to her very essence. Then, he was turning away, whirling toward the man who still stood unmoving, as if frozen by the sight of his daughter bound and at the mercy of the monster that he had spent months trying to find.

She fought against the tape across her mouth, trying to move it to one side so she could scream a warning to her dad, to somehow break the paralysis that held him so he could defend himself from what she saw was coming. But she failed. Although the tape was somewhat loosened, she could only manage stifled mumblings, her agitation only seeming to fix her father's attention more firmly upon her. Alex watched in horror as the man she knew as Walter grabbed the front of her step-father's jacket and swung him forcibly around and toward wherever it was the door led. As if in slow motion, she saw him react, finally shaking himself from his mesmerized state. It was too late, however, to resist the inertia of his fall forward. Walter was too strong and her father's reflexes were too slow. As he moved past the man, however, she saw her father grab him by the front of his trousers, pulling him down after him. Then, they both were gone, falling into, what Alex deduced, was a basement as the sounds of the men's painful descent were obvious. A gunshot and a scream sounded, followed by an eerie silence that descended upon the house, punctuated only by the subdued whimpering of the dog outside the patio doors.

Alex realized she may only have seconds to act, that this may be her only opportunity to free herself. As she bounded into the kitchen, she silently thanked her high school soccer coach who had devised exhausting hop drills to get her team into shape. She looked about frantically, searching for anything she could use to sever her bounds. Abruptly, she saw what she had been looking for. A knife block stood on the counter; its slots filled with what she hoped were very sharp knives. She made her way to the counter, but the block was too far back, she couldn't reach it with her hands still secured behind her back.

Come on, Alex, think! she prodded herself frantically, knowing her abductor could reappear at any moment.

Noticing the sharp corner of a cabinet, she placed her cheek against it as tightly as she could.

Ignoring the pain, she rubbed her face against it over and over, seeking to rid herself of her duct tape gag. It finally pulled free and a cry involuntarily escaped from her lungs, that of "Daddy!"

She received no reassuring reply, however. Whatever had happened to her step-father had left him unable to respond and probably unable to help her as well.

If I'm ever going to get out of this mess, I'm going to have to do it myself.

Her mouth now free, Alex bent over the counter, moving her head past the steak knives in the front row of the block and biting on, what she hoped was, a large chef's knife. The knife slipped easily from the block, revealing at least a seven-inch blade. She tried to place the knife on the corner of the counter, but it slipped off, falling to the floor.

Shit! She thought, *can't I get some sort of a break?*

Rather than attempting to pull another knife from the block, Alex fell painfully to her knees, then onto her side on the floor. She located the knife and, after a few seconds of fumbling about, ecstatically gripped it in her hands. A few sawing motions separated the tape from her hands and she pulled them free. Bringing her hands to the front of her body for the first time in several hours, she nearly passed out from the pain, her muscles screaming from their pent-up agony. She ignored the aching in her body, however, and quickly cut the tape around her ankles. Alex struggled to her feet, simultaneously considering her options as to what to do next.

Well, the smart thing would be to get the hell out of this house just as fast as my legs can carry me. That would certainly be the sensible thing to do, she thought to herself, yet already discarding it as a course of action. *God's put me here for a purpose, and that purpose is waiting down that hole somewhere, not running to save myself. The man in that basement is evil incarnate, he's molested and killed several girls no different than myself. My work has never been clearer than it is right now. For better or for worse, I've got to finish this.*

Alex took the knife in her right hand and walked purposefully toward the basement doorway.

From the top of the stairs, she peered down into the dim room below. It seemed to be finished as some sort of a den with a beige sofa and at least one matching overstuffed chair, among other sundry items of furniture, sitting on a large area rug. Incongruously, a long work bench with a myriad of tools ran along one wall. She could not see the extent of the room in the other three directions from her current point of observation. The dominant feature in the room, however, was the inert body of her step-father, resting motionless on its side adjacent to the stairs. It may have been her imagination, but she thought she saw a small pool of blood formed around his head. Of the other man, there was no evidence. But he was down there, somewhere, of that Alex had no doubt in her mind.

In a balanced crouch, Alex descended the stairs in an excruciatingly slow pattern of one step down, pause, observe, shift her weight, and then bring the other foot down. All thoughts of her various aches and pains had vanished, to be replaced by adrenalin-fueled anger against the man who had abducted her. A glance toward her comatose step-father confirmed he was definitely bleeding, although she still could not confirm the source of the blood.

This bastard is going to pay for this, she thought, as white-hot rage coursed through her veins like liquid fire.

Suddenly, part way through her descent, her heightened sense of hearing detected a small scraping sound at the far wall of the room. Two quick steps brought her down to where she could see to the extent of the room, where she immediately identified the sound's source. There, sitting in a wooden kitchen chair, was the man she knew as Walter. He was in the process of tying a brightly-colored gingham cloth napkin around his upper thigh, the red and white of the napkin losing definition as bright red blood began to blend the colors into one homogeneous hue.

He looked at her with a sardonic smile on his pallid face, that and the perspiration dotting his forehead ample evidence of the severity of the discomfort of his wound.

Through slightly clenched teeth, he said, "Why hello there, honey. Glad to see you haven't left. I was afraid you were going to stand me up for our date."

Although his voice was weak, its insinuating quality remained, solidifying a knot of revulsion in the pit of Alex's stomach.

Oh yeah, Walter, I wouldn't miss this for the world, she thought.

"Well, what's the matter, babe? Cat got your tongue? It seems to have gotten Detective Caldwell's, hasn't it? Or should we call him 'Daddy?' Now, isn't that a peculiar turn of events? My father always used to say, 'Love is strange.' It is, isn't it? I go to meet your dear friend Britt because I was falling in love with her. Then, I see you and, just like that, you steal my heart away from her. Then Daddy comes to save the little girl he loves and oops! So, what happens next? Either you've come down here because you actually find me quite irresistible or to save your dear old Dad instead of running away like the frightened little girl you actually are. I wonder which one it is. Do you know yourself?"

"Shut up you fucking bastard," Alex spat at the man. "You sicken me!"

"Temper, temper," he shook his right index finger at her in mock admonishment. Then, more seriously, "My dad always used to say, 'Don't judge someone until you've walked a mile in his shoes.' Are you judging me? Did you know I watched my father kill my mother, then I helped him cut her up into little bitty parts and put her into garbage bags? No, of course not, but do you even care? After they took him away to prison, I was put into foster care. The things that happened to me there would sicken you a lot more." The man began to weep, his chest heaving from the force of his violent sobs.

Alex looked at the man incredulously, suddenly uncertain what to do next.

Then the man slowly lifted his head, revealing a wolfish grin. "Pretty good, eh? You see, you're not the only actor in the house. With a story like that, any jury in a state as liberal as Washington will have at least one do-gooder who will buy it. That is, if I'm not judged 'not guilty by reason of insanity' first. A few years will give me a lot of time to imagine all the different ways I could have enjoyed that hot little body of yours, Alex. You know what? I'll bet you'll be thinking about me too. What say we get together some time in the future and pick up where we left off? That is, of course, unless you're ready right now? I don't know if I'm up for a fuck, but a blow job sure would be nice." The man got shakily to his feet, nearly collapsing from the effort. He began to shuffle slowly across the floor toward Alex.

She matched his pace, moving warily in his direction in a slight crouch, balancing on the balls of her feet. She held the knife firmly in her right hand slightly in front of her.

"You've been watching too many movies, little girl," his contempt clearly expressed on his face. "You think it's so easy, don't you? Just flick somebody with a knife and they lay down and cry. Well, this isn't the playground. You're going to have to stick it in real deep, but I don't think you have the guts for that. I think you're going to freeze up at the last minute. Then we're going to have some fun, aren't we?" As Walter finished his sentence, he suddenly sprung forward, hoping to use surprise and his additional strength and weight to compensate for his impeded mobility and faintness from blood loss.

Alex had anticipated the man's strategy, however. As he lunged to grab her, she leapt nimbly aside, slashing hard and fast at his throat as he stumbled past. Distracted by the sudden pain of yet another wound, Walter lost his balance, falling toward the floor, but catching himself on the side of the armchair. Alex moved away warily, alert for another of the man's tricks and realizing that, even in his weakened state, she stood little chance against him if he was able to get her in his grasp. She looked at the gasping, injured man before her. Although she had missed her intended target, she was gratified to see a stream of blood flowing from the deep wound that ran from his jawline to midway up his right cheek.

Walter had seemingly not lost his sense of humor.

"Well done, little lady. 'Go for the throat,' that's what my dad always used to say. To tell the truth, I didn't think you had it in you. It's almost like you've done this sort of thing before. I can't see you rumbling with the gang-bangers, though, I'm sure Daddy wouldn't approve. Say, there's been a couple of killings where guys had their throats slit, saw it on the news. At first, the cops were trying to attribute them to me. Pretty stupid, eh? Sorry, probably your dad, huh?" He stared at her for a few seconds, then continued slowly, "Well, congratulations are doubly in order now. Seems we have more in common than I thought."

Alex returned the man's stare, refusing to blink. "Let me make one thing perfectly clear you bastard, you and I have nothing in common. You're an egotistical rapist and murderer, completely amoral and a hideous blemish on God's earth. I do what I do to rid the world of filth like you, to stop the wickedness of you and others like you from happening again."

"A regular little avenging angel, aren't you?" the man sneered, then coughed, blood now frothing at his lips.

"Not really," she said evenly. "If anything, I aspire to be a crusader in the fight against the evil intentions of eviler men. "Therefore, to him that knoweth to do good, and doeth it not, to him it is sin," she recited to herself with conviction, knowing the verse would be wasted on the man before her.

With a set look of determination on her face, she began to move forward. Suddenly, she heard, "Stop, Alex!" She looked toward the stairs and saw her father, now turned slightly on his side, his eyes pleading for her to obey. "You can't do this. Let the law take its course. Frank Chapman will be here any minute now and we'll put this lunatic away until they drag him out of his cell for execution. Please don't, Alex, I'm begging you."

"What about the others, Daddy?"

"We'll get you the best lawyers in the state, medical help, counseling. Anything it takes, Alex, your mother and I will help you get through this."

Alex looked at him sadly and shook her head. She stepped toward the man who had brought such pain to others without remorse. Anticipating what was to be his fate, Walter panicked, attempting to rise and run at the same time. Alex leapt forward, however, plunging her right knee into the small of his back and using her weight to drive him violently to the ground. She grabbed his hair in her left hand and jerked it backward viciously. She drew the knife deeply across his throat. Looking back, she would sometimes wonder whether he had been conscious as the knife had severed Walter Harrison from his life or if he had been knocked unconscious by the ferocity of her attack. She hoped he had felt it.

She rose from the body of the man and walked toward her step-father. The tears in his eyes matched those that welled within her own. Alex sat down beside him.

She lifted the critically injured man into her arms and he said weakly, "Oh, Alex, I'm so sorry."

She looked into his eyes and said, "I am too, Daddy, I am too." She leaned down and kissed him on the forehead, then gathered him close to her body. She hugged him fiercely, tighter even than Britt's strongest bear-hug. "I am too, Daddy."

Epilogue

"Detective Chapman?" The young patrolman reached out and touched Frank's shoulder. "Detective Chapman?"

Frank broke from his reverie and stared at the other officer. "Sorry. What did you say?"

"That about finishes everything here, sir. The medical examiner has already transported the bodies and CSI are just wrapping up. Oh yeah, and the ambulance is on its way to the hospital. Is there anything else you need? If not Stutz and I will be heading off too."

The uniform gestured upstairs, indicating the rough location of his partner.

"No, that's everything, I guess. Thanks."

Impulsively, Officer Willis reached out and patted the senior officer on the back, his empathy overcoming his sense of protocol. The detective turned his head and gave the patrolman a nod of acknowledgement, accepting the gesture for what it was: a sign of condolence. Then, Willis ascended the stairs, leaving Frank alone in the basement of the house at 107 Locust Lane. The place where they had finally broken the Woodsman case. The place where his partner and friend, John Caldwell, had died.

"You dumb son-of-a-bitch," he murmured aloud.

Why didn't wait for me, or at least until backup arrived?

He already knew the answer, however. Not the one John had given him over the phone, but the one he knew instinctively.

You said you had a bad feeling about the case, John. Could you have had a premonition your daughter was in danger? Jesus Christ, he thought. *This is giving me the heebie-jeebies. Next thing, I'll be calling in psychic investigators to help solve my cases.*

Even though he made light of his fellow detective's flash of intuition, it still left him with a funny, chilled feeling, as if something supernatural had brushed up against him.

That wasn't the only thing that was bothering Frank. He had a nagging feeling that something just didn't seem right about the confrontation between his friend and Walter Harrison that had left both men dead.

It's not that the evidence is contradictory, but it seems almost too clear how the encounter progressed, almost as if it had been staged. But who would have done something like that and what possible reason would he have had?

For at least the tenth time, Frank went over in his mind what appeared to have happened.

OK, Harrison had let John into the house voluntarily. Maybe they discussed some of what the Buckley girl had written in her note, or maybe they hadn't. At some point in their conversation, however, John had either convinced or coerced Harrison to show him the basement. Harrison knew he couldn't do that and let John live. So, they had scuffled on the stairs.

Had John let his guard down? Christ, I wouldn't think so. Yeah, John was overweight and undoubtedly had slowed down over the years, but he was a good cop and a veteran. He wouldn't let a possible perp get close enough to turn it into a wrestling match, would he? But, for some unknown reason he had, Frank thought, assessing the evidence dispassionately. *Whatever, the reason, they had both tumbled down the stairs.*

Somehow, John gained some separation during the fall and had been able to pull his service revolver, firing a shot into the other man's right thigh. Good shooting, partner, he commended his deceased friend sadly. *So, Harrison crawls over to the table and ties a napkin around his leg to slow down the bleeding. Now, why doesn't John just shoot him again? The only answer could be that John couldn't move.*

Frank made it a point to ask the M.E. if there was any indication during the post mortem that John had incurred a serious injury during the altercation that would have drastically impaired his mobility.

Taking a quick glance around the room, the answer as to why his fellow detective couldn't have simply shot Harrison from where he was laying became painfully obvious. The sofa was in the way.

Crap, to think John died just because of Harrison's interior decorating decision really sucks. Bad luck, partner, bad luck.

OK, so both men are injured, Harrison over at the table and John here by the foot of the stairs. So, what happens next? Well, John can afford to play a waiting game, he knows he's going to get some backup sooner or later. On the other hand, Harrison can't let the odds against him get any worse. So, Harrison comes after you, partner, or maybe he thinks he can just get past you and back up the stairs. But sooner or later, he's got to come from behind cover, why the hell didn't you shoot him, John? Maybe you lost consciousness, that was one hell of a knot on the back of your head.

Harrison's coming at you, all sneaky like, and you're conked out. What gets you back in the game?

Frank walks over to the table and attempts to retrace Harrison's possible route toward Caldwell's position. He sees the blood stain on the side of the couch. He moves the couch slightly and is gratified to hear an audible scraping sound.

Maybe that was it, huh? So, John wakes up and sees the son-of-a-bitch rushing him. He fumbles for his gun, but Harrison kicks it away. Harrison reaches down for you and . . . Frank shakes his head slowly . . . *and now things just get fucking strange. You grab onto him and the two of you dance ten feet across the room, falling to the floor. Then, a knife suddenly appears and you use it to slash him across the cheek. Maybe he lets go, "Ouch, my cheek!" Then, you reach around him and just about cut his head off. End of story.*

Oh, yeah, Frank added sarcastically. *One thing more. At what point does your neck get broken, John? Pretty hard to bring him down considering that little detail, right? Or did he do it after he had his throat cut? Hard to see him still going after you with that little problem to deal with, don't you think? And where the hell did the knife magically come from?*

It just doesn't seem to make sense, Frank mused frustratingly. *But, hell, any alternatives seem even more farfetched. Could there have been another person down here? If there were, however, the odds would have even been further in Harrison's favor.*

Certainly, no police officer had been on the scene to render assistance and the chance of some do-gooder just happening to be in the basement at that time, assisting the detective to kill Harrison and leave without calling 911 seemed the most implausible of all.

If only the girl would have been able to describe what happened. Yeah, and if frogs had wings, they wouldn't bump their asses when they jump, Frank thought bitterly. In the brief moments Frank had talked to her prior to the ambulance leaving for Northwest Medical Center, Alex had haltingly related she had been unconscious throughout the men's struggle. She had only regained her senses when the police had arrived. Frank didn't press her for several reasons. The large knot on the back of her head would have definitely been enough to knock her out for one. She was also clearly in shock, traumatized both by her abduction as well as the sight of her father sprawled on the basement floor, dead. What's more, the fact she had been securely locked in Harrison's homemade cell made her active involvement impossible.

Most importantly of all, Frank told himself, *she's John's daughter and the least I can do is not make this any harder for her than it already is. Poor kid, supposed to be getting away to college in a few weeks. What was she going to do now? Worse, what was Claire going to do?*

Oh shit, he thought suddenly.

He thumbed his cell phone to speed dial. After a few rings, Captain Phillips' secretary answered. She connected Frank to her boss immediately. Frank quickly ascertained that John Caldwell's wife, or rather his widow, had been informed already of her husband's death. Frank thanked his superior and ended the call. Feeling terrible that someone else had told Claire about John's death rather than himself, Frank stood up and took one last, hard look, around the room.

Yeah, it doesn't make sense, but the whole goddam thing doesn't make sense. How could anyone do what Harrison did to those girls?

He looked at the cell.

And he might have done it to another one if John hadn't stuck his neck out, trading his own life for that of his own daughter. Rest in peace, partner.

Frank wandered over to the work bench, looking at several of the tools that still bore traces of a thick, dark organic residue, palpable evidence of the agony and terror that had been inflicted in this little corner of hell. He shook his head sadly and slowly walked across the floor and up the stairs. He had other cases that needed his attention and there was still a lot of daylight left. First though, he had to go pay his respects to John's widow.

Four days later, as the casket descended into the grave, Claire Caldwell's stoic façade crumbled like rotten mortar. Sobs tore from her lungs and she would have collapsed if it hadn't had been for her daughter catching her. Alex held her firmly as her mother's arm wrapped around her waist. In that manner, the two women supported each other as the body of John Caldwell, husband and father, was laid to rest. Although the city police commissioner had gladly offered a full-honor police funeral, Claire had declined. Although she held no animosity against the force, she had not been able to reconcile herself to her husband's chosen profession taking over his death in the same way it had his life. Despite the ceremony being private, hundreds of her husband's fellow officers and other co-workers had been permitted to attend, paying respectful tribute to one of their own who had given his life in the line of duty. Many other family and friends were also in attendance. Even John's ex-wife, Beverley, and their adult daughters, Samantha and Hannah, were there to pay their respects. When it was all over, Reverend Roberts gave Claire and Alex a final embrace and told them, if there was anything more he could do, they had only to ask.

On the way back to the Caldwell home, George and Grace Stevens kept up a running commentary of small talk, filling the uncomfortable void of silence as best they could. Alex sat in the middle of the back seat of the Stevens' sedan. On one side, she had her arm around the shoulders of her mother, who stared vacantly out the window at the neighborhood where she and her husband had lived their lives together. On the other side sat Britt, holding Alex's hand firmly, willing her own strength into her friend in her time of need. She had not told Britt everything about her abduction, knowing her friend would feel an immense sense of guilt for being at least partially responsible Alex's ordeal. She also did not want to imagine Britt in her place at Harrison's house, confronted by the very real possibility of a fleeting future that would know only pain and abuse.

No, sometimes it's just better to keep some things to yourself, she thought, involuntarily passing a remorseful glance toward her mother.

After an hour, the Stevens' departed, leaving Alex and Claire alone in their house. Sitting in the kitchen, the two women finished their cups of coffee. Rising from her chair, Claire announced she was going to bed for a bit.

Alex said, "Mommy, can I lay down with you?"

Claire looked at her beautiful, vivacious daughter and gave her a smile that conjured a ghost of her past vibrant personality. "Of course, you can, darling. I'd like that very much."

With her left arm lightly draped around the woman she loved so much; Alex breathed the fresh scent of her mother's hair. Neither of them spoke, neither of them slept, instead they each were immersed in thoughts of what would transpire in their lives to come. For Claire, the future seemed overwhelming. She realized this may be the last time she shared her bed, her house, and her life with either of the people she loved most in the world. Alex's departure for California was imminent, their relationship reduced to brief phone conversations and hectic, shared holidays.

How long before those become less frequent as well? she asked herself solemnly, tears coming unbidden to her eyes. *Alex is a grown woman now; she'll have her own path to find in life. Oh, John. I miss you so badly.*

She closed her eyes then, but sleep would not come for a long, long time.

Some of Alex's thoughts intertwined with those of her mother, others strayed down avenues her mother could never guess. She prayed her mother would, eventually, find someone who could bring her as much happiness as she had found with John Caldwell.

It's so selfish, she thought bitterly, *but I want her back like she's always been.*

Alex was enough of a realist, however, to realize hope can often prove the most elusive of human desires.

Her own life seemed set out before her; California, Stanford, then a profession, perhaps even a husband someday.

It seems so unfair. I'm looking forward to a future filled with bright possibilities, while my mother is shackled to a past that ended so darkly. Maybe I should think about putting off going to Stanford for a year. I could help mom get through the worst part of her loss by being around every day. I could even take a few classes at a community college, build up a few transfer credits so the whole year wouldn't be a complete academic waste.

Despite her mother's grief, Alex knew she would throw an absolute fit if she decided to delay going to Stanford, especially since it would be completely obvious it was because of her.

I'll have to think about that one, she thought, defraying contemplation of that course of action for the time being.

What she couldn't put off thinking about was her first appointment with Dr. Martin at the Seattle Counseling Center the next day. Given the emotional and physical trauma her daughter had endured during her abduction, the need for extensive psychological therapy had seemed a foregone conclusion to Claire Caldwell. Not wishing to do anything to upset her mother's own delicate mental state, Alex had agreed without argument. But now, she wasn't so sure she wanted to attend the sessions.

Do I really feel I need counseling? she asked herself.

In examining her own state of mind objectively, she concluded she did not. She was alright, she decided.

I'm a tough, self-sufficient woman who is sustained by my family, my friends, my own sense of self-worth, and a firm belief in God's power over my life.

What about my own feelings about the death of John Caldwell? That is a bit complicated, she admitted to herself, mentally filing this topic for future examination as well.

And what about my calling? She asked herself finally.

She knew she had nearly died at the house on Locust Lane and probably would have if not for a fortuitous sequence of events, chiefly the unforeseen intervention of her step-father.

Will I be so lucky next time?

Then she remembered her encounter with Justin, which had been a close call as well.

How long before my good fortune runs out? What if, next time, there isn't a policeman who just happens to be there to intervene when things go bad? What if the guy is just a little more careful? On the other hand, how long can I expect to do this without getting caught?

Then she thought about the girls who had been in Harrison's basement before her: Angela Simmons, Vicki Redmond, Amy Reiss, and God knew how many more. In the cell, she had seen the lingerie in the drawers, had briefly held the lipstick, the eyeliner, the hairbrush they had used to make themselves presentable for the Woodsman's sick fantasies. They had had no choices. She was sickened by the thought of how close Britt had come to suffering a similar fate.

Whose lives have I kept from being ruined by Robert Jackson or Tom Beach? There are other girls out there, Alex, girls who don't even know they need your help desperately.

Then she recalled the verse from James 4:17 she had used to strengthen her resolve in Harrison's basement.

'Therefore, to him that knoweth to do good, and doeth it not, to him it is sin.'

She realized then that, despite the dangers inherent in her calling, she would not be found wanting.

With that, she wrapped her arm more tightly about her mother, enveloping her in an embrace of pure love. As she finally drifted toward slumber, Alex's features relaxed into a smile. She had no idea what challenges the future held for her, or whether she would prevail in them. She only knew she would face them with courage. Her sleep was serene and uninterrupted.